The Secrets of Married Women

About the author

Carol Mason was born and grew up in the North-East of England. As a teenager she was crowned Britain's National Smile Princess and, since became a model, diplomat, hotel receptionist, waitress and advertising copywriter. She lives in Canada with her husband, Tony, and *The Secrets of Married Women* is her debut novel.

CAROL MASON

The Secrets of
Married Women

HODDER

First published in Great Britain in 2007 by Hodder & Stoughton
An Hachette Livre UK company

First published in paperback in 2007

1

Copyright © Carol Mason 2007

A CIP catalogue record for this title is available from the British Library

ISBN 978 0 340 93275 9

Typeset in Plantin by Hewer Text UK Ltd, Edinburgh
Printed and bound by Mackays of Chatham Ltd, Chatham, Kent

Hodder & Stoughton policy is to use papers that are natural, renewable
and recyclable products and made from wood grown in sustainable
forests. The logging and manufacturing processes are expected to
conform to the environmental regulations of the country of origin.

Hodder & Stoughton Ltd
338 Euston Road
London NW1 3BH

www.hodder.co.uk

For my mam (and not forgetting my dad,
who would have been so proud)

ACKNOWLEDGEMENTS

Sara Kinsella, and the team at Hodder, for their faith in the book.

Jane Gregory, my agent, for her faith in me.

Emma Dunford, for her passion for the story, and excellent judgement.

My mam, Mary Mason, who shared and encouraged my passion to write.

My husband, Tony Capuccinello, whose unflagging support and belief in me went above and beyond the call.

Friends and family, in particular my brother Neil, who cheered me on.

Sincere debts of gratitude to you all!

I

'I'm having a gone-off-Lawrence crisis,' Leigh curls a lip at me as we pack deeper into the Pitcher and Piano bar down at Newcastle's Quayside, holding our wine glasses in the air so they won't spill. Beyoncé's singing 'Crazy in Love'. The walls, my heartbeat, and my big toe in these new leather boots, throb in time to its hell-raising groove.

'After all these years of marriage, Jill, the sex is so tired. He's got this bloody set-piece routine. I tell you, it never varies. I can predict his next move before he does it.'

I look at my good pal who always tells it like it is. Her Botoxed face is like a bare white china plate. The usually lustrous hair, haggard from its recent permanent rinse, hangs black and straight and heavy, like curtains at the crematorium. And she's wearing the sort of mid-life crisis frock that gets you the type of attention you really don't want – a skin-tight, one-sleeved, zebra-striped number that she bought in Jesiré with Wendy and me on our last visit to the McArthur Glen Shopping Outlet.

'You know, last night in bed we were kissing, he was trying to get me going, and I felt . . .' she looks at me in

frank exasperation, '. . . nothing. I might as well have
been kissing the sheet.'

I have a chortle and, despite herself, she manages
one too. 'Oh, Leigh! All marriages get a bit flat.' I say
nothing about my own. Rob's face appears in my
mind's eye, bringing a faint sadness that I quickly blot
out. We've forced our way over to the window, hoping
to nab a table, but they're all taken. Funny, we're at
that age now where rather than eye the fellas we eye the
seats.

'I don't care about all marriages, Jill. I just care about
my own. I know people say you should look at somebody who's got it worse than you – the poor fella with
no legs when you've got two – but I just think, I'm not
even forty and I'm already losing it for him, and I'm
scared shitless by that.' She sends a dour gaze across
the black expanse of the Tyne river. I can't believe the
change in her. Just minutes ago she was cackling in
affectionate despair over Lawrence's obsessive com-
pulsive disorder (one of her favourite rants; that and
his unusual obsession with Christmas), telling me how
he comes to bed after checking forty times that the
front door's locked, only to leave the back one open,
and she wants to smother him with his pillow. But the
smile's wiped clean off her face now. She's on a
marriage-bashing roll. 'I tell you Jill, I'm really resenting him lately. I mean, I work long hours, putting up
with all kinds of petty egomaniac bullshit and he gets to
stay home and watch *Richard and Judy*. A big drama
for him is if ASDA's having a two-for-one and he
forgot to clip the coupon.'

'But you're the one who suggested he give up his graphic design job and become a house-husband,' I remind her. Leigh earns a packet marketing a trendy line of locally-made leisurewear made popular by a famous footballer's wife. She loves barking orders, and Lawrence has a nervous Stan Laurel obedience about him that makes him infectiously cute and annoying as buggery.

'I know I did. I thought it'd help his disorders if he wasn't under so much stress. But I honestly imagined he'd get more done with his day, rather than just sit around reading the philosophers and saying he wants to find himself.'

'Disorders? Plural? He's only got one!'

'Maybe in your opinion.' Her eyes twinkle at me over the rim of her glass before she takes a sip.

I shake my head, playing like I'm aghast with her. It's one thing to poke a bit of fun, but I don't believe in jumping on the bandwagon when friends criticise their loved ones. Take Rob, for instance. Rob is far from perfect; he leaves his banana skins in the plant pot and his shoes on the duvet. It's fine for me to find fault with him, but woe betide anybody else who does. It's hot in here and my throat's already tired from having to shout to be heard. 'Oh, Leigh! You love Lawrence! He's an absolute sweetheart! He does everything for you, all you have to do is ask. He's always there for you, he's a great listener and you're the best of friends.'

'But the sweeter he is, the more he's turning me off.' Her gaze follows a girl's bum that's hanging out of hot pants with the word 'Fatz' – Leigh's brand – written on them in pink sequins. 'I don't want to have to ask him all the time to do things, Jill; he's not retarded. I just wish he'd be a bit more proactive, rather than wait for my orders. It's not even like his routine ever varies, yet there's always about four things he forgets to do.' She sighs, takes her eyes off the girl's backside. Eminem tells us we have to lose ourselves in the music, and we get pushed farther into the corner, away from the seats. 'You know, I swear, even when Lawrence hugs me, he leans on me rather than supports me.'

I get a funny mental image of a friendly ladder against a wall. But I daren't smile because her gaze drops like a sad heart before she meets my eye frankly. 'The thing is, I don't respect him like I used to. He annoys me, so I pick on him. And the more I pick on him the less I want to have sex with him.' Leigh can be a peaks and troughs person but I've never seen her quite this fed up. 'Mind you, nothing ever puts him off. But I suppose that's fellas for you.'

I wonder how she'd react if I said *well, you're lucky, at least you've still got a sex life*, but I came out tonight to forget about certain things, not to be reminded of them.

'You don't feel like that with Rob, do you? Like you're going off him?'

'No.' I hesitate. *More like the other way around*. 'But we have our problems. Everybody has.' Funny how you can make anything sound like nothing if you say it casually enough. But Leigh is one of those people who view their friends' marriages through rose-coloured spectacles. If you tried to tell her that things were a little bit crap at the moment, she'd automatically think that the crapness of your situation paled in comparison to her own. Her attention's already moved on to coveting a passing tattooed bicep.

'Oh, Jill, sometimes it staggers me how different Lawrence is from the men I've had in my past.' She shakes her head in haggard disbelief at her fate. I've heard this line many times. Leigh first saw Lawrence in a swimming pool; he was feeling his way, crab-style, along the gutter. The next was in an aerobics class; thirty pairs of legs were kicking in one direction, and one pair in the other. When she says stuff like this I often think she's apologising for him and trying to say: *Lawrence is not the best I could get; I have bonked more burly blokes than him, men you yourself would fancy* (because this is so important among friends). She looks at me now with a roguish glimmer in her eyes. 'I've been looking up old boyfriends. I've sent a few emails, got a few replies, rekindled the odd little flirtation.'

'You haven't!'

'Why? Haven't you ever done that? Googled your exes?' Then she quickly adds, 'Oh no, you won't have, I forgot. Because Rob was your only boyfriend.'

'That doesn't make me a bad person,' I joke. It's odd, though – sometimes I can't picture a time when I wasn't married. I mean, I know it's not quite been ten years yet, but I do sometimes wonder: was there life before Rob, or was there Rob before life? And I'm sure he must think the same way, which is an even more disturbing thought. 'Do you think you'd ever have an affair?' I ask her, not knowing where I get the question from.

Her eyes come back to mine with that cryptic, playful look in them again. 'An affair? Oh, never! I had so much screwing around in my single days. Maybe it's different for you. You've only ever been with one man so you could be forgiven for being curious. But affairs are so sleazy. It's awful. And besides, I've too much to lose. I have a child. You don't understand what it's like when you're a mother, Jill.'

Leigh sometimes makes tactless comments that make me feel like I'm a member of a very limited club of childless pariahs, and it wounds me more than I can ever let on. Rob and I just found out a few months ago that we can't have children. Leigh's the only person I've told, because Rob, for some strange reason, doesn't want anybody to know yet. It's not as though we ever had a burning desire to be parents. But since when was life so logical that this would make everything uncomplicated and okay? 'So, how's Molly then?' I ask, while we're on the topic. Molly's her eight-year-old, an aspiring Charlotte Church who'll grab the phone off her mam and bleat 'Somewhere Over the Rainbow' in your earhole when you're trying to have a conversation, which can be annoying.

'Brilliant,' she says, because Molly's clearly not what she wants to talk about right now. Her eyes flit around the room. 'Oh, God, cop these two. We'll never look like that again, will we?'

I stifle a yawn and glance at the two dolled-up ten-year-olds in Madonna corsets that she's referring to. The age rant; I've heard it a million times. Honestly, sometimes you can go out with Leigh feeling quite okay about yourself and then you go home and want to stick your head in the oven and slow-roast your own eye-balls. 'Why, like? Would you want to?'

'I'd kill my own mother to.'

'Well, that's not saying much!' She smiles at me. Leigh's mother is a nut who met all Leigh's 'dads' by doing prison visiting. Then Leigh found out she had a twin sister – her mother kept Leigh and gave the other baby away. Leigh recently tracked her down and trooped off to a coffee-shop in Leicester to meet her – with Wendy and me in distant supportive tow at a nearby table – and the woman stood her up; something she won't have mentioned now.

'Honestly, though, d'you even see one fella looking at us, Jill? I tell you, not one has. Not even baldy by the bar who looks like he got that suit free when he bought the tie. Mr Divorced In Polyester. It's so depressing!'

'Well, somebody should just shoot us and send us to the knacker's yard!'

'I know!' she says, thinking I'm being serious, and I just about scream. It's the one thing I'll never under-stand about Leigh. She's bright, she's got a brilliant job, a doting family, yet the only thing she seems to measure herself on is how many fellas look twice at her.

We swell and collide with the pressing tide of bodies. I'm hot and considerably underdressed in my leather jacket, cargo pants and beige drawstring T – something I'd wear to run errands. But getting glammed up on a Friday night to come to a busy bar when I'm married just makes me feel like a big fraud. A bead of sweat makes its way down my spine and my big toe and my calves are now in a serious gridlock cramp in these three-inch, knee-high black boots – my token nod to glamour. Donna Summer's singing 'Hot Stuff' now, and, as if on cue, two young lads latched onto beer glasses walk past us, and one of them – the cocky one with the muscles and the sunbed tan – gives me the eye. Then his mate looks at Leigh and goes, 'Neh. Not her!'

A flaming colour rushes up Leigh's white neck. 'Did you hear what he just said?'

'Oh, God, Leigh, they're pissed. Don't waste a minute thinking about it!'

'Well the good-looking one certainly likes you.' Her eyes do a quick sweep of me.

'Oh, come on, lads his age would shag a bonny carpet.'

'But not me!' She turns away, takes a shaky sip of her wine. I'm stunned to see tears.

'Oh, Leigh, I didn't mean it like that!' I can't believe how fragile she's being. I want to say, why do you care what two horny teenagers and a lonely-heart with a hair-weave think of you? There are bigger things to worry about, let me give you a few . . . Instead I tell her I'm bursting for a wee. I take off, cutting a mission around shoulders, backs, boobs, boob jobs, biceps and beer glasses, barge into the ladies' loos and immediately get gassed by a million cans of Elnett. They're all bombarding the mirror, lifting their boobs, adjusting their thongs, fluffing, puffing and perfuming, or lining up at the condom machine, ranking the merits of strawberry versus peach flavour. What am I doing in this awful place? I left this scene behind me when

I was about sixteen. I should be out with my husband, or at home, snuggled on the settee between him and the dog. There was a time when Rob and I never went out separately on Friday or Saturday nights. We could still see friends, but the rule was we had to see them together. It was a lovely little claim we had on each other; our friends all said it was sweet. Tonight, though, as I was leaving, hovering and hoping for some comment that I looked nice, I got the distinct impression that Rob couldn't have given a flying you-know-what about the weekend rule, he was probably just chuffed I was off out so he could spend his night feeling up the remote control.

I queue for a wee, then I queue at the mirror to wash my hands and get lethally elbowed by a back-combing twelve-year-old Britney Spears. Between all these coiffed heads I manage to catch a glimpse of myself standing quite still. My short 'n' shaggy blonde 'do' that I have to keep Frizz-Eased so as not to look like the Jackson Five. My new tiny, trendy tortoiseshell glasses that replaced my older, chunky ones, that replaced painful years of vanity in the form of contact lenses. And my touch of long-lasting cherry lip gloss. I don't look half bad. I don't think I look thirty-five. But among this sea of fresh young faces, mine is the only one where the surprise has worn off.

'So, I wonder if Wendy's having a nice night out.' I hand Leigh another glass of wine. Our friend Wendy is at her husband's police 'do' tonight. If she'd been here, Leigh would never have ranted on like that about Lawrence, because Wendy's got such a great marriage that a grasping part of your self-esteem makes you want to build your own up, not blacken it. 'So, what d'you reckon?' I elbow her. 'Does Neil look better with his tuxedo off or on?'

The old sense of humour I know and love returns. 'Off. Definitely,' she says. Wendy's hubby, Neil, is a hunk. Plus he's a top policeman, and he only has eyes for his wife. 'But I'd rather you didn't get me started on that thought track if you don't mind. It's a bit like dreaming of a Chateaubriand when you've got to go home to a pale, squidgy, thawed-out pork sausage.' She rolls her eyes. 'Hard choice. Hard, hard choice. A select roast extravagantly carved from the heart of the finest beef tenderloin, versus . . . the pulverised toe-nails and entrails of . . . Miss Piggy.'

'Give over!' I tell her, and we cackle.

'You know, I was thinking about Wendy the other day,' she holds her glass up to her face, scrutinises it, then rubs a secondhand lipstick mark off. 'You know the problem with Wendy? You never get any dirt off her, do you? Don't you just sometimes wish she'd sit down, say life's crap, Neil's an arsehole, my kids should be set upon by Dingos . . .'

'But her life's not crap. Neil's fantastic, and her lads are sweethearts. You're just being a catty, jealous cow.'

'Oh, I am. Haven't the tips of my ears turned green?' She lifts one of her funeral curtains.

'Actually,' I pretend to peer in there, 'you've got a lot of wax in that one.' The smile transforms her face. 'So, have I cheered you up then, petals? You're not going to go home and gash your jugular when Lawrence wants to bonk like a bunny rabbit?'

'Eh? What did you say?' She cups her ear and goes cross-eyed. We hold our grins for a moment then she gawps at the offending lads who are now chatting up the two babies who look like they've forgotten to put their tops on. 'Oh, come on Jill, this place is making me gag. I don't even know what we're doing here. I feel like going home and scrubbing myself in the shower.'

I neglect to remind her that coming here was her idea.

We finish our drinks and leave. It's refreshingly chilly after the sweat-box we've been in, and spitting rain, a fine spray visible only under the blue of the street lamps. I breathe in the oily Newcastle damp, aware that my hearing's gone dim after all that racket. I love this revamped part of the city, especially at night. The Blinking Eye bridge lit up with blue lights; the Baltic Centre for Contemporary Art, a converted flourmill, floodlit against the night sky; and the new Sage Centre for Music that reminds you of a stainless steel seashell, or a giant cream horn, as my dad calls it. The new Newcastle that's lost its scent of coalmines and unemployment lines. A group of lasses jig past us, linking arms, belting out Kylie songs and doing their drunken version of the cancan. Leigh and I walk without saying much, as lights from the Sage Centre bob a reflection on the river and cars drum noisily over the Tyne Bridge. She seems bleak again. Is this still because of those daft lads? Sometimes the people I know the best are the ones I least understand. I listen to our heels clack on the wet cobblestones. Even they seem to be copping a sulk.

The lovely silver Mercedes SL 500, whose alarm I set off when I accidentally nudged it trying to squeeze my VW Jetta between it and a BMW X5, is still parked behind me. I'm about to get into my car when I notice something under my wiper. 'What's that?' Leigh asks.

It doesn't look like a parking ticket. I pull out the somewhat soggy piece of paper and read: *I saw you scratch my car. So instead of compensation, how about a drink?* Under that is the name Andrey and a phone number.

Well! That's cheeky! A mite cleverer than the usual sensibilities of your average Geordie male. I feel a bit tickled pink. My eyes dart from his very fancy car to the steamed-up window of StillLife, where, without looking obvious, I try to see if I can see a man who looks like an Andrey, not that I know what an Andrey would look like. But there's just a lot of silhouettes outlined against the glass. I stand there, lost in a big smirk, staring at the Mercedes and biting the paper. I wonder if he's gorgeous. Like he would be if my life were a film.

'What is it, then?' Leigh's white face peers across the car roof, through a blue-lit rain.

It's on the tip of my tongue to tell her. On better nights we'd have a cackle and speculate about whether he'd be good in bed, and she'd share some sordid story about past high jinks with a man named Andrey. Then she'd wave me off from her door, and I'd sparkle all the way home – that fabulous after-effect of having a damned good night out with a damned good friend.

But I don't want to set her off again, so I shove the paper in my bag. 'Oh, nothing. Just, erm, a silly car-cleaning advert.'

'Leigh threw a wobbler,' I tell Rob when I slip under the duvet beside him, relieved, after a dose of the singles' scene, to have a hubby to come home to. Rob always likes the stories of the girls' nights out. Rob never has stories of his nights out. Rob thinks if he talks about anything other than sport with his pals, they're all being gay or something.

He turns and lifts an arm for me to snuggle under, sniffs my hair. 'Cor! You smell like a brewery.'

'I poke him in the ribs. 'Anyway, what you doing in bed this early? Did your girlfriend just leave?'

'Didn't you pass her on the way in?' I feel him smile against my cheek. 'Why did Leigh throw a wobbler, then?'

The cold steel rain, heavy now, thrashes against the windows that flank our bed, and nestling under Rob's arm is truly the closest thing to my heaven. 'Oh, because some wasted three-year-old made eyes at me instead of her.' I inch my legs over to the side of the bed that he's warmed and tell him the story, lapping up the feeling of his thumb stroking my damp hair.

'She's bonkers,' is his verdict. Rob's deep like that.

Leigh does have issues. But could you blame her, given her upbringing? As she'll often say, 'You know, my mam never once gave me a cuddle or told me I was beautiful.' And I think that's so sad. Because my mother was the opposite. My mother did that every day.

'So, were the flies out again?' he asks. This is Rob's little joke about men finding his wife attractive. 'You're like dung,' he'll say. 'You attract all the flies.'

'Oh, the odd bluebottle was buzzing around, you know . . .' I think of the note and realise I'm still lit up by it. I must chuck it in the bin tomorrow.

'An' you looked like crap tonight, too.'

'God, you know, your compliments bowl me over . . . So, did our very untrained puppy do another whoopsie in the house?' Rob bought me Kiefer, a Walker Hound–Collie cross for my birthday. Don't ask me why. I've never expressed any desire for a dog, probably because I've never had any desire for a dog. So Kiefer's spent the last three months teaching me how to love him – by crapping all over the house, shredding my nerves with his bark, chewing his way through my every last shoe and piece of furniture, and stubbornly foisting himself between Rob and me whenever I try to steal a bit of affection.

'Nah. Just that pile under your pillow.'

'Very funny.' I kiss the smooth cleft of his chin, smell toothpaste on his breath, sneak a hand under his T-shirt, and feel the easy familiarity of my marriage cloak me. Over the years, Rob's middle had become a bit like a lukewarm hot water bottle, but since he's lost some weight recently, he's got a pretty nice body on him again. He clutches my foot between both of his.

'I missed you, you know.' He plants a tender little kiss on my eyelid. 'I always do when I come to bed and you're not with me. I might fall asleep but I've always got one eye awake, waiting for you to come home.'

'How do you keep an eye awake?' I prop myself on an elbow and gaze at him. 'D'you pin its lids back and squirt it with cold water? Or slap it around, or shout at it every two minutes? Shock its socks off?'

He pulls my head back down on his chest again. 'Very droll, funny clogs.'

Strange, Rob's been so soppy with me lately. Normally he's not good with telling me he loves me. Instead, he'll make up daft little songs, and, in his abysmally off-key voice, sing them to some familiar tune: *My wife. I love her. She is beau-ti-ful. I think of her all day. She makes me smile. All the while . . . she has cute little toes, and a turned up nose.*

I plant a kiss in the centre of his chest. His skin smells newly washed, of soap. It strikes me that I can't remember the last time we had a spontaneous bout of clothes-ripping passion. Something that wasn't part of a routine, or timed between two good shows on the telly. I sometimes wonder if we escaped the seven-year itch only to fall into the ten-year ditch. I push these thoughts away, kiss a trail up his body, up his throat, run my lips along his stubbly jaw. But Rob lies very still – a clear case of not-tonight-Josephine. So I stop, noncommittally, as though kissing his jaw was as far as I was going with the mission anyway. I try not to feel flattened. That's how I've been feeling a bit, of late: like a brand new hairdo that got rained on.

'What d'you want to do tomorrow, then?' I prod him. Since our marriage seems to have withered on the vine lately, for reasons I'm not quite clear on, I made Rob make a pact with me. I said, let's make Saturdays our 'date' days. Let's make out we're courting again.

Rob considers my question. 'Anything you want to do, treasure.' Rob will always leave everything up to me, even when it comes to what he wants to do. I never know whether he's just being compliant for an easy life, or whether, over the years, he really has just merged his mind with mine so that he doesn't have one of his own any more. The first theory is sort of sweet and sometimes his amenability suits me anyway. The second theory irritates me.

'We'll think of something fun and brilliant in the morning, won't we?' I stress the *we*.

'You will,' he passes the buck back to me. 'My faith in you knows no limits.' He kisses my cheek then shoves me away and turns over.

What did I read the other day in a mag? That trust, communication, and a little touch of lust are the three ingredients that make a marriage stand the test of time. Bloody hell.

2

'Rob can only keep it up for about thirty seconds,' I tell Wendy on the phone while I sit at my desk at work. (I'm PA to the Head of Finance for Newcastle Football Club.) The girls who sit across from me nearly fall off their chairs.

'You and your dirty minds!' I scold them. 'I'm talking about running! Rob and I are training to run ten K.' It's the new 'us'. It's healthy, it's bonding, it's the perfect way to exercise the dog.

'Glad you clarified that, Jill, girl,' Leanne says to me. 'Otherwise that would account for a lot about you, wouldn't it?'

I grin, then scowl. 'Really?' I cover the mouthpiece with a hand. 'Like what?' I hear Wendy chuckle then I try to tune back into my conversation with her. Wendy's my running guru. She's also about the fittest person I know, even though, ironically – as she will always grumble – she's not the thinnest.

'Well, Jill,' she tells me, 'it takes time to build up your endurance. Your heart's a muscle too, so you have to work at it to make it strong. That's not something you can do overnight.'

'God, if it's anything like how long it took for me to

get arm muscles, it sounds like a good enough reason for packing it in now.'

'Oh, what a defeatist friend I have!' I can hear the smile in her voice.

'It wasn't that bad, though, you know Wend,' I lie. 'The hardest part, I find, is putting one foot in front of the other and keeping going. I'm still trying to work that part out, but we did it exactly like you told us to. We followed the programme.' With our own variation. The first day we started off walking for one minute, then running for two – we did this ten times – sort of. The next day we had to run two and walk for one, and do this twelve times. By day four we had our numbers in a knot and ran for one and walked for about ten and had a good old chinwag, and did this three times. Then, by the end of the week, I had a sore foot and Rob had a pain in his coccyx.

'We're really loving it, though, just like you said we would. And we're certainly going to stick with it.' Once we pick it up again in the winter. As Rob said, it's getting too warm now to be doing all this extra sweating; it'll be better in the dark evenings: the neighbours won't be able to see us; the cold will be motivating. Besides, Rob said, running isn't good for bigger puppies; it can displace their hips. I gave my husband's head a good hard rub, 'Aarrgh, Robby, my big puppy! I wouldn't want you getting your hip displaced now, would I?' Rob said he was talking about the dog.

Shit. I see my boss coming and duck my head down into my shoulders. 'Gotta go,' I whisper to Wendy. 'Adolf's doing the goose-step.'

'I'll see you in yoga tonight, right?'

Oh, God, it's exhausting, this. 'Now, Wend, what would I do without a friend like you, driving me to be a better person?'

'Take the bus,' she jokes. Then she adds, 'Maybe I'll loan you my large backside, then you'll have no problem finding the motivation.'

I'm just about to knuckle back down to work when my phone rings. I recognise the anguished intake of breath and my spirits hit the floor. 'Dad!'

'Love!' he hollers. 'It's yer mam. I turned me back for one second . . . the front door was open . . . She's gone!'

Same as last week. My parents are in their seventies. They had me late in life. My mam has vascular dementia and my dad can't cope, and he's in a right pickle but he won't admit it for fear that somebody's going to suggest she goes into a home. 'Oh, Dad!' My work pals all give me their best sympathetic looks.

'She's still in her dressing-gown. I couldn't get her to get her clothes on this morning. Oh . . .' His voice wobbles; he starts to sniffle.

Hearing my dad cry makes a big lump rise in my throat. 'Dad, you know somebody's going to find her and bring her home. Just like last time.' Silksworth's small. You couldn't run away if you wanted to. I know. I could only escape it when I married outside it. '. . . But, anyway, I'm on my way. I'll be there as fast as I can. Hang on in there.'

'I'm hanging,' he says, pitifully.

I ring off, throw my phone and cardigan into my

bag. I'm forgetting something . . . I used to have a very understanding boss, untill he dropped down dead before our very eyes about a month ago. But this new fella, Arnold Swinburn, goes around like he's got a large, splintery plank up his arse and he's always watching me with eyeballs the size of small planets when he walks past my desk in his slip-on tan shoes with leather tassels that have all us girls giggling. I tap on his door. When I go in, he gives me that preparing-to-not-be-amused look over the top of his glasses, and I've not even said anything yet. 'I'm afraid . . . I'm sorry, but I have a family emergency,' I quake as I tell him.

'Another one?' he says, as though I have them every day.

You'd never think I'd worked here five years and have an immaculate record of attendance, punctuality and efficiency. I put my best monotone voice on, my polite way of making it known that he needn't think I'd put this job – any job, or any thing for that matter – before my parents' well-being, so he really will have to sod off and deal with his disgruntlement, won't he? 'My mother is an old lady. She suffers from dementia. She ran away from the house and she won't know where she is, or where she's going. She probably won't even know *who* she is, for that matter, if it's a bad day for her. Then there are the days where she does remember, but she knows that something is not quite right in her head; she's stuck in some kind of mental maze and she doesn't have the capacity to find her way out of it.' I pause for dramatic effect. 'That's what happens with this illness, and it could happen to any one of us.' *Including you.*

'See you on Monday,' he says. As I creep out of there, I feel his disapproving eyes bore into my back.

Admittedly it didn't help that I was late in this morning and I missed a managers' meeting because that hound Kiefer tried to take our neighbour's bunny rabbit for a ride around our garden in his mouth. I had to streak around the lawn in my underwear trying to catch him, but he just thought we were playing a game. By the time he took my threats to kill him seriously and I got the bunny back in its hut and got dressed, I knew I didn't have a rabbit in hell's chance of being on time for the meeting. So it's two nails in my coffin in one day. But using that line to Arnie about *my dog is only a puppy . . . he barely knows his own name . . . let's face it, being a puppy could happen to any one of us* doesn't work in quite the same way. So shoot me, because I'm all out of apologies.

Of course, because I'm in such a hurry to get through to Sunderland, there has to be an accident on the Tyne Bridge. As I sit there in a frazzle, the passenger of an Alf's Windows 'n' Doors van that's idling beside me catches my eye and winks. Next, his mate's leaning over and doing the same thing, as though they've got a prolapsus of the eye muscles. I fix my attention straight ahead of me and do my utmost to tune them out. She's going to be fine, I tell myself, because I think you have intuition about bad things happening and my gut tells me it's not going to be this time. But still I worry because I am a worrier by nature.

Even when I have little to worry about, I worry. I worry that they might not be sleeping, eating, going to the toilet. I worry whether or not they're warm, getting fresh air, turning the oven off, closing their windows at night or answering the door to strangers. 'What you think we are?' my dad'll say. 'A couple of stool pigeons?'

'I think you mean sitting ducks,' I'll grin at him, and he'll wheeze a laugh, his chest making a melody like a distant orchestra tuning up.

My mam's had this condition for three years now. At first it was little things: she'd put milk in the china cabinet, ask questions we'd just given her the answer to. Then came the big one – Mam forgetting it was Christmas Day. Now she gets it into her head that my dad is her brother who's molesting her. Dementia can have you perceiving things in extreme opposites.

Somebody toots a horn. I register that traffic ahead is moving again. The two fellas in the van pull argh-she's-leaving-us faces and wave like a couple of halfwits. I give them my women-are-the-superior-sex eye-roll then shift into gear. On the way, I ring Rob and sound off about how I'm really going to have to intervene and do something about my parents, and he comforts me and promises me we'll think of something together.

My mobile rings as I'm pulling up at their front door. 'We found her! Jenny Barton found her in the bus shelter. You needn't bother coming, we're champion now!' There's a pause. 'Where are you anyway, chucka?'

'Look out the window,' I tell him.

The curtain twitches. My dad's eyes meet mine. 'Oh,' he says.

I push back an overgrown rhododendron bush by the gate then walk up the path feeling a tad impatient. My dad opens the door, near gleeful. 'Eee! Your mam gave Jenny a good hiding for bringing her home!' My dad finds it funny that a woman as ladylike as my mother has taken to clocking people for the smallest of reasons. Then the smile disappears and he looks like he's going to cry again. 'Oh, Dad!' I go to give him a big hug but he says, 'Geroff!' and swats at me, because we're not supposed to be soft in this family.

The object of our near heart-failure is sitting prettily on the settee, dipping Jaffa Cakes into a cup of tea and staring, bewildered, at her fingers, that keep ending up with nothing in them. Every time I come through that door I die a little, until she recognises me, then I'm reborn. It's called my reprieve from the inevitable. 'Hello, my bonny lass,' she looks at me, benignly. My mother never was benign. Nor was she razor-tempered, like she can be now. I kiss the top of her fragrant head, unable to take my eyes off her, just massively grateful that she's still here and powerfully aware that I must treasure each moment I have with her. I still don't believe the change that this illness has brought about in her, and, as there's no going back to the way she was, I sometimes think that if I stare at her long enough and hard enough I will somehow manage to preserve her, so she'll stay exactly as she is and never get any worse. Because I dread worse. I dread it with an agony that fills every corner of my ribcage and pushes and pushes until it threatens to blow me apart into two pieces that will never be welded together again.

She looks me up and down as though she is about to make a pronouncement. 'Long skirts look very nice indeed . . . on daughters.' She nods her approval. My dad gazes at her, beguiled.

Sometimes, through my heartbreak, I can smile at my mother in the way that you'd smile at a child. That's in my moments when I accept that when we get old, we somehow get stripped of rank, instead of getting awarded the medal of respect we deserve. And then I believe that dementia in some ways is kind, because at least eventually, when it gets really bad, they are too out of it to know. But I'm rarely this generous. Mostly I burn and I rail and I disbelieve there's a God. And I grieve for the lively-minded woman she was, the friend to me. I can still hear her say, with her unsentimental Geordie bluntness that seemed to contradict her exterior reserve: 'Shoot me and put me in a box if I ever get like that.' And we said, 'Oh, ha ha, don't worry, we will.' Because it's fine to joke about that stuff when you think it's never going to happen. What we should have done was bag her off to the doctor early on, have every test and scan under the sun to somehow pre-empt fate. *But*, as Rob will say to me, *you can't do that, Jill. That's not how life works.* And I'll say, *I know. But a good daughter would have tried.*

My dad makes us tea in the kitchen. There is something heart-breaking about his skinny wrists peeping out of the sleeves of his jumper, and the tremor of his gnarled, arthritic hands. 'Other than this episode today she's been champion, you know!' he says brightly. 'Almost like the old Bessie. The other day she even asked when you'd be home from school.'

My heart sinks. 'Oh, Dad,' I stare at the back of his down-like brown hair that's miraculously defied going grey. 'I don't go to school. I'm thirty-five.' He puts the teapot down, studies me for a few moments, like he's trying to recall me, then his chin wobbles and the tears come.

I stay for a couple of hours, valiantly trying to cheer him. Then he waves me off at the door, looking at me with that pathetic little face that will be etched in my memory to my dying day. My dad used to be a manual worker. Everything about him was virile and above-board, and, like Atlas, I imagined he could hold the world on those strapping shoulders and effortlessly run a marathon with it, breaking all records, setting new and unfathomable ones. I can't accept him as raw-boned and in the poorhouse.

I drive around the corner, pull over, and ring Rob. 'Of course he's not losing his mind too,' my husband assures me, through my stammers and sobs. 'He's seventy-five, Jill. He can barely take care of himself, let alone your mam. You've got to forgive him the odd slip. Hell, I forget things all the time and I'm only in my thirties.'

'Do you ever think your wife's still a teenager?'

'Only when you give me reason to. Which, come to think of it, is quite often.'

'Bastard,' I say, my sniffle replaced with a lame smile.

'Cheer up now, okay?' my hubby softly scolds me. 'I don't want you driving home upset or the next time I see you, you'll be wearing a toe-tag on a gurney.'

Rob's ability to always bring me out of my crisis is like some giant safety net I know will always be there when I fall. 'Well, if I am, will you make sure they give me a nice-looking toe-tag? Not one of those dismal "I'm dead" toe-tags. A lively one, the colour of my nail polish.'

'I'll see what they have in stock.' He laughs, then says, 'I love you.'

Going home, I'm stuck in yet another traffic jam on the Tyne Bridge. I don't feel like going to yoga now, but I hate missing things I've paid for.

In the mirrored studio of Better Bodies Gym, Wendy and I deftly try to extricate Leigh from a tricky lotus position. Her stick-skinny body resembles one of those pipe-cleaners I'd twist into my hair to make 'doofahs' as a kid. My exuberant pal Wendy is having thigh-slapping fits of the giggles. Her china-doll skin is flushed like a nectarine. She's got her chin-length bob that she colours a dark auburn youthfully pinned up in tiny clips with messy wet bits around her nape, making her look cute and about thirty-two instead of forty-two. Leigh sits on her haunches with her legs disappeared behind her and her feet flopping over her shoulders. 'I'm getting slowly-bruised flanks here!'

'Gordon Ramsay's favourite,' I tell her. I'm glad I came now.

'I know what her feet remind me of, stuck there,' Wendy turns to me. 'Elephant's ears!'

'Yes, you cheeky sod,' Leigh tries to look up. 'And you know what elephants have got, don't you? Long memories. So I won't be forgetting that comment.'

'I think it'd be better if you somehow tried to get her head out from round the back of her armpit first,' one of the other yogis puts her oar in.

'Pity heads aren't like lids and they could screw off,' Wendy chirps.

'Did you say "screw off"?' Leigh smiles. 'Now there's a suggestion . . .'

'Oh, God, did I tell you Lawrence's parents are coming next weekend?' Leigh blabs, when we have methodically unravelled her limb from limb and are towelling off in the changing room.

'Have you got the beer in, then?' Wendy asks her. Lawrence's parents claim they don't drink. Yet when they visit, the booze miraculously disappears from the fridge and Leigh can never find the empties. Then they turn up in the most mysterious places. Potted in the cheese plant. Lined up in the back of the china cabinet. Stuffing the fleecy hot-water bottle cover.

'Aye, but this time I'm filling the empties with ginger ale!'

'You're not!' Wendy's jaw drops and she looks across at me.

'I am!' Leigh cackles.

'You know,' Wendy looks in the mirror and wiggles a roll of the ab-flab she's always fighting, 'you should rent one of those nanny-cams.'

'What's a nanny-cam?' I ask.

'You know, one of those hidden cameras rich people have to spy on the hired help to see if they're bashing their brats.'

'Maybe I should direct one on Lawrence,' Leigh says. 'To find out what he does all day. Maybe he's into hardcore porn. Or getting laid on the Internet. God, I wish he was. Give me a spell off.'

Wendy and I smile.

As we leave the building, four handsome firemen are on their way in and stand aside to let us pass. 'Cor,' Leigh gawps after them. 'If there's a fire in there I think I'll run back inside. I mean, look at them. Is there such a thing as an unattractive fireman? I swear you never see one.'

'Oh, come on, that's not true.' Wendy, who never has eyes for anybody but the man she's married to, tugs Leigh's sleeve. 'That is such a cliché. There are plenty of very, very unattractive firemen.'

Leigh, duly reprimanded, pulls a playful face.

In the car park, Lawrence and Molly sit on the wall, Molly chastising her Barbie doll for not wearing her blue ballerina dress. 'Well we've both got our men picking us up tonight!' Wendy says, conspicuously looking around for hers. Her BMW's in for a service so she got a lift here from Leigh. Leigh reversed into a pole when she was late for a meeting so she's in Lawrence's old Honda, and Lawrence and Molly have bussed it here.

'They're taking me out to the Gate to see a movie,' Leigh whispers. 'If we can ever agree on which one we want to see.' Lawrence smiles benignly, like he knows he's being talked about.

'Hiya.' Lawrence kisses his wife. Funny, but they do look an odd pair – Leigh in her short, sharp little power suit and Lawrence exuding Make Love Not War in his trademark flowery shirt and ripped jeans, with his blond dreadlocks ponytail and beaded leather necklace. Leigh wraps Molly in a big hug. 'So, what are we going to see, then?' she nudges Lawrence affectionately. I'm pleased she seems back to her old self again.

Lawrence has a beautiful face. Nobody would be slapping it on a composite of their ideal man, but it oozes peace and goodness. And when he looks at his wife, it's with a certain quiet manliness that issues forth from him in the same way that his thinness exudes strength.

'Whatever you'd like,' he looks at her with a warm contentment. 'We thought we'd let you decide, didn't we Molly?' Molly nods, only caring about forcing a resisting glittery shoe on her doll's foot.

'Well, what's playing?' Leigh growls gently.

'Oh. I'm not sure.' He gets the frightened-deer face. 'I've not looked.'

'Well, what time do they start?'

I get the distinct impression that, with the good intention of taking his wife out to a movie, Lawrence knows he's cocked it all up like only he could. 'Oh, well, er, we'll have to go pick up a paper . . . at . . . the . . . store.' I often wonder if he ever just tells Leigh to sod off.

'Well, I'm going to need something to eat first,' she says.

'Ta-da!' Molly produces a brown paper bag, saving her dad's bacon. 'Pasta, mammy! We made it for you!'

Lawrence blanches. 'See,' he says to Wendy and me. 'We're not as useless as we look.'

Leigh makes a face that says *I never thought they were*.

'See you on Monday, boss,' Wendy calls after Leigh, then her perky little gaze goes around the car park again. 'Where is my husband? Neil's never late. And I have to finish reading *Curious Incident* for my book club meeting tomorrow night.'

'It doesn't sound like a novel with a pink high-heeled shoe on the front. I'd probably hate it.' I tell her I'll wait with her. Wendy's just started working at Leigh's company, filling in on reception for a maternity leave. She's been throwing herself at the job market for some time now, but nobody seems to want a forty-two-year-old junior when they can get a twentysomething one instead. It doesn't help that she hasn't worked since before the lads were born. But Wendy sees the forties as the start of life, whereas with Leigh, age is death by numbers. If you're feeling crap, Leigh will ultimately make you feel crapper by relating, with enthusiastic misery, to your problem and thereby legitimising it – which is usually just what you need. On the other hand, Wendy's glass is always so half full that sometimes you don't even bother trying to get her to see the empty bit, because she just wouldn't. You'd just end up feeling rotten for seeing it yourself. Then you might have to snap out of your own misery, and that would be a real pity, wouldn't it?

We perch on the wall and she asks about my mam and dad and I tell her about today's episode. 'Sometimes I feel so guilty, Wendy. I mean, I got there, somebody had brought her home, and rather than just feel thankful she was okay, I felt sorry for myself for having made an unnecessary trip.'

Wendy's face softens, like a good friend's would. 'Oh, Jill, you're only human. I'm sure you only felt like that because you saw her and you knew she was okay.'

'Sometimes I lose my temper with her, though, and I feel so bad. I'll want to shake her and say, "Think, Mam. How can you still be living in Yorkshire when you left there when you were twenty-one? And how can you still be twenty-one when you have a thirty-five-year-old daughter? It doesn't make sense." It's basic stuff. Nobody's asking her to remember the mathematical formula of pi.' Even saying this to Wendy feels like such a betrayal of my mother. 'Sometimes I think she's somehow letting this happen to her. Or I'll think, is this some sort of attention-seeking game she's playing with us? Or is she just being stupid? And then it kills me to think like that about my mam.'

She squeezes my hand briefly, then gives her meaty, freckly arms a good rub. 'I bet there's nothing you're feeling that countless other families haven't felt in the same circumstances.'

I feel the fizz of frustration. 'Well, anyway, how was your first week at work?'

'Oh, very good! Everybody's really nice. Leigh's been fantastic. Clifford's certainly a character.' Clifford La Salle is Leigh's gay, eccentric boss who founded the Fatz empire and interviews a person by asking to see what's in their handbag.

'Does he really fart all the time and light matches to hide it? I often think Leigh exaggerates the hell out of her stories.'

'He must have a gastric problem.'

'Ergh!'

'Poor man.'

'Poor you! But other than that . . . you're liking it, then?' I sensed there was a 'but' coming, and Wendy Robinson's not a 'but' sort of gal.

'Oh, yes. Definitely. When you think but for the grace of God I might have got that job at the call centre.' Wendy had got up and walked out in the middle of one of the rare interviews she'd had, when a very jumped-up nineteen-year-old kept asking her to prove that she had experience of dealing with people. She looks at me with lively candour. 'Oh, Jill, Leigh has a lovely job! She runs that place. The clients adore her. She's so capable.' She inspects her well-bitten finger-nails. Everything about Wendy is sporty, no-frills and down-to-earth. 'I told her over lunch the other day. I said, you've done so well for yourself just by being smart and working hard. You've got your family . . . you hold it all together and nothing has to give.'

'She wouldn't see it that way.'

'She didn't. She said good jobs were overrated.' Wendy gives a hearty shrug. 'But that's easy to say when you have one, isn't it? Don't get me wrong, I'm very grateful she hired me when nobody else would, but it's a bit humbling when you compare yourself to her.' She flashes a big smile at me. 'The whole thing of women juggling a career and family . . . I'd have liked that problem to solve.'

'Well, you shouldn't compare yourself to Leigh. You had twins in your twenties. Your parents had passed away. Neil's had retired to Spain. You had literally nobody to help you. Leigh has Lawrence. And Neil—'

'—was never there.' Her gaze goes around the car park again. 'Speaking of, where is he now?'

'I'll take you home.'

'No. I don't want to tell him not to bother, not when he'll be on his way.'

Because that would be awful for him! I look at my generous, considerate friend. From the moment I met her – through her younger sister, Joy, who I used to work with when we both had Saturday jobs in a pub as teenagers – I liked her massively, instantly, and the feeling stuck. (Joy moved to Australia years ago and married an outback man, and nobody really hears from her now.) Interestingly, though, because Leigh's an open book, in many ways I feel I know her on a deeper level than I do Wendy, even though I've known Wendy twice as long. (Leigh and I met when I did a brief temping stint at M&S where Leigh was a junior buyer, and we just instantly hit it off.) Leigh can sometimes piss you off; Wendy never does. There's a radiance to Wendy that comes from the inside. It's that of a person who is genuinely happy and has no hidden secrets. This makes for a very uncomplicated friendship. 'So, you're not regretting taking the job?' I had misgivings about it, though I don't know why.

'Oh, I'm thrilled to bits! There's a lot to do. It's not brain surgery, but it's detail. So I've got my lists written out and my Post-it notes all over the computer, and I'm trying to teach myself Excel because Clifford said he could use my help with some spreadsheets.' Humour twinkles her straight face. 'It took me a while to realise he wasn't talking about something that goes on the bed!'

Her dark brown eyes soften again. 'Leigh was particularly sweet the other day. She took me out for a nice lunch because it would have been Nina's birthday. She'd have been three.' She searches my face. 'I literally don't know where the time's gone, Jill.'

I squeeze her hand. 'Oh, Wend. I'm sorry. I remembered the date but didn't know whether to bring it up.'

'That was sweet of you both to remember.'

How could we not? Wendy had nearly finished a part-time degree at Northumbria when she surprised everybody by falling pregnant with Nina. It was a difficult pregnancy from the word go. Then Nina was born severely premature, making the possibility of her living as fragile as a snowflake resting on a feather. There were so many problems, but she kept bouncing back. Then she had to have part of her liver removed. But she survived when all the doctors said she wouldn't. Then Leigh and I were at the hospital, visiting. The doctor came in and broke the bad news. I remember Wendy and Neil, Leigh and me, walking to the incubator and watching Wendy's large finger stroke Nina's limp little finger-like arm. And I think that was the day I started to rethink my views about not wanting to be a mother.

'Here he is!' Her face lights up as the black Range Rover rolls into the car park. Neil gets out, his bright white hair striking against such a young face. He saunters around the front of the car in his charcoal suit, the top button of his white shirt undone and the knot of his grey tie yanked down mid-chest. Immaculately dishevelled. As though you could put him just as he is in a magazine ad for just about any luxury product and it would fly off the shelves. That, plus his degree of forgivable cockiness, and the fact that he puts the bad guys away for a living, makes him a real 'knicker-creamer' as Leigh'll say.

'My chauffeur arrives!' Wendy latches onto his arm. His perfectly handsome, young-Paul-Newman-ish face cracks a smile at me. It strikes me that if Lawrence had been half an hour late, then just breezed out of the car and hadn't instantly fawned an apology, Leigh would have tanned his backside the length and breadth of the parking lot, as I would have Rob's.

Neil's mouth meets Wendy's plump, coral top lip. Then his blue gaze, cool as a breath mint, looks over the top of her head, right at me. 'All right, Jill? What's new?' I feel his hand lightly in the small of my back. He doesn't wait for my answer. 'So, how's the job today, then?' he asks his wife. Odd timing for a big question like that, methinks.

Her gaze hangs on his face and she moves against him so he has to put his arm around her. Wendy first met Neil when he was a twenty-five-year-old police sergeant who stopped her car on Christmas Eve and offered her a free ice-scraper, and like a ninny she put her mouth on it and blew because she thought she was being breathalysed. 'It was good. Very good,' she sparkles. I suppose she'll fill him in when they get home.

'So, this Clifford's not got her running the company yet,' he says to me, extracting himself from her. 'She can still find time for yoga.' Wendy playfully slaps him and sends me a look that says, *Oh, isn't he thrash-around-the-floor hilarious!* Then she bends to pick up her sports bag and Neil gazes at my friend's generous backside in its lycra yoga pants with a certain appreciation that makes a quiet part of me pine. 'Our Paul wants picking up at the arena, too. I'm not sure where Ben is,' he says, covertly looking at his watch. Then he runs his hands through his hair in an impatient gesture.

'Movie,' she says, mimicking Ben's grunt. 'Ben speaks to me with one word or a shrug of the shoulders. The men in this family don't like to give too much away,' she looks at Neil then fans her face. 'Phew. Is it me, or is it warm?' Her eyes run over her husband and I feel like you often feel around these two: as though you're gate crashing a raunchy private party. Leigh and I think Wendy and Neil have a rollicking sex life. *And she never has to say to him 'Don't you have a headache?'* as Leigh will say, and chortle. *And he never has to slap her to see if she still has a pulse.*

It's probably all a bloody act, Rob'll say.

'Come on then, driver,' Wendy pushes him ahead and her lovely big bum in its tight pants seems to fold in smiling, self-satisfied creases. Neil puts his hands in his trouser pockets and saunters to the driver's side. And then my friend throws me a look over her shoulder that's not meant to ignite good-hearted envy in me, but somehow it does.

I drive home via Tesco, then Pause for Paws where I leave the dog when Rob can't take him with him to work. As I drive down our street, Kiefer hangs out of the window, barking at the world – at people, other dogs, front doors, stones and traffic cones, giving me a head-ache. In my kitchen I dig in my Tesco carriers for the ingredients to make my quick Thai chicken curry. I'm starving. With being late into work this morning, I missed lunch in my efforts to suck up to He Who Stares At Me Scornfully. I can't instantly find the scissors, so I try to open my bag of rice with a sharp knife. It goes through the tough plastic – and my finger – just as Rob walks in. 'Hiya treasure,' he shouts from the hall, then he sings, 'Why do you have to be a teenager in love . . .'

'Very funny.' I remember the daft little conversation we had earlier.

Upon sight of his lord and master, Kiefer's tail thrashes a tune on the parquet floor. 'All right, there, my angel?' Rob pets him and Kiefer gets hysterical. He stands on his hind legs and the pair of them do a dance around the room. There are three of us in this mar-riage, so it's a bit overcrowded. After they've smooched, Rob plants his gaze on me. He slides my specs down my nose, lays a tender little kiss first on my eyelid and then on my lips. 'Hiya, you. My little Lolita. Are you feeling better now? Did your yoga class help?'

'It did. Ish.' I hold my finger up and wiggle it.

'Good God, Jill! What've you done?' He marches me to the sink, thrusts my hand under cold water. 'You've got to stop doing things in such a bloody hurry! Hang on, I'll get a bandage.'

'Oh, Rob, it's just a little cut.' A sea of blood vanishes down the plughole. I watch my hubby of nearly ten years, in his white T-shirt that strains appealingly over his broad chest, open the junk cupboard above our fridge. And then there's this avalanche of odd shoes, empty gin bottles, Hoover bags, cookery books, panty-liners, Christmas cards, you name it, to which he says *fuck*. He tries to stuff it all back in there and says *fuck* again because everything keeps spilling out. Personally I avoid this cupboard like the plague for this very reason.

'Where do we keep the bandages, Jill?'

'I don't think we do keep bandages, Rob.'

'Well why bloody not? We seem to keep everything else.'

He's sexy when he's vexed.

'And how many times do I have to tell you that you need to leave this by the oven in case there's a fire?' He brandishes the miniature fire extinguisher he bought for me, which I keep trying to chuck out with the rubbish because I get tired of humouring his daft paranoia. But he always drags it back out again and plonks it by the oven, which just gets in my way, so now I shove it up there in the unmentionable cupboard. 'Stay there. Don't move.' He disappears down the narrow parquet passage that flanks our main living area which is essentially three rooms knocked into one. Something builders liked to do in seventies' semis to give the illusion of space. I hear him climb the stairs, his work boots imprinting manly thuds above me. He reappears with a roll of loo paper.

'Oh, Rob! My arm's not hanging off.'

His warm hand holds up my wrist, and his other carefully winds loo roll around my wound; he stops only to pop a kiss in the centre of my forehead, absorbed in the slow and loving process of mummification. 'You could have sliced your finger end off.' His voice is soft and cherishing.

'Pity, it's my middle one, too. I use it so much.' I demonstrate. He pretends to bite the rude gesture. I watch my husband as he works away on me. His serious, fine-featured face, eyes of the darkest grey-blue, the knit of his brows under his tumble of chestnut hair, and his tight-drawn, concentrating mouth. I feel intensely loved, and I fill with this urge to kiss that concentration off his face. He must catch something in my expression, because he does a double take, gives me that Are-you-thinking-what-I'm-thinking? look. So I give him the Oh-you-bet-I-am-baby one back. Our gazes hang there. My heart pounds wildly. Then his hand that was bandaging me slows. His thumb that was pinned to my wrist strokes it. My eyes savour his patient mouth with its upturned edges. And I forget all about my headache, my finger, the curry and my hunger. I close my eyes and drift in to him. My face is tilted upwards, waiting for his kiss; his breath makes little draughts on my skin. Seconds pass . . . Nothing happens.

I open first one eye, then the other. And somewhere deep inside me, a cringe slowly unfurls. Rob is studying me, just peaceably taking the measure of my face. His eyes have apology written all over them: the kind that would choke you if you tried to voice it. For a second he tenderly joins his forehead to mine, and we just stay like that. Then he drops my limp hand and shifts his attention back to my finger, his expression void like a doctor's. 'There,' he pops a chaste kiss on the big fat white bandage, doing a very good job of ignoring my bewildered scrutiny. 'All better now.' The room seems to lose oxygen. I don't move immediately, giving him a chance to rescue the moment. But he turns his back to me and starts making a big fuss of the dog instead. I turn back to my vegetables. Aubergine. Mushrooms. I immerse myself in slicing them as a feeling dies inside me. He wrestles with Kiefer on the kitchen floor. I clash a can of coconut milk on the marble counter, thrust the opener in it. The onions are making me cry. I mop my eyes with the back of my wrist, push cubes of chicken off my chopping board into the pan. 'You've not seen the green curry paste have you?' I ask him as I peer into the fridge. 'I swear I just bought a new one.' My voice sounds fallen.

'Eh? No.' Rob's leaning over the kitchen table now, thumbing through the *Evening Chronicle*. 'Oh, that green stuff in the jar? Yeah. I think I ate it.'

I close the fridge door with my elbow, nail a hand to my hip. 'What?'

'Yeah, I think I had it on toast the other night when you were out.'

'Green curry paste? On toast?'

He scowls over his shoulder. 'Aye. Why? It's dead nice.'

I throw up my hands. 'Well, how am I going to make curry now then?'

'With difficulty, probably.' He sends me a smile.

After we eat our bland dinner in silence, I drag myself upstairs. A pile of clean laundry that I made him bring upstairs yesterday is dumped in the middle of the floor. Well, to give him credit he did put it on the bed first, but moved it to the floor later so he could get into the bed. Rob will happily leave it there, just wearing things from it, chucking them off again, until the pile replaces itself like an exhibit for the clothing cycle of life. You'd never think Rob was a slob when you see him in his spanking white T-shirts, with his thing for Italian leather shoes. Nor when you see the fastidious pride he applies to his job (self-employed carpenter who can build anything from a chair to the house it's going in). I'm not particularly tidy myself – kitchen junk cupboards, say no more. But picking up my own mess after a long day is one thing; picking up his can make me resentful. Sometimes I'll chase him around the house, clipping his backside with a towel, shouting 'I'm not your sodding mother!' Mostly, though, I just tend to do everything myself, because it's less tiring than arguing about it.

I pick his dirty dog-walking shoe off the newly changed, white Ikea duvet cover – scream! – and get some weeny urge to clap his brains out with it. Then I catch myself. Argh! I think of how sweet he just was over my finger. How he constantly offers to have my parents come live with us. Rob is massively supportive in the ways that count. I've just had a tiring day. Fault being the one thing in any domestic disorder that's easy to find. *Get over yourself, Jill. It's hardly the end of the world that he didn't ravish you on the chopping board or playfully threaten to slam you with a large aubergine. Who goes on like that when they're chronically married? Nobody.*

Downstairs, Rob's staring through the window, watching Kiefer having a wee. 'I hate how he squats like that. I think somebody's going to have to show him how to do it like a man.' He beams a smile at me. 'How's your precious little finger?'

'It fell off.'

He reaches for my hand, brings it to his mouth, kisses it. 'A four-digit wife. I've always sort of wanted one.'

3

Rhododendrons are abloom in gardens everywhere as I drive my mam and dad to the beach. Rob didn't feel like coming. 'You don't mind if I don't?' he asked me as I was flossing my teeth, and he balanced a loo roll on my head.

I grinned. 'So long as you don't mind if I do.'

Long ago my dad and I decided it's important to keep my mam looking the way she would have kept herself: elegant, immaculate, even if she was just hanging the washing on the line. So today he's got her in her pink and green sundress and cardi. He's put too much blush on her cheeks, though, and her lipstick's bleeding over her lip-line, making her look like a cross between Tootsie and one of those strange old birds you see in the films who rip their wigs off and are really serial killers underneath. 'How is David?' she asks. This has to be the tenth time she's said this in as many minutes.

'Rob, Mam. You mean Rob. David is a lad I used to date fifteen years ago. The lad I dumped because he was a pound short of his taxi fare so he asked the driver if he could back up a quid.'

My dad titters.

'David,' she says, with an infatuated sigh. 'Ah, David is a lovely boy.'

We park opposite a stretch of white Georgian town houses and the pink Seaburn Hotel where my dad used to bring us for Dover sole and claret for birthdays. My mam's carrying bags – the lunch she said she'd packed us. I was very impressed till I saw they were really carriers full of toilet rolls. *Ooh! We'll enjoy these, won't we!* I cooed at her. We truck over to a spot in front of the white loo pavilion, and set up camp. I feel a bit guilty about not having brought the puppy now, but I was worried he'd hatch a stinker in the car. My dad troops off to buy us 99s from the ice-cream van but comes back empty-handed, saying the driver – disgusting bugger – was picking his nose. 'In it up to his elbow,' is his description.

We sit for maybe half an hour and Mam gets fidgety. She delves into the carrier and finds toilet rolls and asks me, with the haughtiest disdain, why on earth I have brought toilet rolls, and where, pray, are the sandwiches? Morrisons supermarket is across the way so I decide to go buy us something rather than chance my mother in a restaurant.

They've done wonders to the sea front since I was little. New pubs, Italian restaurants and designer fountains front onto cinder-toffee sand and swelling greenblue waves like bolts of velvet in an upholstery store. I pass the amusement arcades and the fairground rides with the music blaring and the kids' high-pitched squeals. In Morrisons I zip around, filling a basket of things I know my mother likes, and in the checkout line I think of my daft conversation with Rob yesterday about how Arnold Swinburn had stood over my desk waiting to sign a letter I was typing, and was pointedly fingering through the *Hello!* mag on top of my in-tray. 'He was doing it to imply that I read magazines instead of doing my work,' I grouched to Rob.

'He probably fancies you, so he's awkward around you and he hides it by being a bit of an arsehole. Men are like that. Especially married ones, because they feel dead guilty. So they want to make out it's your fault for being too much of a temptation.'

'Speaking from experience, are you?'

'What else would I be speaking from?' He gave me his sly smile. Then he said I shouldn't have mags on my desk, though, so I had it coming. So then we got into a fight. He said if I was that sensitive about it maybe it's because I knew he was right. I did a big 'uuuurrrrh' and got the urge to clap a pan over his head.

Rob will sometimes wind me up just because he knows he can. But then again, if he'd just said, 'You're right, dear,' life would be boring, wouldn't it? Even if it would have been the right response. I pay, then I go briskly out of the supermarket.

I vaguely register that there's a lifeguard sitting on one of those white lookout posts by the shore. I get back to the beach where our chairs are and . . . oh, no. The towels are there. The chairs are there. 'Have you seen an older couple? They were sat here,' I ask some kids with lily-white bodies and legs caked with dark, wet sand. 'Naah, missus,' one young lad says. I dump my shopping in one of the chairs and hotfoot it across the sand to the toilets, with this clenched-up feeling inside me. What if she gets on a bus and we never see her again? Or worse, walks under one? I remember the lifeguard. I hasten down the sand in pursuit of his yellow outfit. 'Mr Lifeguard,' I pant to the back of his head, as he gazes off at some kids playing on a crop of rocks. Then he turns and his eyes meet mine over the top of his sporty-framed sunglasses.

'I, erm. I'm . . . erm . . .' Hit by a ton of bricks. He's handsome.

Nothing like I'm expecting. Older. At least forty. With a yachtsman's weathered complexion, velvety black hair that looks wet and is raked back off his face, European-style. And intelligent, inquisitive eyes the colour of new pennies. 'What?' I say, daftly, because he's studying me with a look that – weirdly – you could only call faint surprise.

'What?' he says back, and I think he might have an accent. And then he smiles, a demolishing, testosterone-filled smile.

For a moment I can't speak. Then I remember myself. 'You have to help me. I've lost my mam and dad. They were here, now they aren't and I'm panicked and I don't know what to do.'

He peels off his sunglasses. 'Well,' he says, climbing down from his chair, and I can't help but notice the bracing of his forearm muscles, and the small everyday detail of his having a body like a god. 'Lots of little girls lose their mam and daddy. Is nothing to panic. I will help you to find.'

The accent throws me. The unusual rise and fall of

his sentences. The way he emphasises words we don't. But he's obviously a sexist pig, judging by how he's blatantly enjoying my little denim sundress. I feel a sudden massive hostility, the kind I'll get around very attractive men. 'Look, this may sound like a big laugh to you, but my mother suffers from dementia. If she disappears and something happens to her, I just might have to kill myself.'

'Well, we wouldn't want that, or I might have to take my own life, too,' he says, smiling at me with his eyes. Then he accompanies me back down the sand, asking concerned questions. But his body's angled attentively towards me like he's never seen a female before, and for some reason I've decided he's awful. *Aren't you a bit old to be doing this for a living?* I feel like saying, but don't.

When I get back to the deckchairs my parents are sat there happily eating the sandwiches I bought. 'Oh!' I cry, wanting to heap kisses on their heads and murder them at the same time. 'You're here!' Relief of reliefs.

'You know, if you wanted the lifeguard to come talking to you, you could have just ask.' He grins diabolically.

Oh, God, he thinks I made this up! My mam looks at him and a strange beam of recognition comes over her face. 'Oh, David!' she says, all theatrically.

'Oh, Darling!' the lifeguard gushes back, which makes me shriek a laugh. And then she gives her wide-eyed seal of approval and bursts into a strange baritone chorus of that song she's taken to singing, to the chafe-end of your patience. 'You'll never miss your mother till she's GONE!' I do not know this extrovert person.

Oh, God. I clap my hands over my face. 'Where the hell did you go?' I ask my dad between gritted teeth.

'To the toilet, chucka.'

'You never. I went looking for you.'

'Not them toilets, chucka. The sea toilet. Your mam wanted to go au naturel.'

'Oh.' Her shoes are sopping wet. This man must think we're mental as balls in a lottery draw machine. But he starts having a charming crack on with my dad, who I can tell can't understand a word he's saying. God, he's striking though. He's got one of the nicest mouths I've ever seen: a full top lip, with a Cupid's bow as sharp as cut crystal. When he turns and catches me gazing at him like I'm trying to memorise him, I blabber, 'Well, thank you for your help. But it seems we're fine now.'

'Is pleasure for me,' he says, still combing me with that openly infatuated look some men adopt as a strategy to get into your knickers. 'You walk with me back to my chair, perhaps? For all my trouble.'

My mam and dad are having a set-to now over a toilet roll. Better break it to him. 'Look, I'm married.' I wiggle my ring finger at him.

'Well, if your husband was here he could come too.'

I grin. 'You took that one on the chin, didn't you?'

He laughs, surprising me by understanding me, and his laugh is even more of a shock wave than his smile, if that's possible. 'Want a squidgy chocolate cake?' I tear a carrier bag off my dad's knee. 'Some barbecue crisps?' He puts his sunglasses back on. I can't see where his eyes are now. I feel I'm being ravished by his gaze, and it's lovely!

'You're not from here,' I start blathering. 'Are you Italian? Greek, baby?' *Greek what?* 'Greek *maybe*.'

'Greek!' He scowls like it's a cardinal insult. 'No. I am Ra-shint.'

He's rationed?

'Oh! You're Russian! But hang on, I thought Russians were pale.' And hard-up looking. And this man is burgeoning with everything that's decadent about life.

He seems to find this funny, shows me those muscular tanned arms. 'It's from working outside. Sun, you know, it does this to people.'

'Really?' I try not to smile. 'Does it? I'd never have known.' I love how he says his *w*s like they're *v*s. Rolls his *r*s. Draws out his vowels. Rrrrr-aaah-shint.

'He sounds like Mario Lanza,' I hear my mother's starry little voice. Then my dad growls, 'Does he hell. My backside sounds more like Mario Lanza.'

He asks me my name.

'Mrs Jill Mallin.'

His eyes flick over me. 'Mrs is an unusual name.'

I have to look away, look into my shoulder, scratch my head, anything to . . . 'What's your name, then?' I ask.

'An-drey,' he says, musically, and he peels his glasses off again and his gaze concentrates itself on mine.

'Andrey.' *Where've I heard that name before?* Our pupils lock together. 'You can't be.'

He puts his hand on his heart. 'I swear I am. Ask my mother.'

Ask his who? But he's not *that* Andrey. Of the note on the car? But how many Andreys can there be in the North-East? 'Look . . . I . . .' This is too weird. 'Do I . . . Do I know you?'

'You could have,' he grins that grin which should get him arrested. 'But you never called.'

I clap a hand over my mouth. 'But . . . bloody hell.' This is Sunderland. That was Newcastle. This is now. That was – what? – over a month ago. Then I get what's wrong with this picture. 'Hang on. You don't drive a hundred thousand quid car!'

He does that hand on heart business of pretending his feelings are hurt. 'What? Because I am work as lifeguard on Seaburn beach? You English girls . . .' He wags a finger, tuts. Then his mouth comes close to my ear. 'But as it happen, you are right. I don't drive brand new Mercedes. I drive car that was parking opposite the Mercedes. I just happened to witness your very bad parking. I thought the lady is beautiful. And I am not a man to miss an opportunity.'

'Oh, yuck,' I hear my dad.

I'm already flailing a sceptical hand. 'But even if this yarn is true, why wouldn't you have just got out of your car and come to talk to me?'

He frowns. 'Sometimes, men, you know . . . talking is their first mistake.'

Yeah, right. He probably drives an old jalopy, that's why. A clapped out three-wheeler. His head was probably holding up the roof. I bet he didn't dare get out or it'd collapse like a metal wigwam. I smile inwardly.

'And besides, I wanted to see if you'd call. Women can never resist man with nice car.'

'Oh, that's such an old cliché.' I give him a look that says, *And so are you.* 'I'd never judge a man by his car.' I glance at my mother who's still gawking at him like he's Michelangelo's David.

'Don't mind us,' my dad says, and pointedly clears his throat. 'Carry on chatting up me daughter, lad, I'm too old to give you a thick ear for it. And I'm sure me son-in-law won't mind.'

'He won't,' my mam enthusiastically chimes in.

'Thank you,' the Russian says, clearly not getting my dad's sarky business. A couple of bikinied young lasses walk past us, send Andrey covetous looks, then look at me and giggle. 'But supposing I had called thinking you were the owner of a Mercedes, you'd have had a lot of explaining to do, wouldn't you?' *When you turned up in your old jalopy.*

His gaze travels over me again. 'This may be. But by the time I would be finished, I would have won you with my charm.'

'You reckon?' I'm critically aware that I'm flirting. Like I used to be quite good at, back in the days when Gorbachev was a baby. 'So, well then, d'you live in Newcastle, like?' My dad digs out the *Daily Express* and conspicuously tries to mind his business.

'No. But I go out there, to Quayside, always. Nightlife in Sunderland is too young, even for me.' That cocky smile again.

Ah. He goes out there. Nightlife too young here.

Even for him. Oh, ha ha. Oh no, my eyes just whip down his shorts and he sees.

'And what is more strange is – and you are really going to fall over when I tell you this . . .' He gestures for me to come closer, which I do, noting the warm rays that seem to spill out like sunshine from his smile. 'I see you there, at car. But it is not first time. No. First time I see you in Afterglow, before Christmas—'

'Likely story,' my dad clears his throat again.

'You were in dress of emerald green. Different eyeglasses though. You were with friends. Women friends.' Then cheekily he adds, 'No husbands.'

Leigh and Wendy and I go there all the time! He remembered the dress! My 1940s belted coat dress that I got from the vintage shop in York, which I wore once then felt like Bette Davis in a time warp. And my old glasses! My God, this is beyond unbelievable. My first thought is – is he stalking me? But then again, it's not like he could be accused of following me here, could he? 'Well, I never thought the North-East was so small!'

'Is not. Is just that you are kind of girl a man see once and he remember anywhere.'

'Oh, God, double yuck with bells on,' says my father again.

Okay, admittedly, from anybody else that would have sounded like the corniest line ever. But, I think, he saw me twice in Newcastle, he remembered my dress for heaven's sake, and now I'm seeing him here. How completely, unbelievably—

'Fate,' he says. 'Don't you think?' Then his gaze slides past me to a woman's arse in a bikini.

'I stopped believing in fate and fairies when I grew up and turned thirty.'

'Well, personally, for me, I think things like this happen for a reason.'

Yeah, bollocks. He's practised at this. He's a good-looking, cocky, rather past-it lifeguard who stares at women's bottoms in bikinis and happens to have a good memory for faces. And frocks.

And I'm married.

Fuck.

There. I've sworn.

'Seriously, though,' he pulls me aside now so he's out of my parents' earshot. 'That was real reason why I did not come over to talk to you beside car. I had seen wedding ring in bar. So this way, with note, I think if she call perhaps she not so happily married. Perhaps I have chance.'

'Perhaps,' I hear my mother say.

I'm lost for words.

'So, what do we do with this?' he whispers, and he grins that mayhem-causing grin again.

'*What do we do with the drunken sailor? What do we do with the dr—*'

'Dad, pack it in!' I grit my teeth. Then I look at Andrey again. 'We don't do anything. Remember, I didn't call.'

His smile falters, like a man who's not used to having to take a cold shower. 'Of course. You are married.' His mouth moves in to my ear again, making a warm breeze that sends a tickle around my neck and for some totally daft reason I think he's going to kiss me.

'Happily married.' He pulls away, his pupils directly on mine, starting little flames in me. 'Nice meeting you, heh?' he says, and then he turns and he walks away.

'Oh, he's going? Shame.' My dad doesn't take his eyes off his paper.

4

Newcastle beat Millwall 2–0. It was a good match. Last of the season. Free tickets are one of the perks of my job. I grab Rob's arm and dodge Arnold Swinburn and wife coming out of the private box from where the manager's family and the other bigwigs view the game. 'With an arse like that on her no wonder he's after you,' Rob says. We file out with the crowd that'll soon be stampeding down Northumberland Street like a herd of manic, dyspeptic zebra, chanting 'Howay the Lads!' Then they'll barge into the Bigg Market pubs where they'll swill back beer until closing time before staggering onto the last Metro home with all the wasted twelve-year-olds in their underwear.

Rob's going away tomorrow to suss out a contract job for some show homes in Penrith, so we won't be late home. Besides, we feel a bit guilty about leaving the puppy. 'Don't want him getting depressed,' as Rob said.

'No,' I replied, 'or he might do something really terrible like phone the Samaritans and hang himself with his rope toy when they can't make sense of his bark.'

'You're a hard-hearted woman,' my husband playfully scolded me. But this is our Saturday date thing: my rule. Nothing gets in the way of that, be it animal, vegetable or mineral. Speaking of animals, we go to that Italian ice-cream place that's run by a couple of horn-dog Italian brothers, in the gorgeous building that used to be Lloyd's bank. The younger one sits by the espresso machine and says 'Ciao, bella!' to my breasts. Rob deliberately plants himself in front of the Italian, arms crossed manfully over manful chest ('penis-measuring', as Leigh calls it), waiting to be greeted too. But the Italian completely ignores him. I order coffee. Rob swaggers to the freezer to look at ice-cream flavours, sending me sidelong glances as the Italian carefully flirts with me. I can't look at my husband or I'll set off laughing.

We take my coffee and Rob's espresso gelato and claim an outdoor table overlooking the majestic Theatre Royal that's just turning out its crowd of matinee goers. The sun's high and bright, but it's crisp out, not nearly as warm as it was. 'Come here,' Rob picks a hair off my eyelash. 'Another one of the flies, is he?'

I slump across the table. 'Erm, could be.'

'You get them, mind, don't you? The real lookers.'

'Ooh! Mee-ow!' I mimic clawing and watch his lips fasten around the spoon.

He narrows those sapphire pools-for-eyes. 'Wha'? Me, jealous of an ice-cream man with a funny accent? That'll be the day.'

'Yeah, but they say Italians are good lovers.'

'What with? Their average height's four feet three. You'd probably need an ultrasound to find it.' He shoves another spoonful in his mouth while I chuckle. 'He's generous, mind. I have to hand it to him. It's a big dish, this, for only a quid. I bet it's gannin off.'

'Can I have some?'

'Neh, get your own.' He pretends to move the spoon away, then holds it out to me, spoon-feeds me, catches runny bits down my chin. Next, we play our daft little game where we rate passers-by on their clothes, their hairdos, how fanciable they are. We get through about three victims when Rob says the immortal words: 'I need the can.' Rob's bowels maketh great legend. But Leigh says Lawrence is like that too; all fellas are. Except Neil, I'll add. We've decided that Neil, just like the Queen, doesn't go. 'Told you that ice-cream was off,' he says, as he hurries inside.

I grow old in his absence. Ten minutes. Twenty. Where the hell is he? The Italian keeps catching my eye and smiling in cheeky acknowledgement of how grim marriage can be (although it wouldn't be with him, of course!). Finally, Rob comes back looking relieved. 'Bloody hell!' I hiss. 'Could you not cut it short?'

'Does Niagara Falls have a tap?' He sits down. 'I told you the bastard was trying to poison me. I could have manured Yorkshire.'

'Ergh!' I clap my hands over my face.

'Hard lines for that poor lass, though.'

'Lass?'

'Yeah, good-lookin' bird. Was giving me the eye. She'll not be now, though. She went in after me.' Rob peers inside at the Italian. 'Look at him, still staring over here. He needs to get his eyes on somebody else's wife, the midgety git. I should have taken my ice-cream glass in with me, filled it, and stuck it on his counter with a spoon in.'

I howl till the tears roll down my face. As we leave, the Italian shouts, 'Ciao, bella!' and I crack up again.

'Why's he think you're called Bella?' Rob squeezes me, gives me his sly smile.

The sun seems to bring Geordies out in droves: little ruffians outside the video arcades, girls and mams on the bargain hunt, downtrodden husbands trying to stop their wives spending money, and the lovely legless football fans lurching into pubs. The odd one out for the count, being hauled hammock-style by his mates up the street. Because Rob hates shopping (unless it's for him) we spend a fraught five minutes in Gap while I try quickly to find a pair of jeans. 'What you think of these?' I model a pair.

'They're great.' Rob leans a shoulder against the wall, bored.

'Or these?' I hold up another.

'Them are nice too.'

The bonny young assistant who's folding jeans gives Rob the look-over and smiles, entertained. 'Well, which ones are better, though?' I ask him.

He sighs, stifles a yawn. 'Both of them. I mean, neither.' He musses the back of his head. 'Either.'

The girl grins broadly. A typical bloke, but she loves him for it.

Then we're in Fenwick's men's shoes department. Ever since Rob read an article about how rich people only wear Italian shoes, Rob will buy nothing else. 'Listen,' he'll say, 'there's no way you could ever appreciate the orgasmic joy of wearing shoes that make you feel you're walking on clouds, until you too earn a living clobbering around building sites in hard, heavy boots, in all weather, day after day, growing callouses the size of monkeys' brains.' I've tried saying, 'But maybe you can get comfy shoes – probably about ten pairs of 'em – without having to spend so much.' But he tells me it's his money; he's earned it. I need to try minding my own business. Apparently I have this tendency to stick my big nose into things that don't concern me. Apparently I should just worry about what's on my own feet, not his, then apparently we'd all be a lot happier. Apparently.

So here we are in Fenwick's. I grow old as Rob gets the mumsy sales lady to explain the finer points of Italian shoes. 'You have such a good way of putting it,' he woos her with his quiet charm. 'Can you tell me again how they slice up those specially bred organic cows?'

Walking down Grey Street, Rob stops to gaze at its subtly descending curve, and the ancient sepia-coloured buildings on either side that seem to stand on military parade. 'Come hither,' I pull him to Waterstone's's elaborate window because I need a new pink novel to read. We stand beside a couple of serious, bookish types who are chatting about the latest Salman Rushdie bestseller that's displayed. Rob nudges me. 'So, tell me when you next meet your parole officer?' he says, loudly. The bookish types stop talking and glare at me. 'You sod!' I yank him down the steep bank, pulling him extra hard because I know it hurts his knees. We disappear under the footbridge and come out at the Quayside, chatting about everything from the trousers I want to go back and buy (which he now says he hated because they gave me 'plumber's bum-crack'!) to our puppy having eaten the cord from our Venetian blinds.

I'm just thinking how we haven't had a fun day like this in ages when we cross the Blinking Eye bridge. A handsome young father barrels towards us with his kid in a pushchair, wheels rumbling across metal, the little lad squealing with the thrill. I happen to look up at Rob. And I see it. The quiet, covetous gaze.

When we were first married, we were pretty sure we didn't want children. In my twenties I'd actually pray I wouldn't have a baby because it felt like the end of life as I knew it. And for a sensitive fella, Rob has a very unsentimental attitude to family. Maybe it's from growing up without a father. When his mother was four months' pregnant, his dad went out to get a haircut and never came back. (Rob was raised as the man of the family, which I believe makes him such a good husband.) For years, Rob would grimace at the sight of a baby. 'God, it's got a face like a worm-eaten sprout. Eat, sleep and shit, that's all they do. They've got nowt to contribute to the world, have they? You can't have a sensible conversation with 'em. They don't get any of your jokes. How can they not give a toss about who won the match?'

But then, the longer we were married and the

happier we were, we no longer had a strong enough reason not to do it. So we stopped birth control and decided to let nature take its course. Rob still claimed he was doing it mostly for me, although he'd say things like, 'I hope we have a girl. A little you . . .' and he'd get that quietly pleased expression. Then I caught him making a crib, which was really daft given that I wasn't yet pregnant. 'A bit ahead of things, aren't you?' I teased. He glanced up at me, stain brush in hand, looking very handsome. 'Just in case she gets an earlier boat.' We tried for over a year. I got tested and was fine. Then Rob got tested and found out he had a problem. 'Total sperm count: zero,' he read to me from the piece of paper that came in the mail. We trooped off to see two specialists. I couldn't get my head around the diagnosis. I thought that if Rob could ejaculate he had to have sperm. Some sperm. Enough to do the job. I kept thinking of that little egg I saw on my ultrasound, how mesmerised I was to see my body preparing to create life. How sad now that my little egg would be like the French Lieutenant's Woman in that film, wandering the shores of my Fallopian tubes, waiting for her lover who wasn't coming. It saddened me to think I'd never have the sights, smells and tastes of being pregnant, like other women. I didn't go potty and stalk maternity wards or nick babies at bus stands, but I'd go off certain foods, my breasts would be tender and a strange brewing feeling took up tenancy in my stomach. 'I have to be pregnant,' I said to Rob. 'Why do I have morning sickness? Why is my period late?' Rob would get annoyed. 'Azoospermia,' he'd say. 'I have no

sperm. I'm unable to produce a baby.' But I was sure
we were going to prove the doctors wrong. And then
my period would come and I'd plaster on a happy face
for Rob, but inwardly I'd massively mourn that baby
I'd been so sure I was having. I felt like they say
amputees feel when they lose a limb – knowing it's
gone but feeling it's still there. Then I'd say to myself,
Jill, you can't miss what you've never had. But you can.
You can grieve without having lost.

'You can leave me, you know,' Rob said, in one of
my weak moments when I couldn't mask my despair.
We were in bed. 'If you left me for somebody who
could give you a baby, I wouldn't think badly of you
one little bit.' I felt one of his tears roll into my hair. 'I'd
still love you,' he whispered, 'but with the best will in
the world, I'd let you go. And if I saw you walking
down the street one day with your new husband and
your child, a part of me would feel nothing but joy for
you.'

I bawled my eyes out. 'Of course I'm not going to
leave you! You're my life! Not some baby that I've
spent half my life not wanting.' I planted protective
kisses on him, trying to make that feeling go away, of
catching myself in a lie. Because I did have my moments where I'd see my life in scenes with some other
husband: leaving Rob today, meeting someone else
tomorrow, marrying him Thursday and having his
baby by the weekend. I'd just have to look at a man
who had a kid and find him instantly more attractive,
because he was virile. My old criteria for a partner –
tall, dark, handsome, sense of humour, job, no beer

belly – seemed to come a naive and distant second to that glorious F-word: Fertile.

Infertile. Childless. Barren. We can't have children. At some point we'll have to get round to telling everybody. But Rob doesn't want to yet, so I have to respect that.

I'm okay about it. I've stopped wanting what he can't give me. I suppose I'm like that. I can still feel like a woman without being a mother. And I still have a family because I have Rob. Besides, we could always adopt, which we've not talked about yet – because, well, we've not talked.

Because Rob has taken it badly. Rob's come to desperately want what he can't have. Rob feels a failure. Rob feels less than a man. Rob would never tell me this, but I know. After all these years with somebody, you know the things they cannot say. You feel the things they can't feel. Maybe that's why he's gone off sex. Maybe it reminds him of his failure. I try not to grumble about it. I keep thinking, just give him a few more weeks . . . But then I just get impatient to have everything be all right between us again. The few times we have made love since we found out, our inability to make a baby has lain there between us, like a third wheel on a date. But I worry that the time will come when he'll want to be in the arms of somebody who doesn't have this history with him, who doesn't sometimes cry when they're in bed with him.

I bleed for him. I bleed for us because we've fallen into this dark place. And I just want to make him all right again, see him happy again, but I don't know how to make that happen.

Now, on this bridge, since seeing that dad and his kid, all the joy seems to have been wrung out of him, leaving only a sad and pensive shell. I take his warm hand as we arrive on the Gateshead side, in front of the Baltic, with its banner advertising the new Antony Gormley exhibition. The sun's been dramatically exchanged for that thin, quiet rain that soaks you in seconds. A girl is quickly packing a harp into a case as Geordies scatter onto buses that are switching their lights on. We go inside to take cover, stand by the window and watch the rain coming down. When it eases off, we leave. On our way back across the Blinking Eye, I can feel his sadness. It is palpable. I don't know what to say to him, so I just take his hand in mine again and give it a reassuring squeeze. 'Thank you. I love you, treasure,' he says quietly, as though we've just undergone some sensitive thought transference. His thumb massages my knuckles. We stop halfway over and listen to a Newcastle that's grown louder in the rain.

The Tuxedo Princess, the nightclub boat where we met, still sits there on the river. We often come and look at it, and I'll ask him – again – about when he first saw me . . . 'Well, I saw you standing on the edge of the dance floor with your three mates, in your buttoned-up blouse and poodle perm, and I thought, "There's a rose among thorns". And then when you smiled at me and you didn't look away, I thought, "Please God, let this work".'

Then he'll ask me the same thing.

Rob did make quite an impression. There was something Heathcliffesque about his tumbling dark hair, intense, almost sapphire eyes, and his quiet way of watching me. He oozed a sense of contemplation and reserve, yet he wasn't boring; he was witty and gave me the giggles. I thought, 'Here's somebody who isn't Your Regular Legless Geordie Thug. Peel me off the floor!' By the end of the night there was already something about Rob that made me love him, and the fact that I'd only known him a few hours meant that time wasn't moving fast enough for my liking. What followed was just a close friendship, because Rob thought I was out of his league – was convinced I was waiting for some millionaire. I just reckoned I was too giggly for him, or too loud, but he liked me as a pal. But then came the defining moment. Seated waiting for a Chinese takeaway, him telling me about some famous mobster his aunt married in America, I threw myself on him. He lost his ability to speak. I burrowed into his neck, relishing this new proximity of him. Then two awkward hands clamped themselves, bear-like, around my back. 'I'm in love with you, Rob,' I croaked. I was thinking 'God, I'll have to chuck myself off the Tyne Bridge after this humiliation,' because for sure he didn't love me back. There was this weird little pause, then a voice . . . 'Two order black bean ticken, flied lice.' We could only see the top of a head across the counter. Rob peeled my arms off him, scoured my face, keeping me in suspense. Then he said, 'D'you suppose they forgot the sweet and sour?'

I wondered whether the Tyne was going to feel cold.

Later, when we were opening the fortune cookies,

Rob read me his. 'It says, *A sudden confession can bring a change in destiny.*'

'It doesn't say that!' I read mine, disbelieving my eyes. 'Oh, my God, it says, *Accept the next proposition you hear.*' I waggled it in his face.

'Bloody hell,' he raked in the bag for the last cookie. 'It says, *You are of double character: An active socialite and a serious thinker.*'

We piddled ourselves laughing. When we stopped, he said, 'I'd better ask you to marry me. I think Buddha would want it this way.'

An aeroplane passes noisily overhead, startling me out of my reminiscing. A train slides over the bridge on its way to Sunderland. Everybody moving, going somewhere. Except, I sometimes think lately, us. I climb my free hand up his arm, feel the soft warm hairs on it. I married the love of my life, the first, the only. And when I fell for him, it wasn't because I was thinking I wanted to have his babies. I was thinking that I love him and I can't imagine ever letting him go or not seeing him again. I am so happy when I'm with him. I am this lit-up person.

'Rob . . .' I gently nuzzle up to him. The other day I asked him why he never dances with me in the super-market any more. Not so long ago he'd have thought nothing of snogging me on this bridge while disapprov-ing seniors passed and scowled at us. His arm comes out in goose-bumps, the hairs stand up. As if by reflex I press my breasts into his bicep. But he stiffens, draws his arm back so quickly, and there's an instant where we both register his reaction. Then he brings the arm around me, pulls me into him. Affectionately. Appeasing. But that's about it. We stand without speaking and stare at big ships.

We eat at Saigon Sam's, a new place that opened in a reinvented garage behind St Mary's Church. The food's good but the atmosphere decidedly too funky for our mood. I push chicken around my plate with a fork. The things we can't talk about speaking in a voice so loud that it drowns out even our ability to chit-chat over dinner. All this – what? – because he saw a man and his son? Or was it because I cosied up to him on the bridge? We sit here like two empty eggshells. I keep looking at him, hoping he'll say something, but his eyes are fixed in a blank stare while he chews food he doesn't even taste.

There's a couple at the next table, a good-looking pair a little younger than us, married, drinking matching orange cocktails. She's got one of those elfin haircuts and has on a pastel ribbed top that emphasises the small, attractive swell of her chest. They're not saying all that much. But a cross-current runs between them, in their silences, their glances, their occasional laughs. They're in love. And I can't keep my eyes off them. A lump rises in my throat that I can't swallow back down. I know they know I'm watching them, but my fascination outweighs my manners. As we leave and I slip into my jacket, I glance over again. The girl is slowly climbing her bare toes up his trouser leg.

'Rob, I think it's time we talked,' I venture gently, when we get home and sit in our unadorned front room, me on our chocolate-coloured settee, Rob in the wicker chair by the window. The evening light is making it harder for me to see his face properly and easier, therefore, to confront him.

'Oh, Jill, don't go spoiling a nice day.' He tussles with little Kiefer, who's a grateful ball of excitement.

'We *have* had a nice day Rob. A lovely day.' *Don't you understand? This is what makes this worse.*

'I know. We always do.'

My heart cracks. 'Then why don't you want me?'

He frowns, an expression his face is not used to. 'Want you? Of course I want you.'

'But you obviously don't fancy me any more!'

I can read all that pain backed up in his serious, kindly blue eyes. 'Fancy you? Of course I fancy you.'

'Then why won't you make love to me? We never have sex and when I initiate it you always turn me down! Have you any idea how unfeminine it makes me feel when you keep rejecting me, Rob?' The words fall out sounding shallow and callous. I didn't mean for them to.

He suddenly looks shocked, tired, waxy-pale. I've emasculated him. 'Reject you? We do have sex! I don't know what you're going on about.'

Does he really not? He goes back to wrestling with the dog, catches his knuckles on the coffee table but doesn't even flinch. 'Rob, it's been five months. You've not touched me in all that time. Do you honestly think that's normal?' Maybe it's not a long time to other people. But five days would have

been an eternity to us, before. I stare at his unblinking profile. 'I wish . . . I wish somebody would
tell me how you condition yourself to be sexually
unaware of the man you love . . . because I'm
damned if I know, Rob. I don't know how to act
around you any more.' I rub my face hard with both
hands and when I look up he is watching me. 'If . . .
if you take the sex out of a marriage there has to be
a whole new set of rules and codes of conduct,
doesn't there? But I suppose I've not learned them
all yet. I keep slipping . . .' I never was a very good
student.

'I don't know what you're babbling about,' he says
again, less certain of himself this time.

I try to keep calm. 'Rob, what's worse than the fact
that we're not making love is the way you won't talk
about it. You won't tell me what's wrong.' He tugs on
the other end of a rope toy, and the dog's commotion
just seems to go on around him because he's off into his
sad headspace again. 'I can't get a handle on you any
more, Rob. I don't know what you're thinking. What's
happening with us? You recoiled from me on that
bridge. It was like you couldn't bear the feel of me.
Is it something I'm doing wrong? Have you gone off
me? Tell me and I'll change. I'll do anything. Rob, look
at me!'

He looks at me with sad hostility. 'I don't know what
you're on about.'

'I can't stand this heartbreak between us, Rob.' My
voice breaks. 'You can't withdraw from me like this.
It's cruel. And unfair. And you're not like that. This is

what I don't get. It's like . . . it's like your heart's not in it any more.'

'In what?' he hits back.

'In this. In us. In me . . .'

He sits there on the floor, legs drawn up, elbows on knees. Kiefer walks rings around him, attention-growling, his tail slapping the table. 'Is there somebody else? Is that what it is?' Funny, I think I'm less afraid of this than the alternative.

He gets up abruptly, and it takes a lot to get Rob angry. 'Now you're being stupid. I'm not listening to this.' He walks through the arches into the kitchen.

I quickly pad after him, with Kiefer following. But then he just picks up his car keys off the window-sill and walks down our passage to the front door. 'Where are you going?' I trot after him.

'Out.'

'Out where?'

He throws up his hands. 'Out.'

'I won't let you run away.' I kick my slippers off and waggle a foot into one of my trainers; Kiefer takes off with the other one. 'I'm coming with you.'

'No, you're not.'

I try to snatch the keys off him and he sends me a look that's filled with frustration and despair. He goes to open the front door but I try to block him. My heart is thumping. Part of me wants him to hit me because that would show some bloody emotion, wouldn't it? 'Don't go,' I plead, wrestling my other shoe off the dog. 'I swear, if you walk out this time don't come back.' I don't mean it.

'Don't be a drama queen,' he says, and lightly moves me aside. I make a grab for his arm again but he's already outside. I run after him, thinking about hurling myself onto the bonnet if I have to. God, I don't recognise myself. I've become a raving lunatic.

All this. All this over sex.

But this isn't just about sex. This is my life. I'm only thirty-five.

'Come back,' I beg. I don't want him getting in a car and driving when he's angry. Nosy Eileen Sharrett from down the road passes with her bulldog with the pink nose and glowers at me over our privet. When she's gone by, I start bawling. Rob backs out of the drive, the dog whimpering to see him go. I go inside and the house feels bereft now. I always love Rob more in these dark moments after we fight, where there's the possibility I might have lost him. I sigh, go to the window and stare out at the empty spot on the drive, willing our car to come back. He'd do this after our petty little spats. Walk out. Drive off. Get to the end of the street and come back. The second he'd walk back in that door, we both knew all was forgiven. We'd even laugh about it. We'd go to bed, snuggle, glad to have one another back.

But he doesn't come back. I sit on the bottom stair. Kiefer sits on the dusty parquet and growls at me because I've upset his lord and master. Then I realise something. For the first time, I'm angry with Rob more than I feel sorry for myself or for us. And I'm helpless more than I'm optimistic. My bag is under the hall table. I dig in it for a hankie and come across a folded piece of paper. I open it out.

Andrey's phone number. I never did chuck it in the bin.

5

'They had a row yesterday, Leigh and Clifford.' Wendy polishes off her second glass of wine while I am barely halfway down my first. Rob's worked late all this week. You could say he's avoiding me. 'Jill, I didn't know what to do. They were screaming like an old married couple. It was totally odd, perverse behaviour.'

'What was it over?' I'm agog. Wendy, looking young and sparkly in a tangerine-coloured T-shirt with *Pineapple* written across the chest, crosses her arms and leans on the table.

'Well, Leigh was telling me Fatz doesn't fly with the size sixteens and over. But he's squashed her idea to launch a "Thin's Not In" fashion show, since he apparently spoke to one of his celebrity friends who said you'll never sell any woman on the concept that fat is more acceptable than thin. Leigh said she wasn't trying to change people's perceptions about body image, she was only trying to find a fun way of selling fitness wear to "normal" people, i.e. those of us who don't look like catwalk models. I saw some of the models she had in to audition. They were "normal" bodied Nigella Lawson types – which was supposed to say you don't have to be thin to wear the Fatz brand.'

'What's wrong with that?' *Sounds rather God-who-cares? to me.*

'Well it's all wrong, Jill. The opposite of thin isn't "normal", is it? I mean, I'm a size fourteen at my thinnest, and I'm normal. By saying "Thin's Not In" and showing somebody like me, well, it's supposed to be liberating and legitimising me, but really it's just saying I'm somehow unacceptable. It just perpetuates the notion that if you're not Kate Moss, you're not good enough.'

The waiter slaps our pizzas down. I'm ravenous, but Wendy is far more interested in conversation than food.

'It's Bridget Jones all over again. I mean, she wasn't heavy, was she, Renée Zellweger? Yet the character in the book was so obsessed with her weight that when you saw Renée you just went, well, what's wrong with her body? Many women would kill to have it.'

'I know.' I shake hot chillis onto my pizza, which looks perfectly cooked, moist, and free of too much mozzarella; just how I like it. 'I always said they needed more of a lard-arse in the role.'

Wendy gets her analytical look. 'So, in this case, I would have thought if you're making a powerful statement like "Thin's Not In" you need to have some very real-looking people who are genuinely large and proud of it.' She taps her knife handle on the table. 'I hinted this to her, but she said there was no way Fatz clothing was going to be seen dead on a load of "heifers".'

'She didn't say that!'

'But the very point of the show was to attract heavier

people to the brand! So see what I mean? Sometimes her thinking doesn't make sense.' She rotates her pizza plate between her hands like it's a steering wheel, like she's trying to decide which triangle to cut into first, then she abandons it again, and I think, *Oh, God, can't we just start eating?* I don't want to eat while she just talks. 'If it were me organising it, I'd have the fashion show, but I'd get rid of this "Thin's Not In" business. I'd put a wide range of body types up there to show that it's all about the clothes, not the weight, and that Fatz is for everybody. Then you're making it a positive thing rather than fixating on this tiring issue of size.'

'Makes sense.' *So, Leigh, what she's basically saying, honey, is that your brilliant marketing idea is a load of crap.* I smile. Wendy's like a kid in a toy-shop. Totally carried away with this idea of the working world. I'm happy for her. 'It seems like an awful lot of aggro for exercise pants, Wend, if you ask me. I think I'm glad I have a simple job, with sexy footballers to look at and a group of lasses who work to live, not the other way around.'

Wendy mops some of the oil off her pizza with her napkin. I'm hoping this is a sign she's going to start eating, then I can start too. She's about the only person I know who can quote little gems of dietary wisdom, like the fact that most of the calories in Brie are in its skin. Sometimes she'll use her knowledge as a reason to desecrate the stuff or refuse to go near it, other times, to say, *And really, who gives a damn?*

'Well, poor Leigh's done months of work for the show that he was previously all for, and now he's calling it off. He got hysterical when she told him he was listening too much to his silly showbiz friends and not thinking for himself. He tends to zoom around the place in some battery-operated tizzy, his face getting as pink as his velour tracksuit.' Wendy does some zooming impersonation with her hands and I tuck into my food because I'm tired of waiting for her. 'Poor Leigh seemed embarrassed that I'd seen him belittling her. Because he did say some pretty horrid things.'

'Like?'

She picks a skin of mozzarella off her pizza. 'I can eat this or I can leave it . . .' The two sides of her love-hate relationship with calorie-ridden food. She shoves it in her mouth. *Finally! We have lift-off*. 'Oh, I hate telling tales out of school . . .'

'Well, you must have been embarrassed, sat there.'

'I pretended I wasn't. I picked up the phone and had a very long conversation with a dead tone. Acted like I was sure this sort of outrageous, juvenile behaviour is part of any office.'

'It's certainly not part of mine. Uproarious giggles are about as heated as we get. The lasses and I went for lunch today and gassed about footballers and the latest in who's-bonking-who in the manager's office. We had a grand old time.' Shit, I drop an oily mushroom on my white jeans. 'So, it hasn't put you off working there?'

She seems to measure the question. 'No. So long as nobody is behaving like that with me, then, as Neil said, I've got nothing to worry about, have I? Besides, Leigh and I went for a good gossip about it over lunch. I told her she handled him brilliantly. She told me how she used his private toilet the other day and saw what she thought was toothpaste by the hand basin. It was Preparation H. We had a good laugh.'

I grin. 'Have you ever thought about going back and finishing your degree?'

'Now, why would I want a degree when I have an almost degree?' She always calls it that. Her face gets that look of resigned impatience. 'I do think about it sometimes. In many ways I don't know what's held me back. It's been three years since Nina . . . All I'd have to do is two more courses.'

'So, go for it.'

'Well, it sounds easy when you put it like that.' She shrugs. Which, I can tell, means *end of subject now*.

Then she asks about me. I keep it fairly benign – the usual suspects: my parents, my boss, the neighbours, the puppy and how he would rather garrotte himself on his choke chain than pack in pulling me. 'So, how's being a working woman fitting with your home life?' I ask her, to get off the topic of me. What I mean is, *How is Neil adjusting to not being the centre of your universe?*

'Oh, lately he's been working so much again. So instead of watching the clock until he comes home, I fill the time in with chores that I can't get done during the day now.'

Neil used to do long shifts, and was often gone from home for days. Where to, Wendy rarely knew. She'd live off her nerves, anticipating some ominous knock at the door. But now he's high up, he doesn't go away any more. 'When he's home, I make sure I put everything else aside. If the laundry's not done, so be it. I'll make a nice dinner because that's about the only time my lads will talk to me. Then when they're off up in their rooms, we'll open a bottle of wine, put on a bit of nice music and have some nice couple time.' That's about the closest Wendy gets to referencing a sex life. You never know if she gets constipated before her periods, nor do Leigh and I have any idea how many men she's slept with. I think it's just the one. Leigh reckons she might be a dark horse; she thinks Wendy might have a whole sordid past that she's keeping secret.

'But, I must say, he's been very supportive. Neil is very supportive. Incredibly so.'

'In what way?' I'm visualising piles of laundry he's ironing. Him slugging a ginormous trolley around ASDA.

'Just everything, really. He knew how much I wanted to get back into the workforce.'

Yet, when an admin job came up at Northumbria Police, he didn't want her applying for it. She never told me this directly, but hinted and hedged, and didn't bother to try to fill my jumping-to-conclusion silences.

'He's very supportive.' She smiles, in a last-word sort of way, like a much prettier, more animated version of a Stepford Wife. 'I'm full!' She slumps back in the seat. 'And after all that talk about fat and thin, you'd better not even ask me if I want dessert.'

'D'you want dessert?'

'Yes.'

We order two tiramisu.

It crossed my mind to mention that Rob and I aren't getting on too well lately, without actually telling her all the details, of course. (Perhaps if she'd share something personal about Neil and her, I would open up. But she'd have to go first.) I decide against it. When she opens her purse to pay the bill, handsome, supportive Neil smiles at us from the plastic picture window. I'm glad I kept shtumm.

Saturday morning. Our phone rings. I prop myself up on an elbow in bed, squint to see the clock. I was banking on Rob being around today to see if we could peck and make up. But he's already gone to work, and it's not even 9 a.m. I pat around for the handset on the night table, dreading it being a mother emergency. Things have been ominously quiet since our day at the beach.

'We've got to talk. Now. Fast. Won't wait. H-e-l-p!' It's Leigh. Another crisis. She's always having them: she's just dreamt she had sex with Clifford, or she's developed boozer's nose, or she's bleached her top lip and it's gone blonde and curly and she looks like a walrus.

I sink back on the pillow, relieved it's only her. 'What on earth's the marra?'

'Can't talk,' she whispers. 'L about.'

I yawn loudly.

'I – need – to – see – you.'

'Well, we could always go out for a drink tonight, if you fancy.' Although tonight sounds so far off. I'm suddenly pissed off that Rob's deserted me. I'm fed up of the silent treatment. It's as though it's my punishment for bringing up certain topics. In all the years we've been married, this is the first time we seem to be holding a grudge.

'Tonight? No. Can't wait.'

Why's she so secretive? 'Well, you could come round here this afternoon.' Oh, but then I'd have to clean the house. Weekends are when I should be doing housework but I desperately resent its intrusion on my free time. I struggle out of bed, draw back our white curtains. It's another lovely day. The garden's bathed in sunshine. The branches of an overgrown lilac tree gently knock against our window. Across the fence, next door's bunny nibbles away safely in her hutch. 'It's so nice out, how about going through to Seaburn beach?' I don't know where the idea comes from, but it fills me with a flutter of excitement.

'Seaburn beach?'

'Well, we don't have to. I just thought it'd be something different. It *is* a nice day.' A voice in my head says, *Jill, don't go latching on to some fantasy man to think it's going to solve your problems, because it won't.*

'But what are we going to do there? It'll be full of Sunderland supporters skinny-dipping while balancing beer glasses on their noses like circus sea lions.'

I blackmail her with silence.

'Urgh, well, go on then, if you're so damned keen.'

I hang up and feel terribly guilty but do two jumping jacks in the air.

We park half a mile up at Roker pier, because of course now I'm actually in the vicinity of the beach, I AIN'T GOIN' NEAR THAT RUSSIAN. It was tempting, for about three minutes. But I'm married. It's wrong. And Rob would kill me if he knew. As it's lunchtime we pop into a pub, place our food orders and take our lagers over to an alcove.

'I'm going to have an affair.' Leigh's eyes are riveted devilishly on my face. My glass that was on its way to my mouth crash-lands on the table and I'm suddenly drenched in Stella. 'I've met somebody, Jill,' she tells me, when I get back from the loos, looking like I've weed myself. She makes this *hhh-aar! I'm withering* noise, slumping so far down the bench she practically slides off. 'He's so good-looking Jill. He's a red-hot-blooded sexy bloke, and he's actually interested in me, it's a miracle.' She wiggles her painted-on arches for eyebrows, fans her face, makes gargoyle expressions, and goes 'Pwhoar!' and 'Cor!' like a building-site worker. I've never seen anybody like this, except, maybe, Benny Hill. I tell her this and she grins.

I quiz her and she says he's married, got kids. 'And you met him where?'

'Oh he's been around for a while. He's . . . he works in retail management. High up.'

'He's a client?' She's always said she's got one or two attractive ones.

'I bumped into him on Friday. I was down the town, walked into the bank and there he was. We were both surprised.' She drifts off into space for a moment, smiles. 'It was the way he looked at me, Jill. And when we got talking, there was . . . we were . . .' She claps her hands over her face. 'Oh, hell, what am I going to do?'

'Nothing!' I still don't believe my ears. Leigh? Of 'affairs are so tacky' fame?

'Nothing?' her face falls. 'Nothing isn't an option Jill. All my orgasms have his face on them.'

'But you'd never have an affair. You think the very idea of a married woman—'

'I know. But that was before there was anybody to have an affair with.' She does the Benny Hill face thing again. Leigh, who usually looks like she's spent ten years in a coffin, now seems like she's suddenly come back to life. But it's scary. Part of me thinks she was best off dead. 'I tell you, Jill, he's got me . . . I can't think straight.'

'You're just in heat. It'll pass. You'll forget about him.'

'I don't want to forget about him, I want to fuck him.'

Phew, it's suddenly red-hot in here. I fan my face.

'I'm serious. I've imagined it in every position. Oh, Jill . . . the body on him! And I'm gagging for a bit of rough.' She sticks her tongue out and pants. 'Lawrence's puniness used to be attractive after I'd been with all those macho arseholes. I used to find it cute that he had legs like an eight-year-old Ethiopian. But, you know, last week he went for a blood test and kept the plaster on for four days! And he kept showing it to me like he'd had open-heart surgery. It's such a turn-off.'

This makes me smile. Normally she'd say something like this, or tell me he was on the Internet all weekend looking for holiday packages to Lapland, and we'd crack up. But Lawrence's foibles don't feel like a laughing matter right now. 'But this man's a client, Leigh. You could get fired over it.'

'Oh, no, nothing like that'd happen.' She swings her black hair over her shoulders. 'I know what I'm doing. I'm going to give it an expiry date. Say, six weeks to bang my brains out. After which time it'll get dumped.'

'What? Like a carton of yoghurt?' Or eggs. Maybe it's her ovaries. A mid-life crisis. She told me Lawrence thinks she's having one. My eyes flick over her waif-like body in its trendy little Fatz black velvet tracksuit. 'But do affairs work like that? I mean, what if you fell in love?'

She rolls her eyes, nurses her beer glass between her small breasts. 'You always romanticise everything, Jill. You're the Milk Tray type of gal, which is lovely, but I'm not like that. It'd be strictly the business. No pillow talk. We meet, we bang, see you tomorrow. Go at it hell for leather for six weeks, then that'd be it. We'd both walk away. No harm done. Just something fantastic to look back on.' She takes a long drink, her eyes buzzing around the bar, which has suddenly filled up. 'I mean, don't you think it'd be great?'

I don't know why Leigh's prospect of hanky-panky should get me feeling all wriggly like this. 'Aye, if it worked like that.'

'But I'd make it. I have to Jill. I love Lawrence, and you know there's absolutely nothing more important to me than my family. Especially when you think of my childhood. The ice-cream man moves in on Monday, tells me to call him Dad, that he's waited all his life to meet a woman like my mother, then by the weekend all that's left of him is a bum-print in the settee cushion.' She chortles.

It amazes me how Leigh has the capacity to laugh at her bizarre upbringing.

'You know I would never fuck up Molly's life like my mother did mine. But I have to reclaim a part of me in this equation. Do something, not for Lawrence or Molly or Clifford, but purely to make me feel happy.' She looks hacked-off again. 'The thought of shagging only Lawrence until the day I die is enough to kill me now. Jill, I'm tired and I'm uninspired. I badly need a thrill.'

'Can't you just . . . I don't know . . . get a new job?'

'A new job's not what I need. Besides, that job pays our mortgage and keeps Molly in private school and singing lessons. That job keeps Lawrence at home so he doesn't get too stressed and obsessively compulse himself into an early grave. And, as I always believe, better the devil you know. Cliff, much as I complain about him, is predictable. He knows how far to push me, but because he needs me, he also knows when to back off.'

No mention of her nasty fight with him; she must think Wendy wouldn't have told me.

Her eyes lock onto mine. 'Come on . . . it'd be wild, Jill. Wouldn't it?'

I feel like planting my face in the tabletop. 'Well, I know what you mean about needing a thrill,' I tell her, with bleak enthusiasm. 'Sex is like the Monday morning chore of taking the rubbish out.' Mind you, I wish I got it once a week, but I don't tell her that. She looks at me, staggered, seems to wait for me to dish the dirt that must lie behind a rare outburst like that. 'But I'm not sure an affair's the answer. I mean, think of what you'll lose in your marriage if you have a fling, Leigh. You'll reach your golden anniversary knowing you were the Olympic gold-medallist who took steroids. You didn't win a fair game even if you impressed the rest of the world. You were a cheat.'

She just looks at me blankly and blinks. 'Maybe I don't put such a high value on loyalty as you do, Jill. Or maybe I think there are many other ways of being loyal. Ways that more than compensate for the one way that you aren't.'

I can't believe this is the same person talking. The person who always said that because she screwed around so much when she was single, she got it all out of her system. Unlike me, she always says. I have my fun yet to come.

I get her to spill the beans about this Nick when our food comes. So, she bumped into him in the bank. He said, 'Hiya there, lovely day,' then he sniffed out whether she was blissfully married and made it clear that he wasn't. More such harmless chatter between virtual strangers ensued. Then, as it was her turn to move to the counter, he asked her if she wanted to go and get a coffee. And she was so taken off guard that she said no. So he said, 'Well, maybe another time,' and she's spent the last week analysing what she should do about it, whether it's up to her to make a move, or whether she should wait and see if he makes one.

For somebody who manages millions of pounds of sales for a hip company, it seems hard to believe she'd sit there obsessing over something that doesn't sound to me like it's worth the bother. I hate telling her the obvious, but . . . 'Well, he might have literally just meant go for coffee, and "maybe another time" might have just been his way of politely saying "see you later".'

'Ah, but you weren't there, were you?' she wags a finger at me. 'You didn't get the looks he gave me, or the seductive emphasis he put on the odd little things he said. Or the way his pupils dilated when he was talking about how boring his marriage was.'

'He talked about how boring his marriage was?' All this in the bank? It must have been one almighty queue.

She strums her pearly fingernails on the table. 'We've got to think of something clever to test the waters a bit more. Something that's harmless on the surface in case he really doesn't want to have an affair, but not if he does, eh, Poirot?' She crosses her winter-white arms over her chest. (Leigh can't tan as she had a melanoma ten years ago, from her mam slapping baby oil on her and shoving her in the sun when she was a child.) 'You don't have any instant thoughts do you?'

'Oh, bags of 'em! No, of course I don't! Just don't do anything, and wait, that would be my suggestion. I mean, he's a client, it's not like you're never going to see him again. Has he never made a move on you before?'

She shrugs, shakes her head. 'Waiting's no good, or the moment passes. Affairs have to happen before anybody starts to think up reasons why they shouldn't. Plus, if you think too much, you destroy all the excitement.'

'Well, I don't know . . . What can you possibly do? Maybe invite him to lunch.'

'I was thinking of getting a hotel room and just emailing him the time, the place and the room number.'

'Well, bloody hell-fire! That's harmless on the surface!' We lock eyes and exchange massive grins across the table.

Then her expression changes again. 'Jill, I'm so sick of being surrounded by queenie little men. I want a big burly guy to just take me and give me a good going-over.' She stares at her empty plate. 'You're so lucky, you've got Rob. Rob's such a bloke.'

I don't want her thinking I'm lucky, because for some reason, right this minute, I'm not feeling it. So, as we're on this track, I tell her. I tell her about how since we found out we can't have children, it appears we can't even have sex. Then I tell her about the lifeguard. The note. How he remembered my dress. Conscious, as I say all this, that I'm betraying Rob in more ways than one. But I need somebody to talk to. I'm not like Rob. I can't bottle everything up. 'You know, Leigh,' I fiddle with my beer-mat. 'I've never thought I'd be able to separate sex from love, but the thought of being touched by a man I didn't have to beg it off is just so appealing at times.'

She barely blinks, listens all the way through, without interruption. 'I'm shocked, Jill. I really am. I never

thought you'd have to beg Rob. You're so gorgeous I'd
have said you would have to fight him off every night.
Are you sure he's not having an affair?'

'A what? Of course not!'

'Well, like you've said, he's always working late. He's
gone off sex. Aren't those the two major signs? I mean,
I wouldn't think he would be either, because he always
seems so besotted with you. But that's the point, isn't
it? People aren't always what they seem. And fellas,
even the happiest of them, if they get an opportunity
elsewhere . . .'

'Not Rob!' I hammer a finger into my chest. 'I know
Rob. And you have to understand, since he's taken on
corporate clients the whole nature of his business has
changed. He's so much busier these days. He doesn't
just make furniture any more. Now he spends more
time managing sub-contractors, doing paperwork,
hunting for new business, and I know he doesn't like
it as much.'

'I'm sure you're right,' she says, unconvinced. 'And
having no sperm is a big deal for a fella. I'm sure he
feels less than a man. So that's probably why he's gone
into a shell.'

'Well it's not like he's the only man on the face of the
earth with that problem!' Less than a man! I won't have
anybody thinking that about Rob.

She stares blankly ahead, looking sad. 'No, but you
know how men are about their penises. It affects them
badly, doesn't it? They aren't less masculine because of
it, but they feel they are.'

I am shocked now to see her eyes have filled with

tears. 'I feel for you both, you know, I really do. I mean, if he's not having an affair and this really is all about his masculinity, then that's a big cross he's got to bear. And he doesn't deserve it. And neither do you – especially you. None of this is your fault.' Her pity touches me. I feel bad for snapping at her now. But I wish she'd drop this affair business! Then she tells me Lawrence once sold his sperm to a sperm bank when he was in art college. There could be a million little Lawrences with dreadlocks out there, obsessively trying to find themselves and sending daily letters to Father Christmas. We cackle.

'But aren't you the sly one,' she says. 'You said that note was a car-cleaning advert!'

'I know, but you were in a pissy mood and I didn't know how you'd react.' I can say this now because she's in a good mood and she won't take it the wrong way.

She shakes her head contemplatively. 'That's bloody unbelievable, you know. A coincidence like that. I mean, you'd see it in a movie and say it was too far-fetched.'

'I know.' It certainly is different. The idea of seeing him again ripples through me like quicksilver.

'He remembered your dress! That's so romantic, Jill. It's almost fate.'

That F word again. I get a swift memory of him. I wonder whether if I saw him now, I'd still be as impressed. We order coffee and start hatching daft little plots about how we're going to commit scarlet infidelity with Nick and the Russian.

'Have you told Wendy any of this? About the Russian?' she asks.

'God, no! She'd never approve. As you know, I haven't even told her that Rob and I can't have children; only you know that. It's not like I've lied to her. I suppose if she asked me, I'd tell her. It's just, you know what she's like, she doesn't delve into personal stuff. She's so brilliant at minding her own business.'

'Well, don't tell her about me, either. Promise, eh? Even if you do have to lie for me. I don't want her to know a word of this. She'd judge me something rotten. She'd never understand . . . I just can't adore like she does. My daughter, yes. But not men. It requires a suspension of disbelief that I'm not capable of.' Then she pulls a gleeful little smile. 'Besides, I wouldn't want her thinking I was back to my old slapper ways.' We pay up and leave.

'Oh, my bloody hell, he's there!' I shriek-whisper. We're just emerging around a picturesque marigold-bordered bend with a white picket fence, that drops off like a shelf to the sea, and I see him, not a hundred feet away from us, sitting at his lookout post on the sand. I drag her across the grass, because I swear he's just turned and copped me, and I am dying a thousand deaths. I crucify myself against the side of the bus shelter.

'What're you doing?' Leigh pins herself there along-side me. A young lad and his grandmother give us very peculiar looks.

'I think he saw me,' I hiss. 'Jesus!'

'No he didn't! Where is he?' She peers around the wall.

'Don't look.' I pull her back. 'Up on that white stepladder thingy.'

'The what . . .? Oh . . .' She twists around the corner, leaving one foot rooted next to me. And then she goes, 'O-hh-o! In the yellow? That's him? Come on,' she yanks my arm. 'I need a better look.' She steps one way, and I step the other, and we knock noses and trip over each other's feet. 'Oh God!' I clutch my face. 'Married women don't behave like this!' She links arms with me and hauls me, with zero subtlety, towards the promenade.

'Sure they do. The honest ones.' And then she starts humming 'Lara's Theme', and I dig her in the ribs.

'He was attractive, mind, wasn't he? Omar Sharif?'

She curls her lip. 'I think I'd rather do Julie Christie.'

We pass a line of pubs and fish 'n' chip shops and are almost parallel with him now. As luck would have it, he turns, giving us a clear, unobstructed view of him. Leigh stops dead in her tracks. 'Look at him,' she gushes.

'Honey, I'm looking.' He's like some blazing god sat up there on high, with the sun kissing him and the sea twinkling in the background like a billion diamonds. He's even darker and more rugged and fitter than I remembered, and I feel a big pang of lust. 'But he's a lifeguard, Leigh. A fortysomething lifeguard.'

'So what? He's a complete babe. I can't believe we were in the same bar and we didn't even notice him!' She nudges me. 'Faithful old soul that I am, I'd spread my tiny wings for him in a minute. And I bet he considers shagging part of his life-saving training, so he's probably very good in bed. And he's poor and he's got a crap job, so he's no threat to your marriage. Jill, he's the ideal candidate for a fling.'

Leigh has always said I'd cheat, eventually. Thinks there's no such thing as a one-man woman (and we've sung many a drunken duet over that, let me tell you). Sometimes I think I wouldn't, if for no other reason than to prove her wrong. 'Let's go for a cuppa, Leigh.'

'Aren't you going to go and say hello?'

'Good God, no.'

'Well, what was the point of coming here, then?'

'So you can see him. And I can gaze at him from afar. Besides, it's been a few weeks, he'll probably not even remember me.' And Rob would die if he knew I was doing this. And I'd throttle him if he were out spying on some woman like this, with a male friend. Then I try to picture a couple of married fellas doing this and it would just never happen, would it?

'My arse,' she says. 'The point of us coming here was NOT just so I could see him!'

'Well, it doesn't matter. I've seen him. He's gorgeous. I'm married. Life's a bitch and then you die.'

'And you'll get a coward's burial.'

'Don't you mean a pauper's? Come on, you bad influence,' I drag her up the grassy bank onto the path by the main road opposite Morrisons. 'Give over drooling. I saw him first.'

She gets to the top, stops, pants. 'It's all right. I'm nearly forty. These days I think I can only do one at a time. Although it could be fun finding out . . .' I look at her and shake my head. 'Actually,' she fans her face. 'I think it could be quite utterly bloody brilliant.'

'What could?'

She looks at me, roguishly. 'Simultaneous affairs.'

6

Sex. I'm looking through Leanne's *Cosmo* in my lunch break. One Hundred Ways To Turn Your Man On. I think I read the same article twenty years ago. Apparently I still haven't learned. 'Have you tried any of these?' I ask her.

She squints from her desk across the room. There's a cheese plant behind her chair that looks like it's growing out of her head. 'You wha'?'

I waggle the page.

'Turn 'im on? Got no problems in that department, Jill, my dear.'

'Want this pile of rubbish back then?'

I'm just about to boomerang it when, as luck would have it, Swinburn walks in, catches me. 'Jill's a great reader,' he says, sending me those huge, planet-like eyeballs that Neil Armstrong would be sorry he missed.

'Sieg Heil,' I salute him when he's gone into his office, and the girls chortle.

I'm just putting my jacket on to go home via ASDA as we've been rationing the last loo roll for days, when my phone rings. It's Leigh, summoning me to Au Bar. 'It's a matter of life or death,' she tells me.

'Oh,' says Rob, when I ring him and tell him that I'm in Au Bar and I've just ordered a glass of Pinot Grigio and a plate of yam shoestring fries with dip, because I'm famished. 'So you're not coming home yet? I was thinking maybe we'd go out to dinner.' It's been ten days since our big fight. It has felt more like ten months.

'Well, I'm here now, aren't I? I wish you'd told me earlier.' It did cross my mind this afternoon to go home and make him do something insanely forgiving and fun with me. But it just felt like too much work, with no guarantee of a reward. 'Look, I'd come home gladly, but Leigh needs to see me. Something important. I can't get out of it now.' *I didn't think to check with you first*, I'm about to add, *because to be dead honest, given the way you've been acting lately, I didn't think you'd be bothered*. But I don't. Because that'll only hurt us, not heal us. Having the last word is overrated.

'Well, you've made your plans. You can't go back on them,' he says, like the ever-understanding soul he is, but I can tell he's disappointed. 'I'll just see you later, then.'

I want him to say *Leave. Right now. Come home. I need to see you, I need to kiss you and tell you we're going to change* . . . When he doesn't, I reply with a meagre, 'All right, then.'

There's an awkward pause and then he says, 'I love you. And . . .' A bit more awkwardness . . . 'I'm sorry, Jill.'

'Oh!' I slap a hand to my face. 'Rob, I know you are. Me too. Let's not be sorry any more. It's forgotten

about. Everything's forgotten about.' I let out a sigh
and I think, please let this be our fresh start. When I
hang up, my heart starts a quick ticking. I should just
say 'sod it,' tell Leigh that I have to go home, it's do or
die for my marriage . . . but it's too late. She whips
through the door. I get an ominous feeling that I'll
regret misplacing my priorities. She looks beautiful.
Different. Ladylike. In a loosely-pleated, knee-length
little black skirt with an Audrey Hepburn cowl neck,
slate-grey, silky top. The skirt flirts with her legs as she
walks, in towering strappy black sandals, with that
foxy, Carrie-Bradshaw catch in her step. 'My God,
you look fabulous. Is this new?'

'We're fucking,' she says, and flops into an armchair.

I've clearly misheard.

She peeps around the hand she's clapped to her face.
'Oh, stop looking at me like that!' I see the edges of a
smile. Her neck is blotchy, like you get when you drink
too much, or you have to make a speech, or . . .

'Leigh! How? I mean, when? And who?'

She fans her face. 'Who? Who d'you think? We've
been emailing. I sent him one saying, 'Nice chatting
with you last week, etc.' He wrote back, said we must
do lunch some time—'

'*Do* lunch? Is that how he talks?' He sounds like a
poncey wanker.

'He emailed me at eleven o'clock this morning,
picked me up at twelve, drove me straight to his house.'

'His house!'

'We didn't exchange a word in the car.' She runs her

hand down her face and throat. 'I was barely inside his front door when he got me up against the wall and his face was under my skirt.'

My eyes drop to her skirt hem. 'Good God.' She grips her bottom lip with her top teeth and I don't know if she's going to laugh or cry; she's just this queer, unreadable concoction of emotion. Then she starts waggling her feet and doing the Benny Hill thing again, complete with construction-worker noises. We're attracting attention.

'Where's his wife in all this?'

She shrugs. 'She works.'

'And his kids?'

'Oh, they're . . . I don't know. They're always at their nana's. Apparently they don't have much sex.'

'His kids?'

'He and his wife! Twit.' She goes off somewhere, smiling. Her tongue slides out. She looks slightly touched. But her face is full of life. She's sparkly as a disco ball at her own coming-of-age. She plants her saucy eyes on mine. 'I tell you, Jill, he's wild in bed.'

'Is he?' I try to sound giddy like she looks, like she feels, like I want to feel for her, but I thought all that business about Nick was a joke.

'Oh, I can't begin to tell you.'

Try. I accidentally put my wine glass down so hard it nearly cracks. My eyes keep going to the hem of her skirt. I'm fascinated by the topic of people being good lovers. Having only ever had one, you do sometimes wonder how they compare. 'Why, what's so great about him?' I casually pick up my drink again.

She crosses one leg over the other and I glimpse her white knickers. 'Well, for starters we just connect. You know what it's like when there's that instant heat? It's like a tornado that rushes through you when you look at them, and then you just collide in passion.'

I feel like colliding my brains with the Intercity 125.

She shuts her eyes for a few seconds, bites her bottom lip, the afternoon still very much alive in her mind. 'The fact that we both have partners, that we're doing something wrong, it's the forbidden fruit. It just seems to turn the temperature up seven hundred degrees.' Phew, she whistles. 'And Jill, he's got so much stamina. In the space of an hour we did it three times! I've been with men who are purely animal in the sack, but with him . . .' Her green eyes twinkle softly. 'He's got a tender side, Jill. He's lovely. It really mattered to him that I'd enjoyed it. And most fellas don't give a toss about that, especially when they've got wives at home. I don't ever remember enjoying the feeling of a man's sexual, urgent body like this. Something as simple and basic as pure lust. His sweat. The scent of him. He's just this big hunk of incredible, undeniable male flesh.'

My eyes fix on my cold, limp chips.

When I look up, she's studying me. 'You think it's bad of me,' she says, some invisible truth being erected between us.

I shake my head, over-convincingly. 'No. I just . . . didn't think you'd do it.' I feel awful for Lawrence and Molly. Did our giggly afternoon put her up to this? Part of me wishes she hadn't told me, yet my heart is still pounding from what she said he did behind that door.

'Well, d'you want to hear the rest, or not?' she asks, knowing full well that I do.

'Just don't tell me you did it in their bed.'

She huddles in the corner of the comfy chair, looking gloatingly post-coital. 'No, I made him take me into the spare room. Funny, though,' she smiles. 'He wanted to.'

Why do we love a bastard? Yuck. I hate him. A little bit.

'We did it on the stairs first. I've still got carpet burn.'

The stairs? That film springs to mind, *The Thomas Crown Affair*, with the ever sensual Rene Russo; she and Pierce Brosnan tumbling nakedly all over the house, to that raw, erotic music.

'He took me into the bathroom. Got me up against the counter top—' She sees my face. 'You want me to stop?'

When I squeak a feeble 'Yes' and madly shake my head, she grins. 'We tore each other's clothes off. Oh, Jill, his chest, that broad, fit . . .' She shudders like she's having an orgasm in the chair. Then she looks at me squarely, leans forward, whispers, 'Jill, it was as though my life and my marriage and everything didn't exist. All the stresses just left me and I was young again. I was just me. Only . . . it was better. Because this time I was there for the right reasons. I was doing it because I wanted to. Not because I thought it was something men wanted.' She goes distant. 'Then it was really weird. He . . . well, he did this thing.' She sinks back into the chair again, looks a bit hesitant. 'In the bath. Oh, I shouldn't tell you.'

I give her my *Oh, come on!* face.

'Well, he made me straddle the side of the tub so my lower body was, well you know—'

'Not really,' I fire.

She whistles, fans her face again. 'Oh, I can't tell you.'

She can't bloody leave me hanging now. My heart hammers while we lock gazes.

She grins that grin. I can tell she's gagging to spill her guts. 'Well . . . you know how cold the side of the bathtub is when you sit on it? And you know what that does? The contrast of hot and cold . . .'

I give her my best encouraging blank face.

'Well, we each had one foot in the bath-tub and it was the way he . . .' She whispers, 'you know, entered me, doggy-style. Then he'd get me close, then he'd, you know, pull out . . . Oh, God, why am I telling you all this?'

'I don't know. But you are. So bloody get on with it.'

She rests her elbows on her knees, lowers her voice even more so I can barely hear her over the music – I'm very pissed off at the music. 'Well, he sort of pressed me down so I was straddling the cold porcelain, and his hands held my hips and just moved them with this slow, deliberate rhythm.' She looks at me, then does a double take. 'My God, your face! You look like your head's afire!'

I touch my cheek. 'It's the drink.' I try to act casual,

bored even, like I've been there and done that a million times before. 'Go on. You were saying.' I pretend to look around the room, fixing her with one eyeball.

'What you having, then?' the busy waitress in a thigh-high split skirt really bloody picks her moments. *Something I'm not getting*; I feel like hollering. Leigh grabs the drinks list off the table and scans it distractedly while I gobble her up with my gaze. Now I know how eunuchs feel. Then I look around this bar: the fit lads and lasses and all the throbbing sexuality. I feel old, and staid, and like I've massively missed out. Why did I never dress in navel-grazing skirts? Hold men's gazes until they had to be the first to look away? Be a self-aware, sensual young woman, like a bud before the bloom. Why was I always a good girl? A boring old Wordsworth daffodil that's dead at the end of bloody spring. I look at all these lasses and envy them all their thrills ahead. 'Live!' I want to scream at the world. 'Live!' In case it all dries up when you hit thirty-five.

Leigh orders a crantini. I feel like there's an ocean between us.

'You won't believe it, Jill,' a saucy grin sets on her face. 'He's big, too.'

Kill me, go on. 'B-b-b-b-but they say size doesn't matter. It's what you do with it that counts.' Rob always says he's eight inches. But then again, Rob claims he's six feet two. She just gives me that 'tell that to the marines' look. I reach for my wine glass, can't pick it up. I tell her I have to go to the toilet. I bolt into a cubicle, plant myself against the door. I can feel the blood pounding around my body as fast as the propeller of a helicopter. I stand like this for ages, whirring, listening to people on either side of me wee. When I come out, I have to hold my wrists under cold water to cool my engine again.

When I go back outside, I can't find anything to say. It's weird, but it's like sitting here with a different person, one I'm not sure I have much in common with any more. 'You did use protection . . .?' I finally ask her. I'd hate to think where he's been.

She grimaces. 'It happened so fast. But he says he's clean. He's always been faithful.'

Oh, yeah, right. Mr Gymnast of the Bath-tub who took her to his house! Panic for my friend flies through me. I can't believe how naive she's being! But neither can I bring myself to say, 'Well, he would say that, wouldn't he?' Because if I felt like this I wouldn't want somebody spoiling it for me either.

'Another thing you're going to hit me for,' she grimaces again. 'I came off the pill, remember? Because of all the headaches I was having. But I think that was just all the stress, when Cliff and I weren't getting on, before Lawrence left his job when his OCD was really bad. So I'm going back on it.' She sees my look of horror. 'Look, Jill, don't be my mother. I know what I'm doing. Besides, now's a safe time. I just got off the rag. Stop being so practical.'

'Well, sorry.' Christ, she's going to get pregnant, I just know it.

She titters a bit. Then she looks at me, unseeingly. 'He's nice, Jill. We just click on so many levels.'

'What? Stair levels?' I try not to roll my eyes.

'You measure yourself by who you're fucking, you know, Jill. That's why fellas always want the pretty young things. Besides, you know, he's alive and charismatic, and he's masculine and he's daring, and he doesn't give a shit. That's why he does so well in his job. And there's something very sexy about that.'

There is. I manage a smile. He sounds horrible. I'm eaten up with envy. I look at her knobbly knees and I wonder if she showered before she went back to the office. 'You're going to fall in love. I just feel it in my water.'

'Get out! I told you, this is a fling. I've given it an expiry date. End of the summer, that's it.'

It was six weeks before. It's grown already.

'Besides, he's cheating on his wife, isn't he? You know me, I could never be with a man I couldn't trust. I'm far too much of a psychological fuck-up for that. Why d'you think I married Lawrence?'

'I thought you told me it was because you looked at his kind face and could instantly see yourself having a brood of babies with him. You were thirty. You were done with the boyfriends, the break-ups, the one night stands. You wanted steadiness and something real.'

'And he'd never cheat and he'd never leave me.'

'And you loved him.'

'I did and I do.' She says it quickly. 'But I've always known Lawrence felt lucky to get into my knickers. And at first you sort of get off on feeling like you're doing them a big honour. But that's only good for so long. Then you just think, maybe he doesn't deserve to be there.'

God, she sounds really mean. I wonder if she ever did love Lawrence. Or did she just marry him thinking it'd relieve her of all her psychological baggage?

'You know, I'd forgotten what I was capable of with a man until I saw how I was with him today.' She gives me that dazed stare again. 'It's so different, you know, sex without love, without arguments, without shared history. Just a carefree bonk with somebody you really fancy.'

She misreads my glum face as disapproval. 'You don't understand me, do you?'

'I do. I understand wanting. I just don't understand doing.'

She stiffens, crosses her arms. 'Well, maybe I'm just different. I can't take things too cosy or too the same for too long. What I'm doing with him is just vital to who I am. And I don't have to be proud of it. But I can't deny it, either. And I'm certainly not going to be ashamed. I've not murdered anybody.'

It feels like we're brewing to have words. But as though she senses it too, she says a light, 'Roll on tomorrow lunch!'

'At his house? You can't keep doing that, Leigh, man! You'll get caught. His wife'll come home. His kids . . .'

'I told you . . . she won't.' She takes the martini glass from the waitress, unsettling her drinks' tray. And as she doesn't get out her money (an occasional bad habit of hers that Wendy and I frequently bellyache about), I pay our bill. 'Although, I have to say, the chance that she might . . . it certainly adds to the excitement. Danger is the best aphrodisiac.'

'God, here's me thinking oysters were.' Her eyes do that saucy dance with me. 'It's a lot safer,' I say. 'A few little oysters.'

'Unless they're contaminated. Then try talking horny to the toilet bowl.'

She chuckles and, despite my roaring disapproval, I do too. I've never known anybody who's had an affair. I just want to sit and stare at her. 'Your neck.' I point to the flush on her. 'How'll you explain that when you get home?'

She runs a hand exotically down her throat. 'It's been so long since Lawrence gave me a flush he'll probably think I've got rosacea or something and want me quarantined. He'll read the doctor's book three hundred times.' She does another one of those fling-a-leg-over-the-other-leg things and I catch another glimpse of her underwear. The underwear that I imagine this Nick peeling off with his teeth. 'Eeh!' I stare at her neck. 'I don't know if I've ever had the flush.'

She wiggles her eyebrows. 'Well, I bet I know someone who'd give you one.'

Walking in my door, into my faithful marriage, feels like coming into a snug harbour. But a slightly depressing one that doesn't quite live up to your expectations. Kiefer comes running. I pet him and he wees and I mop it up with a hankie. The TV's on loud. 'Hiya, treasure,' Rob says from the sitting room. Treasure. All's forgiven and forgotten about now. He's not even put out that I went out with Leigh. Suddenly I brim with this desire to salvage us, make us deliriously in love again. Rob's not having any affair; I don't care what Leigh said. He's suffering, and I regret our awful fight so much, I feel like The Evil Bitch from Hell. I stand in the doorway, looking at him lying on the settee watching telly. Blobbed out. But handsomely so.

Does he look all that excited or keen to see me? If he had to live the rest of his life with either me or *ER*, which of us would he pick?

I tell him I'm going upstairs to get changed. My voice sounds strained. In our bedroom, I move his shoes, then flop down on the white duvet and just lie there staring at the ceiling. Leigh's having an affair. Part of me still can't believe it. I wonder if a promiscuous past makes it easier to cheat in your marriage. Funny, though, it's like she's let me down. It was nice believing that a person's wild and wanton ways could be tamed with the right love. It seemed to make anything possible. Now it all just feels like a rather large load of bullcrap. I wonder, in all these years of knowing her, have I thought her a truer person than she is?

I strip off, get into my dressing-gown, go into the bathroom, stand there and gaze at the side of the bathtub. I still can't picture what the hell they did.

The adverts blast out downstairs. Rob turns down the volume. 'Did you have a good night?' he shouts up. 'What was Leigh's big news?'

'Oh, nothing much,' I shout back down. It's weird lying to Rob. Yet I can't tell him. Leigh told me, not Rob and me. And I hate how married friends tell their husbands stuff they've no right knowing. Besides, Rob would be furious if he knew what Leigh was doing or that I was in any way involved. Even though he'd probably think Lawrence had it coming by wearing flowery shirts and believing that in his past life he was a reindeer. 'Room for me?' I ask him when I go back downstairs, having brushed my teeth, combed my hair, put on a bit of perfume for him.

Simultaneous affairs, as she put it. That'll never be me.

He looks up. 'Gaw! Something reeks like a tart's boudoir.' The no-frills side to my husband makes me smile. Jill, I think, this is real. Rob is real. Your marriage is real. I worm my way in next to him on the settee. Rob opens his legs so I can snuggle between them. The dog drags his cushion to the middle of the floor and starts attacking it. 'So, is *ER* good tonight?' I ask, trying to blank out a picture of Leigh and some fella with a lovely body and a large never-mind going at it on the stairs.

'Oh, this is an old one I taped. I've seen it before.' *Me or a repeat. God, there's a hard choice.*

He tickles my ear and down my neck, and a slow sigh comes out of me as I lose myself to the feeling of his fingers, in a delicious vacuum of contented-kittendom. *ER* finishes after about twenty minutes. 'What are you thinking?' Rob asks.

Please just tickle me and let's not talk. 'Oh, nothing, really.'

'So, what did the two of you talk about? It must have been something, for all those hours.'

'Nothing major.' I uncover a shoulder. Rob's hand goes there quite keenly at first, but then his rhythm gets absent-minded. 'I love that,' I tell him and give a small moan. His fingers stop moving. I sneak my dressing-gown down a bit more and inch myself up a tad so his stilled hand now finds itself by my breast. The cold air makes my nipple stand out. Not so long ago he'd have got an instant hard-on and we'd have done it doggy-style over the settee. I will him to touch me there. It doesn't have to lead to anything. I just want something to remind me that he's my husband, not my brother. Mind you, I still can't quite believe that any man could have a bare boob near his hand and not want to touch it. He seems to mind-read. His big hand moves to my breast. I look down at his bashed-up, working man's knuckles, get a flutter in my groin waiting to see what he's going to do. But still the hand just lies there. It's a disinterested hand. Couldn't be more disinterested if it tried.

Then he says, 'So, were the bars very busy?' Then he pushes me up and slides out from under me. I freeze there, half sitting up, with my poor spurned boob hanging out, while he goes through to the back and opens the fridge door.

My throat seizes up. I can't even chirp a 'Not really,' like I might have done in the past to save face. *Jesus, Rob. Jesus.* Kiefer manically humps his cushion. Even the dog's got a better sex life than me.

I get up and go upstairs, smarting from the shame of his rejection. I sink onto the bath-mat, hug my knees, listen to him flicking through the TV channels again. If I go back down there and say anything, he'll say something like, 'Oh, well you can't just expect me to get horny, just like that, when I'm in the middle of watching the telly . . .' And I can't argue with that. Because somewhere in our past I've used similar lines myself. But part of me lives in this dreamworld where marriage is for lovers, and married sex shouldn't need its slot in the bloody TV guide. And I should be able to want intimacy from him without feeling like he must take me for some mad sex pest.

Maybe my ego's too fragile, or I'm too obsessed with sexually keeping up with the Joneses. I rub my aching head. If he'd just say, *Look, Jill, this is just a spell. We're going to be okay.* I take my glasses off and wipe away tears. I run the bath and turn the lights off, feeling like I'm setting the scene for some very intimate encounter with . . . myself. I lift a leg over, sit in the tub, lie back and sigh at the touch of the water. I prop my feet on the green tiles above the taps, gaze down my shapely curves to my newly varnished toenails. This body that I try so hard to keep nice for him. Why do other men fancy it and the one man I want to fancy it doesn't? Then my mind goes back to Leigh. I'm suddenly ragingly jealous of her selfish, testosteroney attitude. It barges in, rattles through me, leaving me stunned from its force. I run a hand over my big boobs and flat-ish stomach, the dark triangle between my legs. My mind flashes up an image of a man's head under Leigh's skirt. My friend is a good person, yet she can hang her conscience on a coat-hanger in a strange man's house.

Maybe I can too.

7

'Ta-da!' Leigh materialises from the lingerie changing room in Fenwick's, her lithe, boyish body clad in a shameless lacy red bra and pants set. She twirls for Wendy and me, then disappears again, casting me a sly smile over her shoulder. Mistress Discretion she's not. Wendy whispers, 'What's come over her? Why does she think we care what her underwear looks like?' Through the gap under the door I watch her bare feet step in and out of an array of lovely knickers. Wendy fingers a lacy thong. 'And they're not even on sale.' We both know Leigh when it comes to shopping. She's got loads of clobber but she only buys stuff in sales or at the cheapie shops. We've witnessed her pull buttons off things to get the assistant to knock it down two quid. Yet last year she got a raise and spent three grand on a Rolex. 'The bloody thing,' she moaned. 'Leave it off for two days and you've got to wind it up!'

Out she comes again, in a purple and black set this time. Flaunting it. Sending me secretive looks. Leigh's not a flaunter. Leigh's the type to stare in a mirror and say, *My bags are so big they're becoming my bottom lip.* Or, *I could get skin grafts from a sun-dried tomato and you'd never be able to tell.* But since she's been seeing her fancy man she's not made comments like that. She just seems so high on her own fantasticness. It's almost irritating.

'I think you look good in all of them,' Wendy says, then adds under her breath, 'So does the rest of Newcastle.' Leigh totters back into the fitting-room. Wendy whispers, 'She's been like this at work. Inexplicably extrovert. And we never go for our fun lunches any more because she's out "to meetings". She keeps asking me to tell Clifford that she's seeing some client. But she never says who. Anybody would think she was having an affair.' If I told Wendy, I don't know whom she'd think less of – Leigh for doing it, or me for letting her secret out of the bag.

'Ta-da!' Leigh reappears and troops off to the till with a hundred quid's worth of smalls! After that we go to Marks & Spencer for a cappuccino in Café Revive. Not that we need reviving.

The following week it's belly-dance. Venus, our instructor, jiggles and jangles and pirouettes, making Egyptian 'pretty hands' in the air. Her ample belly trembles and quivers as she shimmies, rustling up the coins in her hip-scarf. 'Now, girls, belly-dance was traditionally a fertility ritual performed to an exclusively female audience,' she tells us, smiling through her wave of floaty black hair. 'But you might want to imagine you're doing it for your special fella.' I feel like telling her, *Listen, petals, I don't have to imagine*. I recently spent two days sewing tassels on a bra and making see-through harem pants, then I sat my special fella down, lit candles and put my special belly-dancing CD on. Then, with my bottom near his face, I started shimmying my bits and pieces for England. When I turned around, he'd vamoosed. I was doing it to an empty chair.

'I don't get how you roll your belly. I can only manage the shove your boobs out bit.' I look at myself in the mirror. God, I've totally lost the seductive knack. Belly-dance, or the St Vitus Dance. It wouldn't be a hard call.

'Well, at least you've got a chest,' Leigh says. 'I'm like a walking ad for life after a double mastectomy.'

'Oh, that's not funny,' Wendy tells her. 'You don't make jokes about things like that.' Despite being more of a sporty girl than a girlie girl, Wendy has always been better at belly-dance than us. Something to do with her radiating pheromones that come from having curves that her husband appreciates on a very regular basis.

'Clench those Kegels,' Venus instructs. 'Imagine clamping down on a very large penis.'

'Oooooh!' say all us women and I think _Yeah, chance would be a fine thing_.

'I wish she'd not say that,' Wendy scowls.

'I know.' Leigh winks at me. 'It makes me envious for what I don't have.'

'What's that?' Wendy asks her.

'A very large penis.'

Wendy looks Leigh over, deadpan. 'Well, that's something you want to be pleased about. You wouldn't look half as good in those exercise pants.'

'I've had my fair share of them in my lifetime though, Wendy, honey.'

'I'm sure your bedpost's got so many notches on it it's collapsing.'

Leigh grins at her.

'Hip drops!' Venus shouts at us. Then we move on to the raunchier upthrusts. 'Heya!' Leigh manically upthrusts her pelvis. 'A movement I can do.' She winks at me again.

'Lawrence's going to like those,' I tell her. She pulls a *Yuck* face.

Then it's the last Friday of the month, so we're off to Quay, Newcastle's newest, swankiest eaterie. 'I'm having the duck salad with prunes and Armagnac,' Leigh says, before she flits and flirts her way around a floor-to-ceiling fish-tank to the loo. She looks sensational, in a tight white pants suit, with her hair newly cut into shaggy, shoulder-length layers, by our fantastic recently-turned-lesbian stylist, Deb, of Debonhair.

'I tell you,' Wendy says, the second she's out of sight, 'she's so peppy lately. And she keeps going off to lunch to see this client who I think might be Nicholas Barnes, because she once referred to somebody called Nick. She keeps looking at me enigmatically, like she wants me to ask her something.'

'So ask her. She'd ask you.'

'She already did. The other day she asked me if I'd ever had an affair.'

'What did you say?'

'I said "Who with?" and she seemed to find that funny.'

The waiter, an unsmiling Geordie lad, takes our martini orders and is put out when we complain about the price of the wine.

'I've been meaning to ask you,' Wendy looks Leigh over with friendly admiration when she reappears. 'Why are you always carrying your Louis bag around in a plastic carrier?'

'It's the new bag-lady chic.' Leigh plonks herself down in her seat. 'Actually, the effer can't go out in the rain. They don't tell you this when they tell you Paris Hilton has one, and Posh's got ten o' them. This natural cowhide leather that they make a big song and dance about gets watermarks on it.'

'Just spray it,' Wendy tells her.

'You can't! Spraying stains it. So, apparently, does life. I can't even carry it with jeans. The dye transfers onto the leather if it rubs against your leg, and it turns green.'

'What? Your leg?' Wendy again.

'The bag! I'd take it out of the carrier and show you but I'm frightened somebody might breathe on it and it might wizen up like John Wayne's face.'

Our grinning reflections bounce back at us from the mirrored tabletop (That I hate! Ergh! You can see your own nostril hairs. God, I didn't know I had any until now). 'So, how are you supposed to use it, then?' Wendy asks, affectionately. Then she stares into the tabletop. 'Is it just me, or is anybody else getting tired of looking at themselves upside down?'

'On a dry day. If you carry it at arm's length. Dangling off your finger end.'

When our waiter returns, Leigh tells him, 'Mind, these wine prices are shocking, aren't they? Where's your house bottle?'

'We've already had that conversation,' Wendy tells her.

The waiter gives one of those tired faces, says, 'Nobody else has complained.' Leigh narrows her eyes as he walks away. 'Ooh, there's nothing worse than a pompous Geordie, is there? We'll definitely have to pull him down a peg or two.' Then he's back, with plates the size of paving-stones. On them, a square of toast the size of your thumbnail, bearing a pea-sized pink blob. 'A complimentary appetiser from our chef. Mousse of bay mackerel with a cordon of herb syllabub on a warm sesame futon.'

'A futon?' echoes Leigh. 'God, he's bloody putting me to sleep.'

'And he said it with a straight face,' Wendy chimes in, as we gawp at the blob.

'But it's COMPLIMENTARY Wend, you have to remember!' Leigh nudges her.

'Oh, I know. If he hadn't said that I might have thought this place had some class.' Wendy's on to her third martini, outpacing us by two.

'Pretentious little prat.' Leigh swallows her futon declaring it bloody awful.

I wag a fork. 'It's what they call Nouvelle Tapas. I read it in the *Chronicle*. It's basically an excuse for them to give you amoeba-sized portions of substandard food that's dressed up with daft names, and charge you an arm and a leg for it. And you're supposed to think it trendy that you walk out two hundred quid short and have to go home and order a pizza.'

When Leigh sees her main course of breast of duck à la diddle-de-doos, her face falls. 'Right, that's it. I'm never coming here again. It makes airline food look like a hearty meal.'

I look at mine and Wendy's. 'Well, ours is just as bad. It's supposed to be brill but it's more like braille. As in, you can't see it and wonder if it's vanished into the pattern on your plate.'

'Erm, excuse me,' Leigh flags our waiter down so everybody can hear. 'I think the chef forgot to put my duck on the plate.' The waiter stares witheringly at her. '*That* is your duck.' He points to something very tiny and un-quack-like on top of a curly leaf.

'I thought that was the prune!'

He looks tired again. 'It's orbit of Muscovy breast nestled in a hand of forest greens.' He makes a cupping gesture just to hammer the point home. Wendy's hiding her face in her hands and her shoulders heave.

'But it's artistically arranged,' I point out. 'It's an orbit.'

'Orbit that,' Leigh shoots the middle finger. After we chuckle long and hard, she changes the subject. 'Wend, we really have to think of an exciting PR stunt to open the new MetroCentre store.' She's just asked the waiter to send over more bread and he said, 'Would that be a basket each, madam, or one between you?' 'The cheeky get,' she snarled. 'I bet his penis is the size of a long olive.'

'Oh, don't ask me about PR stunts. I'm not very creative,' Wendy tells her.

Leigh stops pushing her 'hand' around her plate and fixes Wendy with a sober stare. 'Try to be.'

Wendy gives me an *Oops!* look. Thank God she's necked three martinis. Personally, I didn't care for that tone.

'Anyway,' Leigh changes the subject again. 'Speaking of being *creative*, Jill and I were just having a *creative* chat the other day about how to *creatively* put the spark back into your sex life.'

Were we? Where's this coming from? I scowl at her. I'm getting tired of this cryptic business in front of Wendy.

'Why?' Wendy stops chewing. 'Is there a difference between putting the spark back and *creatively* putting the spark back?'

Leigh steamrollers her. 'All you keep hearing these days in books and things is about how all single women just want to be married to a good man. Yet women who are married to good men all want to be married to somebody else's good man, at least the truthful ones among us do. Yet who's going around talking about us? Nobody. Because we're supposed to have what everybody wants, just because we've got husbands. So we're not worth talking about.'

'Speak for yourself,' I tell her. She's like a glass of Alka-Seltzer with longer lasting fizz. I'm getting the urge to tip her down the sink. 'I don't want somebody else's man, Leigh. And neither do you.' Obviously, this is all her way of leading up to spilling her guts to

Wendy. I hope she doesn't. Telling one friend is a sanity saver. Telling two is a day at the circus.

Leigh presses on, loudly. 'Argh, I'm wrong actually, aren't I? Wendy's the only one among us who's perfectly happy with what she's got. Wendy just wants to be married to Neil.' It sounds vaguely like a put-down, rather than admiration.

Wendy glances up from her plate of blind man's buff. And I witness one of those rare moments where you can patently see she's not amused. 'How do you know what I do and don't want, Leigh?'

Leigh's jaw drops. 'Well, don't you . . . just want to be married to Neil?'

Wendy runs her fingers up and down the stem of her glass, cool as a cucumber. 'Not always.'

Leigh rolls her eyes. 'Is that it? Or are you adding anything to that?'

Wendy sees the eye-roll. 'I don't know. What would you like me to add?' Again, that look that would make Saddam and his army fill their underwear.

I don't like this turn in the conversation. It feels like it's pick-on-Wendy time, just because she happens to be happy. I jump in with a funny story about how Denise at work told me her husband masturbates to porn on the Internet. 'That's disgusting!' Leigh says, still staring curiously at Wendy. 'I'd lay Lawrence in a box if I caught him doing that. I mean, should a married man be wanking to porn behind his wife's back?'

'Ideally not, but if he has to, he has to,' Wendy answers, surprising us.

'Give over! You're not serious!' Leigh seems really pissed-off now, perhaps because Wendy is somehow getting the upper hand here, and Leigh's not the one doing the shocking any more. 'What if that were Neil? Doing that behind your back? Could you even see Neil doing that?'

'Well, I certainly wouldn't want to see him doing it, and I hope he doesn't. But could I see him?' She shrugs unconcernedly. 'Probably.'

Leigh's expression is priceless. 'Rubbish! You're just being controversial.'

Admittedly, it's not like Wendy to say things like this, and I don't quite know why she is. But I'm tired of this track now. 'Can we change the subject?' I beg, remembering it was me who brought it up.

When Wendy goes to the loo, Leigh whispers, 'I've seen him every day this week, and a few evenings!'

'You're not still going to his house?'

She nods. 'But sometimes we can't make it that far. We have to pull over and do it in the car.'

'Where?'

'In the back seat. In car parks. Down back streets. Wherever we find, when the urge strikes. Look,' she moves aside the lapel of her jacket. She's not wearing a bra and I glimpse her little brown nipple. And next to it is an angry lovebite.

'My God!' My own breasts tingle now with the thought of some man devouring me there. 'What if Lawrence sees?'

'We're not having sex. When he asks for it I just tell him no.'

I just about manage a head shake because Wendy's coming back. 'Shit,' Leigh says. 'I should just damn well tell her. That'd shock her, wouldn't it?'

Probably a lot less than you'd think, I feel like saying.

We order desserts. Molten Belgian chocolate puddings with mint *crème anglaise*. 'It's very nice, this,' Leigh tells the waiter.

'Yes. It's baked in a bain-marie and remains moist in the centre because it's filled with ganache.' He gives us a scathing look and walks away.

Leigh looks at Wendy and me. 'Good ash? What's that mean?'

'Maybe the chef was on wacky baccy,' Wendy says, seeming back to normal again. 'Although I'm not sure how that keeps it moist. Him moist, maybe. But not the cake.' Wendy and Leigh exchange grins.

Our bill, when it gets set down and we recover from heart failure – after trying desperately to fathom what ash, good, bad or indifferent, would have to do with a chocolate pudding – is a hundred and twenty quid and change! 'The bloody rip-off merchants,' I nearly shriek.

'Are we leaving him a tip?' Wendy contemplates our forty-one pence change.

'A small one. We have to. In a place like this.' Leigh reaches out a hand. 'But that's far too much.' She takes away eleven pence. 'Here,' she thrusts thirty pence at him. 'You've been so nice. Buy your girlfriend a chip on us.'

On Sunday, we have my parents, and Rob's mother, who's been away for two months visiting her sister in

America, over for lunch. My mam keeps asking which restaurant we're in, so I suppose that's a compliment. Out of the corner of my eye I watch her chewing away, dainty as a little bird. Occasionally, as though she feels my attention on her, she'll stop chewing, go self-consciously still, slide her eyes around the table, and then shoot enigmatic little smiles at us. My dad's loving gaze combs her hands with their tissue-paper skin, her patient, impossibly unlined face, her butter-coloured hair, then he smiles at me secretively, proudly. 'Tell us the story about how you two met,' I say to my mam, who studies me like she's going to say something very special, then goes back to her food again.

'I saw her at the dancehall,' my dad chimes in. 'She was waltzing tall-backed with a handsome man who had two left feet.' He looks at my mother who continues to eat, looking like she knows she's being talked about. 'I went over to her . . . to save her, of course, from the man with the knocky knees.' My dad coughs, like he does when he's high on his own bullshit. 'I said, "Excuse me, my fellow, but I must cut in," and I didn't say it like I was asking for permission . . . And I took her in my arms, and I danced with her. And we danced, and danced, and danced. By the end of the evening I told her that one day soon, I would put a ring on her finger.'

'Did you take him seriously?' I ask my mother, who looks up, sceptically, from a mound of mashed potatoes.

'Of course not.' She scowls. 'He was half-cut, wasn't he? Besides,' she glances disdainfully at my dad, 'he had too much of a squint in his eye for my liking, when he said it.'

'Eh?' says my dad. 'I had a what?'

'A squint,' my mother repeats. 'You had one of those squints in your eye, young man, and I did not like it.'

'D'you mean a glint?' Rob asks.

My mother slaps a hand over her mouth, humour lighting up her eyes. 'A glint. Maybe that's what I mean. Ooh . . .' she gives us all the evil eye '. . . some people are only happy when they're embarrassing me!'

Argh, my dad's happy! The sun's out. The garden's pretty. The roast's tasty. All in all, this is a very good day where you are over-the-top grateful for small mercies.

Then it's the start of another week again. Leigh keeps ringing after every meeting with the Nick Prick and I tell her I have to cut down on personal calls at the office. But really it's because my head just keeps on turning sex scenes and it has a very disturbing effect. Then Wendy rings and tells me that she and Neil are going away mountain-biking in Scotland for the weekend, so I won't be able to get her on her mobile. 'It's a romantic escape. We're not even taking the lads. We're trusting that they won't throw wild parties while we're gone, and wreck the house.'

'That's brave.'

'And stupid, probably. But necessary. The thing with having children is, you sometimes forget that they're not literally attached to you. You think you have to go everywhere and do everything in a big foursome. But they're getting too old for that, and in some ways Neil and I really don't mind doing a bit of early empty-nesting. It'll be lovely just being the two of us.'

'Have a good time,' I tell her.

'We intend to,' she says.

Saturday. Rob's working again. I'm beginning to think he doesn't live here any more. I get the Hoover out, put it back. Contemplate doing some gardening, go off that idea really quickly. I pace around the front room, twirling my hair. This is essentially my only fun day off and the only person I want to have fun with isn't here. One of my friends is having a great time shagging her husband, and the other's having a great time shagging somebody else's. I pace some more. Okey dokey . . . Bad Jill. Bad Jill. I go upstairs, where I quickly shower, scrub, pluck and shave. I blow-dry my hair and wind up looking like Diana Ross, so I wash it again, gel it and leave it to air-dry. Then, after flinging about seventy-five skirts and tops onto the bed, exasperated that I literally have NO CLOTHES, I finally find something vaguely in style yet 'no effort'-ish that'll do.

I see him coming from my vantage point, on my back, on the sand. I get a fresh reminder of how devastatingly gorgeous he is. He's on a direct course for me. I tent my novel over my face and stop breathing.

'Hello,' he says. I pretend not to hear. But then he kicks me. Just gently doffs his foot to my calf like he's checking I'm alive. I peel Marian Keyes off my face, clamp a hand over my mouth, grin, cringe, die and have an orgasm. His eyes appraise my bikini and he smiles when they land on my belly button, which he fixes with far too much fascination to be called decent.

'You know, I keep seeing you. I mean, again, since time on beach,' he squats beside me, taps my bare shoulder with his index finger. 'Beside bus shelter. I think you with friend. And I was certain you saw me.'

'Nope,' I shake my head. 'It must have been somebody else.'

'Ah, yes. Maybe you have twin?'

'Not that I know of.' God, he's on to me. I die. Time to hoof off back to my marriage. I sit up and start chucking things into my bag. 'I was just leaving.' He's still squatting just inches away from me, the sun backlighting him, illuminating the attractive, wolfish, weather-beaten aura around him. I feel my attraction to him like a meteor that's hurtling unavoidably towards Earth. Have I ever felt like this? Even for Rob?

'When will you come back?'

'Erm . . .' A fight brews inside me. 'In about three minutes. I'm just off to the loo.' *Jill, Jill, Jill, you terrible girl.* He slowly takes in my legs, his gaze settling on my fuchsia toenails like a man who appreciates all the fine points of femininity, as I try to balance on one foot and climb into my cargo shorts, which feels like the most erotic thing I've done for a man in a long time. I don't need Leigh to tell me he'd be good in bed. I always think that a man who notices everything about you as his gaze sweeps over you will be an attentive lover.

'Remember to come back. Quickly. Not in six weeks' time,' he says to my bum as I walk off.

Well, at least I don't look keen. I walk off feeling his eyes on me, so I put on the wiggle. I must either look sexy or like I have a worm. I fling myself into the loo, ring Leigh and tell her what I'm doing, and she's in shock. And a voice inside me says, Just being here is bad enough, but telling Leigh is really making Rob look like a fool, and my marriage a bit pathetic. And this is where I'm getting confused. I'm starting not to know where my loyalties lie. Leigh tells me she's been dreaming of the Nick Prick all day while she was at the Motherplucker's getting her bikini-line waxed. 'Don't do anything I wouldn't do,' she cackles.

I like how he looks at me as I walk back down the sand. It's a grateful, pleased, predatory-beast face. An intoxicating combination for a girl who's a bit attention-starved at home. He grins as I near. 'You were in there so long I was starting to get jealous of toilet seat.'

I replay this. 'Mind, that's a distasteful joke to somebody you don't even know.' I'm beaming my disapproval, of course.

'Well, I would only say to a girl I knew had a sense of humour.' We stand there, beaming at one another as Geordies around us play happy families on the beach. 'Sit,' he says, patting the sand.

I do. My leg touches his and I pull it away and clutch my knees. He asks me how my mother is, which impresses me right off the bat. Then he says my dad doesn't like him and we have a chuckle and his eyes do a little dance with mine. 'So, you work here in the summer . . . what happens for the rest of the year?' He has stubble on his Adam's apple.

'Rest of year, Jill, I am personal trainer, in a gym. I have private clients, mostly women who I put through their pace.' He runs his hazel gaze the length of my bare arm. 'But in summer, I love the smell and the sounds of the sea, so I take a break and I do this.'

'Why do you train only women, Andrey?' I sink my fingers into the wet sand, gripping it into balls, pleased he remembered my name.

He grins mischievously. 'I did not say only. I said is mostly.'

'Well, how many women as opposed to men?' The balls disintegrate; the sand gets down my nails, under my wedding ring.

'Ahrgh, I would say . . .' He gazes up into clouds which, to me, look like white oak trees painted on royal blue china. 'Twenty women. Two men.'

'Oh, and let me guess, the men are gay!'

'Actually,' his handsome eyes roam over my smile, 'one is my boss and other is his brother.'

We laugh. Now, and I'll burn in hell for this, but I am actively picturing what he'd be like in bed. And seeing myself totally letting loose, being some wild and torrid me, the way you can't suddenly be with your husband of ten years or you'll feel a real wally. With Rob, I don't think I've ever been wild, because we were friends before we were lovers. My tongue is stuck to the roof of my mouth. I dig in my bag for my water and feel his eyes on my throat as I tilt my head back and have a guzzle and miss my mouth and essentially salivate all over the place, and he wipes a drop off my chin. It shocks me, feels intimate and highly erotic.

'What sort of exercise do you do to keep in shape, Jill? You have very toned body, but it is still feminine and curvy.'

This thrills me to my split ends. I try to say it with a straight face. 'Belly-dancing.'

'Oh.' He does a foxy whistle. And I think, *If only you could see the state of it, matey.*

A golden Labrador puppy gambols over to us, sticks its head in Andrey's crotch, has a good sniff, then walks around to me and lifts its leg on my foot. The lady owner comes over and apologises – to Andrey. Freezes me right out.

'So, what's Russia like, then?' I ask him.

'Ra-sha? Ahrgh, I had good life, of course, growing up. Yes there was hardship. But when it is all you know, you just get on living. You find joy because you have to. Because we all have to, somewhere.' Then Andrey talks about Russia in a way I wish my history teachers had. All the while, his attention roams around the beach, doing his job. And I'm thinking, it's a pity he's a fortysomething lifeguard and I'm a bit of a jumped-up snob, and I should hurry up, have a bit more eye-sex, then hotfoot it back to my husband.

'Did you manage to get a proper school education, then?' His English is better than most Geordies'.

'Education? Of course. I had education. I had good job.'

He has nice hands. Big hands with juicy, pronounced veins. 'What sort of work did you do back there, then?'

'I was a lawyer.'

'Eh?'

He laughs. 'Don't look so surprise.'

'You were a lawyer and now you're a lifeguard!'

He squints at me in the yellow sunlight, charming crinkles etching themselves around his eyes. 'Well, is not so strange as is sounding. Before I was lawyer I was actually swimmer. I was on the Ra-shint Olympic team when Soviet Union boycotted the 1984 Los Angeles Olympics.'

'You were an Olympic swimmer!' Peel me off the floor.

'I would have been. If my country had allowed for me to go. Twelve weeks before Olympics, Soviet Union pull out.'

'Oh, God, that's terrible!' I scour his face, his hair, his very credible swimmer's chest, which all look fifty times more interesting than they did two minutes ago. 'You must have been devastated. You must have trained so hard.'

'All my life.'

'How old were you at the time of the Olympics?'

'I was eighteen. I am thirty-nine now.'

He knew I was fishing for his age. He looks older. 'So then you became a lawyer?'

'Well, everybody in my family had. It was natural step to me.' He shrugs. 'Then I came to England, where, of course, I cannot be lawyer unless more training and qualify. So now I coach swimmers. Kids. Hopefully next Olympic gold medal winner. And to get by, there is my personal training.'

'But couldn't you just have got qualified here?'

He shakes his head. 'Too many wrong starts. And my heart was never in law. I did it, I think, because I was clever and I could. But what I do now has bigger reward for me. Those kids, I relive my youth again every time I see the dreams on those young faces.'

He runs his gaze over my face, my throat. 'What dreams did you have, Jill?'

I don't want to tell him I don't think I ever had any. Or that I've only just realised that now. Or that I wouldn't have thought he'd have had any either. I feel rotten for having judged him. He knows his work doesn't define him so he needn't be ashamed of it. 'I don't know. I suppose I never really had ambition. For me it was more about earning a pay-cheque, meeting a good bloke.'

'Which you did . . .'

'Which I did.' I skirt around that one. 'So, how on earth did you wind up in the North-East?'

He smiles. 'It was a woman.'

'Oh, I might have guessed! God, I bet you've got them all over the place.'

He beams like a man flattered. 'Yes, of course. There is one under that rock. And two, well, over there.' He shoots his chin in the direction of two old biddies sitting on deckchairs. 'The one on the left is a real goer.' I chortle, and he laughs quietly at my laughing, his gaze roaming haphazardly over my face. He has a lovely laugh. It burrs musically in the back of his throat. 'No, seriously, she was journalist from Yorkshire who was writing book on the former Soviet Union. We met in St

Petersburg; she needed a lawyer. We became involve.
Then she came back to England, so I come. But it did
not work out in long term. So I come here.'

'Oh, I'm sorry.'

'Don't be,' he says, and then, with a twinkle in his
eye, 'I am not.'

'Have you ever been married?'

'I was. Almost. Once. When I was twenty. But I am
not so sure I belief that two people are meant to pledge
themselves to each other, take vows that at the time of
taking them they can't possibly know if they will keep.'
He looks at his hands, at his fingernails. 'I have seen
many marriages where the couples haven't grow together, where after so many years they aren't the
people that either would choose again.'

My guess is he'd have no problem having an affair
with a married woman. Because he doesn't view people
as possessions. 'You wouldn't go back there then, to
Russia?'

'To Ra-sha? *Nyet.*' He shakes his head. Some of his
top teeth are uneven, giving his smile that rakish
quality. I love them. 'No, Ra-sha changed – you follow
in newspaper?'

Oh, God. It rarely makes the pages of *Hello!*

'It changed. I change. And I believe you burn your
bridges in life, Jill, when you make big decisions. But
here is beautiful.' He flourishes a hand around the
beach as a wave breaks noisily near the shoreline and
giggly kids scamper through it and dogs bark at it.
'Every day I come here, I remember how lucky I am to
have choice to appreciate. Whereas at the age I am

now, my father had embolism and died. He loved law, yes. But in end, law killed him.'

He looks at me again. 'Being competitive, in sport, in career, is not always a healthy path to happiness. Besides, Jill, life is not all about where you were and how far you have fallen. It's about joy you find in having some inner satisfaction in yourself, and this often come from having nothing to prove. And it is people you meet. And look, I have met you.' He holds my gaze, says it candidly, squarely, and I feel it in my stomach.

No, I decide. I have never felt like this.

We talk for ages, easily. He asks all kinds of questions. Where I grew up, if I have kids, siblings, where I live, work, my mam's illness. He listens closely, all the while his eyes roaming around the beach at dogs and children in the water. I'm getting the ebb and flow of his accent and don't find it hard to follow any more. I tell him daft things, about my strange boss with the tasselled shoes, my maniac dog and how he's doing my shoulder in when he takes me for walks.

'May I?' His fingers trail the curve of my neck to my shoulder. 'Too much tension here, will create headache here, like gnawing sensation. Yes?' His hand goes under my hair, cups the base of my skull, and kneads gently, more like a doctor than a man after getting down a married woman's knickers. And I have to look away, close my eyes, blow out a small, unravelling sigh.

'So d'you have a girlfriend now, Andrey?' I ask when I get my voice back.

He looks at me. 'No, Jill. No more than you have a husband. Probably less so.'

Oh! Every light in me goes out like a power cut across the board. 'What?' he studies my profile, absorbs the change in me. I get to my feet, every inch of me flooding with Rob and his bright happy trust in me. It's taken a stranger to remind me that he exists. *Andrey, I've just gone off you.* I start hurriedly getting my belongings together. He's still observing me, then he stands up too. 'I didn't mean for to send you running.'

'I'm not running.' How dare he imply that I am? I glance at him. He genuinely looks like he didn't. I have gone off him less.

'Then will you come back, and when?'

'I don't know.' I hate his presumption. I'm critically aware that Rob'll be home now. Waiting for me. Trusting me. And I'm here. And I shouldn't be. Damn him, and what he had to say about vows. I made vows I knew I could keep.

He smiles. 'I am sorry, really. I am sorry for how these things come out. And . . .' he cocks his head kindly, sincerely, duly humbled. 'I am sorry, Jill, that you are married.'

Oh, I wish he hadn't said that. I stare at my painted toenails. Right this minute I am so bloody sad. But I'm sad for all the wrong reasons. I'm sad because I am married. And I like this man and it's wrong. And I hate myself for feeling like this. And I hate that my marriage has come to this. But what I hate most is that I'll never be wooed again, I'll never fall in love again, all that's ahead for me is fixing what's broken. I give a sad, thin, grief-stricken little laugh.

He's studying me with curious disappointment, as though he knows this girl isn't going to forgive him. 'Jill,' his serious voice makes me look at him. 'I don't have right to say this, but that you will come back is my hope.'

I shrug, sigh, shake my head. I walk off across the sand, conscious of him watching me. I climb the steps to the promenade, feeling wobbly. *Jill, you sad little attention-seeker*. I exhale one long breath, forgetting that the rule is you breathe in and then you breathe out again.

It's called living.

8

I lie in bed and pretend to read my novel, ablaze with thoughts of him, playing over what he said, what I said, trying to remember every sentence and the exact order they all came in, the way he touched my shoulder, the tickle of his finger, and his eyes.

A dishevelled, un-hair-combed Rob is sorting through the No Go Zone that is his top drawer, where he keeps a life's work of receipts, old Visa cards, the odd smelly sports sock, empty condom packets from aeons ago, old anniversary cards and what have you. He's looking for the bill to an automatic shut-off iron he bought me that he now claims doesn't work.

A well and truly sobering incident met me when I came in the door, high on my Russian. Rob was sniffing a wad of tangy-looking kitchen roll, while the dog was cocking his head in fascinated curiosity, looking very cute and puppy-like. 'I found this on the carpet.' He brandished the wet handful at me. 'Thing is, I don't know if it's vomit or the other. You'd think it'd be obvious but it's completely got me beat. Here,' he shoved it under my nose. 'Smell it.'

'Ergh!' I plastered myself to the kitchen wall.

'It's got bits of fresh food in it, which makes me think it's vomit, but it's more the consistency of the other.'

'Does it bloody matter, Quincy?'

'Of course it bloody matters. Vomit is forgivable. The other means we're one step forward and two back.'

'Rob,' I said. 'You know something, I'm a bit puzzled.'

' 'bout?' He was still gazing at the paper. 'Cor, it's one of life's mysteries, this . . .'

'Pack in doing that!' God, he can be a lout. 'What I'm puzzled about is . . . well, I'm wondering why we have a yellow dog.'

Rob looked at the dog whose tail started thrashing excitedly against the floor. Then he gave me a close, analytical look, then he tapped the end of his nose. 'We went to the beach this afternoon, didn't we, lad?' He looked at Kiefer again.

I froze. 'The beach?'

'Yeah. We went for a little drive after work, didn't we, angel? And who d'you suppose we saw there, Jill? Hmm?' Again, that look that said he knew something.

I lost the ability to breathe.

He ruffled the dog's ears. 'Shall we tell her who we saw?' he said to Kiefer, then he looked at me again. 'Or shall we keep her in suspense?'

I died.

'We saw Bill from across the street, didn't we? With Sharon and the girls.'

'Bill,' I repeated, thinking, Jesus Hallelujah.

'We had an ice-cream, didn't we, angel?' He glanced sideways at me. 'Yeah, we went to Tynemouth.'

'Tynemouth.' Thank you, Tynemouth. For existing. 'So, what flavour did he have?'

He tutted. 'No. I had the ice-cream. He just ate somebody's snotty paper hankie off the ground.'

I rubbed the dog's head, then rubbed Rob's too. Rubbed it really hard, until he said, 'Pack in doing that.'

'I love you,' I practically sang. 'I love both of you. I do. With my whole heart.' The relief I felt at my lucky escape only barely outweighed the guilt of having something to have a lucky escape from.

'Thanks,' Rob said. 'Seriously, though, can you pack in rubbing my head!'

Then he looked at me, warily, and grinned.

'You sure you don't have the receipt, Jill?' he asks me now, in a tone that implies that the mess of his drawer is something that is somehow my doing. He's just sent me a most peculiar look because I was just thinking of how Andrey said he was getting jealous of the toilet seat, and I've just had a good chuckle – gone 'Hehhhhe!' out loud.

I do a mental eye-roll. 'You paid for the thing. It'll either be in your wallet or in the carrier bag that probably got chucked.' I go back to my book. Start reading the same sentence I've begun thirty times. I can't believe he was a lawyer. And an Olympic swimmer. S-vimmer.

'Well, I didn't chuck it,' Rob says. 'Unless you did.'

I sigh. Pretend to ignore him. Hope he'll go away. 'Did you?'

'Did I WHAT?'

'Chuck it.'

I'll chuck him in a minute. 'No. I didn't chuck it. I didn't even open the bag.' *Get a life.*

'You didn't even open the bag?' he turns around and looks at me, exasperated. 'Don't you think there's something a bit strange about that, Jill? Why d'you think I bought you an automatic shut-off iron if I didn't want you to use it? Or is the opportunity to one day burn our house down so tantalising for you, eh?'

Rob is always on at me about forgetting to turn the iron off. But I'll say, well, that's what happens when you try to do seventeen things at once. But he seems to think his failure to do more than one thing at a time is a lovable handicap all men are born with, whereas mine is a genetic disorder. I give him that face. 'Maybe I was leaving it for you. You know, to acquire the ironing skill before you die.'

He narrows his eyes at me, goes back to raking through the drawer.

I watch him in his mucky stretched-neck T-shirt. *God, Rob, you're scintillating, aren't you? For a Saturday night this is real Rock Your World stuff. The iron receipt. Pass me the vodka bottle.* 'I think Frank Sinatra bought one of those for Ava Gardner for an anniversary present, you know,' I tell him.

'One of what?' He freezes in that I-know-you're-being-sarky posture.

'A shut-off iron.'

He looks at me over his shoulder. 'I bet his bloody worked though.'

I try to get on with reading my book. Where was I?

Ah, yes. The hand on my neck. His fingers under my hair. A shiver goes down my spine and all my arm hairs stand up. I bet he'd be a considerate lover. Just the right touch, at the right moment, in the right place, just long enough to make waves of sensation . . . in Australia. God, I'm hot now with all these bed-covers. I thrash the duvet off.

Then I hear Rob go, 'Ahh!'

Oh, bloody hell-fire!

He's stopped raking through his drawer. He's holding something. His entire body is poised in quiet fascination. 'Remember this?' He comes closer, his face a picture of warmth and tenderness. 'Look at this beautiful little thing.'

I take the little laminated card from him. 'It's my old gym membership! God, I look so young. And that perm!' I chuckle. 'I didn't know you kept this!'

He holds out his hand. 'Give it back, it's mine.' He gazes at it again, his face lit up with nostalgia. 'I've always loved this picture. Your flushed little un-made-up face. Your hair like somebody rolled you in the clippings bin at the poodle grooming parlour.' He looks from my face to the picture. 'Ahh!' he says, 'My beautiful wife who I love and treasure with my whole heart.' And then he smacks three kisses on the little card. Sincere, hearty, beefed-up-with-adoration kisses. I watch him deliberately put it in a safe place among the mess of his drawer, his love for me seeping like some quiet reminder into the air.

I feel like the worst cad.

I put my book face down on the night table. It's time

to bury the Russian. Cheating might not be wrong for everybody, but it's wrong for me. 'You sure the iron's broken, Rob?' I ask my big, soft-hearted hubby of nearly ten years. I clamber over the top of the duvet and go to dig it out of its box, a sudden chastened participant in the trivia of our life. 'It's not a loose wire in the plug?'

He looks over his shoulder, scowls. 'No, it's not a loose wire,' he says, in that *What d'you think I am? A monkey?* tone.

I go over to the socket and plug it in. The little red light comes on. 'It's working, Rob.'

'How?' he says, like I'm a genius.

'You just had to switch it on.'

Buried but not dead. Despite my best efforts, I spend the week with little else but Andrey on my mind. I am not me. I am on fire. On permanent, twenty-four-hour-a-day heat. The wacky things I do: bake chicken à la cling film; take the lead for a walk without the puppy; sprinkle Vim in my knickers instead of talc. It stings, and I have to ring Leigh. 'Ow! What do I do? It's burning like a bugger.'

'Put water on it. But how the hell did you manage to get Vim down your pants?'

I stand beside the bath doing the splits. 'I'd just been cleaning the toilet, hadn't I? Then I had a bath. Got dried. Reached for the talc . . .'

I put water on it. My crotch turns green. 'Oooh!' I call her back, trying to protect my precious bits with my hand. 'God, I can just see me having to crab-walk up to the doctor's looking like I've had sex with a forest of well-endowed tree trunks.'

She gives a dirty laugh. 'Make a paste of bicarb of soda. That's what I do for sunburn. It always works.' So I do. I paste on a white beard, making 'down below' look like a Nestlé Mint Aero with whipped cream. And I lie there on my back with my legs V'd up the bathroom wall. But even this doesn't dampen my libido.

It's been over six months since Rob and I have had sex. I'm trying very hard not to count. But it's been over six months, dammit, bloody hell! If I gave the exact number of days that would make me sound really pathetic, so I won't.

I still have his phone number. I pull it out, stare at his handwriting, every loop and curve. I dial, listen to his voice on the answering machine, hang up, do it again. About fifty times. A couple of times I drive over to the beach, camp out in a strategically inconspicuous spot and stare at him while he does enthralling things like scratch the back of his head, or kick his sandal against a rock to dislodge the sand. You'd think he'd chat up all the girls, but he doesn't, I'm pleased to see. I stop short of following him when he goes off shift, because that's got stalker written all over it. But in my fantasies I hold nothing back. I imagine going over to his place for dinner. We're at it the instant I'm through the door. Then he cooks, with a tea towel thrown over his shoulder, something devastatingly Russian. In the middle of the meal, the other hunger comes over me again. I straddle him in his chair and we go at it again.

At work, the girls comment that I seem unusually

distracted. Then I make two nasty accounting mistakes, either one of which could have landed me the sack had I not noticed in the nick of time. Then I sit at my computer supposedly doing bookkeeping, twirling strands of my hair, thinking of something Leigh said: that the truest test of whether you fancy a man is if you can see yourself giving him a blow-job.

I can.

On Thursday I sit in the dentist's chair and while he rakes in my mouth, I'm wondering if I could fancy him. My old, bald dentist with false teeth. I've been coming here since I was a kid; the thought has never once entered my mind. Then, in my bed, as I try to fall asleep, I'm a livewire. Andrey courses through my red-hot-blooded veins, refusing to let me rest. Andrey, the boy, growing up in Russia; Andrey's smile; Andrey's humour; Andrey's hopes and dreams; the feel of Andrey's fingers on my bare skin.

Not Rob's. Lately I'm not imagining anything physical to do with Rob.

By Wednesday I'm exhausted. Wendy rings me at work. She sounds flat. 'I'm not coming to work out with you tonight,' she tells me. 'I'm a little tired. I had a bit of a bad argument with Neil last night so I didn't get much sleep.'

I have never heard her say she's had an argument with Neil. 'Is everything all right, Wend? What was it about?' The second the words are out, I regret asking.

'Oh, it was nothing. Trivial, really.'

Trivial but a bad argument? Sometimes I wonder why she bothers telling me anything at all. 'Well, why

don't you come out anyway? Exercise makes you feel
better. Aren't you always telling me that?' I realise I
want her there for my own selfish reasons – to change
the track of my thoughts, and the mood and inevitable
conversation between Leigh and me.

'Erm, no. I think I'll give it a miss. Leigh was getting
on my nerves a bit today at work. I think I need a bit of
Leigh-free time.'

She doesn't sound herself. But, honestly, if she's not
going to tell me I'm not about to drag it out of her.

In the gym changing room, a static current of sexual
frustration crackles around me as I pull off my shirt.
Leigh stands there in scarlet bra and knickers, swinging
her new raven hairdo, jangling her gold double-hoop
earrings. She looks exotic, like a flamenco dancer. We
claim treadmills beside each other and start pounding
away. She's still seeing him every lunchtime. It's been
over a month now. The other day he came to her office.
Wendy was at a doctor's appointment and Clifford was
out. They did a frenzied pelvis-grabbing grind against
a wall by an open window, with Northern Goldsmith's
clock chiming in the distance. 'The sex is only getting
better, if that's possible, Jill,' she pants. 'It's true,
women are at their prime in their thirties; I've never
had so many powerful orgasms. Yesterday, I was so hot
for him I made him pull over at a Burger King. He
snuck me into the men's toilets and we did it in a
cubicle!' She cackles. 'Now I know why everybody
loves those Whoppers!'

'Aren't you horrified Lawrence is going to notice
how different you've become?' I pound it hell for

leather, watching all the fit fellas lifting weights while this need for a hot, sweaty tangle with some male flesh runs loose in me, faster than my legs.

'Look, I do what I do with him then I go home. I don't sneak out at night. My life goes on as normal. So my mind might be somewhere else? Lawrence doesn't know that. We always assume people are mind-readers, Jill, but they're not. They've got enough to think about with their own lives.' She's panting, giving off a golden glow. A bead of sweat disappears down the V of her top. 'Actually,' she says, 'affairs are a lot easier to have than you'd think.'

In the sauna, we lie on opposite benches in our towels, our heads turned to one another. 'Oh, God, Leigh, tell me something bad about it. Tell me a downside.'

She seems to think hard. 'I can't. Doing this just makes me wonder why I was faithful all these years. And the funny thing is, Jill,' she sits up, her towel falling from her breasts. 'You know, since I've had a lover, I pick on Lawrence so much less. And you can tell that he's more relaxed because of it. Even his OCD's better.' She wipes away her running mascara. 'In a peculiar way this affair is saving my marriage. Fucking another man is actually doing Lawrence a favour.' The door opens and somebody comes in. Our gazes slide apart. In the changing room we dry off. 'Are you still thinking of going for it with the Russian?' she asks me. 'I mean, now that your marriage is back on track.'

I lied the other day and told her it was. I didn't think she believed me for a second, given that it came about two minutes after the Vim episode. But if this thing that Rob and I are going through turns out to be just a blip on an otherwise happy landscape, I don't want my marriage remembered by the bad things I've said about it, because they have a way of obliterating the good.

'Well, I'm not sure it's exactly back on track,' I say, knowing the only reason I can't tell her how bloody dismally un-back on track it is, is that she'll then know I told her fibs. Then she'll think things are even worse than they are. 'Besides, he's not exactly said "Come on, let's do it." He knows I'm married.'

'Boring,' she sings.

'No, actually, I like that. If he were all over me it'd put me off. At least he's got class.'

'A classy lifeguard.'

'Don't take the piss.'

'Well, you initiate it, then!'

'I can't.' My eyes suddenly brim with tears. 'Oh, God, Leigh, I don't know what I'm coming to.' I plonk myself down on the bench. She stops drying her legs and looks at me, shocked. 'I thought all I wanted was to fix my marriage. But now . . . I don't know what I want. I'm scared I want something I don't want to want . . . Another problem, instead of a solution. Maybe I'm just fed up with the whole concept of being only thirty-five and married all this time. Maybe – like you once told me – a part of me is just burning to go out and make up for all the fun I should have had in my twenties.' *When I was taking life too seriously, and settled down ahead of my time*. 'I'm scared that I'm starting to doubt not just my future with Rob, but my past, too.'

'Look, Jill,' she sits down beside me. 'I know you love Rob. He's a great lad. And I'm certainly not going to encourage you to be unfaithful. But you're my friend. You're the one I care most about. And you've not judged me. So I'm certainly not judging you, no matter what you do. And I can tell you're unhappy. There's a cloud hanging over you. So if there's something you badly need to do, do it. Do it, and fuck guilt. Guilt is only something invented by people who are too scared to do what they really want.' She looks at me directly. 'You're not going to get your life back once it's over. I'm convinced you don't have some burning desire to shag around and make up for lost time – because, believe me, that's not the fun it sounds. But maybe you were destined to meet this man for a bit of fun to get you through a tough period in your marriage. Maybe he's come along to somehow save you.' She stands up, starts putting things in her bag. 'But if you're not going to go for it, then forget about him or you're just tormenting yourself. Basically,' she rolls up her leggings, 'piss or get off the pot.'

My very ladylike mother used to use that expression all the time.

At home, I lie in the bath and contemplate my menstruating body. My breasts, which always seem bigger at this time of the month, spread and float on the water. Little pieces of my endometrium unfurl into the water like sea anemones, which reminds me what the root cause of all this is. Why couldn't we have been able to have a baby? Weren't we allowed to change our minds?

Maybe it was wrong of us to say we never wanted children, when to most people kids are a blessing. But is this some sort of divine punishment – our marriage biting the dust? I will not let it happen.

So why am I wavering? Why does Leigh's Elasto-plast solution sound a little bit appealing? Why do I rack my brains to make a mental list of all Rob's flaws and make them add up to enough of a reason for me to cheat? Why does part of me wish I could find out that he were having an affair, so I could have my own in revenge? It's terrible and it's shameful and I hate feeling this, but I do and I just can't help it. If only I were like Wendy: happy and still in love. Or, if I can't be her, why can't I be Leigh, and just not give a damn? Good girls, they can't be true to themselves.

In bed I lie awake next to a mound of snoring husband, thinking about marriage and fidelity, temptation and honest friends. But what was it Leigh said? That being with Nick makes her realise she'll never enjoy sex with Lawrence again. So she did answer my question. The one thing bad about her affair: when the party's over, she'll feel like she's gone home with the consolation prize.

I smile to myself with some sort of smug satisfaction about my righteous commitment to my ailing marriage. I glance across at Rob's back, his heaving barrier of shoulders. Then I shut my eyes, slip my hand under my nightie and take the only course of action I'm left with.

9

'Something very odd's happened.' Wendy's voice is missing its bounce. I sit on my bed with Kiefer next to me and stuff the phone under my chin while I try to put on my socks. Rob has just come out of the shower with a bath towel around his waist. Kiefer watches him walk across the room. 'You know how Leigh wanted ideas for opening the flagship store at the MetroCentre? Well she's decided she wants to give away five hundred pounds' worth of merchandise to the first person who's through the door naked. She thinks half of Newcastle is going to be lined up at the door in the buff.'

'She's probably right.'

'Well, she wants to invite the national media. She thinks it's brilliant publicity for the brand. And Clifford happened to ask me my opinion of it.' She takes a deep breath. 'So I said, well, I can certainly see it attracting attention. But I actually have a problem with that on two levels. One: it's wrong to ridicule people even if they do very stupid things and don't know that people are laughing at them, not with them. And two: if this gets on the telly, well, I just don't think it sends the right signal to the rest of the country about the North-East. I mean, I hate it how the few times this region ever gets on the national news they'll always manage to interview the most toothless, illiterate moron who punctuates everything with "man", "why aye" and "like", and that's supposed to be representative of Geordies! It just keeps fuelling those old Andy Capp stereotypes and I get fed up of it. So having a load of silly girls embarrass themselves for a bag of free clothing . . . I don't know. I think it's wrong. And if it were my company, my brand, I'd want to associate it with something with a bit more class than that.'

'And you told him this?'

'Well, I was a bit less vehement, but yes.'

'Good God!' Rob's doing that thing of dressing where he'll put his T-shirt on before his underpants so his dangly bits hang there. I used to find it comical. Today it pisses me off. 'So, what's he say?'

'He completely agreed. He really latched onto the point about class.'

'Well, that's good then!'

'No it's not. Because five minutes before that he thought Leigh's idea was the best one since sliced bread. In fact he thought it was so good that he actually thought it was his idea. And now that he loathes it, he's coming down very hard on Leigh for "leading the brand astray". And she's mad and seems to think it's all my fault.'

Tits up. I tell you, I predicted it. Never work for friends. 'Well, what's she say?'

There's a pause. 'She just looked at me like she actually might kill me. Then she said, "Well, just because ONE PERSON has no sense of humour . . ." So I suppose that meant me. Then they had this massive fight. The production manager was on his way in the door and just rolled his eyes and crept away.' She takes another deep breath. 'Jill, what do I do?'

'Nothing, I'm sure it's over with now. Leigh doesn't hold grudges.'

'Doesn't she? Yesterday morning when I went in, there was a note on my desk. It said, "Please phone the MetroCentre and find out the fire hazard policy for crowds outside stores. FOR MY IDEA YOU TRIED TO SABOTAGE".'

'Sabotage? She used that word?'

'She did. She didn't spell it right, but she did. She even put it in block capitals.'

'Well, go tell her that was completely uncalled-for!' As I say this, Rob, who is listening in on the conversation as he dresses, gives me a curious scowl.

'I can't. I've mulled this over half the night. There's going to be a very strange atmosphere if we end up having a big row. I mean, she's my friend. I can't just switch her off at five o'clock. And I don't want her thinking that just because I've never worked all these years that I'm too sensitive . . .' There's a pause. 'Jill, I did something really cowardly.'

'No you didn't. You gave your opinion. So she didn't like it. Tough tits.' Rob gives me the thumbs up. Kiefer leaps off the bed and takes off with a pair of Rob's socks.

'No. I don't mean that. I mean, when I saw that note. For some reason I just thought, Oh, I can't face this. I just couldn't be bothered with the silliness of it. So as she hadn't come in, I went in to see Clifford clutching my cheek saying how I had a really bad toothache and I'd just got an emergency appointment at the dentist.'

'Oh, no.'

'So now I'm sat at home nursing a toothache I don't have, trying to work out how I'm going to never go back to a job I'm not even sure I want any more, and all this feels . . . beyond childish, and ridiculous to say the least.'

'It is childish. She's being childish.'

'I thought about telling her I'd changed my mind, that the more I think about it, it's actually a good idea. But why should I do that? Why should I pander like that and take back what I believe in?'

'I don't know, Wend. Maybe for an easy life! But what's Neil say about all this?'

'Oh, he thinks I'm overanalysing. Mind you, I didn't tell him the toothache part. But he did say I should be on my guard about her – she's obviously not the person I thought she was. Which is taking things too far.'

'Well, I think you should go back in, say your tooth's fine now, and act like none of this has ever happened. And if it ever happens again, you'll take her to task then.'

'But that's a bit lily-livered too, isn't it? Isn't she probably testing my mettle here a bit?'

'Oh, I'm sure she's got better things to do. Who knows, maybe she meant it as a joke.'

'But when I told you what she wrote you didn't think it was a joke did you? SABOTAGE is a strong word,

Jill. It's not like she just said "for my idea you don't like".'

'Wendy, you know, maybe Neil's right. Maybe you are making a bit too much of this.'

Rob, who is scrounging through his dresser drawer looking for something, glances at me and rolls his eyes, while the dog growls and prances around him, trying to get him to play Chase-Me with the socks.

She sighs. 'Maybe I am. But lately I just wonder what I'm doing, Jill. Marketing. Exercise wear. I don't know . . . all my life I've fantasised about standing for something. Just . . . if I could get into a company where the work is a bit more relevant to something I'm interested in, or has some bigger meaning . . . I wouldn't mind just being the receptionist. I'd gladly be it.' She sighs again. 'Sometimes I think I should go and finish my degree, go and get more degrees, even, until I'm so degreed that somebody finally takes me seriously. I mean, I have a job that I'm supposed to be grateful for because I can't find a job anywhere else, yet in many ways I feel too good for this job. So where this leaves me, I'm not quite sure.'

'Well, go and do it. Go back and finish your degree.' I've lost count of the number of times we've had this conversation.

She pauses. 'Neil doesn't think it's a great idea. But then again, Neil has no respect for education.'

'Neither does Leigh.'

'No. Because they did fine without it. But they're the exception, not the rule. And that was then and this is now. Today, at the very least you need a degree. And if you're my age and trying to get your first job, you need a degree and a miracle.'

'Well, nothing's stopping you. I'm sure if you decided to do it, Neil would support you.' I put a finger in my ear to block out Kiefer who has exchanged his growl for a high-pitched bark.

'I know. I just don't know what it is with me. I seem to have this mental block where this topic is concerned. I mean, I am *able* to finish it. I want to. Yet, for some reason, I can't. There's always been Neil or the lads stopping me. Way back it was my A-level grades that prevented me going to read law, which is what I always really, really fancied, when all I had to do was resit them instead of taking a job at the Civic Centre. Then it was the job that prevented me from going back to school. Then it was my parents dying, then Nina dying. And now that nothing's stopping me . . . *I'm* stopping me. I know I'm not afraid of failing,' she sighs, frustrated. 'Maybe I'm afraid of succeeding.'

'God, I'm very glad I was a complete ambitionless no-hoper, because this ambition business just seems like more trouble than it's worth.'

Kiefer adopts a new strategy to get Rob's attention and abandons the socks for an Italian leather shoe. 'You devious little fucker!' Rob cries. There's a pause on the line, then Wendy says, with a smile in her voice, 'Does your husband talk like that to you a lot?'

Sunday is Lawrence's fortieth birthday. We're all invited to a barbecue at Leigh's. 'Oh, Christ, do we have to?' Rob groans. It's funny how, after all these years, our husbands have nothing to say to each other.

'I've got this really bad toothache . . .' Wendy says, when I ring to make sure she's coming. I laugh. 'Oh, come on, now you're playing silly beggars. She said she put it in capitals for a joke!'

'Oh.' She flattens. 'You talked to her about it?'

'Well, she never brought it up—'

'Well, of course she wouldn't. Not when she knows she behaved rotten.'

Shit. 'Wendy, honey, you know . . . I think it's time to put this baby to bed.'

'I didn't get the wrong end of the stick, Jill,' she says flatly. 'She was annoyed. The face doesn't lie. Even if the block capitals do.'

Leigh and Lawrence have a lovely home, a four-storey Edwardian terrace that they bought for next to nothing, fixed up, and now it's worth a bomb. The rooms are tiny and unusually shaped, with uneven floors and high ceilings. Before you can climb the steep, narrow stairs you have to duck your head under a sort of hanging ceiling. Lawrence creatively attached a brass bar across it so that when you get to the bottom stair, you almost have to limbo under it. Cute. Loads of character. But it's a patient person's house. As Wendy once remarked, perfect for some rather 'with it' dwarf.

Lawrence keeps poking the hamburgers that are sticking to the grill.

'Don't do that, they'll disintegrate!' Leigh barks at him. 'Come and grate some Parmesan cheese instead.'

Lawrence slinks away. He takes a bashing so well. I suppose having seven sisters he was sort of born for it. Leigh can never get their names straight. When she's being particularly vicious, she calls them Happy, Sleepy, Dumpy, Dopey . . . Rob slaps Lawrence's back as he walks past him. 'Don't worry, mate. I can't barbecue either.'

Lawrence gives Rob a look of quiet humour. 'Marriage is the process of finding out the kind of husband your wife would have preferred. I didn't make that up. I read it in a book.'

Neil, who's been leaning against the fence with a beer in his hand, volunteers to take over the barbecue. 'You good at it?' Leigh quips over her shoulder as she comes out and puts olive oil on the picnic table.

'Me? Good? The best,' Neil says, and Leigh grins at Wendy and me.

Maybe it's just me, but whenever we get together there's something a little bit painful in Neil's attempts to appear at ease. I watch him standing there, holding his bottle of Stella, the muscles in his forearms flexing as though even they feel the strain. Maybe it's being an important detective; he can't relax. As though Wendy notices it, she walks over to the barbecue and stands right beside him, their arms touching. Being a good foot shorter she has to look up at him when she talks, which appears sweetly idolising.

'Here,' Leigh thrusts the Parmesan at Lawrence. 'Do half.' Molly follows her mam, singing, making scissor movements with Barbie's legs. Wendy's lads sit on the patio steps, hunched over in a shared desire to send a signal that being here with their parents is too uncool. 'Wend, give the lads a beer,' Leigh tells her.

Wendy looks lovingly at her lads. 'I think they're okay.'

Paul, the cheeky one, says, 'No we're not. Speak for yourself.'

'You're not, son?' Wendy rubs Paul's shaved head with its zigzag lines that match the ones in his eyebrows. 'No, you're really badly done to, aren't you? I'm just a really horrible parent, aren't I?' She looks up at Neil proudly, but Neil is watching Leigh walk out from the house holding two bottles. Rob is watching her too, noting the denim miniskirt. He's already told her she looks great, although later he'll probably tell me she looked like mutton dressed as lamb in that skirt. That's Rob: master of insincere compliments when he's got nowt else to say.

'Here,' Leigh thrusts the beer at the lads. 'I can't have them thinking we're a bunch of geeks now, can I?'

The lads' faces light up. 'Right on there, Leigh, man,' says Paul.

Leigh's studying gaze moves between the two lads, who look almost identical, and so much like their dad. I wonder, reading her expression, if she's thinking of her own twin. If she's thinking that somewhere out there is another woman who looks just like her, maybe even thinks just like her, only this woman wants nothing to do with her.

Ben looks up and grins with triumph at his mam.

'There you go,' Wendy says, deadpan. 'My lads now think my best friend is cooler than their mam. It'll never do.' Her hands lock around one of Neil's forearms.

Leigh takes her eyes off the lads and looks sad for the briefest of moments. Then she turns and sees Lawrence grating Parmesan for England. 'That's enough!' she grabs the block off him.

'What else would you like me to do?' he says as she chortles at him.

'Book a one-way ticket to Papua New Guinea and shack up with a cannibal,' she mutters, her eyes smiling at me and Wendy. And then she tells him, 'You could top our glasses up. But first go and see if Rob and Neil want another beer.'

'Great idea.' Lawrence pops a kiss on her cheek and gets right onto it.

How does she do it? I watch her sail around her kitchen, assembling food. Act so normal? God, she's got it down to an art. It's almost pathological. From time to time she catches me watching her, sends me that secretive, defiant, this-is-all-bearable-because-of-HIM smile. Call me old-fashioned, but it seems hypocritical putting on a big 'do' for your husband while you're rogering somebody else's. I said to her the other day, 'You're not really going to have a big knees-up for his birthday, are you?' She looked at me like I was wrong in the head. 'Why not? He's not dead, is he?'

I go back to watching Rob now, without him knowing I'm doing it. Yes, he's lovely, and yes, if I met him for the first time today, I'd be attracted to him.

Very.

Ish.

I get the urge to relieve Lawrence of a bottle of beer, take it outside and plant a desperate smacker on my husband. So I do. 'Thanks, treasure,' he says, and chinks the bottle to my wine glass. Then, with a wink, 'For the kiss, too.'

'So, what did you buy him then, Leigh?' Wendy comes back into the kitchen looking curvy in white Capris, white runners, and a four-quid black M&S cap-sleeved T that shows off the lovely worked-out V of her bicep.

Leigh's face turns devilish. 'Botox.'

'Botox!' Wendy nearly chokes. 'But he hasn't got wrinkles!'

Leigh tuts. 'It's not for his face, is it? It's for his feet. You can use it to stop you sweating. Didn't you know?'

'No!' we both chorus, and she gives us a look that says we have to get with the times.

Lawrence comes into the kitchen, smiling benignly, and Leigh says, 'Shush! I'm giving him his pressie later.'

'Later?' Lawrence glances from his wife to us. 'What do I get later?' By his face, it's obvious what he's hoping for.

'The burgers are about ready. I take it we want them well done? No salmonella,' Neil cocks his boyish face and platinum hair around the door, and smiles at his wife. The sleeves of his gun-metal grey shirt are rolled up and his stainless steel watch beams from a sun-tanned arm. He looks almost funny doing something domestic. His out-of-placeness makes him look effort-lessly fanciable.

'I love samon-ella!' Molly chirps, going over and hugging her mam's backside.

'No sweet pea. You love salmon. That's a bit different.' Leigh grins at Neil.

'I may have to go in for a little procedure,' Wendy says, as she watches Neil go back outside.

Leigh stops stirring the parmesan into potato salad and we both look at her. 'On your tooth?' she asks her.

Wendy glances at me, half-smiles. 'No. Not on my tooth. Actually, the tooth's fine now.' She tops up her wine glass. 'It's nothing, really. I had my smear and they've found abnormal cells.'

My heart sinks. 'Abnormal?' I say, as Leigh fires, 'You've not got cancer?' Her bloody sledgehammer tact!

'No, I don't think it's cancer. But I have to have this procedure, something called a colposcopy. It's a type of microscope that gives them a better look at the cells.' Her eyes are looking out of the window, fixed on Neil's back again as he tends to the burgers.

'My God,' Leigh and I say in unison. *All that fuss she made of this silly SABOTAGE business, when she knew she had far bigger things to worry about!*

'It's most likely nothing. Lots of women have abnormal smears, don't they?' she snaps her attention back to us. But beyond that bravado she sounds vague and unconvincing.

'Well, how do you feel?' I hope she doesn't think I'm prying.

She shrugs. 'Fine. But I've been having a bit of breakthrough bleeding. That's why I went for a check-up.' Her mam died in her forties from some sort of female thing, I forget exactly what. My heart flutters.

'Don't you have regular smears?' Leigh asks, agog.

She shakes her head. 'I hate people messing around down there.'

'But you always said you went!'

'That's because you two do, so I lied.'

Leigh looks at me. I sink into the chair at the kitchen table. 'Does Neil know?'

'I'm not saying anything until I've seen the specialist. What's the point? Why worry him?'

'He's your husband, Wendy,' I tell her. And she looks at me, as though to say *precisely*.

We eat at the picnic table under a loganberry tree. Leigh and Lawrence's back garden is all climbing wisteria and hidden paths and birdbaths, thanks to Lawrence's eye for design. Wendy's news has sort of put me off my food, and Leigh doesn't eat much either, although I suspect for different reasons. I happen to look over and catch her off in enraptured space and I think *Jesus, can't you think about anything but yourself just for two minutes?* The conversation inevitably turns to the murder at the university that Neil got interviewed on *Look North* about. I watch Wendy watching him as he talks, how her eyes comb over him, in that interested way you might study a person you don't know very well. 'Well, as far as I see it, Neil, there seem to be two truths,' I hear her saying. 'What the police are saying, and what the media are reporting.' I still can't believe she hasn't told him. Rob would be the first person I'd tell if there were anything wrong with me. 'I think you've had too much wine,' I catch his response, which comes off like a real put-down, and I wish I hadn't missed what they're talking about, because the atmosphere round the table becomes very cuttable-with-a-knife.

It's a lovely meal. Afterwards, Leigh materialises from the kitchen carrying a two-tiered yellow-iced cake, a bewitched smile on her face. 'Ta-da!' she and Molly sing. 'Happy fortieth, Lawrence!' Leigh pipes. And Molly bursts into a soprano chorus of 'Happy Birthday to You!'

It's here. This weekend. 22 July. Our tenth wedding anniversary. Rob will get me a card. And on it he'll write the original, thoughtful sentiment: 'Happy Anniversary, love Rob'. Two years running he's given me the exact same card: a watercolour of a vase of flowers, which could have come from the Sympathy section. I'm certain he must have just dug it out of my drawer and stuck it in a new envelope. When they don't make much effort you start matching their behaviour, thinking things like *If he came in with a big bouquet of red roses, I'd come down to breakfast in a garter and suspender belt*. But it never happens. And it's far easier to blame Rob for not taking the initiative than to actually take it myself. Sometimes having to put the effort in just feels like a synonym for trying too hard. My nagging must have penetrated, though, because for my birthday he got me the dog. I'm certain it was to ensure I'd never ask him for any-thing again. But this year's different. I'm giving it my all. Ten years deserves nothing less. Rob deserves nothing less. I keep thinking of him kissing my little picture.

I have it all planned. I'm going to pick him up after work and whisk him away to Bamburgh for two nights at the Coach and Horses Lodge where we spent our wedding night. I've even booked the same room. I've splurged on an expensive bottle of champagne, a new dress for when we go out for dinner, and, wait for it . . . a sexy nurse's outfit. I was trying it on in The Pervy Store, and the bloody fire alarm went off in the mall, didn't it? There was me, running outside in fishnets and a white vinyl miniskirt with a scant red-cross nipple-revealer for a top. Got some very strange looks from people, and the firemen had a field day. Anyway, I'll probably feel a real wally in it but I'm giving it a go. I'm trying my hardest not to think the words Last Ditch Attempt.

But I swear, as I was shopping for the dress, I was looking for something I could wear if I go back and see Andrey. As if that wasn't bad enough, I was mid-aisle then did a sudden shift-of-mission and made right over to the Wheels and Doll Baby section – Clothes to Snare an Affair (my version of its tag line). And I found just the top. It gave me cleavage on my cleavage and a thoroughly whittled waist. I got it to the till when I was hit with The Great Big Guilt Attack. The assistant was holding out her hand and could I hell give the thing to her? I stood there, mouth open, frozen, clutching my solar plexus. Her eyes looked deep into mine, as though she knew. 'You're not going back,' I thought she said. And I vigorously shook my head. 'You're right. Honest. I promise. Never again.' Then she looked at me funny and said 'Eh?' And I looked at

her funny and said ' "Eh?" What does "Eh?" mean?'
She snatched the top off me. 'I said, do you want me to
put it back?'

Before I whisk Rob off for the weekend, though, I go
to pay my mam and dad my regular visit. When I walk
in their door, I've obviously just missed some big
eruption because I can feel the desolate wake of it in
the air. My dad's stooping to pick up bits of broken
teapot. A harrowed, pathetic little face looks up at me,
his eyes sunken in his head. 'I dinna kna what I said to
upset her. She was champion one minute, then she
started saying how I'd taken her pension money, that I
was stealing off her.' He wipes the back of his hand
across his brow, which has a fine sweat on it. 'I said
dinna be daft. Why would I steal off me own wife? But
she said I had some other woman. I tried to tell her,
dinna be daft! Some other woman! But she wouldn't
see it . . .' I know this is the hard part for him; he knows
he can't reason with her because she's past that, yet the
stupidity of some of her claims makes him have to try.
'I told her I wasn't listening to this, I was off to make a
cuppa tea – but, the bad bugger, she followed me in
here, took the teapot off me, dropped it.' He mimics
dropping something from high up. 'You shoulda seen
the temper on her.' He shakes his head disbelievingly,
sadly. 'She loved this teapot. Had it for years. Remember how she kept glueing the handle back on?' He
half titters.

'I loved that teapot, dad. It feels like it's been in this
family longer than I have.' My dad puts his head in his
hands and I hear a tiny whimper.

'Oh, Dad,' I go to cuddle him, but he flaps me off.

'Give over, you're making me sweat,' he wipes at his eyes. Together we pick up bits of broken brown ceramic, like chunks of a kid's smashed up chocolate Easter egg.

'It's only stuff, Dad. Just stuff. It should have been binned years ago.' Not true. I'd never have binned it. If there were one thing I could have taken from this house when the time comes for everything to go, it would have been that teapot. My dad stares intensely at the ground, fresh tears welling in the corners of his eyes. 'I kna, love. I kna.' But he doesn't know. None of us knows anything any more. We sit down at the small formica kitchen table.

'Dad . . .' Now's as good a time as any to bring this up, I suppose. 'I've been looking into care homes that'll take her for a weekend. Just like a little holiday—'

'Holiday?' His sad eyes bore into mine. 'Give over. Would you gan in one of them places for a holiday?'

'But Dad, it would just be—'

'Oh, Dad!' he mimics my voice. 'Rob and me aren't bothering with Spain this summer, we think we'll gan in a nut-house!'

'Dad!'

'Holiday!' he spits, disgusted. He gets up, throws a hand in the direction of the front door. 'There's the door. Walk through it. Dinna come back. You're no daughter of mine.'

'Okay, now you're being ridiculous!' I get to my feet. 'All it would be is for the weekend. To give you some time off. Nobody's suggesting—'

'I dinna need time off, I'm not in the army. I didn't marry her to abandon her in her hour of need.' He sinks down into his chair again. I stand there and watch him hold his head in his big, upturned hands, his elbows up by his shoulders, bony fingers clutching at either side of his skull. 'Once they get their hands on her she'll never come home. I'll never see her again.' His voice wobbles with anxiety.

I keep standing there, looking at him, and I don't know what to say because part of me knows he's right. We stay like this in silence for a long moment, then he looks up at me. 'I'm telling you one thing, and it's final: *she's* not going anywhere!' He's annoyed now. 'I'll tell you another thing, if you like. If *she* goes, *I* go. So think about that.'

I'm about to, but then the kitchen door flies open and I just about get knocked off my feet. My mother glares from my dad to me, lucid eyes of sea-foam green. 'She! She!' She says indignantly. 'Who's she? The cat's mother?' She continues to stand there, staring at us, indignant, like some spinster headmistress in a tizzy.

My dad looks at me and I look at him. And in that instant, everything diffuses and we have a little chortle. Then comes the weirdest baritone song from my mother's tiny little body: 'You'll never miss your mother till she's gone!'

'I thought we'd go to Stolley's and have a look at a carpet,' I tell Rob when I've got him in the car after I've dropped the dog off at the kennels. 'I fancy a new one for the bedroom.'

He groans. 'Carpet? Bedroom? On a Friday night?'

I try not to smile. It's raining again. The wipers are going like the clappers and I can barely see.

'This isn't the way to Stolley's, Jill.'

'God, you're quick on the draw.'

'Well, what are we going this way for, then?' He studies my profile and I try not to smile. Then I tell him and he's floored. 'You booked this?' I nod vigorously, squeeze his hand.

'Shit, Rob, I pressed your shirt before I left and now I think I've left the iron on.' I'm just braking hard as the traffic's slowing down. The car aquaplanes.

'Which iron?' Rob gives me that look.

'The shut-off one.' I wink at him.

When we get moving again I floor the accelerator, but it drags. 'You're driving like a senior citizen,' my husband says.

I barely get the words, 'I think there's something wrong with the car' out of my mouth when my 'battery low' light comes on. 'Oh, sodding buggers, the battery's going flat.'

'Ignore it. Those lights have come on before when there's been nowt wrong. We're not far now.'

'Shouldn't we call the AA?'

'Well, you know how long we'll wait. Let's just get there. We'll call while we eat dinner.'

I do my 'you win' sigh. Rob gives my hand his 'I know best' pat. We turn off the motorway and follow a trunk road. But it looks suspiciously like we've arrived in a field of sheep. 'I think you missed the turning,' he says, in that God-you're-useless tone.

'I don't think I did clever clogs!' I peer through the splashing rain, hoping to find the main road again. I don't get far when our car stops, the dashboard lights up, and then everything dies. 'Right,' I say, in my this-is-all-your-fault tone.

'Right,' he says back.

I want to kill him. I always listen to him and it always buggers everything up. Any minute now he's going to bloody say 'I told you so' and then I'm going to bloody kill him. We sit there for a while, me mentally counting down to it coming.

'I tol—'

'Hup!' I wag a finger. 'Don't even think about saying that.'

The rain pelts an irregular rhythm on our roof. We have some daft argument now about who's going to truck to the nearest sign of civilization to find out where we are, so we can tell the AA where to find us.

'You are, cos you got us into this mess and I'm not wearing a coat!' he says.

'You are, cos I've got good sandals on, plus I did all the donkey-work for this weekend to start with because you couldn't think of a romantic idea if your life depended on it! And besides, in case you haven't noticed, you're the fella and I'm the woman, and this isn't going to be another example of Me Tarzan, You Jane, where I do everything and you just cop out. And besides, it was me who wanted to call the AA right away, or did you just forget that, Mr I've Seen The Bloody Lights Come on Before?'

'All, right, all right!' he says. 'Pack in nagging, sodding buggering hell!' He gets out of the car, pulling his collar round his ears, and I watch the navy blur of him disappear down the road and swallow a small chuckle.

An hour later I'm shivery. Te-che-te-che-te-che go my teeth. Some sheep come up to my window and go 'Mehhhe!' God, this is great, isn't it? Where'd he go? Canada? I bet he's taking longer just to piss me off. And I'm cold and I'm famished and my gastric juices are devouring my stomach lining. I always keep chocolate in the glove compartment for these sorts of emergencies. I pull the thing open. Pity I always scoff it when I'm not supposed to. Rob comes back days, weeks, God, months later, like a drowned rat. 'The tow truck's on its way and it'll tow us to the closest garage. Fuck,' he says, water dripping off his nose end. I start to laugh.

'It's not funny!'

I hear another 'Mehhhe!' and get a fit of the giggles.

He sits, his teeth chattering, smelling deliciously of rain and woken-up cologne. 'Are you very cold and very wet, chucka, or by any chance just very wet?' I hide behind my hands while he playfully bashes me. I peep at him out of the corner of my eye. Rob. I love him. I do. My head, my heart and soul are just filled with him. I wish he'd just take me right here in the car!

Look up there, I see a pig flying past.

Another hour later, some tattoo with a central nervous system tallies us up at his big back-end, then we hop in the front and off we go. Rescued. Rob slides an arm across my shoulder. We fall into the nearest pub and eat. By the time we get to the hotel it's after ten o'clock.

They've let the room. We didn't guarantee it for late arrival.

Twenty quid in taxi fees and seven guest-houses later, because apparently the world and his wife come to Bamburgh since it got written up in the *Mail on Sunday*'s Best Romantic Getaways, we manage to find a room. It's hardly the place you'd open a bottle of expensive champagne in. More like the home for a cheerful glass of Henkell Trocken. But do we care? Let's get this straight: we do not care. We are just so knackered, and I have an awful, burpy stomach because I went so long without food, then ate greasy crap.

Rob goes upstairs to the shared bathroom to take a shower. When he reappears, he says 'I hope you've brought your own Andrex. There's none up there.'

I look at him, all sexy with his towel around his waist. His chest hair is glued up with white stuff. 'Ergh!'

'Yeah, the shower's not working, either. Bastard sears you like a minute steak, then after you get soaped up . . . nothing. He puts his T-shirt on, climbs into his underpants. 'You smell something funny in this room, eh?'

I sniff. 'Like what?'

'Death. Formaldehyde.' He climbs into bed.

Methinks I'll save the nursey outfit for tomorrow. 'Ow, Jesus!' I catch the front of my shin on the bed-frame and go hopping around in a circle. It's Rob's turn to smile. 'God, Rob, these sheets smell like dirty old man's hair.' Plus the carpet's got these sticky, leathery black marks. I must remember not to stand on it in my bare feet when I get up to wee in the hand basin in the middle of the night. I just knew this was going to be a ball. Balls up, more likely. I climb into bed. Rob moves his arm for me to snuggle under. 'Happy anniversary, treasure,' he says, and then, 'Thanks for bringing us here' – like he actually means it! Two minutes later he's snoring, like the Northern Sinfonia drowning in the North Sea.

When we wake up, the rain hasn't let up. We go to pick up the car, then walk around the town, looking in gift shops and ducking into cafés for cups of tea. Tonight's the night. Oh, yes, baby. Champers. Dinner. Dress-up outfit – pathetic attempt to prostitute myself to my own husband. I can't wait. We wander around Bamburgh Castle and stare across one of its walls at a very foggy Northumberland beach that's completely deserted except for one of those birds with a very long neck on a rock. Where is everybody? Probably in the hotel we should have been in, having sex. There's something serenely beautiful about this, though. The castle, the beach, the fog. Nobody around but Rob and me. We stare across the sea that, today, looks like a big grey undulating prison blanket, and I remember our honeymoon when we had sex in the dunes and I got sand-mites up my you-know-where. Then I say something brave. 'I was thinking, the other day, Rob, that maybe we should adopt a baby.'

Some seagulls let out a shocking scream overhead but Rob doesn't even look up. I wait, look at his profile, his long, slim-bridged nose with its perfectly rounded tip, his right eye that's not blinking, the dark blue of its iris and the fringe of long black curly lashes.

'I thought you said you weren't bothered about having a kid.'

'I'm not, really. But sometimes . . . Well, like the other day at the barbecue, I just thought how I could see myself having a daughter like Molly, who I could be close to like I'm close to my own mam. I think that would be very nice.'

'Not one that sings all the time.'

'Good God, I hope not.' He's being remarkably good-humoured. 'But also, Rob, my main reason is I sometimes think when we're old who'll be there to call in on us? Who'll come for Christmas? Whose weddings will we go to? We'll have literally nobody. There'll be nobody to care whether we live or die.'

Still his gaze doesn't budge. 'I can't live my life worrying about when I get old, Jill.'

'I know. Neither can I. I mean, I'm not. It's just, well, in some ways I think it'd be good for us. For you. To be a dad. You'd make a lovely dad.' I take a risk here. 'I was even thinking I could get an appointment and find out about sperm donors.'

He glares at me. 'Sperm donors? You want some other fella's semen in you, who you don't even know? Who you've never even seen? You've just picked him off some list?'

Ergh. 'Well, when you put it like that . . .' My heart's thumping now. I clutch the cold castle wall. 'But who said you pick them off a list?' Has he been researching this?

'What if you got HIV?'

'Oh, Rob, it's pretty regulated. I'm sure—'

'You won't know the first thing about him! His family history . . . What you're passing on!'

'I think they have to declare stuff like that.'

'Oh, yeah. Some fella who sells his sperm for money. He's probably dead honest.'

I want to tell him Lawrence did it. But then he'll know Leigh and I have talked about this and then he really will kill me. 'Rob, let's not make a big thing. It was just a thought.'

'Well from all this thinking you've obviously been doing, Jill, I'd say you've made your mind up.'

'I've what? How can you draw such conclusions? That's not true! I punched in "sperm donors" on the Internet, read about three pages on the subject, now you're making it sound like I'm giving you some ultimatum.' I want to throttle him and say I just want to bloody talk about it! Like normal people. But I try to keep it cheerful. 'Look, really, the way I feel right now I'm probably about fifty-fifty wanting a kid. But then other days – most days actually – I'm like, twenty-eighty, as in hardly wanting it at all. It's true. I'm not just saying this to make you feel better. In fact, it's the strangest thing that I can be so ambivalent to something as primal as a woman's desire to give life.'

He stuffs his hands in his pockets, leans against the wall with his back to the beach, looks at his shoes encrusted with sand. The wind blows his hair round his face. 'I told you this before, Jill, if you want a kid that badly, I understand. It's not right of me to deny you that.' He looks up, scours my face, looking more handsome and more pained than I've ever seen him. *Want a kid that badly*. Hasn't he just been listening? 'If I could give you a baby, Jill – if there was a pill I could take or an operation I could have – that'd make me the proudest fella in the world.' He moves his hand towards my face but takes it back. 'But I can't. And there's not a damned thing I can do about that.' He moves a lock of hair from his eye, puts his hands in his trouser pockets, looks back to his feet again. 'But you *can* do something about it. You could go and find somebody else and be a mother. But I hope to God you'll do it before it's too late.' He turns and looks across the water and the mist seems to blow in a close, cold circle around his head. 'What would hurt me the most is if I'd thought you'd stuck around another ten years and then realised that staying with me was the biggest mistake you'd made, and then you'd live the rest of your life bitter because of it. I don't want a bitter wife. I don't want to have to carry around your regrets as well as my guilt for the rest of my days.'

God, it sounds like he wants rid of me. I press the corners of my eyes. I mustn't cry. Tears will only affirm in his stubborn mind that I really do want kids. So instead, I link arms with him, force my words out through a big smile. 'You're being daft. I don't have regrets and I'm not bitter, and I never will be. I just thought that if we decided we still wanted a family, adoption would be one way for us to have it.'

He stares darkly ahead. 'I don't know, Jill. If I can't have one of my own . . . How do I know I could love somebody else's?'

'Oh, give over! Look how much you love Kiefer and he's a dog!' He gives me a penetrating, querying, washed-out look. 'I know you. If somebody put a little baby in your arms, Rob, and said it's yours, you would love it instantly and madly with your entire being. Because you'd know it was a little baby that somebody gave away, that somehow found its way to you.'

'Well . . .' he says, still not blinking. 'Maybe you're right.' Which means, *I've had it with this topic now.* He turns and starts walking. The seagulls squeal again, and he looks up at them, and his feet walking away make a lonely sound that reverberates through the castle walls.

We go and sit in another tearoom and drink tea, but our mood hangs over us, damper than the rain. And then we drive back to the guest-house, calling in at the same pub for a plate of mince and dumplings and a beer, which we consume in that grave silence again.

I don't know how much more of this I can take.

We go to bed early because there's nothing else to do. Rob lies with his back to me. With hurt and anger etched into my tone, I ask him, 'Rob? Are you going to talk to me, or even say goodnight?'

He extends an arm over his shoulder, pats me consolingly.

'For the fifty-fifth time, Rob – and this is the last time I will ever say it – I swear I'm not bothered if we never have a kid. I really, truly, am not. I thought you were. I thought that's why you've gone into this shell. So adoption was my solution.'

'I'm not in a shell,' he says, in about as sorry a tone of voice as you could ever hear from somebody who's supposedly not in a shell.

It pains my soul that our day has ended this way. All my plans for it gone out the window. 'Hold me. Please,' I say to him. There's a resistant pause, then he turns onto his back, lifts an arm for me to settle under. Just holds me, and lies there thinking. I can feel his blinking eye against my temple.

Sunday is more of the same. Weather-wise, every-thing-wise. We decide to head back early. Rob drives, and I sit there quietly staring out of the window, my champagne, lovely dress and tart's outfit burning a hole in the suitcase. I think Rob needs to see a doctor. It's no good me doing my tired old trick of planting magazine articles on infertility around the house. This is bigger than that. Bigger than me. But if I mention a doctor, he'll think I think he's sick. Besides, Rob's a macho Geordie lad. He'll not be lying down on the quack's couch. Suggesting it will only make him think I don't even know the man I've been married to for ten years. Maybe I don't. Maybe it's me who should see a doctor.

The dark green Northumberland landscape slides by. Am I to give up on Rob ever being anything other than a rather withdrawn but abiding partner to me? But I'm too young to settle for that. And none of this is my fault. And then my thoughts drift to a certain Russian.

And unlike other times when I've stopped them, I just let them fly. They carry me home, playing like some soothing background track on the iPod of my mind.

When we pull up at our front door, my eyes latch onto something on our 'Welcome' mat. 'What's this?' I ask, opening the car door before Rob has even put on the handbrake. Lying in plastic wrapping on our doorstep – a very rained on plastic wrapping, I might add – is a massive bunch of two dozen long-stem red roses.

A pain builds up between my eyes. 'Where did these come from?' I scoop them up in my arms, their dewy fragrance punching me in the gut.

I turn and look at my husband of ten years leaning on the open car door, head cocked, watching me. His sad face takes on that quietly-pleased-with-himself look. 'I had a man deliver them yesterday. I didn't know we wouldn't be here, did I? They were supposed to be a surprise. One that doesn't bark and crap on the carpet.'

10

'I'm gagging to give you an update on the shag of the century, but first, how was your anniversary?' It's Leigh. I'm in Boots, filling a basket.

At the best of times, if-I-must-ask questions from friends deserve very brief answers. 'It was nice, Leigh. Very nice.' I find myself, coincidentally, in front of the condom shelf, my eyes going over colours, textures, sizes. I walk further up the aisle to get away from them and find myself staring at men's deodorant. Old Spice. A sea of it.

'Was he impressed with the nurse's outfit and the bubbly?' She's giddy, giggly and annoying.

I wish I'd never told her. 'Very.'

'Did nursey-nurse and her medicine chest mend things in the old penis department?'

'There's nothing wrong with his penis, Leigh. That's never been the problem.' I say it a bit too loudly. A woman next to me looks at me with startled fascination.

'So I can assume you did it, then?'

Oh, I can't have my personal problems reduced to this level. I walk off down another aisle to get away from people. 'We did.'

'Thank God,' she says. 'For a moment you had me really worried for you two.'

I tell her I'm at the till so I have to go. I hang up, abandon my basket in the aisle, and flee. I keep running until I'm halfway down some side street, bending over with a painful stitch, the crowds of shoppers dissolving into a blur behind me.

I can't go home. So I walk around the town, full of the ailing state of my marriage, wondering if I'm blowing it out of perspective – if there's a bright, light side I'm not seeing because I've convinced myself I can't. It's a sunny evening. Stores are closing, metal shutters clanging to the ground. Somebody is picking expensive watches out of a jeweller's window, and the barrow-boys are loading their unsold goods into vans. It's a lonely feeling, the town emptying. Suddenly, the sky goes very dark. In about three seconds my white T-shirt looks like it's been lifted out of a pail of water. I pelt past Grey's Monument, as people who've been sitting there soaking up the sunshine run into Eldon Square for cover. Under the awning of a pie shop, I stand and watch it coming down in one long spectacular sheet, bouncing noisily off the ground like grey lightning. Behind me, people disappear down the slippery steps of the Metro. Everybody going home. To their families. Why don't I want to go home to mine?

My phone rings. I want it to be Rob, telling me that he's as sad as I'm feeling, but it's Wendy. Her voice anchors me again, though. 'Actually, Wend, I've been ringing you all day but your mobile's been switched off,' I tell her.

'Oh, I've just bought one like Neil's – a fancy one

with all the bells and whistles – only like everything we
seem to buy, there was a problem, so it's being fixed.
How was your anniversary?

'Not great. We had a fight.'

There's a pause. 'I thought you sounded flat. Is it
anything you want to tell me about?'

*Yeah, my husband's gone off sex. But then again, you
could be dying, so I can see how my problem might pale . . .*
'Not really. How did your appointment go?'

'All right. Although you know me, I find that whole
business of people looking down there so unpleasant.
You'd never think I've had three kids.' There's a pause
with the obvious reference to baby Nina. 'But they
were very nice at the clinic.'

'When will you find out?'

'Not for a few weeks. They also did a biopsy.'

'A biopsy?' She's still so vague and it worries the hell
out of me. 'Have you told Neil yet?'

'Not yet. He'll only worry.' The rain turns from
noisy to quiet. 'By the way, the naked scramble for a
bag of free clothing at the MetroCentre is back on
again. Leigh has convinced Clifford it'll make him a
national name like Antony Gormley. Because Gormley
did it in *Domain Field* – had people of all shapes and
sizes strip naked before wrapping them in cling film
and covering them in plaster. That was art and this is
exercise pants, but Clifford doesn't see a difference.
Leigh's busy writing the press release.' There's a
pause. 'Oh, Jill, it's a silly little place to work.' We
ring off, the rain eases off, and I go home.

*   *   *

'Don't go,' I say unconvincingly to Rob on Saturday, when he announces he's off to York for a job for a few days. 'Send somebody else.'

'You know I can't do that, Jill.'

'Can't, or don't want to?'

He's honest enough to shrug.

As our front door shuts I think, *That's it. You desert me and whatever I do from now on is your fault.* I even go as far as to tack *You bastard* onto the end, but it doesn't fit. In my car, I have every intention of going to see my mam and dad. Only at the Board Inn, instead of turning right, I keep going straight.

I sit on the wall, hugging my knees, a little bit mortified to be here. A part of me still seeing those roses on my doormat. With these dark sunglasses on, I can pretend I'm just looking around. But my eyes keep sliding past him up on his lookout post, grabbing information. He's seen me. He keeps cocking a look over his shoulder, like he wants me to know he's seen me. What? Is this a game? He's not made any effort to come over. It's rapidly feeling like the end of my world.

The beach is busy. Kids and dogs, and an advancing tide. Plenty for him to keep his eye on. And he's doing just that. The longer I sit, the more embarrassing this feels. At the very least he could come and say hello, couldn't he? Or wave. If he doesn't come over in the next ten minutes, damn it, I'm leaving.

But why doesn't he come over? Is he making a point? The point that he isn't interested? Maybe he's gone off me. Given up on me. Him too.

Ten minutes turns into an hour. 'Oh, God,' I mutter

under my breath, my eyes sore from looking in one direction, at him, while I've got my head turned in the other. 'Please come over. Please, please . . .' I need his attention like I need a drug.

He's snubbing me. I'm certain. Well, if he thinks I'm going to do all the running . . .

My breath comes shakily. If I just get up and leave, it's going to look like I'm bothered, like I'm in a huff or something. So I make the quick decision that I might as well be adult about this, just go over there, say a casual hello, and then leave. And then never, ever show my face here again.

'Never again' feels like a big pain cracking my ribs. I can barely breathe. I'm right on the verge of getting up, but then . . . he's climbing down his steps. My chest tightens. He walks on a direct course for me. My heart crashes in my eardrums. I quickly pretend I don't notice him coming, to hide my rabid delirium. But he's smiling. That smile I only have to think of and I get nothing done with my day. It registers in me with that quick, stomach-lifting thrill of being on a small boat bumping over a large wave. I give up the act, smile back with pleasurable, painful relief. 'Hi,' he says, looking me over quickly and plonking himself down beside me on the wall. His leg touches mine, so I shift a bit. His eyes go straight to my two-inch high green slip-ons with their criss-cross spaghetti uppers. 'Nice,' he says, in that appreciative way of his. 'Can you walk in them?'

Walk. *Valk.* 'Not really.' I bury my toes in the sand.

He smells of sun-cream, has a white trace of it that's

not rubbed in on his neck. 'I have looked for you. Every day, you know,' he tells me, while he gazes out at the waves and I make a quick study of his profile, engraving it on my mind. 'I have want to see you again.'

'I bet you say that to all the girls.' There's a nervous tremor in my cheeks as I try to smile.

He meets my eyes. 'No. Actually, I don't. I have not felt that for a girl in such a long time.'

My heart lifts. I look out to sea and I feel him study my face now. 'Do you want to go have cup of coffee, my shift is nearly finished?'

I don't answer and he says, 'Maybe you'd like to think about it. For an hour. Maybe two weeks. How about I go away, give you some time, and you come back in three years . . .'

I grin and his eyes smile back at me. 'I wouldn't mind an ice-cream.'

'I did not think you would come back,' he tells me, as we stand in line at the van. 'You are too nice a girl.'

I've missed the lilt of his sentences. 'So my coming back makes me not a nice girl?'

His eyes look at my mouth like a man does before he kisses you. 'An exciting girl, I think.'

We get our ice-creams – he orders and pays, which embarrasses me – and I stand there sneaking covetous eyes over him. We claim a bench on a jetty of rock that overlooks the sand. The ice-cream runs down the side of his hand and he licks it quickly, and his wrist hairs flatten and stick to his skin. He asks me how I've been. Then he says, 'It was with regret I said last time those words, Jill. When I mentioned you having a husband.'

'Don't worry about it. I'm thick-skinned.' I'd almost forgotten how what he'd said had offended me. I'm surprised he even remembered. He watches me eat, takes occasional glances at my legs in my shortish khaki skirt. 'I imagine it must put a lot of men off when the woman's married.'

He shrugs those hefty shoulders. 'Some men.'

'Nice men.'

'Some men.' He grins roguishly.

An engine starts up in my stomach. His eyes travel down my legs to my shoes again. It feels grand to be alive.

'You know, Jill, I take my lead from the woman. If she give me sign . . .' His eyes meet mine. 'But then, sometime, you know you just think, to hell with sign.'

'You're a to hell with it guy, aren't you?' I feel utterly nauseated with bravery.

He looks at me, surprised. 'No. I am not.' He shoves the end of his cone in his mouth, licks the tips of his fingers. 'But it's the old competitive swimmer's instinct. It will appear at surface when there is something it wants.'

My mouth goes dry. 'I don't want this,' I tell him, holding up my half-eaten cone. 'Here,' he says, and takes it off me and stuffs it in his mouth.

And then I say it. I will never know where I get the nerve, but I do. 'I've never had an affair before. I wouldn't know where to start, what to do. I'd probably be really crap at it.'

He doesn't even flinch. Just looks at me long and openly, while my heart pounds. 'You don't have to do anything. I would do everything.' His eyes roam over my mouth. 'All you would have to do is turn up.'

Then his gaze meets mine. And without a second's warning, he leans in and he kisses me.

11

Don't ask me how we get from a kiss to my being in his car. But we do. Something about my jumping up, him grabbing my wrist, saying, 'Don't go,' his eyes searching my face. And I couldn't go. So now I'm here. Sitting in a beaten-up white VW Golf outside a block of flats. Mortified. Terrified. Electrified.

As he drove us here, I sat cringing, with a hand over my face. My other hand he held, his thumb massaging my palm. Treading carefully. Like he's doing now, sitting here as the engine turns, his foot doing a discreet, rapid tap. Giving me time to change my mind. He knows one clumsy move will send me packing. His gentlemanly consideration for me is a massive turn-on.

In a moment of bravery, I hear myself say, 'Let's go inside, then.' One part of me is saying, God, you tart. The other is telling me it's just a fling. People have them all the time. Leigh's having one. For a lot less reason than I'm doing this.

My heart hammers up three flights of stairs, leaving me rattling like a windy radiator, which he jokes about. I notice how he keeps behind me; I feel his eyes on my legs and bottom. It does terrible things to me. We reach the top floor and walk the threadbare carpet of a dim corridor that smells of stale cigarette smoke. The crackling reception of a radio filters under somebody's door: Oasis; that song – something about Sally waiting. He stops at a brown door with the number six nailed on wonky. A number for my sins. He wiggles a key in the lock and the door squeals open. He gestures for me to go inside. I do, cringing a bit.

It's funny when you see a person's home for the first time. It's no palace. But what can I expect? He'll not make great money. The living area is no bigger than our spare bedroom. The blinds are dipped and it smells of sleep. I take in the sparse furniture. A settee. A portable telly with a crane-shaped aerial. A coffee-table bearing a clenched can of Stella Artois. An armchair with his laundry dumped on it. The sparse living of a single man. It's very much him: pared down, nothing fancy. But empty, so empty compared to my own home.

He sees me having a good look. 'Would you like drink?' he bumbles. 'You know. I am meaning tea, of course.' He's awkward at this too. I feel strangely comforted.

I start babbling, 'Ah, there's that place, isn't there? The Russian Tea Room . . .'

'Ah, yes.' He nods overenthusiastically. 'Yes, in America. In New York. I have been,' he says, keenly.

'Oh,' I say keenly back.

That conversation dies on the vine. I don't know what else to say. Neither, apparently, does he. A sense of imminent conquest buoys up the atmosphere. A fridge ticks over, making me jump, and he sees. And

I'm pleased. Because, daft as this sounds, it makes me feel more respectable. There's about six feet of distance between us. He's standing in front of a battered settee that belongs in the charity shop window and has tartan slip-on covers on it that don't fit at the corners. I'm on a clawed-up doormat, barely inside the door. Half here. Half unfaithful. My eyes tick around the room like the second hand of a stopwatch.

'You look like girl who is going to run.'

His telepathy makes me smile. I look at that face and get a fresh reminder of how handsome he is, and how nice he is, and how much I've wanted this. 'I'm not. I promise.'

He smiles warmly, his eyes make a slow sweep of me in a universal language, and I feel it in my gut. My thoughts start thrashing around, wrong and right in one big face-off. The note on my car, the meeting on the beach; all this was meant to be. He's not just anybody. He's the man who saw me round Newcastle and remembered me because he couldn't forget me. I take a few steps towards him, feel the give of wooden floorboards under my feet, like I'm balancing barefoot on swelling waves. I stop close enough to feel the heat of his body, and look up into his eyes, which are focused keenly on my mouth. As I go up on tiptoe his arms go round me, sweeping me an inch off the floor. And then he is kissing me. Nothing like on the beach, when I was too startled – by the kiss, and my own response. But easily, like he's pushing an open door. Amazing how instinctively we fall into rhythm. We fit. We glide. Oh, little *Mmn*s pour out of me, and

he mimics me: '*Mmn* too.' Kissing a new man after all
these years is like some delicious shock. He kisses my
smile, coats me with this incredible feeling of being
sexy, sexual and wanted. My eyes flutter open and
closed, like I'm fading in and out of consciousness,
noticing the open pores under his eye, a few wrinkles,
dashing imperfections. 'You saw me in my green
dress,' I whisper, into his skin that smells of sun-cream,
salt and ice-cream.

'Hmm. It did very nice things for your ass.' His
hands go there. He smiles against my lips.

'That's a terrible thing to say to a lady.'

For a moment our pupils bounce and bob with each
other. And then . . . We collide, with doors and walls,
stumbling over shoes, sending a small table scraping
along the floor, making it, somehow, into a bedroom.
He's well versed in this. His clumsy navigation has a
swift expertise, while his hands find the skin he's yet to
lay eyes on. As he pins me up against a wall and we go
'Oops!' and laugh because a framed print slides to the
floor, I say, 'I think I've fallen for you.' It comes out in a
husky whisper. Strands of my hair stick to his lips, and
I peel them away between kisses.

He swiftly hikes up my skirt, puts my legs around his
waist, grabs my bum. 'You're such a sexy girl,' he tells
me. In the small of my back I feel the pointing finger of
a light switch. Then his thumbs are under my knicker
elastic and he pulls me into his pelvis.

'Not so fast!' I gasp. But his thumb is in me with its
sharp fingernail.

It all happens so fast. We fall onto a bed, which has

no give when we land on it. My shirt is tugged at. My breasts grabbed out of the tops of my black balcony bra. His mouth clamps on my nipple in a frenzied bite that makes me go, 'Ow!' I look down and see him pulling it between his teeth, turning it deep red. And I disbelieve the strange face I see down there.

And then I see them in my mind. Those red roses on my doormat.

Suddenly it's as though this is not really me. I'm acting a role that somehow doesn't fit. My body shuts down, turns off all electricity. He hovers above me, fumbling with his belt, a drunk passion on his face. 'Bebe,' he says.

Baby?

My eyes home in on a damp patch on the ceiling that looks like bodily fluid. 'Bebe,' he says again. 'Bebe, bebe.' I'm mesmerised by that stain. And then I'm up there, floating, looking down at myself. And I see this person – me – near-naked, breasts out, skirt hiked up, knickers askew, not much poetry to it at all.

This is a let-down. The realisation is a hard shock. I catch sight of his penis and think *Oh, Jesus, ergh!* But he's in me so fast. I feel him now, chafing, because I've gone so dry. I shove his shoulders. *No!* I want to cry. I want to cry *No!* I push with the heels of my hands, and his fingers dig into the cheeks of my bum, but he clearly thinks I'm enjoying it and he says, 'Oh, bebe!' in that accent, and I want to yell *Oh, bloody yuck!* But I can't. Nothing will come out. It's all choked somewhere far inside me. Heartache blazes in my chest.

His breath is thick all over me, coming in grunts,

smelling not quite nice. Mine's barely coming at all. 'Stop,' I say. 'For God's sake, stop.' Or do I say it? I don't know. Sadness is raging in me. If I do, he doesn't seem to hear. He flips me onto my stomach then slides in from behind, embedding disgust deeper and deeper in me. I'm aware of his bad breathy grunts on my neck, my breasts thwacking against a hard mattress, and my head slamming repeatedly into the wall. God, it's killing me. Doesn't he realise?

Rob would realise.

Rob.

'Stop!' I yell, hearing it come out of me this time.

And he says 'Sorry,' and then, 'Sorry bebe, sorry bebe.' And he eases up on sending me through the wall, flips me onto my back instead. And I feel so cheap. I feel so bloody cheap.

He humps away, smelling bad and making awful noises. But he's a raging horse that's out of the gate. I don't know what to do to bring him back. The tears pour out of me, and I wipe them away, leave my arm there over my eyes so he won't see the sad sight of me. And my mind slips away from this. And I do what I've done on the odd occasion with Rob, in the throes of sporadic tiny crushes on footballers. I picture another man's face. Only the face I'm picturing is my husband's.

Somewhere deep in me, I heave a silent sob.

He comes with a big stomachy grunt, sinks on top of me like an athlete who's just finished a race. And I want to throw up at the warm injection from a strange man emptying himself inside me. I shove him. He moves in to nuzzle me, but ends up smacking his face into the pillow, because somehow I'm out from under him, scrambling for my clothes. My head's spinning. I'm seeing stars. I'm seeing Rob. Sex with Rob sits there like a burnt-out fire in some warm place in my mind. The sob that was strangled somewhere in me comes out now. 'What is wrong?' he asks, clearly oblivious to the fact that this has been anything other than a great time for me. 'Where you go? Why you cry?' He goes to get out of bed. I put my hand up to stop him, getting a quick view of it all hanging there. I can't get the words out for my sobbing. The tears are rolling down my cheeks. His semen is trickling down my thigh.

The lonely music is still wafting under a door when I get out into the passageway, which is a fog of cigarette smoke. I hurry towards the exit sign, my feet slipping out of my stupid sandals. I can barely make out the stairs through my tears, but I take my shoes off and pad down them. I get outside and then it hits me.

I've left my bag up there.

My bag with my wallet, credit cards, keys . . . I pat my pockets. Oh, thank God, not my keys.

But where is my car? He drove us here. I don't know where I am. I wasn't paying attention. I'm like some prostitute thrown back on the curb. My shirt's not even done up properly. I rub hard at my eyes and squint in the sunlight both ways up the street. A man is walking towards me. An elderly man, in a Hawaiian shirt and bifocals. He's walking an obese sausage dog that has its head in one of those lampshade things. He looks at me, then does a double take when he sees my face.

'Nice day for it,' he says.

12

I walk upstairs to our toilet and throw up. It cascades from me, nearly taking my eyeballs along for the ride. Then I sink to the floor by the bowl, hug my legs and shiver. The dog sits straight-backed and alert in the doorway, watching me.

I manage to run a bath, cock a leg over the tub into the too-hot water, almost numb to the scorch that slides up my body. I let the water run, draw my knees up and rock on my bum, feeling the soothing wake down there where I feel so sore. I stay like this, with my chin resting on the surface, until the water goes cold. Then I crawl out, shiver, and throw up again before I reach the bowl. The phone rings repeatedly. I hear it from the floor of our walk-in wardrobe, where I somehow find myself, sitting wrapped in a wet bath towel. Even as a kid, I loved to cry in cupboards.

I should have told him to stop. Or did I? Why can't I remember? All I know is he had me up against a wall and I mumbled something about how I had fallen for him. Did I really say that? Then there was that grubby ceiling and him calling me 'Bebe'.

He was like a different person. He wasn't the man I

met on the beach. I screw up my face and press the heels of my hands into my eye sockets.

I don't sleep on Saturday night at all, but by Sunday I'm so worn out I sleep for half the day. When I wake up some time in the early evening, with a groggy headache, it hits me – strangely, only now – that we didn't use a condom. My mind rattles through dates. I think I'm safe. I brighten. The damage doesn't seem quite so devastating.

On Monday morning, I wake up with a whole other panic on. I'm at the doctor's as the doors open, convinced I'm riddled with diseases. If I've not got the major ones I've at least got herpes. When you think how old he is, all those years of bachelorhood, he must have had hundreds of women. And he clearly doesn't care about condoms. What if he's one of those blokes who takes the attitude *Well, somebody gave it to me, so I don't care who I give it to* . . .

I don't know him, do I?

I never did.

What if I give Rob something? I think of his gorgeous clean body. How would I live with myself?

Diane Wilson, my doctor, doesn't work on Mondays, the receptionist informs me. So I'm forced to tell a sheltered-looking young male locum that I've had extramarital sex and I'm going to need testing for STIs. He asks me, dispassionately, if my partner and I used a condom. I feel like I'm back at school. I can't tell him why we didn't, because I'm not even clear myself. I want to say, 'Look, I've been married for ten years. My husband was my only lover. I don't just carry a box of them around in my bag, on the off-chance. I'm not that sort of girl. The entire condom culture is something I feel passed me by.' But I don't tell him anything. I just sit there, cringing.

Then he tells me to undress from the waist down. Next, my feet are in stirrups and my crotch is about two millimetres from his face. The tears roll quietly down my cheeks as he scrapes away beyond the turquoise sheet. He gives me the morning-after pill just to be certain, looks at me like a disappointed parent, and I skulk out of there clutching my prescription.

I can't drive. I just sit there in my hot car gripping the steering wheel. A burly traffic warden taps on my window, tells me I have to either move or feed the meter. I tell her I've no change, hoping she'll see the state I'm in and take pity. 'Then move it, will you,' she orders. So I do. It's a miracle I get home alive, or that I don't kill somebody.

Rob calls that night from some hotel in Yorkshire, and I am feeling violently ill, probably from that damned morning-after pill. He says he's been ringing and ringing and when he tried my mobile some fella with an accent answered. I'd completely forgotten my phone was in my bag! So now I have to make up some story about how I was mugged, to account for this, and for why I had to cancel our credit cards, and our bank debit card. We got new PINS recently and I could never remember mine, so I've been carrying it around in my wallet. Rob would kill me if he knew.

I babble out my pack of lies. The agony he clearly feels for a trauma I've not been through shames me almost more than the trauma I have. I have never lied to Rob beyond your average white one.

'Well, I can't believe you'd not call the police!' he says, after he's asked me to describe in precise detail every last cut or scrape I'm tired of telling him I don't have. He can't seem to believe the bloke could have mugged me without at least leaving a bruise.

'It was a bag grab,' I keep telling him. 'He pushed me. I fell, but just went down on one hand.'

'Please tell me you went to see the doctor, Jill.'

'Like I've said sixty times, Rob, I don't need a doctor. I'm fine.' God, what if the doctor's office calls if they find I've got VD, and Rob answers? How will I explain that?

There's another exasperated pause. 'For Christ's sake, Jill, just do me one favour, call the police. Just call them. Right this minute.'

I break into a cold sweat. 'But they never go after muggers—'

'That's not the point! You can't go around not reporting crimes because you think the police won't do anything. What kind of society would we be living in if everybody did that?' He sighs again. For a brief and shining second I think he's giving up, then he says, 'Look, I'll phone them for you. In fact, I'm going to hang up and ring them right now.'

'No!' I bleat.

'What d'you mean, no? Why can't I call, if you won't?'

'Because . . . because I don't want you to!' I'm practically shrieking. 'This is my business! I'm the one that was hurt!'

'I thought you said you weren't hurt.'

I pause. 'I'm not. I mean . . . I'm not.'

I can hear his frustrated breathing. 'Jill, you're acting very weird. What's wrong with you? You've got me very worried.'

I start to bawl. 'Don't you understand, I want to try to put this behind me.' I am incoherent. I am over the top. For somebody who has supposedly just been mugged.

He pauses. His voice softens. 'Don't cry like that. Please, don't cry, when you're there and I'm here and there's nothing I can do.' He breathes deeply through his nose and I hang on to the phone, thinking, *My God, Rob, please don't ever stop caring about me like this*. But I've got an awful sixth sense that my days are numbered. 'Look,' he says, 'why don't you call Neil? He'll tell you what to do. I'll even call him if you—'

'Rob, please, please pack in wanting to call people. Just drop it.'

He's silent for a moment or two. Then he says, 'Hang on a minute. My God, I've just realised something.'

I hold my breath.

'Your mobile got stolen. So when I rang . . . that must have been your mugger! The bastard answered your damn phone!'

My heart stops.

'Right then. I'm calling him back. The fucker. This'll shock him . . .'

'No!' I scream.

'Yeah! Never mind "no"!' He sounds excited, like he's relishing putting the boot in.

'No! Leave it. Just leave it. Please, please bloody leave it.'

I can tell by the heavy sigh, and his even heavier silence, that he's throwing his hands in the air. 'I tell you, Jill, I really don't understand you sometimes. All I want to do is call the bastard and give him a piece of my mind. Or maybe I'll call the police and give them the number—' He's thinking aloud.

I bawl. The bawl of all bawls.

'Christ,' he says, clearly shocked. 'Okay. Okay. Keep your hair on. I won't if you don't want me to.'

My hysteria comes down a peg or two. 'D'you promise?'

'I don't know why it matters to you, but . . . look, all right, it's forgotten about.' Then he says brightly, 'Why don't you come down here, instead of me coming home tomorrow? Take the train in the morning. Put the dog in the kennel. We'll check into a hotel in York. It'll take your mind off this.'

'No,' I snivel.

'Ahh!' he says, in a loving, sympathetic, frustrated sigh. 'Why not, Jill?'

I ache at his concern for me. 'Because I don't want to. I just want to be alone for a bit. Can't you leave me alone?'

'Why are you acting like a freak?' he asks me, with his peculiar brand of affection. 'I mean, you said it yourself, you just got your bag nicked. They didn't hurt you. You've not been raped. I don't know why you're acting like a nutcase.'

If I don't get my act together my behaviour's going to give me away. 'You're right. I'm fine. I'm being stupid. But I'd still rather not travel all that way there.'

He sighs. 'Well, if there's no persuading you then I'll just come home. I'll see you some time tomorrow.' There's a pause and then he adds, 'I love you.'

'I love you too,' I cringe.

We hang up. I immediately ring up and cancel my mobile which I completely forgot to do when I cancelled my cards, then wrack my fuddled head to see if there's anything else I've overlooked. Then I crawl onto the bed and hug his pillow and tell it the one thing I can't tell him: how sorry I am for what I've done, what a disgusting disgrace of a human being I am.

That corridor. The wonky number six nailed onto that door. Why didn't I run when I saw that hovel? The thin bedsheets. His penis inside me, and however many other he's been with. I look at Rob's pillow. This pillow used to belong to my one and only lover, on my sanitised bed, in my fragrant life.

I run another bath, dumping some salt in it to act as a disinfectant. Then I dig out a turkey baster from our kitchen drawer. Then, crouched in the water, I fill the baster and inject the warm salty water up inside myself. It feels melodramatic, like something I've seen in a Mike Leigh film. But with every squirt I imagine I'm cleansing every bit of his disgustingness out of me, ridding myself of him thoroughly.

Some time on Tuesday – or is it Wednesday now? I

couldn't tell you – I remember I have an animal and I take him around the block. He charges down the street, scanning the scene for entertainment and mischief. So when he finds it, with people and their dogs, I have to stand and pass the time of day, and act normally, which is a massive strain. As I come back through the door the phone rings. It's Leigh. 'Wendy and I have been ringing you at work but they said you've been off, they think you're sick but they're not sure. Your mobile's dead. We're worried. What's the marra?' So I tell her the mugging cock and bull and how I had to cancel my phone.

'Jesus, are you all right?'

'Yes.' It's an unconvincing yes. I cannot, I must not tell Leigh. Nobody, for that matter. Ever.

'Well, in that case, given that you're okay, can we go out tonight? There's something I'm bursting to tell you and it won't wait.' She has that irritating glee in her voice.

'Look, I'm not well enough. I think it's – a bug – on top of the mugging. I really can't go to any bars.'

'Do you want me to come over?'

She wants to for her own reasons, I can tell. I just want her off the line. 'Look, no. I'll ring you when I'm feeling a bit better.'

'Well, don't take too long, because like I say, we have to talk. It's bordering on being gravely threatening to my mental health if we don't.'

A bit later on, I hear my doorbell. The impatient ding-a-ling-a-ling. The dog barks up a storm. I hold my breath until I'm convinced they've gone away.

Then the phone rings. It's Wendy. I don't answer, but hear her message:

'Where are you?' The concerned voice of a friend seems to reverberate off the four sad walls of my heart. 'Leigh was insisting on coming round so I thought I'd come with her to see how you are. We're worried about you. But you're not there. We thought you were sick . . . well, maybe you went to the doctor's. Anyway, we brought you something. It's on your doorstep.' Then I hear Leigh chime in, 'Along with your belated anniversary present. I researched high and low on the Internet for this company, so you'd better use it. Anyway. I hope you get better. I'll try you later.'

I go downstairs when I'm convinced the coast's clear, and peek out of the window. On my doormat is a big carton of 'homemade' soup from that lovely new place, Stockpot, that's just opened in the town centre. And under it is an envelope. I open it and it's some sort of registration papers . . . to Canine Obedience School. Leigh has attached a Post-it note that says, 'They're the best in the area. Trust me, I am now an authority!!! I've got you eight lessons. If the little effer doesn't pass with flying colours I want my money back!!!'

I go back into the house, look in the mirror. I'm a weird shade of taupe and I've still got burst blood vessels all over my cheeks from throwing up so violently. I have good friends. For some reason this makes me sadder. I crawl back into the wardrobe and cuddle one of Rob's sweaters again. Kiefer sits sentry outside champing through a shoe.

Next thing I know, I hear my name. I open my puffy eyes and I don't know if it's day or night, except that I am still sitting there, and Rob is crouching in front of me, with the dog in a cinnamon bun shape at my feet. 'What the . . .?' he touches my face. 'Jill?' his thumb brushes my cheek. 'What're you doing sitting in here, for God's sake?'

Slowly coming round, I shake my head.

'What's the matter? Oh, treasure,' he pulls me into his chest, his arms encircling me. 'This is all because of the mugging?' He sounds sceptical.

I lay my head on him. 'I don't know,' I say sceptically back. 'I'm not feeling very good.' I wasn't planning on being like this when he got in. I was planning on being washed and made-up and ready to do a very good impression of Jill being Jill. But he's come home early. My sweet, worried husband. Of course he would.

He kisses the top of my head, plucks me from the floor. 'Oh my God. The bastard, I'd like to kill him,' he says of the phantom mugger, and I bury my face in his shoulder. He carries me over to our bed, where he cradles me like I'm a little bundle of vulnerability. 'You're all right, little treasure. If he comes near you again, I'll tie his feet in a knot and ram them so far up his backside they'll come down his nose.' He kisses my head again, as though his life depends on healing me. And I mumble something about how it's not just the mugging, but I think I've come down with a bug too.

We lie there for ages until he's comforted my tears away, and I've got the pattern of his breathing and I'm breathing in sync with it. The two shall become one. Forsaking all others.

Later on, I tell him I want to go out by myself for some fresh air. 'Well, just take my phone and call me at some point to let me know you're okay. And for God's sake, don't carry a handbag,' he tells me.

I am pitifully aware that I don't deserve this man. An odd change for a girl who, not so long ago, thought she deserved better.

I walk down the Quayside, umbrella-less in the lashing rain, and stand on the Millennium Bridge overlooking the Tuxedo Princess, the floating night-club where Rob and I met. Then I drag myself up Grey Street, the street that today looks like its name, dodging squashed chips on the pavement, smelling the reek of urine up the walls. An argy-bargy is going on outside a clothes shop between a young security guard and a pensioner who has a shirt dangling from a coat-hanger that's somehow got itself attached to the back of her mac. I disappear down another back street and come out at Fenwick's, where I order a cappuccino and get the urge to throw up again. I try to will the feeling away by being very, very still. Other than the odd crust of bread, I don't think I've eaten in days. My lips are chapped, my mouth is parched, and I've still got that ache in my pelvic region.

I walk back to the Monument Metro, get on a train with half a million single mothers and buggies, and babies with tattoos and pierced ears. I go to the end of the line and back, my head resting against the window, staring, as we pass through tunnels, at alternating light and dark. And then I go home, not having found any sort of clarity that I hoped coming out would give me. As I walk through our front door, I register how different everything feels now, once something's done that there's no taking back, since I let a third person into our marriage. Rob is on the settee, in a room with no light, no telly on, the dog beside him cracking through a bone. The air is filled with loss.

I will win him back again. Even though he doesn't know I've lost him. I get an odd comfort from this.

'Something terrible happened while you were out,' he says. His face is pure end-of-the-world wretchedness, like he's newly bereaved.

Good God. I reach backwards for the nearest chair. Andrey's been here. He must have. I sink into it, a weightless collapse.

'What, Rob?' I can barely croak.

He looks at me with that face. I've never seen Rob quite this distraught. Then he holds up one of his best leather loafers. 'The fucker chewed it, didn't he? Look. Two-hundred-quid shoes and it's got a sodding tongue now,' he shakes the shoe so the sole flaps against the upper, like the mouth of a leather puppet.

I'm so relieved I could practically kiss the dog. I can't speak. If I as much as crack a smile he'll divorce me on the spot.

'How are you, anyway, after your walk?' he asks, once he's got over his grief about his shoe.

'I'm fine. Really. Back to normal again.'

He looks at me with uncertain faith.

We eat fish fingers and oven chips, which he throws

on for us. I watch him covertly as he lines up three chips on a bun, rolls it up and stuffs an end into his mouth. Poor, naive Rob. I should have put such a higher price on his love. I stare at his fingers, the upward-turning tips, his jaw, his ears, the expression of concentration as he eats. And I cannot, cannot believe that I've had another man inside my body, that I told another man I might have fallen in love with him. Did I say that? I really think I did. What was I thinking?

'I don't want to push it, but are you sure you're feeling better? You seem . . .' He looks at me across the table.

I nod energetically.

'That's not very convincing.'

I fake great interest in a fish finger. Thank God he doesn't know. And as long as only I do, he never will.

He tells me about his weekend away. As he talks, I have a horrible thought. Shit. My mobile has my entire telephone address book in it, including Rob's work numbers. What if the Russian copied numbers down before the phone got disconnected? What if he rings Rob to tell him? Tell him what? Why would he ring my husband? He'd have to be barmy. But what if he wants to return my bag? Shit. He might ring a friend. Or my work. I told him where I worked. What if he comes looking for me? If he waits for me outside work? No, Jill, I think. Calm down. He's not going to ring your friends or your work. He's not going to come looking for you. You were nothing to him.

I tune back into Rob, who is looking at me strangely.

I flounder, not sure what expression I am supposed to pull because I've not heard a word he's said. 'You know, Jill,' he says. 'I sense this is about more than the mugging.'

I focus on my food, eat like nothing's happening. But my eyes burn from holding the tears back. Then I look up. His eyes, his whole face, are filled with despair. 'Please tell me. Whatever it is. You can tell me.'

Oh, I can't chew. Why does he have to be so nice? So damned there for me? Unswallowed chips clag in the back of my mouth.

'Oh, God, why are you crying again?' he asks me.

I just shake my head.

I'm going to have to tell him, aren't I?

No. Good God. I can't.

He starts to say something but stops. A frustrated sigh comes out instead. 'I'm sorry,' he says finally; his voice sounds choked and he clangs the cutlery down. 'I feel like you're about to tell me you're leaving me for somebody else.'

I stare at him. 'Why on earth would you say that?'

He shrugs. 'Dunno. I suppose . . . I'm sorry, I don't think that. It's just . . . I'm obviously making you so unhappy. Because it's me, isn't it? I know I'm the root cause of this.'

Sometimes I think I don't give Rob enough credit. He gets up out of his chair, shaking his head, walks down our passageway with a sharp intake of breath, rubbing a hand over his face. He's got his shoes on. The pair with the one the dog chewed. His socked foot sits in the middle of it like filler in a leather sandwich.

I put the greasy pan in the sink and start washing it. I stare out of our window at the lilac tree on the other side of the glass. I drop a glass on the floor and it shatters. I stare at it, slap a hand over my mouth, suppressing a scream. This scares the dog, who trots off with his tail between his legs into the dining room.

I hear Rob's feet up there on the other side of the ceiling; he must have been brushing his teeth. Then it all goes quiet. He's obviously gone to bed. Rob will sleep a lot when he's sad. When we first found out he couldn't have kids, he'd sleep half his day away. And I'd do anything to make him get up, throw the sheets off him and yank him back from whatever world he was in. Because I didn't want him sliding over there, being lost to me. Now I think, at least if he's up there in that bed he's still mine. Just knowing he's there makes my life feel full and safe again.

I sit down and stare at Rob's empty chair. The few abandoned chips on his plate. The piece of fish finger on the end of his fork. It's no use. I'm going to have to tell him.

13

I lie awake all night analysing the pros and cons of clearing my conscience versus ruining Rob's blissful ignorance. By the weekend I'm in a state of panic. If I don't talk to somebody I'll explode. And right this second – although my mind changes about every two minutes – I know that the last person I should tell is Rob. Oddly enough, Leigh keeps ringing and asking what's the matter, like she's on a mission to prise it out of me. And it's on the tip of my tongue to tell her. But all my instincts say *don't*. So I don't. Neither do I tell Wendy, who rings and exercises her more round-about approach. In my 'up' moments, I'm glad I'm keeping it secret. At other times, I sit there moaning to myself about how ironic it is that I am a good friend to everybody, yet when I need a friend I don't have one. I mean, I do. But I have one who wouldn't understand me, and another who would understand me too much. I don't feel like opening up either can of worms. A problem shared is a problem doubled.

On Monday, I call in sick again at work. This makes it – what? – a week. Jan from personnel wants a doctor's note. But I can't face the doctor again, so I tell her I'll see what I can do. And then I don't do anything.

But I do put on an act for Rob. I make dinner, I smile, I chatter, I deceive – not easily, but at least with a degree of accomplishment. There's a part of me that needs to pour my soul out to Rob in his role as my best friend. But Rob's also my husband, and this time there's no separating the two. Then one night, over pork pies and chips, I can tell something's troubling him. Predictably, he lays down his knife and fork and looks at me. 'Jill, there's something that I have to tell you that you're not going to want to hear, but I feel I have to.' He's got that face that says he's about to drop a large bomb – it's showing the same kind of misery as when he told me about his shoe. Only I know this is worse than that.

'I've done something that I'm not proud of. It was very, very wrong of me . . .' He shakes his head piteously. 'I've thought about not telling you, but it feels like a bigger crime to keep it from you. So while you're already annoyed with me, and disappointed in me, I might as well just come out with it . . .'

The pork pie sticks in my throat.

He rubs the back of his head, looks at me while I hang there in agony. 'I betrayed you,' he says. I can hear the beat of my heart as though it's right beside my eardrum. His sad eyes bore into mine.

'I rang the coppers, didn't I? About your phone. Right after I promised you I wouldn't. I hung up and I rang them right away. Told them that the bastard probably had your mobile and all they had to do was ring it and they'd have him.'

I soar. Then I sink. This is good. No, it's bad! 'You rang them? Moments after you rang me? Jesus, what did you do that for?'

'Because he had the balls to answer your phone after he'd just ripped off your bag! That really pissed me off.'

'Oh, God!' I clutch my head between both hands. 'Oh, God! Crap! Shit!' When I rang to cancel my phone I was held in a queue for ages. What if Rob got through to the police before I got the bloody phone disconnected? 'Rob, what the hell did they bloody say?'

Rob shakes his head, bewilderedly taking the measure of my panic. 'Not a lot. If you don't report it yourself, there's not much they'll do. So it's sort of gone away.'

Relief surges out of me so hard it almost whistles.

We don't say much after that. He just seems to look at me like I'm a raving lunatic. I barely hang on to my sanity for the rest of the evening. Next morning, Rob goes off to work and I am in a flap again. Wendy rings and I'm relieved it's her because I still keep thinking it'll be the Russian. 'Leigh's gone out and I was going to take my lunch break, and I wondered if you'd like to come.'

If I told her, at the very least she'd have advice for me that I don't have for myself. But I don't want to put Wendy in the same position that Leigh put me in: having the burden of somebody's secret. 'Oh, I'm actually just about to go through to see my mam and dad. I've not checked in on them in a while,' I tell her. She seems disappointed; she has no idea what I've just spared her.

Come to think of it, the thought of seeing my mam feels like a good one right now. So because I don't exactly feel safe to drive, I take the train through to Sunderland. My dad, who rarely gets a change of scenery these days, is more than happy to be sent off out for a pint. Then I curl up on the settee and put my head on my mam's pillowy stomach as she watches some silent drama on an afternoon soap. She strokes my head, which feels like priceless therapy, and I find myself looking at the photo on the mantelpiece, the one of me in my PE kit when I was about thirteen, with my face full of spots. I feel this awful tug of nostalgia and loss inside me. I want to be that girl again. I want to live in that house we lived in, in that bedroom I slept in, with my mam and dad there with all the answers. It's weird because my mam suddenly gets hold of my hand. 'How old are you again, flower? I always forget.' She gets these moments of near-clarity, and you can see they frustrate her.

'I'm thirty-five, Mam.'

From my upside-down position on her lap, I look up at her face. I can see her brain ticking over. 'Thirty-five,' she repeats and squeezes my hand in her hot clammy one. 'I have a thirty-five-year-old daughter.' She says it with such pride, and searches my face as though I am a foreign language she is desperate to understand. Then her hand smooths the hair away from my brow in a repetitive, cherishing rhythm, like you'd stroke a dog or a cat. 'Live your life, my darling,' she says. 'Because it passes all too quickly, you know.'

Her eyes go back to the telly. I squeeze mine tightly shut and feel my insides lurch with the urge to bawl.

'There's something the matter with me, isn't there?' she says, after a few minutes of her silent staring at the telly. There's a deep frown between her eyes. Then she looks at me, the frown disappears before I have a chance to answer her, and she seems to brighten. 'What's important, though, is are you all right, love?' And I don't know if we're for real now, or if we're in this other world that has taken her.

'I'm not especially all right, no,' I say. Then, without taking my eyes off her face I tell her. 'I did something bad, Mam. I had an affair.' Calling it that somehow sounds better. Just hearing myself say it is both agonisingly unreal and a massive relief. She plucks tendrils of my hair, pulls them through her fingers like thread. My mam who was always my best friend, who always took my part, even at times when she shouldn't have. I wait to hear what she's going to say.

She keeps on playing with my hair for a while, like it's just enthralling her. Then her eyes wander back to the telly and the fingering motion stops. She points to some very good-looking blond man with a white rose in his buttonhole. 'Chase is getting married,' she says, and then she smiles, proudly.

The following Saturday – the two-week anniversary of my infidelity – Rob and I have a wedding to go to. A friend he went to comprehensive school with: Simon Hicks. They got back in touch just recently through 'Friends Reunited'. It's the very last thing I feel like doing. I consider telling Rob I'm sick, but I can't use that excuse on him any more than I can the folks at work. I'm going to have to come up with new and better ones to account for my 'off' behaviour. Besides, there's so much atmosphere between Rob and me lately that if I bail on his friend's wedding it just might be the last nail in my coffin.

The weather stays ideal for the day. The church is pretty. The bride, a picture. Fortunately, the bit I'm most dreading – the vows – I needn't have. The bride and groom have written their own, the vicar tells us. Rob mutters, 'Oh, God help us.'

And so the serious, cherubic-faced, well-fed groom clears his throat and starts blushing even before he gets the words out . . .

Diane, I stand here before you in pursuit of a lifelong commitment. You are my best friend, my soul mate. You have made me a better man.

Rob imitates playing a violin and I try not to smile. Very nice mush. I bet there's not a dry eye in the room, but I'm just numbed by the old clichés I've heard a million times before. And by the groom's pathetic inability to memorise something he's read without sounding like he's reading it – like a dyslexic four-year-old. As the groom takes another breath, I'm just rolling my eyes and Rob's muttering, 'God, don't tell me there's more', when the groom takes hold of his future wife's hands and says, deadpan, and with heartfelt sincerity:

Diane, we complement each other beautifully. I wear the trousers and you are the belt that holds them up. Together we will face the world knowing that—

Rob leans in to me and whispers, 'Our trousers will never fall down.'

Oh my God, I set off laughing. I have to practically swallow my hand so as not to embarrass myself. Rob digs me in the ribs because I'm making a definite ripple in this sea of transfixed, obviously far less cynical faces. 'Bloody shut up,' my husband tells me off with a small laugh. 'You'll get us thrown out.' I bury my grin in his bicep.

'Belts and trousers. The daft bugger,' Rob is still saying, as he holds my hand and we stroll around Whitley Bay market to kill some time until the reception. 'Where d'you reckon he got that piece of poetic brilliance from?'

'Byron. Keats.'

Rob chuckles.

'It was the blatant sexism that got me, though. If he'd said that she wore the trousers and he was the belt, then I almost could have stood it.'

Rob's thumb strokes my palm. 'He always had everything arse-backwards, even in school. God, these days people have always got to get clever and muck everything up, haven't they? I mean, what makes somebody who can barely speak English a poet on their wedding day, eh? I mean, what's wrong with the old vows? The ones we said. The sincere ones. The time-honoured ones.' He brings my hand to his mouth and drops a big kiss onto my knuckles. 'Those ones don't need dressing up in bloody belts and trousers.'

I feel bleak again.

In the function room of a large pub, we find ourselves seated with some of Rob's old school friends who also got back in touch thanks to the Net. But making conversation's like pulling teeth. Rob bumps shoulders with me and whispers, 'God, they're a bunch of boring wankers, aren't they? They've never changed.' It's true, once we've established what we all do for a living it seems there's nothing else to talk about. And then when they find out Rob and I don't have children, it's like we don't count any more – because they all do.

I lean in to Rob and spit tipsy sarcasm in his ear. 'Thank God for their wives, though. I mean, they're the real life and soul of the party.'

Rob does a small 'hee-hee!' He's got his arm draped around the back of my seat, and his hand rhythmically strokes where my bra hook is, and I love this hand. I love this hand. 'Well, Jill, if this is what having kids does to you – makes you sit there like a bunch of bloody Roman columns – all I can say is, I'm glad we've been spared.'

I scour his face and it's perfectly serious. 'Yeah,' I give him a big nudge with my elbow. 'Because we're so fascinating, aren't we?' Dig, dig. 'So vivacious and interesting and perfect in every way.'

He winks at me. 'Never a truer word said in jest.' He raises his glass, 'Cheers to that!'

Next, we eat the same meal they've been serving at North-East weddings since the year dot: The Dreaded Prawn Cocktail (canned prawns in watery mayo, on limp, pale lettuce, with paprika on top). Rob leans in to me and says, 'Innovative.' This is followed by dry

breast of chicken with string beans, carrots and tatties
in their skins. Rob leans in to me again and whispers,
'Does life get any better?' It's all capped with – 'Abra-
cadabra . . .' says Rob, 'Heart-failure ward here we
come!' – profiteroles filled with cream, sitting on a blob
of cream, with cream plopped on the top, and a glass of
Ge–worst–traminer wine: Rob's favourite.

Rob and I belch and pass wind all the way upstairs to
the disco, where, in a square room bedecked with
balloons and flashing red-amber-green traffic lighting,
we dance to a nostalgic blast of eighties tunes – Rick
Astley meets 'Pump Up the Jam'.

Dance? Yes, I actually manage it. A few hours ago
I'd have thought it a physical and emotional impossi-
bility. But it's actually fun. Takes me back to when we
were first courting.

At ten, it's endless drunken speeches washed down
with wedding cake and Asti Spumante. The speeches
do touch me. Not what's said, because that's actually
worse than the vows. But the faith that's placed by
everyone present in these two lovebirds to defy the
odds; it's bright as the noonday sun. And the cynic in
me says *enjoy your moment*, and the forgotten romantic
in me envies them for it, longs for some fickle finger of
fate that could make Rob and me swap places with
them.

And then it's the first slow dance of the evening; time
for the bride and groom to take to the floor.

Rob and I never had 'our song' on our big day, for
several reasons. One: we could never agree on a song
we both loved (our differing tastes in music used to be

cute until we were married, then it became just another excuse for a bit of tasty nitpicking that would some-how, irrationally, escalate into us rupturing a lung). Two: the idea of launching our wedded love-boat on a particular tune that a million other married couples had sailed around the floor to, felt a bit like checking in to an exclusive hotel and having to share a toilet with everybody else on your floor. Three: the whole idea of 'our song' is, was, and always will be, cheesy as hell, to say the least.

The bride and groom's song is Rod Stewart's 'Have I Told You Lately' (alas, not the infinitely preferable Van Morrison version). 'God, Rod should really have given it up once he turned thirty, shouldn't he?' Rob mutters to me, and I smile and remind him, 'Yeah, well, Rod Baby gets the hot young babes. Will you be able to say the same at his age?'

The next tune, the DJ tells us, is Bonnie Tyler's 'If I Sing You A Love Song'. I've never heard of it and neither has Rob, but the DJ introduces it as probably THE most romantic song of all time, in a gigolo voice that says either he fancies his chances of getting on the radio one day, or he just fancies himself, full-stop. Rob and I sit there, waiting for it to get going, to see if it's something we could dance to. It's a nice tune, touching from the word go. Rob pulls me up and we fall into step, not exactly dancing, more doing a sort of mobile embrace, as Bonnie says that if she sings her man a love song, he will always remember her by it. Rob lays his forehead on mine and we inch without skill, but with honesty, around the floor. Just me and this sentimental man I call my husband, who'll always pretend he's not really crying at sad films. Me, who always used to be embarrassed by too much lovey-dovey business on dance floors. Then Bonnie gets to her last line. As she sings to her man about how love songs don't leave you like lovers often do, and she's afraid that's what's going to happen to them, I feel something that makes me look up – Rob's heartbeat quickening under the palm of my hand, the sudden pressure of his fingers on my back. And through the changing red-amber-green haze of colour, his quiet blue gaze plunders mine. By his expression, you'd think I was a rare white diamond attracting and refracting light. One that, unfortunately, he's not going to get to keep. I scrutinise his face. His eyes are full of tears.

14

'You still haven't heard anything about your tests?' I ask Wendy as Leigh and I sit with her in Café Espagne. I can't keep avoiding them forever.

'Probably not for another week.' She seems so completely unconcerned. Leigh seems agitated, in a distant sort of way, if you can be distantly agitated. Her attention's somewhere across the room, inhabiting another body, another life. This behaviour is really old hat now. When Leigh goes to the toilet, Wendy gabs, 'I have to leave that job, Jill! I can't stand it any more. All the petty fights. A twenty-hour argument over whether the sequins on the new hot pants should be gold or baby blue. They're a couple of dizzy, deranged prima donnas. They're completely dysfunctional. I've never seen or heard anything like it. I have to get out. Urrrrrhhh!' I've never heard Wendy sound this desperate before. 'Jill, I have a brain. I have an almost degree. I don't have to have some massively important career, but I can't do this any more. Act interested in things I don't give a damn about. I need to get out of bed every morning and feel like something I do helps improve one person's life, or even just . . . helps improve my own. That would be a start.' She glances in the direction of the toilets, hurriedly whispers, 'She's so changeable. Especially lately. One minute she's telling me I'm great and the next she's saying I didn't make enough media calls because none of the journalists across the country are coming to the event. Clifford overheard me mutter to myself, "Well, maybe that's a reflection of the event . . ." And then he told her the whole reason nobody's coming is because the idea stank from the start.' She shakes her head again. 'It's so silly. It's overpriced exercise pants that, let's face it, despite all the claims to the contrary, go bobbly after you've washed them twice.' Leigh comes back from the toilets. Wendy shuts up.

Then Wendy goes to the toilet, and Leigh says, 'I have to talk to you, Jill! It's urgent.' And I feel like an elastic band being pulled at both ends and it's about to snap, and it's not going to be pretty.

'I've fallen in love,' she declares a few hours later, over a low table in a turquoise candlelit bar in Gosforth, when it's just her and me.

I stare vacantly at her through a fug of exhaustion and apathy. For a second I think she's talking about Lawrence. I'm about to congratulate her.

'I love him, Jill. I don't know how it happened. But it did.' She positively glows.

'Oh . . . you mean Nick?'

She scowls. 'Who d'you think I mean?'

'Oh. You're in love with Nick?'

She looks momentarily hesitant, then says, 'Like I've never been before. With anybody.'

'But what about Molly and Lawrence?' Bloody hell.

Fear for somebody other than myself suddenly takes over. 'My God, Leigh! What about Nick? How does he feel? Is he in love with you?'

There's a guarded look in her eyes. 'Which do you want me to answer first? He's not one of these fellas who uses the love word easily, Jill. A part of him is afraid to show his true feelings. His wife is the weaker one in the relationship so he's never been able to be vulnerable. And he's never been able to tell anybody that but me.' She averts her eyes, picks up her martini glass. She sounds angry on his behalf. 'But he says he's crazy about me, which is the same thing.' Her tone is chirpy, over-convincing. She looks thin, like you could snap her in the middle, in skinny leopard-print trousers and a black ribbed V-neck top. Well turned-out, but nervy and fragile somehow.

'You've got to end it, Leigh. You said it was just going to be a fling, that you'd pull the plug after the summer. What happened to giving it an expiry date?'

She looks at me as though my reminder is in bad taste. 'I can't! I have to leave Lawrence.' Her eyes fill up.

'Leave Lawrence? What about Molly?'

'Obviously it'd just be until we got ourselves sorted. Then she'd come and live with us.'

'You can't leave your own daughter!' What is she? Mad?

The glass she's holding tips slightly, sending vodka onto her trousers. She sets it down. 'I said I'm NOT leaving her! It would be temporary, to cause her as little upheaval as possible.'

'And what about his family? His wife? What about his poor kids? Where does that leave them when he ups and walks out on them?'

She stares at me through the thin darkness of this near-empty room, looking like a balloon that's suddenly losing air. 'His wife! His wife! You're taking everybody's side but mine.' Then there's a heavy silence. She puts a hand over her mouth, clutches her face as though the magnitude of what she's saying is only properly dawning on her as we speak.

'Leigh! The only side I'm taking is the side of sense.' I lean across the table because the waitress standing by the bar is watching us with a bit too much interest. 'You're going to leave your family for a married man with kids who can't even tell you he loves you? Has he asked you to do it?'

She shakes her head grudgingly. 'Not in so many words. But I know it's what he wants. I think he's waiting for me to initiate it because he doesn't want to be the bad guy in all this.' Her voice is a valiant tremor. But then she cups her hands over her nose and mouth again. Tears roll down either side of them. 'Oh, Jill, I feel so bad for Lawrence. It's going to kill him. What am I going to do?'

'End it and forget about it. You don't have any other option.'

She wipes under her eyes where her mascara has run and there's something desperate and pleading in the way she looks at me and I don't know whether I'm more angry or sorry for her. 'I can't,' she says. 'I love him.'

'Oh, come on. You love the fact that he's charming and he's into you. You love the sex and how he makes you feel.'

'Isn't that enough?'

'If you were both single, maybe! But this isn't long-haul stuff, Leigh. It was a fling, and you've got all carried away. God, he'll probably crap himself if you go telling him you've left your family for him!'

She is shaking her head vehemently, her double-hoop gold earrings he bought her tinkling like wind chimes. 'You don't know how unhappy he is in his marriage. It's all been an act. He's only stuck it out for the kids. She was never right for him. All she's done is stick to him like a leech. She doesn't know what he needs. She's never known. But I know.' She's stabbing a red-painted fingernail into her chest.

Smart, cynical, worldly Leigh. Has she really fallen for the 'my wife doesn't understand me' line? She narrows her eyes at me, 'I might have known you'd never understand.'

'Oh, give over. If I wouldn't understand, why are you telling me?' My bluntness stuns her. But I'm on a roll. 'God, Leigh, you've always said you could never fall for a cheat. You said trust and fidelity were everything.'

'But he's only cheated with me because I'm special. That doesn't make him a bad person. If anything, it's a clear sign we're meant for one another. And despite what you think, he doesn't take it lightly. He's got a conscience about what he's doing.'

'He took you to his wife's home, after you'd ex-changed two and a half emails. He wanted to screw you in his wife's bed! That's having a conscience?' I'm getting loud.

She shakes her head, wordless. I glance across at the bar and the waitress is staring at us goggle-eyed. So is the barman.

'He's my soul mate, Jill.' She snivels, looking wistful. 'He – he completes me.'

'Oh, bollocks. Tom Cruise said that in *Jerry Maguire*, man! It was on the telly the other night!'

Her long, heavily made-up eyelashes flutter open like a chorus line of centipedes doing the cancan. 'Speak your mind, why don't you!'

'Thanks,' I fire back, and she looks astonished; then she titters.

I titter too. I don't know why, because none of this is funny. 'Look, Leigh, if nothing else, think how much your life is going to change if you leave Lawrence. Who's going to do all your laundry? Have your favourite muffins toasted in the morning? Put you at the centre of his universe, because he loves you even more than he loves himself? Will he do that? Mr Big Bloody Position In The Retail Industry who walks out on his wife and kids? I don't think so somehow.'

She watches a tea-light flame bounce in its turquoise holder. 'It's not like that,' she shakes her head, certainly. 'How do I leave him when I'm in love with him?'

'Just don't go back! Don't see him again! Oh, God, you said it yourself. It wouldn't matter who you were married to. You need risk and adventure.'

'It's more than that. I know you think like that, but the hours I'm not with him I don't know where to put myself. I can't bear thinking that he'll go back to her, and I'll limp back to Lawrence and the old routine.' She shakes her head again. 'Jill, I'm not like you, I'm not gorgeous. Fellas don't do double takes when I walk past them. I'm very realistic about the level I attract. And I never imagined a man of his calibre would be interested in me.' She looks at me hard. 'You know all my life men have made me feel like crap. I've never been with somebody who makes me feel so good about myself.'

'Lawrence doesn't make you feel like crap,' I remind her, and she glares at me, as though, again, I have no right saying that. 'Leigh, you can't want to be with a man because he makes you feel good about yourself. You've got to feel good about you, regardless of men.'

She twists a paper napkin into a sausage. God, her mother really has a lot to answer for. 'You don't understand,' she just keeps saying.

'Well, you're right. I don't. Maybe I can't.'

But it hits me how ugly all this is. How ugly we are. I had standards for how I lived my life. And the gulf between them and what I've done is more than I can bridge. My face has gone into an involuntary tremble. I'm trying to stop it but I can't.

I'm aware of her studying me, of the easy shift in the air from her crisis to mine. 'What's wrong?' she asks quietly, her green eyes gazing into mine. 'Look at you, Jill. What's the matter?'

I try to breathe, but even my breath is shaking. Inside of me is rage and regret. She will not get this out of me. As tempted as I am, I must never, ever tell her.

So I tell her.

I tell her the lot.

And as I do, I rue it. Because when I get to the part about how I fled from his room practically pulling up my underwear in the hall, I see something in her eyes. Glee.

She gawps at me for a moment, her jaw hanging open. Then her look hardens. 'Well,' she says. 'I think the pot just called the kettle black.'

'What?' It takes me a couple of seconds to register this slap. 'I am nothing like you! I never was!'

She crosses her arms over her chest in some sort of physical standoff with me. 'Oh, because you're so beautiful and you've only ever had one fella? Give it a rest.' She rolls her eyes. 'I've always known you judged me. You and Wendy took pleasure in being the good girls who never felt they missed out. I've always been different, haven't I? Somebody you both liked to have around for entertainment, but whom you couldn't quite approve of.'

'But that couldn't be farther from the truth!' Surely I didn't do that? Laud my virtue over her? I mean, I know I've always taken such pride in having only ever been with Rob . . .

'Yes, Jill, all along you sit there and you listen to my secrets and you want all the details, but in the back of your mind, I've known you were looking down on me.'

'Looking . . . what? I've envied you!' I feel a pain build between my eyes. 'How can you think this? Damn it, I've always known that my having only been with one man has bothered you, for some unfathomable reason . . . You've waved your promiscuity in my face but I've always sensed you secretly regretted it and would try to make yourself feel better by making me feel I'd missed out.' Her eyes widen in speechless shock. 'But I never thought your resentment would run this deep.' I shut up because I really don't want to get into a big fight. 'But, Leigh,' I keep my voice down, 'you're dead wrong if you think I've never felt I've missed out. A part of me has thought that maybe I should have lived it up more in my twenties, then what happened in my marriage might not feel as bad. And that's not a reflection on my love for Rob. Maybe it's just a natural response under the circumstances. We all have our demons, Leigh. We all do.'

She contemplates me as though she doesn't give two stuffs about my demons. And I register something. That I am losing a friend. And with her she takes my biggest secret. In my mid-thirties I catch myself learn-ing one of life's tough lessons – that there's no such thing as friends you tell everything to: only on *Sex and the City*.

'I'm sorry,' she says, after a long silence. 'I don't know why I turned on you like that, Jill. I suppose I'm just pissed off you didn't tell me before about the Russian, after everything I've told you. I sometimes feel like my personal business is everybody's business. But yours and Wendy's . . . You're both so careful. Especially her. I sometimes think you must tell each other things, but you keep everything from me. Because you two are the good girls and I'm the bad one.'

'Oh, give over saying that! You know Wendy's guarded. She never says anything to anybody.' *What are you, a child?*

She holds my gaze for a moment. Then she does that thing of looking shiftily around the bar, and I know something else is coming. She sits up tall in her chair. 'Well, Jill, now that we've said all this, I might as well tell you everything. You've not been honest with me; well, I've not exactly been honest with you either.'

I look at her. Something in her face, a quiet gloating, is frightening me.

'I'm going to tell you something that you're not going to want to hear, but you have to promise me that you'll still be my friend.'

'Stop it. I don't like this, Leigh.'

She leans forward. 'You have to promise.'

'That's not fair!'

She titters. 'I know, but I'm making you.'

I titter a bit too, more because her look of leery triumph has made me nervous. 'What the hell is it, then?' I gabble.

She sits back now and primly weaves her fingers together in her lap, staring at her steepled, red-painted thumbs. 'Jill, you've been a good pal to me, but it seemed easier at the time not to tell the whole truth. Back when I thought this thing was going to be very short-lived.'

I've almost forgotten we're in a public place. The waitress comes and asks if we want another drink. We both hurl 'No!' at her, and she says, 'Gawd! All right!' and walks away, glaring at us.

Leigh suddenly looks quaky and unsure of herself again. 'I have to tell you something pretty terrible, Jill, so you'd better brace yourself. Something I'm not exactly proud of.' She holds my eyes. I hold my breath. 'See,' she says, 'thing is, I've not been having an affair with any client at work. There never was any Nick. It's Neil I'm in love with.'

15

I sit on our chocolate-coloured corduroy settee with a wine glass clenched in my shaky hand. And, in the twilight of our room, with the dog snoring on the cushion beside me, I tell Rob everything.

Well, not *everything*.

'Keep out of it, Jill.'

'But she's going to do something terrible, I can just tell. She's got this mad idea they've been harbouring feelings for each other for years!'

'No they haven't! I never had the impression he was even remotely attracted to her.'

'Well, I know, neither did I.' I mean, I know she's always thought him gorgeous. But Wendy having a drop-dead gorgeous husband has always just been a bit of a giggle, something to pep up the conversation. As though if he didn't exist, we'd have had to invent him.

'She's obviously menopausal.'

'I think she's more than that. She's ready to walk out on her marriage for him. On her daughter!'

'I always knew she was crackers.'

'Oh, come on! Who could ever have predicted this? Not me, and I was her best friend!' With more than a bit of irony, I wonder who would ever have predicted what I did.

The dog stretches, yawns a bored, whiny yawn and pushes me with his back paws as though he'd rather have the settee all to himself. 'To think she utterly abhorred her own mother for having twins and giving one baby away. Yet here she is—'

'It's not quite the same thing.'

'It is. It's abandoning your kid.'

'I suppose. But . . . I mean, it's very weird that a mother would keep one baby and give the other away, but at least she put the kid up for adoption. That kid probably grew up in a happier home than Leigh did.'

'So, what you mean is, it's worse what Leigh's doing?' I thought he was implying that it wasn't as bad.

'Of course it's worse. It's running away from your responsibility. No kid wants to grow up knowing they were a product of some crap, failed relationship. And no kid wants to grow up with only one parent. Frankly, I would never wish that on a kid, having been there myself.'

I sometimes forget that Rob's dad buggered off before he was born. Rob's mother tried to love him even more to compensate, but, as Rob once told me, 'You don't want that. You don't want a mam who tries to be a dad too. You want a mam. You want a dad. And you want to be a little boy.'

'And there's Wendy's lads, too. What happens to her and them when he runs off into the sunset with Leigh? What am I going to do, Rob? I can't sit by and watch Leigh do this, take Neil away from his family.'

He leans forward in the chair, resting his elbows on his spread knees. 'Yeah, you can. It's not your business.'

I wish he'd pack in being so logical. 'It *is* my business, in some ways. Remember it was me who introduced Leigh to Wendy in the first place? She says she was besotted with him from the word go. How does that make me feel? Like I somehow helped get them together!'

'Oh, give over. That's daft. Anyway, that was years ago, and they've only started bonking recently, if that's to be believed. Anyway, you make it sound like you've got some control over what Neil does. You don't. If he leaves Wendy, then he obviously wants to. And, who knows, maybe he does love Leigh. God. Hard as that is to believe. But either way, there's nothing you can do to stop any of it.'

'Well, thanks Rob, but that sounds too rational and simplistic to me. And another reason why this is my business – Leigh made it my business by putting me in this position. She's forcing me to take her side because I was in on the whole thing from the start. She thinks that gives her a right to my vote, or something.'

'Well, sod her! She thinks wrong! But I really can't believe that you knew she was having an affair and you went along with it.'

'How do you make that out? That I went along with it? I didn't stand there and cheer her on!'

'It's the same thing though, isn't it? If you don't disapprove, they think you support them. I mean, I wouldn't sit there with Gav or Macca and listen to them talking about screwing around on their wives, would I? Or it would look like I approved. Maybe it'd look like I even do the same thing myself.'

Make me feel like crap, why don't you? 'But I didn't know it was Neil, did I? Our friend's husband! She said it was somebody called Nick.'

'No, but you knew he was married with a family. You knew he was somebody's husband. Somebody's dad. He was somebody who was loved and depended on and highly thought of in people's lives.'

We sit there registering my silent shame. Rob yawns, because my shame is obviously far less soul-shattering to him than it is to me. Even the dog groans, like he's clean out of sympathy.

'I'm sure he never loved her. He probably just wanted to get his rocks off.'

'Don't say that! God, you've got such a way of reducing everything!'

'Well, he must be hard up, that's all I can think. And some fellas, when they just want to get some action, they're not too picky.'

'I know you always say she's poor to look at—'

'A mutt.'

'You don't have to use that word!' I suppose because I know and love my friends I always see them as beautiful. 'And how can he be hard up? He's married! I can't believe he told Leigh that Wendy doesn't give him everything he needs!'

Rob lies back in his chair, clasps his hands behind his head. 'Well, I'm sure he just added that to get it signed and sealed. You know, the sympathy vote. But maybe she *doesn't* give him what he needs. Maybe she's spent her life resenting not having a career and a life of her own. You don't know what their marriage has really been like, Jill. There's three sides to every story. His side. Her side. And the truth.'

'There's only two sides to this story. And Wendy's is both of them.'

'Well, there you go.' He looks like he's moving to get up.

'Where're you going?' I pin him there with my eyes, before he has a chance to get any ideas. 'It's so disappointing, though, Rob. I mean, I always imagined he'd be so upright. I thought they were the perfect couple. I thought I'd actually encountered one.'

'As opposed to us, of course . . .' he says sarcastically.

'You know what I mean.'

'Well, them buggers are the worst, aren't they? The upright ones. But he's a good-looking fella, I'm sure it's hard for him to stay faithful.'

'But just because somebody's good-looking doesn't make them more likely to cheat, does it?'

'I don't know,' he cocks his head and studies me with interest. 'You're good-looking and you've not cheated. Have you?'

'Well, that's what I mean.' I look at the dog.

We go on, and on, and on. Forwards, backwards and in circles. The room grows darker. The dog slides off the settee to the floor. Rob slinks farther down the chair. 'Tell me what to do,' I plead.

'I have. Seventy-five times.'

'That's not being helpful.'

He yawns again. 'Well, like I've said – seventy-five times – you can't tell Wendy, that would accomplish nothing except to destroy her. Some people would rather not know that their partners have had affairs. Your only choice is to try to talk some sense into Leigh. Now, can we go to bed and pack in talking about this?'

'But I've tried talking to Leigh.' In the few days I've known this, I've done nothing but. And she's not budging.

'Well, I'm starting to sound like a stuck record, but like I've said, you've done your bit then.' He yawns again, only his yawn has an 'oh Jesus' tacked onto the end of it. He moves to get up. Does he think this conversation's over? I still have another ten miles of it to run.

'Where are you going?'

'Oh, I was just leaving the country, I mean I was going to get a drink of water.'

'Well, can't you wait until we're finished here?' I know once he leaves the room I'll never see him again. He'll be like one of those men who go missing and all they find at the shoreline is their shoes.

He groans, sits back down again on the floor beside the dog.

I begin my rant all over again, with renewed enthusiasm. The clock ticks loudly above the mantelpiece. Eventually there is only one voice in the room. Even I'm getting sick of hearing it. 'I can't believe it, Rob. I can't believe *her*.' Rob's responses have trailed off to the odd jerky grunt. 'All these years and then they suddenly start having an affair.'

'Right then!' he says. Meaning *Right, that's bloody it, I've heard enough*. He gets up.

'But we've not decided anything, yet!'

'Oh yeah? Maybe you haven't, but I did ten hours ago.' He stretches his arms over his head and lets out another   oh-my-God-this-has-been-an-agony-worse-than-being-eaten-by-Rottweilers groan. 'Kiefer and I are going to bed.' He gently rouses the dog with his foot. 'Just keep your big nose out of this, Jill. That's my last word.'

I nod. 'You're right.' I watch the dog pad after him across the floor. 'I'll stay well out.'

A few days later I ring Neil.

Thursday lunchtime I am seated opposite him in the stately oak-panelled dining room of the Stannington Hotel. Where businessmen lunch. Or come to have affairs. It feels peculiarly appropriate. The place was his suggestion when I rang him and said I wanted to meet him. Across a white linen tablecloth decorated with white place settings and silver cutlery, I say the immortal words: 'I know about your affair with Leigh.'

I could just as well have said I know where you buy your socks. He is unflinching. Everything I'd rehearsed I was going to say evaporates into the ice-green walls with their oil paintings of the Tyne Valley. And I see a Neil I've never seen before. A curious, cold bastard. Cold, like his glacial eyes.

'And?' is all he says to me. He quickly drinks back his Scotch and soda and waves the approaching waiter away. I take it that means we're not ordering lunch now.

'And?' I repeat back at him, defensively. I can suddenly picture him as a copper. If I were a bloke in his custody, I'd rather just skip the interrogation and be sent down for life with men who might put unpleasant things up my bottom while I was bending over to do the laundry.

'And you've come to tell me to stop seeing her.' He resettles his grey-blue and white tie against his pale blue shirt. He sits back confidently in his chair, sliding down it a few inches, crosses his hands at his chest with the cocky art of the interrogator. Turning the tables on me with just a stare. 'You don't have to. It's stopped. I mean, it was never really started as far as I was concerned.'

This isn't the Neil I've known all these years. Been on holiday with, for God's sake.

He looks at me now, seems to note my speechlessness, shrugs. I run my eyes the length and breadth of him. I'm having a hard time picturing this man with his face up Leigh's skirt. In his own house. Bathroom. Bath-tub.

'That's not how she sees it. She's in love with you.'

An eyebrow shoots up, as though he's mocking the very idea. 'In love with me?' Something in his expression seems to humanise him again. 'Ah, well, that's her misfortune.'

I pick up my wine glass. It feels weird sitting here drinking with him, but I need the Dutch courage. 'You *are* still seeing her. She said you are. So there's no point in saying it's stopped.'

'Well, frankly, my friend, that's none of your business,' he says, with smug flippancy, and I hate him. I'd rather he'd said *Keep your big bloody nose out*. There's a lone, crusty-looking bread roll sitting on my side plate and I feel like pelting it right between his eyes.

'Do you know your wife might not be well?' Around me I hear the chink of crystal water glasses being filled. Two creases form between his eyes; the only two imperfections on his blank, impenetrable, handsome face.

'I don't know what you're on about.'

My pulse pounds in my temples. 'She's been for tests. Did you know that? Why don't you go home and ask her how she is, how she really is?' I bet he never does. I suppose I've always sensed she loved him more.

He knows I know he didn't know. But again, he doesn't flinch. This time his Mr Cool act seems just a touch less convincing, because I can see a twitch just under his left eye. 'She's never said anything to me about any tests.'

'No, because she didn't want you or the lads to worry. That's how strong and unselfish she is. But while you've been busy with Leigh, she's been seeing doctors.' I'm exaggerating, and that feels wrong, even cruel, but somehow necessary.

He flushes; it comes and goes quickly. He studies me for a few moments, as though he's deciding what to say, then he says, 'Well then, it's good she's got such a good friend in you, isn't it?' And I don't quite know what he's getting at. Then he leans to one side, slides a hand in his trouser pocket, pulls out ten quid. Then he stands up. And I realise I've lost. Rob was right – I shouldn't have done this. You can't play cat and mouse with Neil.

'I have to get back to the station, Jill,' he says, almost with affection. 'Don't worry yourself on that score, though. Leigh and I . . .' He doesn't finish. He tosses the ten quid on the table, glances at me with finality and shakes his head, as though he just can't be bothered to finish the sentence, or he doesn't feel he should have to.

I watch his confident, unfaltering walk as he cuts around occupied tables. A few faces look up as he passes them.

The next day comes and goes, and the wrongness of my confrontation with Neil takes root and grows in me. Go to see Neil! Oh, God, what the bloody hell did I do that for? Rob was right. What did it accomplish? Nothing, except to infuriate Leigh. Because I'm sure he'll tell her.

Rob keeps asking me what the matter is. 'Been up to anything?' he'll say, narrowing his eyes. I go into work and am haphazardly efficient. The good thing is that Swinburn's off on holiday – Torquay is being blessed with his presence (I hope he's stopping in one of those *Fawlty Towers* guest-houses with Basil after him, doing the goose-step). So at least I don't have him glaring at me with those big, Nazi eyes. Only a lot of phone calls, and a lot of accounting to do, and a couple of urgent billing matters that he's left instructions for me to handle. 'He discovered you made an accounting mistake just before you went off sick,' Leanne whispers, as though she shouldn't be telling me.

'Mistake? Shit. I did make a couple of big ones, but I'm sure I fixed them. What sort of mistake?'

'No idea. He wouldn't say.'

'Well, what did he look like? Was he furious?'

She shrugs. 'If he was, he didn't say anything. But I'm sure he'll let you know about it, if it's anything.'

Damn it. I've never made mistakes in my job. I've always taken such pride. Well, I suppose if it'd been anything major he'd have delighted in telling me.

Rob and I seem to heal. Or rather, since the news of Leigh's infidelity we haven't had a wrong word between us. He doesn't look at me strangely. All that business about the mobile and my mood seems to be off his mind. And, strangely enough, the business behind the mobile and my mood seems to be off mine. Even though I still have the dim feel of the Russian in my body. And he's there, waiting to be my next thought, if I let myself.

When I come home in the evening, Rob's got dinner made. He heaps spaghetti alla puttanesca onto two plates. The M&S box sits torn up on the counter. I love him for it. But the pasta, me, him . . . it all feels too easy, this returning to normal. *Affairs are easy*, didn't Leigh say?

We're just eating and I am counting my blessings yet again, when the phone rings. I pick up and I hear two words. 'You bitch.'

'Leigh!' My heart falls. He's wasted no time telling her.

'You unimaginable, double-crossing bitch! And to

think I thought you were my friend and I could trust you!'

This verbal hail of bullets sends me collapsing onto the kitchen chair. 'Oh, Leigh I . . .'

But Leigh is having none of it. 'Don't "Leigh" me, you cow!' she barks. 'You went to see him to tell him to leave me! After I'd told you I loved him! That I was ready to leave my family for him! You went to break us up!'

'It wasn't like that . . .' I'm cut off by her screaming.

'Like you've got some right to start telling people how to lead their lives, you hypocritical little cow. You of all bloody people!'

She goes on bawling me out, but I'm thinking only one thing. I knew I should never have told her. I feel the need to say nice things, to get on her right side again.

'He's ended it now!' She's sobbing. 'Do you realise what you've done? He's gone back to them. Doesn't want to see me again. Won't even give reasons. He was furious that I told you, and even more furious that I hadn't told him about Wendy and the tests.'

'Well, maybe that's his reason. I mean, the possibility that his wife – your friend – has cancer and you knew about it while you carried on with him. It *is* a big enough one.'

I feel her seething. 'Even Wendy says it's more than likely not cancer.'

My refusal to dignify that makes her silent. Then she says, 'Well, I suppose you're happy. You've really done it for me, haven't you? Tell me, Jill, what am I supposed to do now?'

'Forget about that idiot! Start focusing on your marriage. Because you were happy, generally, before you started this mad affair. Nobody's happy all the time, but it's if you're happy most of the time that counts. And you were.'

'I can't,' she says, in a destroyed tone. 'I've already told Lawrence I'm leaving him.'

'That was Leigh,' I tell Rob when I put the phone down.

'Glad you clarified that. I was wondering.'

Rob opens his arms for me and holds me till I stop shaking. 'She's already told Lawrence she's leaving him! She was screaming. She hates me.'

'I take it you didn't keep your big hooter out, then?' he says. My head gently bounces off his shoulder as I shake it.

In bed, Rob holds me and calls me his treasure, scratches his chest, says the dog's given him fleas. His parting words before falling asleep are: 'You'd better prepare yourself, because something tells me you've not heard the last of this. What do they say? Hell hath no fury like a woman scorned.'

For the next few days, Leigh's call haunts me. She's right to hate me. What sort of hypocrite am I? Me, a cheat, betrayed a friend who had an affair because I didn't like her choice of lover. And I did it with complete disregard for what this would do to her. And despite what Rob says, I do believe she thinks she's in love with him. And I believe her when she says she really did intend it to end. Some people are just naive to think they're never going to get found out. But what troubles me most is that never for one minute did I consider that the affair might blow over, that Leigh would finally see sense, or Neil would dump her, and life would go back to normal again. I never even gave it time to happen. I just barged right on in there and buggered everything up.

'Don't feel too sorry for her, Jill,' Rob tells me. 'People who cheat on their partners don't deserve your losing sleep over them.' We're in bed again, and he knows I can't get this off my mind.

My heart sinks. 'But people stray for all kinds of reasons, Rob. Surely they deserve some empathy; the benefit of the doubt?' He loosens my tightening grip on his chest.

'Not when they've been unfaithful. You should be angry that she ever told you any of this, when you were Wendy's friend too. She should never have put you in this position.' And he's right. She shouldn't have. But she did. And I can't use that to justify betraying her. But somehow, I suppose I have.

The next phone call I get, some time the following afternoon, is from Wendy. I see her number on my call display and think *Oh, God.*

'Why did you tell him I've been for tests?' she asks me in a subdued tone, which is as close as Wendy will ever get to telling you off. 'He said he bumped into you down the town. That you happened to mention I was seeing a doctor.'

He lied. And now, by default, I have to. Again. Neil

must know that I chose to confront him rather than tell Wendy. So he's using that. He's using me, expecting I'll keep up the story. That I'll lie to protect my friend, and somehow save his bacon in the process. So my first instinct is to stick it to him and just come out with the truth. 'Wendy . . .' I take a bracing breath. But what am I thinking? I can't just come out with the truth! This is my friend's life, here. 'Look, I'm sorry . . . I know I'm a big wally . . . It was inexcusable of me. It just slipped out.'

There's a silence. I hate lies. Even the kind kind. 'I'm not sure how it really happened, actually. I reckon I think—'

'It's all right,' she says. 'I'm not hauling you over the coals.'

'Aren't you?'

'No. Worse things could have happened, couldn't they?'

If only you knew.

'I'd better go, though. I've got to clean up this house and then get some dinner on, and there's a job in a solicitor's office I'm thinking of applying for. Half of Newcastle is probably going to apply for it and get rejected, so I might as well be one of them.' Her humour sounds strained. We say bye. It bothers me as soon as I put the phone down. I know Wendy. If she were really furious with me, she'd be strained. Then she'd probably freeze me out of her life. So I quickly call her back and apologise again and check that she's still my friend. I feel her smile. 'It's all right, Jill. Like I say, forget about it.'

A few days later I have to go through to Sunderland to take a piece of cushion flooring I bought for my mam and dad's bathroom, because my mam has been wee-ing on the carpet in there. I'm on my way back, stuck on the A1 in traffic – immediately ahead of me, a BMW has just rear-ended a VW hippy van. Out of the van pour a fat young lad and lass who look like two packs of ASDA sausages with heads on, then the father, a tattooed ball of blubber with a bottle of Newcastle Brown in each hand, and the granny, one of those hardened council-estate hags with smoker's hair, whose face is gradually capsizing into the space where she used to have teeth. And they're ganging up and laying into the civilised, besuited driver of the BMW. I thrust the heel of my hand onto the horn. The noise feels nice. They all stop their argy-bargy and look at me, probably wondering what the hell my problem is. I leave my hand there, blaring, staring at them with an intensity that equals the noise I am making. Then it hits me. Oh, God, how am I going to explain to Wendy that Leigh and I have fallen out? What's Leigh going to say to Wendy about it? I stop blasting the horn and put my head in my hands.

The dispute is over. Somebody behind blares their horn at me, because I'm still sitting there not moving. I'm just slipping into second gear when I see it. In the opposite lane, zooming up to pass a slow-moving Micra, is a beaten-up white VW Golf. I don't see his face. Just a blur of dark skin and hair.

My hands clutch onto the wheel as I attempt to drive in a straight line. Of all the cars on the road in Sunderland, what on earth were the chances of that? How many more times in my life is this man going to just coincidentally appear?

I get home, safe but hardly sound. Relieved, that much is true. Kiefer's going scatty for a walk because I didn't take him to Pause for Paws today. I'm hungry, but I've not been to the shops and don't know what we've got in for dinner. All the strands of my togetherness unfurl again. Our answering machine says we have four new messages. God, what if he saw me and it's him ringing? Maybe all that commotion across the road made him look over. I can't breathe. I go round the sitting room doing a quick nervous-energy tidy, picking up newspapers and putting them in the waste-paper basket, one hundred per cent convinced his voice will be on that machine. Then I press *Play*. The first is from Rob, saying he'll be late home so not to bother with dinner – maybe we can go out – that he loves me, that he'll see me soon. Every time I hear Rob's voice, loving and trusting, I fill with a glorious reprieve, a fawning inner gratitude to a God I never knew I believed in until now. If Leigh were going to ring Rob to get her own back on me, she'd have done it already. Knowing her and her anger at me, I can't see her waiting five days, trying to decide whether or not to do it. So with each day that passes, I am one step farther away from my worst living hell. The second message is from Mrs Towers from the puppy obedience classes that Leigh bought me for my birthday. Talk about poetic timing. And the third message – Good God – is from Lawrence. The distress in his voice! 'Did you know this was happening, Jill? You're her friend, are you really going to tell me you didn't know? All those times you went out, were you talking about this all along? Or maybe she never did go out with you. Maybe you covered for her while . . . Maybe there were no exercise classes all along.' He sounds beside himself. But even when he's angry he sounds gentle, which makes my heart bleed for him. 'She's gone!' he says, as though to himself, in disbelief. 'Neil doesn't want her now, and I told her I certainly don't. She's moved in with Clifford.'

Her boss! Who she has blistering fights with, as Wendy said, like an old married couple.

He sighs, as though he might cry. 'Molly's howling and won't eat, and since Leigh recently bullied me into taking contract work, I'm now on a project deadline and I can't get to it because Molly's howling and won't eat. My client's pissed off. I'm pissed off, and I'm hurt and I'm confused, and I miss her and I hate her and I still love her, and I don't know what to do, and I had my parents over but they didn't really help and they've gone home now and everywhere I look I'm finding beer bottles in weird places, and I want her back! I want her gone. I want her dead. I don't want to live without her . . . I – I'm so confused.'

He stops abruptly.

'Argh,' he adds, like he's worn himself out. 'Don't bother ringing back. You're as bad as her.'

I wonder if she's told him. I quickly press *Delete*.

The last message is from Wendy, a total contrast to Lawrence's. 'Hi, Jill,' she says, her voice flat. 'Give me a ring, will you?'

'Wendy!' I say, when she picks up.

'Oh.' Her voice is a mere whisper. 'Hi there.'

There's a tense silence while my heart beats like the clappers. 'Wendy, what's the matter?'

'Well,' she says. 'I know.'

16

She looks raw. Her face is bare, as though the make-up's been traumatised off it. I've never seen my exuberant friend this undemonstrative. Wendy, but not Wendy. As though Wendy has left the building. We sit in her car around the corner from where she lives, overlooking Jesmond Dene, and a motley group of teens smoking behind a wall.

'That's why she's been behaving so off-it at work. She comes in, doesn't even look at me or say good morning, goes into her office and slams the door. Clifford comes in virtually right behind her and does the same thing. I came home from my doctor's appointment. My phone rang as I was walking in the door. It was Neil, telling me I had his phone.' She looks at me. 'I looked at what was in my hand. He was right: the subtle difference of the orange screen versus the green . . .' Her voice cracks. She looks at her bitten fingernails. 'I didn't feel like driving all the way to the station to take it to him. I wasn't feeling great. I'd just stopped by the house to make a cup of tea. But he said he needed it, so I told him I'd bring it before I put the kettle on . . .' Wendy – a level, more subdued version of herself – looks at me now. 'I happened to notice there was a new voicemail message. I've no idea why I did it, but I checked to see who it was.' She leans sideways, reaches in her pocket and pulls out the phone.

Leigh's distraught voice fills the quiet car. 'Neil, you've got to talk to me. You can't just say it's over. This is my life, here! I've left my husband for you, you bastard!' Leigh bawls. 'Oh, I'm sorry. I didn't mean to call you that. I love you! I always have. I need you. I miss you. I miss your face, I miss your body, I miss you in my body. You can't do this to me, you bastard! You've got to talk to me! Answer the fucking phone!' By the end she's hollering like some mad person. It's *Fatal Attraction* all over again.

I clap a hand over my mouth as Wendy puts the phone back in her pocket, the fine hairs on her arms standing up. The lads by the wall catcall after some girls who toss them grins as they walk past. 'My God. Does he know you know?'

She shakes her head. 'I told him I couldn't bring him his phone because I wasn't feeling well. Then I rang Clifford and told him I couldn't come into work. I didn't tell him that I'm never coming back again, though.' Splotches of red surface on her forehead. 'I thought I heard her crying in her office the other day. I tapped on the door, asked her if she was all right. She didn't even reply. I thought she must still be sulking about the stupid store opening . . .' She looks at me frankly. 'Jill, I'm assuming you know what's going on. I'm getting the feeling I'm the only one who doesn't.'

'Wendy, it's not me you should be hearing this from . . .' The last thing I want to be is any more involved than I already am. But I am. And I owe her my honesty. 'I did know she was having an affair, yes.' I talk to her hands that are clenched around the base of the steering-wheel. 'But she said it was with somebody called Nick. She said he was one of her clients. She only told me it was Neil the other day. That's why I went to see him. I was frightened he was going to do something terrible like—'

'Leave me.'

'I was convinced Leigh meant to have him at all costs.'

She watches one of the lads idly kick the wall. She's unusually calm. She doesn't comment on what I've just said, just sits for a while – a long while – staring over the top of the steering-wheel. Her chest is all that moves, a shallow rise and fall. But her pallor frightens me. Even her hands seem to have lost their tan. 'All those times she kept telling me to tell Clifford that she was out with some client. She was obviously seeing Neil. She was getting me to cover for her while she was having sex with my husband.' She looks at me with vulnerable, abject bafflement. Then her shoulders shake almost imperceptibly, her brows knit and form two vertical ridges between her eyes. 'I don't understand. Neil doesn't even think she's attractive. He says she's brittle.' She searches my face. The intensity of her scrutiny makes me lower my eyes again. 'How long has it been going on? Years?'

'Weeks,' I say quickly. 'Since June, maybe.'

'Weeks,' she repeats, distantly.

I feel as helpless as I did the day that Nina died, knowing no amount of comfort can ease the pain. I stare at her sorry hands, her platinum wedding band, the only piece of jewellery she ever wears, and I don't know what to do for her. 'Look, do you want to come home with me? Stay with us and we'll work out what you're going to do together?' I don't know Wendy's heart. Maybe she can't leave him. Maybe they'll have a big row, he'll say it's over, she'll get a new job, never talk to Leigh again. Life will somehow mend itself, as my own seems to be doing, after a fashion.

She shakes her head, her eyes still not moving as she replays the scene in her mind. 'I covered for her. I actually covered for her while she was out screwing my husband.'

I look at her unblinking profile, the sturdy, speckled shoulder nearest mine. As though she reads my help-lessness, she looks at me for a long time, still completely unable to comprehend what Leigh did. Then she says, 'I have to go into hospital.' She pulls an ironic smile. 'They've found something wrong.' And then her eye-brows go up and she gives a tiny little huff. A huff that says, completely without self-pity, 'Can you quite believe this?'

I follow Rob round the house, breathless in my distress, as I recount my conversation with Wendy. The good thing, apparently, is that the cancer – carcinoma in situ – as she called it, which sounds even worse than just calling it cancer – is at a very early stage. But she has to have a procedure that's supposed to remove the af-fected tissue. If it works, she'll be fine. If not, she'll have to have a hysterectomy. 'Have my womb out,' she said, and she put her pale hand on her belly.

Later, Rob holds me in bed while the word 'cancer' hovers over us, making every other drama pale by comparison. I feel the rhythmic tickle of his eyelashes on the side of my face. 'Rob, I feel like an evil chain-letter.'

'Don't be daft,' he whispers and smooths my hair down with his hand. 'It's not your fault she ended up with his mobile phone.'

'But if I'd never gone to Neil, he'd have never dumped Leigh, and she wouldn't have rung his mobile in hysterics.'

'Yeah, but Wendy would have found out some other way. I bet that's why she checked his messages, because she suspected something. I mean, I would never even think to check your phone messages because I trust you. Surely you always know, deep down, if your partner's cheating? People who have affairs always get found out, don't they?'

The next day is a reasonably quiet one at work, thank God. Swinburn's back from his holiday but he never mentions this error I'm supposed to have made. Nor does he ask how I am, or in any way refer to my time off and the fact that I didn't provide a doctor's note, nor does he say he's glad to see me back – but in some ways all that feels like a long time ago now. I try to get Wendy on her mobile all day, but it's switched off. And she's not home when I call the house. And of course I know she won't be at work. I have a mountain of accounting I've not got done because I've been in la-la land, so I stay until past six to catch up. Then

I drive home, after picking up the dog, subconsciously noting every small white car – my new habit. When I get into the house I try Wendy again. She'd usually be home for the lads at this time, making dinner. I'm getting a bit worried now. I have visions of her standing on the Tyne Bridge, staring into the depths of the water . . . A headline on the news . . . Somebody witnessing a body, as if in slow motion, falling through the air. Rob and I are in the middle of eating when she rings me back.

She's left him.

Or rather, she's thrown him out.

'I went home after I'd sat with you in the car,' she tells me. 'Neil came home and I gave him his phone. He went into his study, presumably to listen to his messages, then he came back out again. Seemed fine.' She's keeping her voice down; maybe the lads are around. 'The next morning he went to work while I pretended to be asleep. Then I made tea and toast. Then, when the lads went out, I took four large suitcases down from the cupboard. I packed Neil's clothes, Neil's toiletries, Neil's paraphernalia from his desk drawers, even Neil's dirty laundry from the bin. Then I put Neil's name on the labels, got in my car and drove to the headquarters of Northumbria Police. I parked across the road and watched the building for a bit. Then I hauled those suitcases across the road, two at a time. I dragged them to a spot right in front of the main doors. Then I turned and . . . I just walked back to my car—'

'Good God, Wendy! What did you do next?'

'Nothing. I looked one more time at the suitcases abandoned in the middle of the street. I said, "Goodbye, you son of a bitch," and then I drove off.'

'You didn't! What happened?'

'Oh, he was furious I'd humiliated him in front of people at work. I think he was more upset by that than the fact that I knew about him and Leigh. Security had to bring the cases up to his office. They'd checked them. Were worried there might have been a bomb.' She goes silent for a second. 'I never even thought of that, Jill. I probably should have . . . I just didn't want him coming home and I didn't want to have to see him. Anyway, I don't think he was too impressed to know that the first thing they'd seen when they opened one of the cases was a great pile of his dirty underwear. By the time he came home I'd had the locks changed.'

'That fast?'

'That fast. It was pointless in some ways, though, because I had to let him in. To have a talk. There was no other place to have it. Your home is the only place you can respectfully hurl things at people.'

'You hurled things at him?'

'I did. Yes. A few.'

'Are you all right?'

'Oh, yeah. I aimed a few plates at him, then he walked out – and you know what he said? He said, "Look, I really don't feel like being made into the big villain in this." '

'He didn't say that!'

'That's Neil for you . . . I've told the lads that their dad's gone away on business for a few days. I have to buy some time to think how to handle this with them. That's my biggest fear, Jill,' she whispers. 'I don't know who they're going to blame.'

'What d'you mean? Him, of course!'

'But I'm the one who's thrown him out. Maybe they think parents are always supposed to work everything out.'

'So, what d'you think you're going to do now?'

There's a good pause before she says, 'Cry.'

It strikes me that what I'm doing every day now is living with new information. It gets hurled at me, I intend to try to make sense of it, but it just gets pushed along the great conveyor belt in my head, because more crap just keeps getting piled on board, and the wheels of my sanity have to be kept in motion.

A couple of days tick over. Wendy clearly does her grieving in private because when I see her she's in fully-fledged survival mode. 'We've got joint bank accounts,' she tells me, 'and it wouldn't surprise me if Neil tried to do something devious . . . Do you think he can put a hold on our credit card without my consent?'

'I haven't a clue.'

Ring the bank she writes, on a 'to do' list that I'm supposedly helping her compose as we sit under the Tiffany lamp on her kitchen table and she knocks back three quarters of a bottle of wine without even registering that she's doing it. 'You know, I can't even remember what accounts we have. I can barely even remember which bank we're a member of.' Her pale, harrowed face looks at me. 'I've been this cliché that lets the man take care of all that. But it wasn't intentional. It was mainly because I had other things to do and I just wasn't all that interested in money.' She is now, though. She's particularly concerned about the loss of her own pay-cheque. 'What should I do? Should I ring Clifford and tell him that for personal reasons I can't come back?' She rests her elbows on the tabletop, her chin in her upturned hands.

'I don't think you'll have to. Leigh's living with him. I'm sure she's told him everything.'

She shakes her head. 'I still think I should at least email him. He did employ me. I owe him some sort of explanation. I don't want him thinking I'm the bad person in all of this.'

'I don't know why you keep saying stuff like this!'

'Hang it. I'll think about it later,' she says.

We're just going through a pile of bills when she suddenly drops a pen and stares at me in the soft light. She has black lips from the red wine. She rubs her face hard with both hands, messing up her eyebrows. 'Jill, I don't even know where the deeds to the house are. Would you think me really stupid if I told you that I don't even remember if Neil put the house in both our names?'

Some time later she rings me on my new mobile when I'm at a managers' function at work that I couldn't get out of. 'It's all sinking in now, Jill. All those afternoons when she'd come back from lunch and look at me coyly, secretively. They must have actually talked on the phone while I was in the next room, planned their shenanigans.'

I walk outside the functions suite, with my glass of untouched wine, to get some quiet. I remember Leigh telling me they'd had sex in her office. Wendy was at the doctor's, hadn't Leigh said? Although Leigh wouldn't have known why. And that small fact makes her marginally less contemptible.

'Then there was the day she was trying on underwear in Fenwick's. Do you remember, Jill? She was parading around and acting very off-it. She must have been buying them for Neil. She was parading her affair with my husband right under my nose! Who would do that? A friend? What satisfaction could that possibly give her?'

Lots. Because, deep down, I think Leigh envied Wendy's blithe uncomplicatedness. I put my glass on the window-sill, nod to a few of the footballers who walk past and look me over, like they think they're God's gift. 'I'm not so sure she was parading it for your benefit, Wend. I think she was just so high on the whole thing that she didn't even register her own inappropriate behaviour.' It's weird that Wendy's more concerned with fathoming Leigh than Neil.

'Mm,' she says, not convinced. 'And the barbecue . . . They were obviously carrying on then and none of us were any the wiser. We never saw a sign.'

'No.' But I did. The way he watched her when she came out of the back door, carrying beer. I suppose I didn't want to see it. Or maybe the integrity I credited her with made me blind. But there was something in his face. It was the look of a man rediscovering somebody.

'It all started, apparently, because she bumped into him in the bank,' Wendy tells me the next day, over coffee.

'Ah! She told me that bit. I didn't know if it was true.'

'She asked him if he'd come with her to get a coffee at Pret a Manger, and then quite out of the blue she told him she'd always wanted him. Ever since day one. She laid this big confession on him in Pret, can you believe? He was stunned. He said he wondered if she was taking some strange pills or something. But then she emailed him at work to apologise, asked to buy him lunch, to make it up to him. He said he didn't want to go, but he went. And it kicked off from there.'

He didn't want to go, but he went – my arse! And Leigh told me that he invited her for coffee and she turned him down, because she was too taken aback. 'Well, fancy,' I say.

'It's odd, though, isn't it? They've known each other all these years, and only recently they started having an affair.'

'That's what Rob and I can't fathom.'

She pushes her coffee cup away. 'I can't drink this.' She scowls at me. 'Do you think it's true, that she wanted him all along?'

'She told me she did. She obviously picked her moment to make a big play for him. Or maybe she'd just reached a point in her own marriage where she was so hacked off that she just decided to go for it.'

'I don't think you should tell me that. Or I might have to go and kill her.' Wendy rotates her wedding ring on her finger. 'Neil always loves to be admired,' she smiles at the ring. 'He's as susceptible to it as we all are. Even though it tends to happen every day to him.'

Is she going to take him back? Because she's suddenly seeing him as a victim – of Leigh the devious predator who has been biding her time, and of his own irresistible good looks?

Deception: one's own or other people's, I'm not sure which is worse. Either way, it all gives me a headache. I come home from work emotionally and physically done in. Rob and I eat dinner, then Rob makes me come with him to walk the dog. Kiefer with his new training collar that the obedience woman recommended (thanks to Leigh) is walking almost like a dream. When we get back to the house I tell him I want to go to Ikea to stock up on the water glasses I like that we're running low on. It's not really that I've got some urgent need for glasses. I just have to do something normal, ordinary, reassuring, small.

'Do you like the clear ones or the blue ones?' I ask him, holding up one of each.

'Yeah, they're great.'

'Which ones?'

'Neither. I mean, the blue ones.'

'But they won't match. We've got the clear ones . . .'

'Well, get the clear ones, then. They're nice too. I think I like them best.'

'Rob?' I stand still, holding a glass. 'Where are the deeds to our house?'

'You what?' He's bending over to tie the lace of his

running shoe and he looks over his shoulder at me. 'What's that got to do with water glasses?'

'Not a lot, but where are they?'

'In our safe. In the spare bedroom.'

'I don't know the combination.'

'Yeah. Have you ever wondered why? Because knowing you, you'd write it down and shove it in your bag along with the words 'bedroom safe combination'. You'd probably even draw a bloody map to go with it. And the mugger who nicked your bag would be having a field day by now.'

I smile at him and he stands up and kisses me. Then he turns. A pretty young woman goes past in a pair of very tight white jeans, and Rob's eyes follow her.

'Are you looking at her bum, by any chance?'

'Never,' he says. 'I mean, who would look at bums when there are glasses to stare at?'

I slap him and he grabs me. He pulls me into him, wraps me in his arms. A woman holding a glass candlestick looks at us. Rob starts singing one of his little songs: 'My wife, in the middle of I-k-ea. My wife, oh how much I really love her,' to the tune of Madness's 'Our House'.

His warm breath makes my hair fly around. Then he tangos me down the aisle and dips me at the end. I giggle and feel a real wally. The woman with the candlestick stares warmly at us.

'I thought I'd lost you, you know,' he says, pulling me into him again, turning quite heavy and serious. 'I know I've been hard to live with lately, for reasons I can't explain, Jill . . . I thought you'd lost patience with

me . . . that I'd driven you away.' His warm hands
clutch my face, I can feel the callouses on them. 'I love
you, Jill. I'd die if we broke up. It'd kill me to think I
ever drove you to do what Leigh did. Two out of three
marriages here have split up, but I swear I'll never let
that happen to ours. You – and we – mean more to me
than anything in this world.'

I burrow my shameful face into his shoulder, breathing in his smell. Thank God I never told him. Owning
up would have been selfish. Guilt isn't some kind of
time-share arrangement. It's something that only I
must, and should, own the lifetime lease to.

'You'll never lose me, Rob. I love you, I always have,
I thank God for you.'

'Why d'you love me when I've been so bad to you?'
he strokes my cheeks with his rough thumbs.

I put a hand over his mouth. 'Sssh! You were never
bad. You deal with things the only way you know how,
like we all do. And you've a right to do that and to not
have to hide it all away from me behind some front.' I
stare intensely into those two sapphires for eyes.

'I don't deserve you,' he says and kisses me, an
earnest kiss that, by its very nature, is passionate. The
woman with the candlestick backs into a pyramid of
water glasses and sends them crashing to the floor.

Later, in bed, I lie with my face on his chest, deploring
myself and wracked with guilt that he thinks I'm such a
good woman. Occasionally in this life we get a lucky
break. What happened tonight in Ikea was mine.

I lie there for ages, taking in the silence of our room,
the gentle rise and fall of his breathing carrying me

away from these awful thoughts that sabotage my happiness – thoughts about coming clean. Then he moves his head, tilts his chin to mine. I feel his lips, the light suction of his mouth moving tentatively over mine. For a few moments we do this gentle, slow, beginners' dance, then . . .

'I can't.'

'I know,' he says. He plants an understanding kiss at the corner of my mouth. 'It's okay. I just want you to know, Jill, that I . . . I promise to be a better husband to you, to be the man I was—'

I stop him by rolling onto my back, pulling him into a position where I'm cradling his head in my arms, trying to keep my voice from choking. 'Can we not talk, Rob? Can we just take this slowly? Recover slowly?' And then I just hold him there.

I don't know in what order things happen next. What I do know is it all happens so quickly that I feel like travelling sound. My dad rings me at work. My mam tried to iron her petticoat while it was on her body. When my dad tried to stop her, she went for him with the iron. He says there's barely a mark on him, but I hurry over there after work. He's got a long-sleeved shirt on even though it's quite hot out. 'Roll your sleeves up, dad,' I order him.

'It's nowt!' he flaps his arms, brushing me off him. 'Roll them up!'

His forearm bears the clear inverted V of an iron mark.

My first reaction is anger at her, then I think, God, it's not her fault! It's not her will.

'You can't go on like this!' I snap at him. 'At this rate, it could be you going before her – do you realise that?' And it'll all be my fault because I failed to intervene and make some tough decisions for him, which he can't, or won't, make himself.

'I know,' he says. 'Something'll have to be done.'

We sit in the living room, me in the armchair and my mam and dad next to one another on the couch, none of us saying much, but the silence speaks volumes. My mam must remember something, though, because she keeps watching him guiltily out of the corner of her eye. 'Oh, come here,' she finally says to him. She takes his limp arm in her hands and gently runs a finger around the burn. 'That looks nasty.' She tuts, as though some bad person has done this bad thing to him, and woe betide them when she finds out who it was. Then she lowers her head and kisses beside the mark.

'You're my lady-love,' my dad says to her, practically singing the line, and I just about cry.

I stay a while, then drive back home, not knowing what I'm going to do about the pair of them. I hear the date announced on the car radio. 16 August. Shit. Tomorrow is Rob's mother's birthday and I forgot all about it. I rush to the corner shop and grab the first 'Mother' card I find. The checkout girl makes some crack about how she must be a real special old soul as it took me so long to find the right verse. Then I get home. Last night, on our way back from Ikea, Rob said he thought we should go on holiday to get away from all this misery. Somewhere nice. The Caribbean maybe. 'How about Barbados?' I had said, not taking him seriously for a second. Now, sitting on our hall table, is an envelope with *Jill* written on it. I open it. Inside is a copy of the online booking for two weeks in Barbados at the end of September.

'Rob?' I shout. 'Rob?' There's no reply. That's weird, the telly isn't on. I wonder if he's out walking the dog. 'Rob?' I go into the sitting room, and his jacket's tossed over the back of the settee. The dog is lying on the floor on our white rug, looking at me mournfully. 'Rob?' I shout again, when I see his shoes under the coffee-table. Rob hasn't left his shoes lying around since the dog massacred his best pair. Funny, when I walked through the door the air felt ominous. I hurry upstairs.

I suppose, in a way, I know. Doom has an atmosphere of its own.

I barge into our bedroom. Rob is lying in bed, the back of his arm laid across his eyes. He doesn't move. 'Rob,' I say again. 'What's wrong?'

He moves his arm just enough so he can look at me. His eyes are bloodshot, raw. 'I've just had Leigh on the phone.'

17

I feel like you feel when you're running fast and you fall and there's that stunning smack of concrete.

He knows.

I pat around for the edge of the bed, lower myself beside his feet. He looks at me with pitiful sadness and regret. We sit like this, locked into a study of each other, for what feels like an age.

'How did you do it, Jill?' he finally asks quietly.

A couple of tears land on my khaki trousers. I shake my head.

He breathes a long sigh. 'So, she's not lying, then?' He sits up against the bed-head, draws his legs away from me, grasps his shins. He's got that harrowed, waxy pallor that always worries me when I see it.

'You know, I thought maybe she got the wrong end of the stick, or just blew something way out of proportion, or she'd plain gone off it and made the whole thing up. That's what I thought, Jill.' The anger mounts in his voice. 'I was waiting for you to come home and tell me it wasn't true.'

I stare into the space where his feet were, tears dripping off the end of my nose. He's done with me. I feel it in the way he stares at me, in the loss that hangs in the air. I push the heels of my hands into my eye sockets, hard, until I see a kaleidoscope of black stars and flashes. 'Rob,' I moan, then look up with blurred vision.

'Who is he? I couldn't make sense of what she said. Something about you met him down the town, or the beach . . .' His voice is ratcheted up with anger and disappointment. There is not one iota of love left in his expression. I try to swallow, to speak, but my throat feels constricted. I can barely breathe.

'Who is he, goddamn it? Tell me.'

I clutch my mouth, the urge to vomit stirs in my throat. 'He's . . .'

'He's who?'

'A lifeguard. At Seaburn beach.'

'A what?' His cheeks flush red. 'How old is he?'

'About forty.'

'Forty? A forty-year-old lifeguard!' His face fills with mocking disgust. 'I didn't know there were such things.' Then he springs off the bed. 'Jesus. Fuck,' he shakes his head, goes over to the window where he stands and looks out blindly. Next-door's kid is chattering away to her dolls in the garden. The air is pungent with my disgrace.

I start making a sound that's caught somewhere between a cry and a gasp. 'Look, he wasn't some . . . He's Russian. He was a lawyer in Russia. He was a nice man.'

I can't believe that I've just told my husband that the man I was unfaithful with is nice. I retch, my insides just quietly coming up into my throat and sliding back down again. He doesn't seem to notice or care.

'Why would she say you met him down the town, then? Were there two of them?' He shoots me a look over his shoulder. 'I mean, is that what you did on your Friday nights? You and her? Go scouting for fellas? Were there others?' He glares at me. 'How many others have there been, Jill?'

'Of course there've not been others! What do you think I am?' He stares at me like he knows exactly what I am. 'Oh, I'm not going to talk about this, Rob, I'm not. Not if you're just going to stand there with some dim view of me—'

'You fucked a forty-year-old lifeguard!' he shouts.

I bawl. 'It wasn't like that!' There was the note. How he remembered me. I scramble off the bed, stand facing him, rail at him. 'You don't understand! Why d'you think I did it? Eh? Tell me why?' My knees buckle and I hit the floor.

For a moment he just looks at me, stopping my drama. 'I don't know, Jill. You tell me why.'

He sits on the edge of the bed, now, with his back turned, unfeeling to the pathetic hump of me sitting on the carpet. Memories of him tenderly plucking me out of our wardrobe flood me. I'm vaguely aware of incoherently apologising, begging; and him standing now, watching me.

I feel my way back to the edge of the bed, sit cross-legged and cling on to an empty bit of the duvet cover. I sit like this for ages and he doesn't speak, still just stands there. 'I was so lonely, Rob. You pushed me so far away. You didn't seem to see me as a woman any more. I was just this . . . flatmate. A flatmate you barely spoke to. I was like a wallflower in my own marriage – sitting there waiting for somebody to come along and ask me to dance.'

Just saying it now, it feels so insignificant, like I'm exaggerating for effect. I'm trying to remember how awful it was for me, to somehow support my case. I'm trying to recall the despair I must have felt to do what I did, but I can't. I don't understand. It. Me. Anything, any more.

'A flatmate?' he says, sceptically. 'What the hell are you on about? A wallflower?'

'You never touched me!'

'What d'you mean? I always touch you. I hold you. I treasure you . . .' He genuinely looks like he's got no idea what I'm talking about.

'You never wanted to have sex!'

His waxy cheeks flush with colour. 'Oh, for fuck's sake! So we didn't do it for what, a few weeks? A few weeks in ten years of marriage! So that was enough for you to run off and go and fuck some loser on a beach?'

'He wasn't a loser! And it was more than a few weeks, Rob. It was months. Nearly six months.' God. Six months. Under two-thirds of the term of a pregnancy. Was that all it was?

He flings his hands in the air, gets off the bed. 'I suppose you bloody wrote it in a diary. Six months in ten years of marriage. Good God. I mean, I cannot believe you, you know. How insensitive you are. What happened to 'in sickness and in health'? Did you ever stop to think what I was going through, Jill? How responsible and bloody guilty I felt? How horrible I felt for what I was denying you? Did you ever think that maybe that put me out of the mood? Maybe there was a bit more going on in my head than getting off.'

I have never heard Rob shout. I don't think even Rob has heard Rob shout. We stare at each other, fiercely startled, my heart hammering while he hovers over me in that posture that says he's resisting the urge to kill me.

'Do you know what it's like to come home and lie nearly naked on the settee and have your husband take so little interest that he actually walks out of the room? Or to repeatedly try to look nice, smell nice, dress up, plan anniversaries, do stupid belly-dances . . . anything to coax some kind of life out of the man you're married to – yet nothing works? And he won't even tell you what's wrong. That's the worst part. He won't talk to you and, worse than that, he just seems to act like everything's normal. And your friends and the girls you work with all go on about how they've got to keep fighting their men off, and you just sit there thinking, what on earth is wrong with me? What's happening to me? To my life?'

We stand there, eyeball to eyeball, in a grizzly stand-off, fighting for the title of who deserves more pity. I calm down. 'I know you were going through a lot of pain, Rob. But so was I. And I didn't ask you to feel responsible for being infertile. It had to be one of us. It could have just as easily been me. I told you I wasn't bothered if we never had kids. But you would never listen. You seemed to want to refuse to believe that.'

'Oh, yes, I wanted to. I really fucking wanted to.' He rubs a hand over his mouth, shakes his head again. 'Jill didn't want a kid. Jill wanted a kid. Jill didn't want a kid again. Jill loves kids. Jill hates kids. Jill sits and cries because she can't have a kid.'

'Well, it was the same with you! I distinctly remember you saying there was far more to life than raising little snotnoses. Those were your words. Then you even stopped going out with your mates because they were always on at you about when you were going to have kids, and they were all having kids, and kids were all everybody our age was talking about. Every fella in the street with his baby . . . it was like walking through a minefield. But try to get you to open up—'

'Yeah, and you would have been so supportive, wouldn't you? You go and run off with a fucking Russian bloody lifeguard. Thanks. Thanks for the support and the sympathy.'

'It wasn't like that!' I yell as he walks back to the window again and stares out. 'I gave you as much sympathy as anybody can give a bloody brick wall. But what was I supposed to think? That because we couldn't have kids we were never going to have a sex life again?' But maybe I could have tried harder. Maybe I should have found some other more effective, less emotional way to deal with Rob's crisis. Did I give up more easily because the Russian came along? If he hadn't have, would I have fought harder?

'Don't be ridiculous,' he says calmly, doubtfully.

I put my hand on my chest and I can feel my heart pounding into my palm. We're just going round in circles. I don't even know what we're arguing about any more.

He does a sharp intake of breath; moments pass, bringing the tension down. 'So, are you in love with him? This lifeguard? I mean, Jesus, Jill.'

'In love? God, how could you even think that? It was only . . . It only happened once.'

He holds up a hand. 'I don't want to know.'

But I know he does. Certainly some things. So I tell him. How we met, the coincidence of the note on my car, his having seen me before around the town. About Leigh and my loneliness. 'This man made me forget myself, Rob. More than his good looks and anything else, he made me laugh. He made me light. And he looked at me as though the presence of my body in front of him was some irresistible tease. And I loved that. I was turning him on in a way that I could no longer do with the man I most wanted to. And until I could decide what to do with that pretty significant detail in my life, I allowed seeing him to somehow save me.' It strikes me that I borrowed that particular piece of poppycock from Leigh.

He stands there with his back to me, in that I'm-not-listening-but-I'm-listening posture, shaking his head from time to time. When I say the bit about seeing Andrey saving me, he groans. I think of us in Ikea, him singing me his little song, and I mourn that little song, because I know he'll never sing it to me again. 'I never meant for it to happen, Rob. You won't believe that, but it's true. It was just . . . I don't know, something essentially harmless. A distraction.'

'Distraction?' He huffs. His hand goes to his face. He seems to wipe his eyes.

'You have to forgive me. Please tell me you will, Rob, I have to know we're not over.' Over. The word kills me. I bawl from the bottom of my lungs.

He turns, looks at me, and there are lines on his face that were never there before. Lines I've put there, and tears in his eyes. And I hate myself for making a big guy cry. 'My God, Jill, were things so bad between us? Had you totally given up on us?'

'I don't know. I don't know how I felt then, Rob, because I'm just so overwhelmed with how I feel now.'

Passion. Sex. How trivial it all sounds now, against what I'm standing to lose.

'Why did it only happen the one time?' he asks, after a long, sad study of me. 'If I'm supposed to believe that.' He perches on the window-sill and I can't believe how handsome he is with the sun backlighting him. I cannot lose this angel of a man.

The feeling that I'm about to vomit returns. 'I don't want to talk about it, Rob. I don't think I can.' My voice is barely a whisper.

'But I want to know. Why weren't there more times?'

I rub my eyes. That tawdry little flat comes into my head again, and Andrey banging into me the way he did, the way that Rob never has, like you see in bad porn. I pinch the bridge of my nose. 'Because it was terrible! He was like some monster.' Part of me can't believe I'm telling my husband about revolting sex I had with some middle-aged lifeguard.

'But five minutes ago you said he was a nice man.'

A small sob escapes from me. 'Because I thought he was.'

He's staring at me hard. 'He was nice to me, so I thought he'd be nice. I thought he thought there was something special about it too – the way we'd met and everything. But it was awful, Rob. I don't know how it got so far . . . I wanted to stop it but he was just so carried away. By the time I realised . . . I told him to, but it was too late.'

Didn't I? Why is there still this fog in my head?

I look at him and wonder how a man who is already standing still can suddenly seem to stop moving.

'What're you saying, like?' A look passes over his face: a stunned, sad, gentle humanity. 'That he raped you?'

Just for one second I think, is he going to forgive me if I say he did? Even though I went willingly to his flat? We hold each other's gaze. My heart hammers with the adrenalin of a very bad lie poised to pass my lips. But Andrey wasn't a rapist. I shake my head.

His face hardens. 'So, it was just bad sex.'

I remember the shock of his private parts touching mine, his mouth on my breast, a strange man trespassing on Rob's territory. 'I know, Rob, that this will sound like the oddest thing in the world, but I am probably the only woman I know who would take a lover only to get down to it and lie there wishing it was her husband.' He looks at me curiously. 'See, I wanted to feel wanted. But when it came down to it, I only wanted it to be you.' It should somehow make me less unfaithful, but it doesn't.

He sinks down on the edge of the bed, with his back to me. 'So, I take it there was no mugging? You made that up?'

I nod. 'I left my bag at his place.'

He processes this, then snorts. 'So the phone . . . when I rang, it was him who answered?'

I shut my eyes. 'Probably.'

'Him I reported to the police? That's why you were so upset about it?'

I nod, and he says 'Fuck' again. Then there's silence. Then he says, quietly, 'What a fool you've made of me.'

I have.

'I trusted you.' He says it so innocently, frankly, vulnerably. 'If there was one person in this world I'd have said wouldn't have it in her to do this, it would have been you, Jill.' He shakes his head in quiet disbelief, almost laughs.

We don't say much after that. Rob lies down on the bed, on top of the duvet, the sunken shadows under his eyes seeming to darken the more I stare at them. I remember my mother once saying that marriage is a series of tests. How's he going to stand up to this one? I curl up at his feet, feeling bled of all energy. We stay like this, me waiting, vacantly watching the red numerals of the clock click over as though they're the last moments of my life, hoping for a stay of execution.

'Rob,' I eventually say, startling him. 'I have to know what you're thinking. Talk to me. Will you tell me what we're going to do?'

He stares, unblinking, at the ceiling. Then his eyes

slide to mine. 'Well, what are *you* going to do is more the question.'

I struggle to sit up. His face has a ruthless sadness to it that panics me. 'What d'you mean?'

'Well,' he says, with an almost flippant finality. 'Obviously you're moving out.'

18

I have to keep pinching myself as I load my car with the six boxes and three suitcases that contain everything that's 'mine' and not 'ours'. 'Make sure you're not here when I get back,' Rob said as he went off to work with his dog.

I'm moving in with my mam and dad for now. Until I can think how to get him back. But it'll not be easy. Rob may be a bit more sophisticated than your average Geordie male, but like all grafters whose grandads were miners, he's a 'no messing' bloke. Once he's made a decision, he rarely goes back on it. In ten years of marriage, I can't think of a time when he has.

We've already agreed to sell the house. He says he wants to get on with his life! 'What?' I asked. 'You mean try to meet somebody else?'

'Maybe. Or maybe you've put me off women. Maybe I'll be just fine on my own. Me and the dog.' He gave Kiefer's collar an over-zealous rub.

I stand on the curb, fish in my pocket for my hankie, look back at my house and get a massive hit of separation anxiety. I don't blame him for wanting rid of me. I'd be the same if the shoe were on the other foot. But the point is, it's not. And I'm not feeling very fair and square and noble right now. I go back in and plonk myself on the settee. I look around at our sparse but solid furniture that Rob made, the bare rectangles on the walls where the framed photos of us used to hang until I packed them to take them with me. Taking them down felt like emptying a house after a death. No, I think, Jill and Rob live here. Not Rob on his own. Not some other lovers who might move in and have the luck we didn't.

'I love you,' I told him, after our terrible fight.

'I love you too,' he said. 'And I always will. But Jill, you've sickened me. My pride won't let me be with you any more.'

If he'd said he didn't love me, I would have felt this situation had hope.

I hug a cushion and try to squeeze those horrible words from my brain. I will make him change his mind. And if we never have sex again, that's fine. It's a small price to pay to go to bed with him, wake up beside him, live my life beside him as he lives his.

'You're still here,' he says, when he comes in and finds me attempting to put together a tuna fish salad. I've unpacked the photos and hung them back up again.

'Like Hadrian's Wall.' The dog pads over to me, slurps a tongue up the backs of my legs.

Rob rakes in the cupboard and opens a can of salmon as though defiantly showing me that he's not about to eat anything I've touched. I abandon slicing cucumber, go and sit and watch him eat the undrained fish that he's just dumped on a plate, bones, skin and all. Kiefer pushes two moist, black, twitching nostrils under his elbow.

'Go,' he says quietly, when I follow him upstairs to bed. I try to snuggle him but he arches his spine, pushing me away. 'Please, Jill. Just leave me alone.' When I don't he flings off the duvet, grabs his pillow and storms into the spare room, locking the door behind him.

I spring out of bed, rifle in the wardrobe for a wire coat-hanger. Many a time Rob will pick the lock when I'm on the loo. Shocking me off the pot. His idea of funny. I go to the door and jiggle the end of the wire in the lock. 'Shit,' he says, when I go in. 'If you're going to do this, I'm leaving.' He gets up, storms back into our bedroom, and starts filling his sports bag. Bloody hell, he's not kidding, is he?

I follow. I cling on to the door-frame, feeling close to collapsing. I see him being available for somebody else the second he walks out of this door. Falling in love again. Replacing me. 'Don't leave me,' I say, clinging to his shoulders as he zips his bag. He stands there, clearly not wanting to go – because there really is nowhere for him to go, except to his mother's, and I can't see him doing that and having to explain everything. He abandons the bag, takes hold of me and gently shoves me out of the room and locks the door. I bang on it for a bit, ashamed at my appalling behaviour, but relieved, too, that he's changed his mind. Then I suddenly feel so knackered and destroyed, I slump to a heap on the floor.

★   ★   ★

In the morning, I wake up still there, sore all down my right side. I can hear him in the shower in our en suite. When I try our bedroom door, he's unlocked it so I go in. His bag is on the floor. I go into the bathroom, sit on the toilet lid watching his moving silhouette through the glass door. When he comes out, he towels off like I'm not there. I sit across from him in the kitchen as he eats his Rice Krispies. The air has a sad, silent understanding to it. I've been bad. This cold-shoulder treatment is my punishment. I have to weather it because I'm praying that forgiveness will be the silver lining to this dark cloud.

On his way out, he turns and fixes me with a frank, unforgiving face. 'Jill, if you're not gone before I get back, I'll just move out myself. Your choice.'

'My God, you really do want rid of me.'

His eyes hold mine over his shoulder before he disappears out of the door. 'I want rid of you, yes.'

Those words, they engrave themselves on my heart as I drive through to Sunderland. God – me, a cheat. There's really nothing original about it, is there? I'm like a bad joke. But cheating is weak. It is so bloody weak and I never was weak.

I switch the radio on as I swing off the roundabout and head towards the Board Inn, and Linda Ronstadt's singing 'Blue Bayou'. I don't even notice the traffic lights, and sail right into the back of a red Toyota. I register the crunch of metal, the way I lurch slightly forward. The driver, a middle-aged chap with a big gut, is out of his car, having words with my unresponsive face through the glass. As I wind down my window, he mumbles something about having to get to hospital because his wife's gone into labour. I look at his belly, catch words: damage, insurance, phone number. He waggles a pen and paper at me. My lack of reaction flusters him. I mechanically take his pen. Before he cocks a leg into his car, he looks back at me and shakes his head like I'm a very bad person. Then off he drives to his wife and new baby. I realise I've just given him Rob's and my home number.

When I get to my parents' bungalow I put my big dark sunglasses on like some fallen Hollywood starlet. My dad opens the door, does a double take. 'Good God, are you gannin on holiday, or is this your impression of Ray Charles?' I peel off my glasses. 'Gaw!' he says. 'What's the marra, chucka?'

'Everything,' I tell him. But I'd never tell him what. My dad has some pretty old-fashioned ideas about women behaving like ladies. His lady-love looks up from the telly when I walk into the sitting room. 'Hello, sweetheart,' she says, in some mental twilight of detached recognition. I want her to stand up, hold me and make everything better. But in her pretty, transparent gaze she feels gone from me. Elizabeth Mallin might be sitting here, but she's just a shell in which my mother doesn't live any more.

And that about characterises the next little while. We are shells in which we don't live any more. I try to settle into the clutter of the spare room among all the old furniture that my parents brought with them from their last, much bigger house, and couldn't bear to part with. I sleep in my old single bed, the one I slept in when I dreamt of meeting a man like Rob. My first night I wake up and it's dark and I don't know where I am. I struggle to sit up, and smack my head off a wall I'm not expecting to be there. As I clutch my sore head, it dawns on me, and I fill with plainspoken loss. I peer at my watch in the moonlight. 4 a.m. Will he be lying there like me, beset with grief for us, wanting to run to me, forgive me and take me back? Somehow, I can't see it.

On my first morning, I come out of the bedroom to find my mam and dad having a set-to in the hall. My mam is trying to get out of the door with four carrier bags filled with clothes on her arm. My dad has her arms in his grip and there's a right old tussle going on.

'She's packed her bags and she says she's leaving. She said she's going to stay with her mother in York.'

She goes for the front door handle and I immediately rush to stop her.

'It's locked,' my dad tells her, patiently, like he's reasoning with an imbecile. 'You can't go anywhere, Bessie. I've got the key.' But my mother keeps rattling away at the handle, like a tormented prisoner who has found a window of opportunity to break out. 'Bessie,' my dad calmly strokes her hand. 'Come on now, love. Howay, lass.'

'You brought her here!' my mam turns and fixes me with her gaze that is, today, unfairly lucid.

'She thinks you're my girlfriend,' my dad explains.

'Floozie!' she spits at me, with sharp contempt. 'Can't keep your own man so you want to take somebody else's!'

I clap my hands over my face. 'That's it! I'm calling the doctor! We can't go on like this! This is mad! It's a madhouse in here!' I fight back the urge to cry. I should be coming down on one of their sides, but it feels like I'm coming down on my own.

'Don't be coming here and ordering us about! If it's a madhouse, it's our madhouse, so go home, we don't want you here.' Then he looks at me, shocked, appearing, by the heightened purplish colour of him, to be about two minutes away from a heart attack. 'Oh, I'm sorry, lass. You kna' I didn't mean that.' He wraps my mam in a big cuddle. 'They'll take her away from me!' he wails, and my mother stares out at me across his shoulder, quietly, innocently.

When she settles down, I manage to persuade my dad to at least let me call a doctor out. I ring the health centre and they send Dr Reilly, a good-looking lad with smiling eyes and red hair that looks steamrolled straight. 'Irish,' my dad whispers. 'Don't they have room for him in Ireland? How old do you think he is, thirteen?' Dr Reilly says that the last entry on my mother's file was in 1976. 'That's because our family doesn't believe in doctors,' my dad tells him.

The doctor asks my mother her name. And she tells him, 'Elizabeth. Or Bessie, as my husband calls me.' She gives my dad a lucid, disapproving, superior smile. 'Makes me sound like a black Labrador.' The doctor looks at me sceptically, as if to say, *You sure there's something wrong with her?* My dad looks at me like a man triumphant. Dr Reilly gives us some pills to supposedly calm her, and an emergency phone number. He tells us that, of course, the very best thing would be for my mother to be admitted to a home where they can take proper care of her.

'Aye, aye, right, lad,' my dad gets hold of him – one hand on the seat of his trousers and the other on the scruff of his neck – and frogmarches him out of the door, then down the garden path, so fast that the doctor trips over his own feet trying to keep up. 'Go and push your prescriptions on some other poor, unsuspecting bugger.' Free of my dad's clutches, the doctor flees to the safety of his car, turning only once to catch my apologetic expression and giving me a thin, aghast smile.

I can't face work again, so I ring in sick, rattle off some rubbish about a bug. Wendy rings me. I had almost forgotten about her. My heart sinks. Oh, God, this is where I have to start telling everybody, isn't it? I stare at her number on my call display. I don't pick up. I can't do it.

At some point I throw up. My dad keeps feeding me tea. Then he messes around in the kitchen and somehow produces mince and Yorkshire puddings. We eat by the small bay window overlooking the lawn that's surrounded on all sides by old person's semi-detached bungalows. 'What happened to her place?' I nod to the house opposite, with newspaper over the windows.

'Dolly Oliver? She snuffed it, love. Stroke. About a month ago.'

I look at my dad's hand furled around his tea mug and get a fresh reminder of how frail he is and how he's not going to be here for many more years. 'Is it strange, Dad, to see people you've known all your life die?

People who were young with you, had kids when you had kids . . .'

He leaves his carrots. 'Not really, love. We all have to do it. So long as we've lived a good life and we've treated those we love well, there's no need to be frightened to leave this world.' He searches my face.

Who will I grow old with now?

More to the point, who will Rob?

'What you doing the Ray Charles for, again?' He squeezes my hand. 'She never knew you cared.'

'Who didn't?'

'Dolly Oliver,' he slaps me playfully.

Somehow I make it through a week. A week of my mam's tantrums and my dad's tears, the fire on full blast, the telly blaring, my mam's dirty underwear showing up in strange places, my dad's lectures about not switching the lights on and off as it wastes the electric, or his tapping on the loo door every time I've just got into a bath, telling me he's bursting for the toilet . . . My dad screaming like a banshee in the middle of the night. I'd forgotten about his nightmares. He's had them from as far back as I can remember. They consist of him squealing in progressively higher notes until he reaches a blood-curdling squeal crescendo, at which point my mother usually sends her elbow right through his ribcage, and he wakes up. He never remembers anything afterwards, and they've never seemed to harm him in any way. And then there are the comings and goings, the routine non-events of the neighbours and people passing by the window.

Of course, amidst all of this, I ring Rob. Listen to his voice on our answering machine. About fifty times. It strikes me that I've done the same telephone stalking business quite recently, only with a different prey. If he answers, I hang up. The other day he said, 'Hello? Hello?' And then, 'Jill, is that you?'

'No,' I replied, and hung up. Since then he's stopped answering.

I drive home. I sit parked on our street, staring at our house, waiting for Rob to come out. Then I follow him. To work. To the grocer's. To the dog park. I reckon that if somebody saw me and tried to have me arrested for it, Rob would probably happily watch while they threw me in jail.

And then I pluck up the courage to ring Wendy. And in the dimness of her Tiffany-lit sitting room, holding a glass of wine I can't drink, I tell her what I did. She listens for hours, slowly polishing off an entire bottle of wine with a certain mechanical lift to her arm. I have to be a bit careful what I say, though. I mean, I can hardly tell her, *Oh, Wendy, Leigh was having such a great time shagging your husband that the idea of having my own affair became irresistible.*

But as for what happened in Andrey's room, I don't tell her that. I just say it only happened once and I felt too guilty to do it again.

Of all people, I have most dreaded Wendy's reaction. Yet she listens with an almost therapist-like understanding, completely without judgement, in a way that I wouldn't have thought she'd be capable of, being the wife of a cheat. But she says one thing that stings me to my soul. 'What surprises me, Jill, is that I would have thought nothing and no man would have ever tempted you to stray. I wouldn't have thought it would even be a last resort for you.'

'But what are you supposed to do in the circumstances I was under, Wendy? When your husband won't have anything to do with you physically and you can't even talk about it?' *But that's not true. He was physical. He was loving. He just wasn't sexual. Was that so bad?*

She seems to think hard. 'When you know the reason for it? When you know he's just learned some shocking news about himself, and you know that fertility is a very tender subject for a man . . . I don't know. I suppose you give him time.'

Time.

Yes. Why didn't I?

Next, I get the letter. I recognise who it's from by the envelope. They've sacked me. Too many unexplained absences. Unreliability. Refusal to provide doctor's confirmation of blah blah blah . . . The paper falls from my hand.

My lovely job at the football club! All my lovely pals I go for lunch with. They all ring me. They hate Swineburn, as they now call him. They think he had it in for me all along. But they can't understand why I didn't just go on the sick. Heather tells me a friend of hers did that when her husband had an affair. So they think Rob cheated. And, dreadful as it is, I don't feel like disillusioning them. I'm flattered they care. I want them to go away.

My dad gives me a hand-out from his pension. 'Don't worry,' he tells me. 'Gordon Brown needn't know we're splitting it three ways.'

'Don't worry' – but I do. I mustn't be hiding it well, because in the dead of night I wake up conscious of a presence in the room. I think I smell her talcum powder first. 'Mam,' I whisper.

She hovers above me then she bends her face to mine. 'Jill, my precious daughter.' Her warm hand lightly touches the side of my face. 'No matter what happens in this life, I want you to remember one thing. Remember that I love you. And nobody will ever love you like your mother.' Then she kisses me, a wet smack of proud ownership on my lips. And then she goes as softly as she came, into the still of the bungalow with the fridge softly whirring in the background.

How fast is a person supposed to recover? Well, I'm not. Wendy tells me I absolutely have to get back up to the doctor's because my face is so gaunt. 'You're remarkably together,' I tell her, proud of her.

'I'm surviving. I look like this when I'm out doing things. But when I'm on my own with all my thoughts, it's a different story. I'm a lot like you.'

The doctor gives me more than the standard ten minutes, which feels flattering, or worrying, depending on how you look at it. Probably because when she asked what the matter was, I burst into tears. She drags the skin under my eyes down, tells me she's going to run a batch of blood tests. I didn't for a minute think I was depressed, but when she suggests prescribing me uppers, this of course sends me into a right downer. I tell her I'm not ready to take pills for depression. I tell her, actually, I'm fine now. I straighten myself up, walk out of there, and burst into tears outside.

On the weekend I go to Seaburn beach. I know he won't be there, it being September. In fact, the whole place is a ghost town on this pallid, grey day. The fairground has shut down. The coffee shops are closed. Only Morrisons supermarket is showing any signs of life. I walk along the deserted promenade, arrive at the bench where I sat with Andrey when I said that terrible, 'I've never had an affair before . . .' Staring at a melancholy beach, everything comes back to me. I relive it, large as life, like I somehow need to, to forgive myself.

It wasn't all bad, was it? It just should have stopped at a nice flirtation. Nobody can punish you for those. It could have been the summer I almost had an affair. There's some glamour in that. I would have had a whole corridor for my imagination to wander down in my lonely old age, with Rob in the rocking-chair beside me.

Speaking of Rob, later in the week I do something brave. I drive home and knock on my own front door, which is a whole other level of weirdness, let me tell you. I barely recognise his face under three weeks' worth of beard, hair that needs a good cut. His dark blue eyes stare out at me like he's a man in hiding. Then his gaze runs quickly over me. He leaves the door open as he walks back into the house. I go in. The house feels so empty. It's missing me.

Walking into the kitchen feels foreign, like I've been away on holiday and have to reacquaint myself with my life again. Rob opens a can of soup. I'm amazed how thin he's got. The counters are a mess of opened cans, empty bread packets, empty milk and juice cartons, food stuck to the stovetop; his shoes are all over the place. 'I want to come home,' I tell him.

He tips the white soup into a saucepan. 'Not an option.' He turns up the heat and watches the soup sputter.

Something about his disappearing bum in his faded jeans makes me put a hand over my mouth to stop any sound coming out. 'You'd better stir that or it'll stick,' I tell him, trying some form of cajolery. I can already imagine this pan with burnt stuff stuck to the bottom, waiting for me, just like so many others in the past. And I'd clean it, cursing him, resenting him, as though this pan was the end of my world.

Why do we let the small stuff bother us? I'd give the world to have Rob and his gluey pans back, Rob and his shoes on the duvet.

He pours his soup into a bowl, takes a dirty spoon out of the dishwasher, doesn't bother washing it, comes and sits at the table. 'I'll go if you want me to,' I say.

He bites into half a stale French stick. 'Please yourself.' The soup burns his mouth. He gets up and takes a can of pop from the fridge. *Rob*, I wonder, *will I ever kiss you again?* But I think I knew the answer the second I saw the state of him at the door. I will never kiss Rob again. Even if he could forgive me, he would never forget how I made him feel.

I watch him skim the crinkled skin off his soup. I'm not here, as far as he's concerned. His body is healing itself and that means tuning me out.

'How's your mam?' he finally asks. Dinner table chatter of the past; it gets my hopes up.

'Not good. But I suppose not really all that much worse, either.'

'So what you going to do, then? About your job?'

He asks it not without caring, but as though it affects only me, not both of us. It fells me. 'I can't think about that now,' I say. Or I barely say.

He studies me unsympathetically for a few seconds, scrapes his bowl. 'Well, what are you going to do about the bungalow? I mean, I can't see you wanting to live there for too much longer. Are you going to look for a flat or what?'

I stare gauntly at him, disbelieving his cruelty, but he refuses to look at me. My eyes fill up.

'Well?' he asks, finally looking at me again. I want his eyes and his heart to melt for me. Aren't I the person he used to least like to see suffer in the whole world? But he looks at me coldly. 'No good crying over spilt milk,' he says, and he scrapes his chair back and goes to the sink with his bowl and runs the tap. I sit there and tears drop into my lap.

'I hate you,' I say, unconvincingly.

'Yeah, well, I'll live.' He starts washing dishes. He's even got the gall to hum a tune.

That's it. This is so belittling. I get up, too choked even to say goodbye. But I register something as I walk down our passage to the front door. He's stopped washing dishes, and he's listening to the sound of me leaving.

19

Wendy and I go for a day out to Durham. It's the first change of scenery I've had in the month since Rob threw me out, and I've been living 'on death row at the bungalow', as my dad puts it. Again I note Wendy's conspicuously unmade-up face. But other than that, she's turned out like her old self, even tries the same smile. We attempt pie and mash in a falling-down corner of a seventeenth-century alehouse just up from the cobbled market-place by St Nicholas's Church. We drink a draught lager and my misery gets to go first. I fret and she consoles, both of us doing a good job of it. Never once does she pressure me about what I'm going to do, or ask questions she knows I don't have answers to. 'God, I wish I'd confided in you instead of Leigh,' I tell her. 'It's just you only ever had eyes for Neil . . .'

She studies me wisely. 'You're wrong. I think both you and Leigh wanted to think that about me, but it's not true. There have been, over the years, one or two who've caught my eye. With one of them, yes, I suppose something could have happened if I'd have wanted it to. But I never thought a fling with somebody who didn't really know me could be better than all the years invested in my body by somebody who did.'

Yet we do, don't we? Why do we?

'Neil and I were both very inexperienced with the opposite sex. I'd only ever had one other lover before him and Neil had had two. We met so young. But that was never a problem for me.'

'Men are different.'

'Are they, though? I think we like to believe they are, to somehow make them easier to blame. But look at you and Leigh. You both were married.' Then she adds, 'I'm sorry,' when she sees my face. 'I didn't mean it in a recriminating way. I'm just saying I don't blame Neil because he's a man. I blame him because he's Neil.'

I tell her I need fresh air. We walk outside, join the gathering crowd in the market square and listen to a curly-haired student playing 'Clair de Lune' on a violin. A homeless person is sitting on the wall. He's swaddled from head to toe in a commercial fishing net, and there's a ginger kitten crawling all over it, having a field day. We watch its antics for a bit, then go. We take the narrow high street that's closed to traffic and join the slow, quiet milling of people walking down the cobbled road, gathering at shop windows. When we come to Elvet Bridge, we pause to gaze at its unbeatable view of the three majestic towers of Durham Cathedral, set high on the green banks of the River Wear. The day is picture-postcard perfect. But it's missing a feeling that neither of us can bring to it. It's even missing Leigh, and the high old times. I have an I-wish-I-were-here-with-Rob moment, but push it away. I reckon there's enough missing going on already.

'He's living with her, you know,' she says, eventually, flatly, staring down-river at the rowing boats that roll into the distance. 'He's renting one of those new lofts down the Quayside.'

I am almost too floored, and disappointed, to speak. 'Living with her!'

She plucks blades of grass that jut through the stone wall. 'Neil needs somebody to pander to him. He needs to come home to his comforting pile of ironed underwear.'

'Well, he's picked the wrong girl there, hasn't he?'

'Who knows? She was tired of being the one who wore the trousers all the time. Maybe now she'll be content to wash and iron them.' She looks at me and smirks and her eyes are like two dark marbles held up to the sun. 'Isn't that what Denis Thatcher said to a reporter? That he wore the trousers in the relationship, and he washed and ironed them too? That's about the only thing I remember about a lengthy era in British politics. Isn't that sad?'

Her face quickly takes on that distant, dismantled look again. 'He wants to come home. Came round last night. His words were, "Give it another try".'

I scrutinise her hair that she's forced into a cute little ponytail that sticks up like a palm tree from the centre of her crown. 'What did you say?'

'I said "What do you mean, another try? We were never giving it a try in the first place. We've been married for eighteen years. We have two sons."' She looks at me with a harrowed face. 'He said he can't bear her, and now that he's living with her it didn't make sense. Apparently she wants them to buy a house and have Molly live with them.' She goes to bite her nails but stops herself. 'What's really strange about this is that Neil isn't a person to just get bobbed along with the tide.'

'Maybe he just can't be bothered dealing with her right now. I mean, his life has changed radically as well, hasn't it? Maybe he's just catching his breath.'

'Poor him.' That was a rare feat of sarcasm. 'He'll not want Molly. I know how much he didn't want to have a third child, to start from square one again. Sometimes I think he resented being a father because it took him away from the two things he loved most: his job and himself.'

'I'd never have thought, Wend. I assumed he was pleased about the baby.'

'I was hardly going to tell anyone. It doesn't exactly make him look very good, does it? And it's sort of disrespectful to the memory of my daughter, thinking her own father didn't really want her in the first place.' She straightens up from leaning on the wall. 'Come on, let's walk.'

We take a stony short-cut down to the riverbank. Fishermen are casting lines into water that looks like a sheet of green opaque glass. On it quivers the reflection of the cathedral. She stops and gazes across to the other side, to a neat line of moored rowing boats. 'It's not the first time he's cheated, you know.'

'Eh?' Peel me off the floor. Her eyes scan my face for my reaction. She almost smiles. She starts walking again, leaving me lagging there, mouth agape. 'I can't

believe this!' I trot after her. 'Wendy! I had no idea!
How d'you . . . How d'you know?'

'You know,' she says. 'Although I never had any
concrete evidence, if that's what you mean.' She
pushes up an overhanging bramble and we duck under
it, minding our eyes. 'The thing with Neil is he's very
good. Maybe spending your career around dishonest
people, you learn the ropes. You'll never catch him in a
lie. None of Neil's behaviour is typical of the cheat. He
never gets too nice all of a sudden. Never has strange
hairs on his clothing or lipstick on his boxers. He's
never gone off sex – quite the opposite. He doesn't
make excuses to pop out and be gone for hours. He's
not forgetful and I don't have to tell him everything
three times.'

She's a walking magazine article.

I look at her profile, the flush of her cheeks, the half-
inch of grey at the temples where her hair needs
colouring again. 'Well, how do you know, then?'

'D'you want to sit here a minute?' She points to a
graffitied bench missing its central plank. We sit. She
sits forward, hands either side of her knees. I notice
she's not wearing her wedding ring. When will Rob
take his off? When will I take off mine?

'Something happened. Years ago. We'd gone to
Edinburgh for his job. We were in a bar.' She looks
at me briefly, her neck flushed peach. 'There was
hardly anybody there, except this young waitress.
She was a cute little thing in a short tartan skirt, with
long, runner's legs; strawberry blonde hair in bunches.
She was instantly taken with Neil.' She shrugs,

straightens her legs, looks at her clean white running shoes. 'I thought nothing of it. Women always look at Neil. It's par for the course. Anyway, we went and sat down in a corner. It was a nice evening outside and it seemed a pity to be in there, but Neil didn't want to leave, given the girl seemed so happy to have customers . . . We just ordered mineral water. She brought them to us. Neil gave her five pound and told her to keep the change.'

That sounds like Neil. A little bit flash, but not enough to be criticised for it.

'So, she gets this good tip and she looks at him. I can still picture her face. Pretty, but a bit hard, like a young Meg Ryan. She stood there chatting with us. Why were we here? Etc. Then Neil told her he was a police detective.' Her eyes comb my expectant face. 'Women react to that. Every time.' She swats a fly that keeps dancing before her eyes. 'Anyway, a few more people came in. But every time she walked past us she'd look over, not directly at him, but almost as though she was inviting him to look at her. And Neil . . . he was talking to me, but it was the same thing: they were very much aware of each other.' She shakes her head. 'Funny thing is, I don't think either of them was particularly aware of me noticing this. We had our drinks, then he asked her where the toilet was. I remember the offhand way he got to his feet, stood tall and buttoned his jacket, like a man who knows he's handsome. It was a very assured gesture. Everything about him was confident of himself, I thought, as though he held all the power. The girl said it was downstairs, she'd show him.' Wendy shifts on the uncomfortable bench, hugs her knees so her black Capri pants ride up her legs that could use a shave – something you'd never see, back in the days of Neil. 'And I'm sat there thinking, why does this girl want to show my husband where the toilets are? Isn't he big enough to find them himself? And I got a really bad feeling. Just . . .' she punches a fist into the middle of her rib cage, 'I don't know, like I was somehow at a disadvantage. Anyway, she led him down the stairwell. I remember it had prints of jazz musicians on the walls. And just before they were out of sight, I saw her turn and look back at him. And it was all there in her face: that rapt, mischievous, illicit understanding.'

'No! God. Was he gone a long time?'

Her grip tightens around her knees, pushing pockets of muscle out on her arms. 'Long enough.'

'How did he look when he came back up?'

'Well, not like you'd think he'd look if he'd done anything. But I knew he had.'

'How?'

Her pupils drill into mine. 'I knew.'

'So what did you do?'

'Well, I asked him what had gone on. He said I was being ridiculous. It was my bad mind.'

'You don't have a bad mind.'

She smiles. 'I didn't think I did, either.'

She gets up now and we start walking again. 'You have to remember, I wasn't looking for anything to upset my world. I had two boys. I loved him. I was very happy with my life. The last thing I wanted was a reason to leave him.' Our feet crunch stones. We pass a fisherman who turns and says 'Hello,' and three young Chinese girls in a rowing boat whose giggles cut an echo across the still, opaque, green water.

'I never actually saw her come back up again.' Our walking trails to a stop and she seems breathless. 'Whether she left . . . I thought about going down to the ladies' room, but then I thought, what if she's down there? You know, cleaning herself up, or putting her clothes back on. What'll I do? She'd know I knew, then. And I'd know Neil was lying. And I'd have to do something. And I didn't know what I'd do.' The remaining colour drains out of her face.

'My God, Wendy.'

'You always think, when you hear things like this, that "Oh, I'd flip out . . . or I'd kill her . . . or kill him . . ." But when it does . . . I tell you, I didn't know what I'd do. I was intimidated by the situation.' We start walking again, my eyes on the slow forward rhythm of our shoes. 'We got back to the hotel and had a massive fight, because of course I had to bring it up again. But it all boiled down to his word against my suspicions. The way I saw it, I had two choices. I either had to leave him, or believe him. So I believed him.'

'Jesus. So how did you feel towards him after that, then?'

She laughs a little, humourlessly. 'Alert.'

A picture of Neil flashes up in my mind. Neil, who I have always felt was a little bit unknowable, but it added to his appeal. Then I think, hell, he's not the man Leigh thought he was either, is he? The loyal man who was only cheating with her because she was special. 'So, was that it, then? Or did anything else happen?'

'Oh, phone calls to the house. Hang ups. There'd be none for ages, then a run of them. A few other things . . .' She shrugs and I know she's not going to elaborate. 'In the beginning I'd be checking his pockets all the time, his credit card statements. But not trusting the person you live with is the most exhausting state of being that you can be in. It's completely emotionally knackering and poisonous. Besides, I didn't want that sort of unhealthy relationship. That's not who I am.' She stares off into the distance. 'Funny, though – when I found out about Leigh and I asked him how many others there'd been, he hesitated, just for a second, before he said "None."'

'So how many do you think there've been?'

She shrugs. 'Lots.'

'Lots! You're kidding?'

'No,' she almost laughs. 'I know this is a shock to you.'

'Wendy, you never let on . . .'

'I couldn't. It's not something to be proud of. Besides, I'm good at being happy but I'm not good at being sad.' She looks at me, sadly. 'And like I said, there never was real evidence. I wasn't going to walk out on my marriage and rob my lads of a family on a hunch, was I? Even a very strong one. But, I don't know, I feel so . . .' She shakes her head, doesn't finish.

I think of that day in the restaurant when Wendy said *Not always* to Leigh's comment about how she only ever wanted to be married to Neil. Leigh took her two-word response to be – how did she put it when we were talking about it afterwards? – humouring, as though Wendy said it to condescend or just to fit in. But I'm sure she was really just being honest, only we refused to believe it. We pigeon-holed Wendy into being this poster-child for happily-marriedness. Why? Maybe to give us some ideal that we felt our own lives fell short of, to justify our gripes. We walk to the end of the path, and then come back up onto the high street again. 'I did something the other day that I'm quite proud of,' she eventually says, brighter. 'There's a course at Northumbria Uni. It's basically a conversion course for people who think they might want to be lawyers, who have a non-law degree. I'd have to study for the Common Professional Examina-tion, which takes a year full time, and I'd not be able to start it until next September, and that's assuming that I enrol almost this minute to complete my two credits to get my degree. But the CPE would guarantee me a place on the Legal Practice Course, and then after that I'd be working as a trainee solicitor for two years, but I'd be collecting a salary. After that, there's the Profess-ional Skills Course, but that's really only twelve days.' She looks at me, a bit like the radiant Wendy of old again. 'So, Jill, I reckon that by the time I'm fifty I could just about be a fully-fledged solicitor!' She laughs a bit. 'So I think I'm going to go for it. What do I have to lose?'

'That's incredible, Wendy.' And amazing that, as far as life goes, she seems to be back on the horse. 'I can see you making a brilliant solicitor.' She analyses the hell out of everything as it is. 'Would it not just be easier to become a law clerk or something, though?'

'Yes. But I don't want to be a clerk. I want to be a lawyer. I always did.'

I mourn my own job now. She has a goal now. What's mine?

'My problem is, I always tend to need to do things well. So I was a good parent, a good wife. But the whole ultra-domesticated thing has been something I've taken a false pride in. It's not really me. It never was, much as I thank God for my lads . . . I don't know, I suppose if I'd never had children I could still have been happy. A part of me has always felt I short-changed myself by marrying Neil, even though I've always convinced myself that by landing him I'd hit the jackpot.' She huffs; shakes her head. 'Neil knew about the law thing but he showed so little interest in the discussion that he even managed to convince me that I wasn't really interested myself. Because Neil has to be top dog. But I think it's because, deep down, if he didn't trade so much on his good looks, Neil's not really a confident man. And men who lack confidence in themselves don't want successful wives; they don't want wives with brains. Besides, he detests lawyers. Always says they get the bad guys off. So imagine how ironic it'll be . . .' She looks at me, widening her eyes.

We walk to Crook Hall, the medieval manor house that does a smashing home-made afternoon tea, as she tells me the ins and outs of the studying she'd have to do, the courses she's most looking forward to. We claim a table in the shade in a pretty little rose-filled courtyard by the fountain. Then she's flat again. 'Where do you suppose they went to do it? Leigh and my husband.' We've already had the conversation about how we can't believe she made up the name Nick, which is so close to Neil, and she managed to call him that without a slip of the tongue. But then again, she didn't really use his name all that much, I don't think. It was usually just *him*. Come to think of it, I didn't really ask all that much about him. And I was so trusting of her that I never looked for flaws in anything she told me. But now I'm ashamed that I believed so completely in the existence of a person who wasn't real. I should have seen some sort of sign. 'I always wonder that about people who have affairs. Where do they go?'

She holds my gaze before I drop my eyes. I know where they went. And I know where I went too. 'I have no idea, Wendy. Probably to a hotel. Isn't that what people do?' People. Adulterers. Me. The judge and the judged.

I feel her probe me with her gaze. 'What, Newcastle people? Maybe the ones on the television, but this is real life, Jill. In real life people have bills to pay. Responsibilities. They don't run around throwing money at hotels for cheap sex.'

Obviously she must think that's what I had. She knows I know where they went. But she's got too much class to press me.

'You always liked him, didn't you? You and Leigh,' she says after a bit, as we stare at a three-tiered tray of goodies that's been set before us.

'Yes. I suppose it's because he's so damned good-looking, Wendy. You don't see past it. You see his looks, the job he does, and you imagine everything else must be great about him, too. And it didn't help that you seemed so besotted with him. He was so perfect in your eyes, so that made him doubly perfect in ours.'

She gazes through the spray of the fountain and we listen to its silvery sound. 'I was besotted with him.' Her face pales and red patches appear on her forehead. The fine hairs on her arm stand up. She looks chilled. She has picked up her teapot but she has to put it down again. An inch of milky liquid sits in the bottom of her rose-festooned cup. 'But you were wrong to assume I thought he was perfect. I was never blind to his short-comings. I just thought him . . . essential. Essential to me. Isn't that weak?'

I pour her tea for her. 'Well, maybe now you regret not having acted on your instincts, but that's only because what he's done now makes what you thought he might have done back then more likely. Wendy, you stayed in a relationship mainly for your kids. You booted him out the second you found out he was sleeping with Leigh. And you're forty-two and thinking of going to become a solicitor. Weak is the last word I'd use to describe you. You're probably the strongest woman I know.'

She pulls a wry smile and I know she's thinking about her diagnosis. 'But did you know I only ever exercised for him? I hate exercise! I love eating. I love my food. And it loves me – too much.' She laughs ironically, picking up a Yorkshire ham and Brie sandwich. 'But I thought that if I looked as good as I possibly could it would give him less reason to stray. Can you believe somebody could be so soft? I kept thinking that by marrying me so young, he'd missed out. And I know he got opportunities with women far better-looking than I am. I almost felt sorry for him at times.'

'But he married you because he wanted to. Nobody put handcuffs on him.'

'I know. And he loved me. And he was attracted to me. And I know he still is. He just . . . Neil has to live on the edge. That's why he's so good at his job.' She looks around the small cobbled courtyard, tilts her sad face up at the near-cloudless sky. 'Oh, we shouldn't be talking about this. Not here. Not today. Look at it, it's too nice . . .'

It's funny, but suddenly I feel closer to her. With Leigh I suppose I had to know her really well to learn that we were strangers. Yet Wendy has had to open up to me to let me know we really are friends.

Her sandwich sits on the plate with just a half-moon bite taken out of it. 'I'm all right though. I am. I've spent a lifetime suspecting him of being unfaithful. Finding out that he actually has been is surprisingly not that much worse.'

'Why haven't you had it out with her?' I have to ask this, because this is what surprises me the most, along with the fact that Leigh still hasn't phoned and apologised to my friend or offered any explanation. She's just disappeared. It's as though the near decade of our friendship had an embolism and dropped dead.

She shrugs coldly, stares at the bread she's absently poking holes in. 'I can't. I just can't see it happening – me in one corner of the boxing ring and Leigh in the other. Can you? All this over him.'

'No. You have too much dignity for that.'

'I don't have the balls,' she says, surprising me. 'Mind you, if she'd rung me I'd probably have let her have it. But am I going to ring her? Say "Oh, hello, Leigh, I heard you've run off with my husband . . ." It's like being back in that bar again, all those years ago. It fills me with a dread that locks me, immobilises me.' She makes a philosophical face. 'Besides, I don't want her explanation. I just want never to lay eyes on her again. Him neither. All that counts is being there for my boys, now. They're at that age where sex and life, it's all just starting to make sense, and they're getting slapped with a harsh truth. That people who we think would be the last to fail us sometimes go ahead and do it, and leave us with this legacy of never being able to trust. You know, this is the age that I really do believe shapes who we become, whether we become cynics or not, later on.'

'Don't think like that. They've got your influence as much as his – maybe more.'

She lays both hands on her stomach. 'Jill, I don't want them being brought up by his example.' She looks at me vehemently. 'And I never want them living with Leigh.' She says it in a way that suggests I might have some control over that.

'Don't talk like that!' This sounds, morbidly, like she's planning on going somewhere. Not at all like something Wendy would ever say. 'They're never going to live with Leigh. They're only going to live with you – always – because you're their mother.'

She looks at me and I see a glint of humour saving the moment. 'Well, not always. I mean I do eventually want them to get married and move out. Imagine if they were both fifty and still living at home. And I was the breadwinner – the eighty-year-old lawyer, hacking out a living.' We chuckle. We walk out through the rose garden, leaving a tiered tray of goodies we can't eat. 'You know, I spent years thinking if I left him, where would that leave me? Who would I have? And the funny thing is, now I know the answer. I have me. You're born just you, and you go through life buffered by other people, but first and foremost you are just yourself. And then you die just you. So the sooner you get used to yourself, the better.'

Her words won't leave me. She drops me off at the bungalow, gives me a kiss. I watch her car pull away, suddenly very moved by our day. I sneak in the front door and am just picking my way across the floorboards when I hear a quiet, 'Goodnight, lass,' from my parents' room. I'm thirty-five, yet my dad still waits up till I'm home.

'Goodnight, Dad,' I whisper. I get into bed and lie there staring at the ceiling, wide awake.

Maybe that's exactly what I am now. Just me.

20

I drive along the A19 with the radio on. I'm going to look at a flat for rent in Jesmond. Wendy told me about it. Somebody she knows is moving out. I drove by our house the other day again. The 'For Sale' sign still hasn't gone up. It's been nearly two months.

I pull up at the house – number thirteen; lucky for some. It's one of those white three-storey Victorian terraces with well-tended gardens and quiet children playing on the path. I park across the street and sit staring at it.

'You can have both tickets,' Rob said on the phone when I rang him about our Barbados holiday the other day, which is supposed to be this Saturday. 'Take your Russian.'

'Don't say that!'

'Well, then, take somebody, take Wendy.'

'You take them. You go. The holiday was your idea.'

'Well, maybe I will,' he said.

'Or,' I took a big breath. 'We could both go. I mean, we could get separate rooms. But the point is we'd be there together, away from here, we could talk, maybe with a change of scenery we could sort all this out—'

'Get serious,' he said.

I was being serious. And I didn't mean forget it ever happened. What's he take me for? 'Well, I don't want the sodding tickets, so you do with them what you will,' I said and hung up. I am getting truly sick and tired of this.

I stare at this house now, the top window, which is the floor that's available. It's so weird sitting here, looking at a room to rent as a single person, when two minutes ago you were married and you owned your own home. I can't go in.

I go back to my mam and dad's, lie on the bed and stare at the same crack on the ceiling. Sometimes, like now, my memories of kissing Rob are so real that I have to stop what I'm doing and recover from the effect of them. Today I tell myself I'll do this one more time, then I have to stop thinking thoughts that will continue to destroy me.

Wendy asks me if I want to borrow her *Divorce for Dummies* book. Strangely enough, I actually manage a smile. 'Maybe you should become a divorce lawyer,' I tell her. She screws up her face. 'No,' she says. 'I'd have an unreasonable urge to castrate the husbands.'

On 25 September she has her 'procedure'. I go with her and am the first face she sees when she comes round. 'No sex for two weeks. Doctor's orders,' she tells me, and she manages a pained laugh. I stay over a few nights at her house to help out. When the lads go to bed we sit up for hours nattering, her at one end of the settee, me at the other, under the chenille throw. You'll never hear Wendy saying anything self-pitying, but somewhere in the scheme of things she feels it was a

cruel blow to have lost a child, a husband and now – if
her op isn't a success – a womb. 'I've been dreaming
about that strange experience I had when I was pregnant. Remember?'

'I do.' It always gives me the creeps. Wendy was
about six months' pregnant with Nina and she was in a
yoga class, doing relaxation at the end. The instructor
asked them to picture a scene – a personal place that
gave them a sense of calm – a beach, or a spot of
sunlight filtering through trees. Wendy couldn't think
of one. But then something came to her. She saw it as
clearly as if it were real. A dark, outdoor clearing; and
in the centre, risen earth. On the earth was a clutch of
flowers. White flowers, she said. A bouquet. It took a
while for her to realise that she was seeing a burial
place. 'That's how I knew that something awful was
going to happen,' she told Leigh and me, after little
Nina died.

'Jill, I keep dreaming of that feeling I had. When I felt
there was something awful going to happen in my
womb.'

I squeeze her hand. 'If you lose a womb, Wendy, it's
only a very small part of you that'll be taken away. It's
not your brain. It's not your heart. It's not the air in
your lungs. It's a small price to pay for still getting to
have your life. And your dreams and ambitions.' She
nods.

'You all thought I got pregnant with Nina by accident, didn't you?' She looks at me, her uncovered
secret blazing. 'So did Neil. But I didn't. I stopped
taking the pill. I think part of me was scared my lads

were growing up and motherhood was all I knew. And I'd vowed to myself that when they were older I would probably leave Neil because I didn't want a cheat or a liar. Yet I could never actually *see* myself leaving him and being divorced. That fear of the unknown was worse to me than living a lie. So I think having another baby was my way of stalling for time.

The next night she whispers, 'You know what bothers me the most when I think of them together? It's not the sex. It's the thought of them talking about me. You know, intimately. Discussing my body . . .'

'You don't know they will have—'

'Oh, come on. She'll have coaxed it out of him. I can imagine her wanting to know things about me. Very private things.'

'No,' I say. But I'm thinking, Yes. Because I can see a person with dodgy self-esteem behaving like that.

'I'm angry,' she says, suddenly. 'Oh, Jill, I'm hopping mad about her.' She gets up, clatters glasses and bottles in the drinks cabinet and pours us both a large something.

'Maybe you shouldn't be drinking, Wendy, with the pills . . .'

She stands in the centre of her sitting-room floor, tosses back her drink, then refills her glass. 'Fuck the pills,' she says. I have never heard her swear. 'I'm angry, Jill. I'm so angry I want to kill her. I have this inner rage. I want to critically harm her. Isn't that awful?' She bites the side of her hand with the glass in it. 'I want to ring her and call her a thin, ugly-hearted, titless, decrepit bitch.'

'Do. Titless and decrepit would probably be enough to see her off. But not tonight. Not while you're so angry. And not right after your op. It'll do you no good. Come on,' I pat the lovely burgundy velvet settee. 'Sit down.'

'Titless and decrepit,' she chants again. Then she puts a hand on her lower stomach, winces. 'Oh,' she turns to look at me. 'That hurt.' Then she sinks into the settee; and it comes out in a distraught whisper. 'I loved him.' And then it comes out again. But I get the feeling this is one of the last times she's ever going to say it. For one last time the room seems to fill with the ghosts of a bygone marriage.

My house must feel like this, to Rob.

Then she looks at me and says a short, 'I suppose you're right.' I've almost forgotten what she's agreeing with me about.

I pull the chenille throw over our legs again and sink the brandy she's poured for me – and then the measure she's poured for herself, just to stop her having it. 'You know what I could never get over about her?' Wendy says calmly, some time later, when our voices have become yawny. 'Why she didn't get those horrid little teeth fixed. I mean, she made all that money, she'd buy those bags and fancy watches, yet she'd live with those horrid little back teeth.' It's true. Leigh didn't have great teeth. She claimed it was from taking asthma medication as a child. She often joked that she hoped her adopted identical twin had better teeth than her.

I can't help but have a small chuckle. I've never heard so much bitchiness come out of Wendy's mouth, and I love her for it. 'We're talking about her as though she's dead.'

'No,' she says. 'I wouldn't want her to be dead. I think of what a good friend she was to me when I lost Nina. Both of you were.' Then she looks at me. 'Besides, death would be too kind. Let her have Neil. How long do you think it'll be before he cheats again?' She cocks an eyebrow. 'Judging by how deliriously happy he is to be living with her, I'd say not long.'

'And she once told me she could never, ever, be with a cheat,' I say. 'She said her self-esteem just couldn't take it. It'd kill her. She said that's why she'd married Lawrence, because he was a sure, safe bet.'

'Oh, well, poor her. Poetic justice. What a shame.'

One night Wendy's son Ben walks into the room just as Wendy is busy enlightening me with the fact that Neil didn't have half as big a penis as Leigh made out. Her lads have been fabulous through all this. They seemed more shocked that it was Leigh than anything else. Not because she was a friend, but because, as their Paul said, 'Gaw, I thought when married people had affairs they were supposed to, you know, upgrade the model. Park the Peugeot in the back alley and take the Ferrari out for a spin.' Then he told her that she was far better-looking than Leigh. Any day.

Neil will try to get custody, Wendy told them. But their Ben said, let him. There was no way they were going to live with him. And, as Wendy said, they're big lads. Try making them.

'Make way, make way,' Ben says now, and he's holding something at arm's length, pulling a face. It's

a sock. Obviously one of Neil's. We watch in disbelief
as Ben walks over to the kitchen bin, puts his foot on
the pedal, and drops it in there with a 'right, then'. He
dusts off his hands, nods to us, then goes back upstairs.

'It's all an act,' she whispers. I think it's so sweet how
they keep taking turns making sure she takes her
painkillers. 'They hug me and ruffle my hair, watch
videos that I choose. But I see it in the strained silences
as we try to rearrange our simple little routines – like
who gets to drive whom where, now that we have to
factor out Neil – and a second car. I hear it in their
bitter little grunts about how they're never getting
married.'

'They'll be all right.' I envy Wendy her lovely lads.

On my last night at Wendy's I get a surprise. Well, two.
The first is that we're watching the North-East news
with the sound down, and we suddenly see this gaggle
of naked bodies outside a shop. Wendy stumbles for
the remote control. We just get it turned up in time to
hear Mike Neville talking about how fourteen-stone
Madge from Cleveland was the first person over the
threshold when the new Fatz store opened at the
Gateshead MetroCentre. Madge, whose bare arse
looks like curdled cake batter, pads like a pet elephant
into the store to claim her prize. Wendy and I have a
good chortle.

Then . . . Over chicken pie and salad from a bag, she
generously offers for me to move in, as a temporary
alternative to staying at my parents'. The lads say
they're all for it. For a minute it feels like I'm even

being strong-armed. And for a minute it's tempting. But a connectivity of adultery runs between our mutual circumstances, and as long as we're together under the same roof, it's all we talk about. And I'm sure that in the long run it'll pull us down more than it'll help us move forward.

Speaking of which . . .

I manage – miraculously – to get my act together enough to actually go to work. I've got a temporary secretarial job through an agency. It's down the Newcastle job centre, which, let me tell you, is nothing like working for United. Instead of sexy footballers to gaze at, and glamorous lasses to go for lunch with, there are bespectacled Nora Batty types with a meat-and-potatoes sense of humour, and a parade of unemployed Geordies coming to collect their pittance of a dole cheque. I didn't think they existed since Newcastle became so upwardly mobile. But they do. In droves. The employment agency said they just want somebody short-term, so that suits me fine, because I'm just taking life day by day at the moment. Since moving back in with my parents though, and not having Wendy to distract me, I'm not good again. But I go through the motions of filing claims until five o'clock, and have a bit of a crack on with some of the Noras. Strangely, it helps. Then coming back to the bungalow pitches me back into despair. But I see it as a sort of halfway house. If I'm there, instead of in some flat I've signed a lease on, I am halfway back to Rob.

The next day at work, something terrifying happens.

The manager of Claims, Bill Crushing – an intense, overly affable chap who's on Prozac – asks me out. His wife left him for another man. He's not bad-looking for a middle-aged civil servant, but he's nobody you'd set your sights on. I wouldn't care, I've not even been looking nice lately. I know I still look exhausted because my dad will keep gawping at me like I'm the Bride of Frankenstein, and when I glower at him he quickly pretends he wasn't doing it. And unlike at the football club, which was a bit of a daily fashion parade amongst us lasses, I've not been wearing my good clothes to come here, for fear the punters might think I have it too good.

God, if only they knew.

But he must have sniffed out my situation, this Bill, and he wants a kindred soul in misery. He hovers at the side of my partitioned cubicle. I stop him mid-sentence, tell him, nicely, that I've only been separated a short time; that I'm nowhere ready to date again. Voicing the word 'separated' freaks me out. He looks mildly embarrassed. I go and hide out in the toilets. Am I back on the dating scene, after thirteen years? Will I have to dodge predatory divorcees on the happy pills? Is this the type that's going to set its cap at me? That I'll somehow end up being grateful for? Good God. I'll have to tell them, won't I? That I cheated. Then the nice guys won't want me. I'll become, in their minds, somebody who I know, in my own, I am not. Yet we are what we do.

All I can say is, thank God I told them I'm going away on holiday for two weeks. Even if I'm not.

On Friday night, I'm pacing the bungalow, manically twirling my hair because tomorrow's the day. That business of being 'just me' is overrated. 'If he doesn't come, get on that plane regardless,' Wendy told me.

'What, and do a moonlight flit from my life?' If it weren't for my parents, it'd have sounded appealing.

'Have a holiday,' she said. 'Go away. Relax. Come back fresh, maybe seeing things a little differently.'

'It's a nice thought,' I said. But it's not.

Our flight is at 10 a.m. I stand by the dustbin outside the bungalow to get a bit of privacy and make an impassioned, pride-swallowing call to Rob's mobile. Of course he's not answering because he probably sees my number, so I leave a message. 'Look, Rob, I don't for a minute think this is really going to do any good . . . only I have to try, this one last time.'

I take a deep breath. I have vowed I'll not cry or be a drama queen, as he sometimes calls me. But what happens? What do I say? I say 'Rob . . . Oh, Rob, my life is not going on without you! It's not, Rob. It never will. I'm so sad, I can't function.' My voice squeaks, then it turns into a fully-fledged bawl. 'Rob, every day we don't talk is a day I feel I'm giving you to get over me. And I can't let you. I can't let you get over me . . .' My voice cracks now with a jagged ache. 'Rob,' I say, after I've faked a big coughing fit to disguise the state of me. 'I'm so, sorry for what I've done. I'm a heinous person. I've said this so many times it's starting to sound like I don't mean it, and I don't mean it to, I mean, I mean it to . . . well, what I mean is, oh, never mind.' Oh, God. I pause and snivel. This monologue's sliding quickly down the tubes. I dry my eyes with my free hand, lean a shoulder into the pebble-dashed wall, talk to the dustbin. 'Well, anyway, without grovelling, which I know you wouldn't respect, I'm just going to say this one last time. Rob, I did wrong. Very wrong. But please forgive me. Or at least give me another chance – for the happy couple that we were for ten years, not the people we became for a few months.' I get a blast of cheery strength in my bones. 'Rob,' I wag a finger at the dustbin. 'I for one am going to be at that airport tomorrow, and I . . .'

I what? I beg you, I want you, I need you . . .?

'I hope you'll be there too. Let's go on our holiday, and let's see if, away from all this, we can talk better and maybe work this out. And if we can't, and you can't forgive me, I promise I will accept that, and I'll leave you alone and you will never hear from me again.' I grimace and bite my lip. Please, God, don't hold me to that, or I'll never get into heaven. Not that I hold out much hope of getting in, in any case. I'm sure there's a separate loading dock for cheaters and there's probably a big bin they fling them in first, full of boiling tar and feathers; they probably even feather your eyeballs. 'Right then,' I draw breath. 'I've said my piece. I'll leave it at that. Like I've said, I'll be there tomorrow. At eight. In the morning. Eight a.m. I'll be waiting for you. So I'm hoping . . . with every ounce of hope in me, and all of my heart, that you will come.'

Somewhere in there, towards the end, I'm convinced I've heard a beep and I've been cut off. So I ring him up again and leave the message all over again, this time at breakneck speed.

When I hang up I lean back into the wall and sigh, looking from the dustbin to the stars, where I make an impassioned plea to God, my new best friend, to deliver Rob to the airport tomorrow morning. Mrs Parker next door – nosy parker, more like – is peering around a sheet on the washing-line, gawping at me, mid-peg. She must have heard every word. Now the whole of the colliery will know and my dad will never dare show his face in the pub again.

On Saturday morning I get out of bed, a barrel of anticipation, and put on the cargo trousers and navy tank top I laid out the night before. It feels, ridiculously, like I'm going on a blind date – only blind as in, he may not be there. What am I doing? He's not going to come, is he? I mean, it's daft even thinking it. Going there hoping he might is like admitting I don't really know the man I've been married to for ten years. But maybe there are such things as miracles. So I have a quick cuppa, brush my teeth, tell my puzzled dad that I may or may not be going away on two weeks' holiday.

'When, like?'

'Now, like.'

'What d'you mean now, like? When now, like?'

'Now, like, as in, I'm leaving for the airport in three minutes.'

'Eh? Hang on a minute. A holiday? This morning. You might be gannin but you might not?'

My dad's thin comb-over is practically airborne. I

lick my hand and pat it down and he goes 'Ergh, ger off!' and flaps my hand away.

'That's right, Dad.'

He looks at me with those red, watery eyes that used to be a vivid, young-blood blue. 'Are you all right, chuck?'

'Wouldn't go that far. I feel okay. That's about it.'

'No, chuck,' he knocks on his temple. 'I dinna mean in your body. I mean, in your head.'

I wrap him a big cuddle that he can't extract himself from no matter how he tries. 'Oh, dad, I probably never was, from birth. But there's not much I can do about it now.'

'Be good,' he tells me, with a big grin on his face, as I venture outside into the autumn air. 'And if you can't be good, dinna come home because me patience has about reached its limit.' He chuckles. He's kidding. He waves me off.

I get to the airport early, feeling like a prize plonker, three hours before the flight. Now that I'm actually here, I know with crystal certainty that Rob's not going to just show up to go off on some holiday with me. I imagine him sitting at home thinking *Is she really sat there at the airport, waiting for me? Does she really think we're going to gaze at the sunset and toast ourselves with pina coladas?* But still, I give the reservation clerk our e-ticket number, ask if he's checked in yet, and hold my breath until she tells me what I already know – that he hasn't.

I quietly die.

I go and buy a Costa coffee, hoping the caffeine will pep up my flagging adrenalin. I take it to a bench that faces the revolving door and watch the toing and froing of the holiday-makers. It always fascinates me what passionate places airports are. The goodbye, feel-like-I'll-never-see-you-again-yet-will-see-you-in-three-days snogs that make the disenchanted-and-trying-not-to-be-cynical among us roll our eyes. The orange people coming from the arrivals levels, fresh from two weeks of roasting their you-know-whats off on a beach in the Algarve. I get carried away watching a couple my age with their little boy in the check-in queue. The wife is toned and lovely with her belly-ring and blonde and black streaks and her little cropped tank top. She's having a tiny bit of a disagreement with her sexy hunk of a hubby about whether little Nathan should take his big coat on the plane or not. Deciding not, she bends over and shoves the coat in the carry-on bag and her hubby's hand instinctively touches her bum when she stands up. She gives him a smile and a quick, promising kiss. It's lovely. They are. And I wish I could just lop their heads off and stick Rob's and mine onto their bodies and their lives.

For some strange reason I think about that time when Leigh, Wendy and I, and the hubbies and kids went on a trip together. Leigh was pregnant with Molly. We rented one of those honking great caravans in St Ives. Imagine all of us in a caravan, even though it was big – oh, it was hell. Rob got gastric flu on the way down, and by the end of our first day there, Wendy's lads and Lawrence had got it too. Then the toilet in the caravan packed up, so Lawrence, who was the last to fall ill, had to trek across a great big field to go to the site facilities. In the middle of the night he was crawling back, clutching his poor gurgling belly, when he realised he'd left the door key in the toilet but he didn't have the strength to go back for it. He didn't want to wake us all up by knocking, so he peeked in the window where he thought his and Leigh's bed was. Only the poor sod had got the wrong caravan. What he saw was not his sleeping wife, or a sleeping any of us, for that matter, but a fella and a woman having sex. Oh, it was like a *Carry On* film. The moment he saw them, they – or the woman, to be precise, who was on top – saw him, and then, oh dear. The fella ran out of there stark naked, jumped on Lawrence and gave him a bare-backed hiding. We all woke up with the commotion, hearing somebody calling somebody a 'fucking peeping Tom'. Rob tried to pull the fella off Lawrence, but it was Neil who eventually split them up. Poor Lawrence ended up in a police holding cell! Neil had to use his influence. Lawrence spent the rest of the trip in the caravan manically locking doors and peeking around curtains and doing his business in a bucket. We laughed about it for years. Even Lawrence eventually saw the funny side.

Argh. What will never be again! I feel it like a great big pain, have to plant my fist in the centre of my ribcage. We were all just individuals towing the line of life, and then our lives somehow became connected, and serious investments were made. I cannot accept that suddenly they all count for nothing. Or that we'll never all be friends again. Or that I've lost Rob. I stare out of the glass doors, at arriving cars, coveting some vision I have of him pulling up in a taxi, leaning forward, reaching in his back pocket to pay the driver. And then he'd climb out, hair cut, beard shaved off. The gorgeous, immaculate Rob of old. The sexy apprehension in his eyes that would turn to look for me. And then he'd see me, standing by the door. A sea of people would bob between us, but they wouldn't be able to separate our locked gazes. Nothing would. And in that moment, we'd know: that our love was stronger than whatever came to try and break it. And Rob would smile – a happy-ending smile. And I would run to him.

I shut my eyes now. And I will that when I open them, what I have imagined will be real.

I open them. Nothing. I look at my watch again. It's twenty past. Our flight leaves in forty minutes.

If he's coming, he's cutting it fine.

EPILOGUE

The baby is born in May. Hannah, I name her, after my nana on my mam's side. We bury my mam one week after the birth of her only grandchild. The grandchild she saw but never knew was hers. My mam surprised us by dying in her sleep – the day before she was to be admitted to a home. I had finally got my dad to agree to it. A cousin of my dad's hugged me, looked at Hannah, and made the remark about one life ending to make way for another. I could never have imagined I'd ever look at my mam's dying like that – as though you can somehow trade in a mother for a daughter – but, strangely, in a way it helps to do just that.

It turns out that's why I was so sick. The doctor left a message to call, but I never did. A combination of me just not being very 'with it' at the time, and maybe fear that I was going to be told something I wouldn't want to hear. Who knows? But I never, ever, thought I could be having a baby. I was pretty certain of my dates. I'd taken the morning-after pill for God's sake! Of course, the doctor never mentioned that the failure rate is ten per cent. Anyway, I found out I was preggers soon after Rob never showed up at the airport.

The airport. I'll never forget how I felt when I stood there and watched that plane take off without us both. I couldn't pick my heart up off the floor on the Metro back through to Sunderland, carrying my suitcase, my bag full of hope.

It was an awful shock at first. Andrey's baby. A child who would be forever attached to a terrible memory, and the one mistake I would undo if I could. A baby who came along when I was quite sure I could live happily without kids. And a child that meant Rob would never have me back now.

I'm ashamed to say that my first thought was to have an abortion. But I try not to think of that any more, or of the past, or of the life I had and what I've lost. At some point you've just got to stop punishing yourself. I still feel a blackguard about cheating and always will, but that's just me, and my strong but momentarily misplaced morality. But I don't wish it had never happened. Not when I look into Hannah's little face and see her pout her moist pink mouth that I keep plopping kisses on, or feel her little sausage fingers tighten around mine, like squidgy curlers around a section of hair. I can only thank God for her. It's hard to believe that I ever thought I didn't want kids, because now, of course, it's the old cliché: I can't imagine my life without her.

The loss of Rob is the gain of Hannah. A weird way to look at it, but such is life.

And life does have a way of rolling on. Between working, being fired, being pregnant, being hired somewhere else, being split up, being shacked up in the spare room of a senior citizen's bungalow, I've been very much just coping with life as it's been flung at me, but coping, I suppose, is the operative word.

The flat I moved into before Christmas is hardly my dream place to live, but I suppose I shouldn't complain. At least it's in a nice part of Gosforth, in a professional, family neighbourhood. I'm on the first floor of a three-storey town house owned by a couple of retired teachers who live downstairs. I was worried at first about the baby crying, but they don't have grandkids and said they actually find the noise quite soothing. Which is more than I can say for myself. Hannah does cry a lot. But nowadays, strangely, I don't. I often wonder if she detects sadness in me, and decides to cry to save me the trouble; if this little bundle of baby is somewhat telepathic.

I tried to find him – Andrey. It's odd calling him that. I like to think of him as nameless, faceless, everything-less. That was a hell of a decision to make. I didn't think he'd be bothered; he certainly didn't strike me as the family type. But I felt his right to know he fathered a child was bigger than all my reasons not to tell him. The main reason I did it, though, was for Hannah. I just had to think of Leigh or Rob to know how hard it was to grow up knowing nothing about your own dad. I remember Rob's speech to me about the fractured family. I didn't know where to start, of course. I couldn't go and knock on his door because, strangely, I've never had any memory of where he lived. Certain events of that episode are just locked out of my mind. So I went to the Civic Centre, his employer, and

managed to find out the sort of confidential information they're not supposed to tell you, but if you catch
the right girl on the right day and bawl your eyes out to
her, you might get lucky. She was a single mother
herself. Yes, she said she remembered him: lovely-
looking fella. It turned out that Andrey left his job at
the end of last summer. She believed he moved out of
the area. That was pretty much in keeping with what I
knew about him. I was ready to leave it at that, but then
I thought, well, that's not exactly trying very hard to
find him, is it? And what if the girl was wrong? So I put
an announcement in the personals of the *Sunderland
Echo* and the *Evening Chronicle*. For a second I wondered if Rob would see it, but I can't really see Rob
looking in a newspaper to find love. It was a very weird
message to write, and what I ended up putting sounded
daft, really. '*To a certain Russian on a beach. You have a
daughter. From a married woman who you thought would
be impressed by a fancy car.*' He'd get that, if he read it. I
included a PO box so he could get in touch with me,
dreading that he actually would. I still check it. Seven
weeks on and I'm still getting mail. Mind you, it's very
bizarre stuff. Men wanting to meet me, take me on
holiday, marry me. One sent me a picture of his penis!
Some fella who claims he's in the Rolls-Royce Enthu-
siasts' Club. A lesbian couple who offer to buy Hannah
for ten thousand pounds. A very old man who sent me
a picture with the caption: '*Let me be your sugar daddy.*'
There's a lot of oddballs out there. Makes me feel not
so bad. But seriously, though, one day, when my
daughter asks, I'll be able to look her in the eye and

say that I tried to find her father. And I'll probably tell her stories about how she's related to the Princess Anastasia, the only vaguely interesting bit of Russian history I ever remember.

As for her ever calling anybody else 'Daddy', I don't hold out much hope there. It's been ten months since Rob and I split, and I've never so much as thought of another man. On the rare occasions I do think of sex, it's still sex with Rob. This doesn't bode well for my future. I don't know how I'll ever move on to anybody else, because Rob was, and always will be, my one and only. In my heart – if not, alas that one time – in places farther south.

A little newsflash here . . . Wendy is doing very well. The operation was a success and she's been given a clean bill of health. She's got a job working part-time for a solicitor – a much older, Jewish gentleman who she'll say, with great understatement, is a very nice man in a 'father-figure' way (translation: I think she might actually have shagged him). And a few weeks ago she finally got her degree. Okay, so she didn't just 'go for it' like she vowed she would that day in Durham. She actually dithered and self-doubted for a few more months with the result that she now won't be able to apply to Northumbria Uni to do the qualifying course that she was on about until next year. But I actually believe it will happen. I'm convinced that before she's fifty (as she joked) – or maybe in her mid-fifties – she really will be a lawyer. Then it'll be the old middle-finger salute to Neil. I can tell that she's dying for that day. Not that she's doing this for the wrong reasons, but revenge, even to good people like Wendy, is sweet. 'Sometimes I still have to take time to mourn him,' she'll occasionally say. 'But mourning him is better than living with him, and I'm happy I have the sense to recognise that.' Her lads are doing well, although Ben developed psoriasis, something that the doctors say can be triggered by stress. Interestingly, they still point-blank refuse to see their dad.

Leigh and Neil are a bit of a different story, though. They ended up having a massive bust-up and she went home to Lawrence. Lawrence, not surprisingly when I think of his phone message that day to me, took her back. But – and here is the surprise – only for about a week. Then he threw her out. Told her he was a happier person before he ever clapped eyes on her. So where did she go? She went right back to Neil, who still says he doesn't want her, who still makes the occasional pitch to Wendy to take him back. Little Molly lives with her dad, although she sees her mam every weekend, supposedly until her mam gets herself sorted. But apparently she's not – getting sorted, that is. Wendy saw her by chance down the town centre and said she looked almost unrecognisable, lots of grey roots growing through the black hair, no make-up, dark glasses, and wafer thin.

I got a card off her. A 'congratulations on the birth of your baby' card. I don't know how she found out. Maybe it was an olive branch. I'm sure that in her own way she loved us, as we loved her – although she still hasn't apologised to Wendy. She probably just can't bring herself to. But she did send her a Christmas card;

she wrote on it, *Wishing you peace, from Leigh*. Not Leigh and Neil. And 'peace'? It doesn't even sound like something Leigh would say. Wendy and I tried to fathom it, but, as usual when it comes to our once best friend, we can't.

I think of her quite a bit, though. How could I not, when you think how close we were? I've run the gamut of emotions but in the end I just come back to pity, because Leigh was, is, and always will be, a very damaged person. I suppose for what she did to me, I've forgiven her. I can understand her desire to get back at me. But much as I've tried to blame her for my going astray – trying to convince myself that I only did it because I somehow followed her example – I know deep down that I can't pin that on her. I was a big girl. And even if she'd never ratted on me to Rob, I'd still have got pregnant, so he'd still have found out and dumped me. No, actually I find it hard to think too badly of somebody I thought so much of. I'll often catch myself smiling over some of the daft little laughs we had. There is a massive void in my heart where a good pal once had a very special place. Sometimes it saddens me, because I think I'll never put that sort of faith in a friend again. A part of me will always be a bit guarded. But maybe that's not a bad thing.

As for myself, Rob still won't talk to me.

He took my getting pregnant very badly. I had to tell him, of course, because I was sure he'd find out. The North-East, as I learned to my cost, is a small world. In light of our history, it seemed like a very cruel blow that the man I was unfaithful with should succeed where my husband had failed. There was a big silence down the phone when I broke it to him. And then he said, 'Well, be a mother and be happy, Jill. Don't have any regrets.' And then he hung up.

He still claims he's selling the house. It's funny, though – I regularly drive over there looking for the 'For Sale' sign on our lawn, but I still haven't seen one.

Ironically, today happens to be our wedding anniversary. It's hard to believe how different my life was just over a short year ago. Today is also Hannah's christening. I wasn't going to bother with all that business because I've never been what you'd call religious, so it seemed hypocritical, but my dad nearly had kittens: 'You have to christen her! Or you know what she'll be, don't you?' he whispered: 'A bastard.'

'I don't think women can be those, Dad,' I said, reeling. 'Only men.'

'No, they can, lass. If she doesn't get christened that's what she'll be. A bastard.'

He's not quite got the right end of the stick has he? Although, as usual, my dad hits close to the mark on the conscience front. My dad still doesn't know Rob's not the father; I want him to leave this world still having some respect for his daughter. But one day I caught him stuffing photos of Hannah in an envelope with Rob's address on it. I snatched the package off him. 'Don't ever do anything like that behind my back, Dad!' He didn't say a word, just narrowed his eyes at me, like he knew something.

My child will never be fatherless, though. I plug her arms into the cream and white knitted cardigan that she's going to be wearing overtop the cream and white knitted dress that was mine when I was christened. I will be both a mam and a dad to her. And whenever I've got my paternal hat on and I don't know what to do, I'll try to imagine what Rob would have done under the circumstances, and I'm sure we'll bluff our way through it somehow.

Hannah's taking my name: Mallin. Hannah Mallin. I wrote it down before I chose it. Wrote it, spelled it out out loud, went around saying it, liking the flow of it, the rhythm, the 'n's and the 'l's. When I married Rob I kept my own name, because I thought Jill Mallin sounded better than Jill Benedict. I regret that now, though. I regret not taking all of him while I had the chance.

Rob. Still his name conjures up this searing loss in me. I pick Hannah up and squeeze her to me by her podgy little shoulders. Sometimes I get these moments where I can't believe how my life has turned out. This is one of them. Hannah starts to cry.

My dad taps on the bedroom door. 'Howay, lass. You ready? We're going to be late.' I look at him, dressed in his suit and cheerful mauve tie that's already got a tea stain on it and he's only had it on two minutes. My dad who lost my mother and acquired a single daughter with a baby, and has never for a moment been anything other than a trooper. 'No more doing the Ray Charles . . .' I keep hearing him say, a thousand times a day, even when I was just thinking of doing the Ray Charles, and it makes me smile. Yes, family sticks. Friends don't always. Not even husbands. But, my God, I thank my lucky stars that I was born into a close family. I lift little Hannah above my head, and there's a pull in my groin because I'm still sore from the delivery; it was a bit of a grisly one, just like my mother's was when she had me.

'She's a beautiful little babba, yes she is!' My dad coos to Hannah and thumbs her little cheek. My daughter's head looks like a white eggshell that you might have started gluing a bit of dark carpet fluff on to, but gave up. Her skin, with its rosy pink cheeks, is just like my mother's. But in every other respect – her eyes, her nose, the shape of her face and her mouth – she is, uncannily, the spitting image of her father. Every time I look at her, I see him, and I probably always will.

Sometimes I'll catch my dad staring at her. 'She's the living double of Rob, mind, isn't she?' he'll say, like he's only saying it because he knows damned well she isn't.

'Really? Hmm. You think so?' will be my reply. Then we'll stare each other down until one of us – usually me – has to break away first, with some excuse about how I have to go to the toilet, or it's time for dinner. I often wonder, though, if he connects it all to the Russian, and our day out at the beach. My dad has always been a man to think more than he'll ever let on.

'Sweetie-pie sweetheart,' I settle Hannah on my shoulder, patting her big, square nappied bum, and she nearly pulls out a handful of my hair. I walk into my parents' bathroom and look at the two of us in the mirror, then I comb my hair where she's messed it. My hair was lustrous during pregnancy, but has since gone thin, I think. But I did get my figure back quickly, all but a few pounds. Although nowadays I really don't care. I think of all the time I spent moping and staring at my body and feeling sorry for it. Don't they say that sometimes you just need something bigger than your biggest problem to realise you never had anything to worry about? However, considering I sleep only about two hours a night because of all the crying she does, I actually think I look pretty bloody good.

'Come on, lass,' my dad says, patting my shoulder. 'It won't get prettier the more you stare at it.'

'Oh. Thanks! God, you're all tact.'

I think about putting on some perfume but decide not to. I don't want the vicar thinking I'm a tart. 'Come on, Miss Hannah Mallin, let's get you to the church on time,' I sing. Last time I went to this church it was for my mam's funeral, and in the back of my mind, I was hoping that Rob might come. He didn't, of course. How could he come and comfort me? And how could he come and not? But I know how much it would have hurt him to stay away. He loved my mother.

Rob. My head floods with him again, like it's prone to do at all the worst times. Hannah lets out a great big bawl. Saves me the trouble.

The other day, cleaning out my stuff, I came across something I had long ago forgotten about. A pocket-sized blank book with a silver cover, in which my mother had written quotes that she had collected over the years: quotes about love. She gave it to me as a wedding present. I remember ten years ago thinking it was very sweet and sentimental and typical of her, but not much more. I suppose I hadn't lived enough, back then.

> *The most powerful symptom of love is a tenderness which becomes at times almost insupportable.* Victor Hugo

> *Real love, I've learned, is a very, very strong form of forgiveness. I don't think people yearn for love because they hate staying home alone on Saturday night or because they dread going into restaurants alone. People want love because they want their taped-together glasses or ten extra pounds to be forgiven. They want someone to look past the surface stuff like bad-hair days, a too-loud laugh, or potato chips crunching in their living-room couch when anyone sits down.* Lois Smith Brady

> *To love a person is to learn the song that is in their heart, and to sing it to them when they have forgotten.* Anonymous

> *I ask you to pass through life at my side – to be my second self and best earthly companion.* Mr Rochester in *Jane Eyre*, Charlotte Brontë

That last one always gets me. Maybe in ten years' time I'll be able to read it again and it won't.

The church isn't exactly packed, but there's enough of a turn-out for it to have an intimacy as we enter it. I decked out the aisles with a string of fat white roses. None of the mothers of the four other babies who are getting christened today wanted to chip in and help pay for it, but I didn't care. It's weird being here twice in such a short space of time. When I last came here, before we buried my mother, I was a child. Now I come in today as a mother myself, with my own child. Something about that gets me right in my gut. Hannah starts to cry again.

I gaze at the small, stained-glass rose window while the vicar does a reading and his voice drifts peacefully through me. The organist sits by the organ studying her fingernails. All of the babies' names have been printed into a small white book with a flock cover, which I stare at as it sits open on my knee. Hannah Mallin. I look down the list of names and my eyes keep coming back to my daughter's. It's by far the best, of course. I glance across at my daughter in her god-mother Wendy's arms. And so is she. Better, brighter, bonnier than any other baby in the room – nay, in the world – and she's all mine. I made her; I baked her in my oven. Oh, I hope I'm not going to be one of these obnoxious mothers who other mothers hide from at parent–teacher meetings. No, I think, looking at her and just wanting to plant kisses on every square inch of her little sausage body; I hope I am.

I take my daughter from my best friend's arms, my friend who very bravely accepted the role of godmother to my daughter, despite having lost a daughter herself. I look down the short pew at my dad, his gnarled hands resting on his kneecaps as he listens solemnly. This is all that matters now, I think. This moment that I wouldn't change if I could; not all the things that I would change given half the chance. It's all water under the bridge. My dad looks across at me, and his eyes are full of tears. I know it's hard for him. I know he's thinking of my mam.

I pass Hannah to the vicar when he nods to me. She scowls and twists and puckers her mouth. I look up at the stained-glass rose window again. Rose. I think of her little cheeks, her rosebud blooms against the dark, wild, colouring of her eyes and hair. Damn it, maybe I should have called her Rose.

The vicar starts giving her his blessing and I'm lost on this sentimental journey of thought about this weird state of screwing-up we all go through until we finally accept that life is just something we have to take, however we get it dished up, with all its associate baggage, pitfalls and mistakes. That I am a mother shocks me again afresh. The vicar is just at the point where he is asking for her name, when something strange happens. Somewhere in the distance, I hear a dog bark. I mean, you couldn't really miss it. It's such a loud, crisp bark, a get-right-on-your-nerve-ends bark.

I've heard that bark before. It seems to stop everything, including my heart.

My head instinctively shoots round to the back of the church, and just as it does, the door opens, giving one of those low, burring groans.

The dog comes in.

And so does Rob.

Kiefer gallops down the aisle towards me, starts jumping around me in circles, then quickly forgets about me and latches onto the vicar's cassock. The vicar passes Hannah to me like a hot potato.

I gaze across a sea of curious faces and look speech-lessly at my husband.

You could hear a pin drop. And the dog playfully growling up a storm. And the vicar saying, in his thick Geordie accent, 'Bloody ger off!'

'I'm sorry,' Rob says, looking even more Heathcliff-like with his wild hair, his arms bent stiffly by his sides. 'I thought I'd get here and catch you outside. But the car acted up again.'

How did he know about today? I look across at my dad, who's looking at me, with 'Okay, so shoot the messenger, I'm nearly dead anyway,' written all over his face.

I look back at Rob. He's dressed in his old jeans and navy Gap sweatshirt. He walks towards me, down the aisle, makes straight for my daughter. 'So this is Hannah,' he says, softly combing her with his gaze. Then he looks at me. 'D'you think I can I have a word outside, Jill?'

I look speechlessly at Wendy who says, 'Go on, then,' and holds out her arms for me to pass her Hannah. I'm aware of walking down the aisle, to a sea of bemused faces, all turning to watch us walk out of the church doors.

I'm hot. There's a ticking of blood in my temples. 'What are you doing here, Rob?' I ask him when we're outside in the bright sunshine, on the narrow gravelled drive framed by headstones, hearing the quiver in my voice. I look at his pallor, his pained eyes. I've never seen Rob look so changed. Last time I saw him was that day I went round and begged him to let me come home. I imagined in all this time he would have been back to his old self again.

He kneads his temples with one hand, blows out a big breath. 'I've come to give Hannah my name. I want to be her dad . . . if you'll let me.'

He looks right at me, his pupils latching questioningly onto mine. A breeze rustles the tall trees, and it takes moments for me to speak. 'But you said you—'

He shakes his head, turns from me, props himself against the dark blue church door with an outstretched arm and leans forward, looking at his feet. 'Am I not allowed to be wrong?' His forehead goes down onto his arm. I think his shoulders are shaking.

As much as I've dreamed of this moment, of course never expecting for a minute that it would happen, there's another force taking hold inside me: the mother in me. I can't have Rob barging in and botching it all up, trying out forgiveness at Hannah's expense. 'But you said you could never bring up another person's kid. That's why you didn't want to adopt.' That awful anniversary conversation. A year ago to the day.

He sighs, that big manly sigh I've so missed. 'I didn't say I could never. I said I wasn't sure if I could. But that was . . . I don't know . . . maybe my anger. A part of me didn't think I deserved . . .' He looks up at me, straightens his body away from the door. 'I don't know what that was, Jill. I'm not a psychiatrist. But I know it's not how I really felt. Or, more to the point, it's certainly not how I feel now.' His eyes search mine, and birds tweet in the trees behind us. 'Of course I'd have loved a kid of my own. I never realised how much until I

couldn't have that. But I can't have that.' He smiles,
gets a quietly enlightened look on his face. 'But I've
come to see that having one that's half yours is the next
best thing.' He touches a stray bit of my hair, tucks it
behind my ear, his eyes soften, scour my face again;
there are tears in them now. 'I love you, Jill, and I'll love
your baby and I want you back, if you'll have me. I
wanted you back the second I made you go. But a part
of me thought maybe I should try and live without you,
because I was so damned hurt by what you'd done. I
just couldn't understand it. But now . . . I don't know,
in some ways maybe a part of me does. Or maybe I just
don't think it matters as much as I always thought
something like that would.' He shakes his head, and the
birds vacate the trees in a flurry of wings. 'See, I'm just
not happy without you. These last ten months . . . I'm
a very sad man without you. I keep waiting until I'm
going to feel better, until I'm going to feel any excitement at the prospect of going out with another woman.
Until I'm not going to wake up every morning and
dread another day without you. Until I'm going to
come home and not register your absence as I walk in
that door.' He digs the heel of his hand into his eye. 'I
miss you with my whole heart. And I just want us to be
a family again.' He takes hold of my hands. 'The three
of us.'

I choke. A big surge of love and massive, massive
respect for him makes my throat constrict in a choked
agony.

'You know what was on Metro radio the other night?
Before the phone-in? That song, you know, the one we

danced to at the wedding. "If I Sing you a Love Song." '

I nod. Because I remember that song and I love that song. I meant to go and buy the CD and forgot. Then after we split up, I couldn't.

'It was a nice song,' he says. 'It's our song.' He takes hold of me and very slowly moves his feet, dancing with me.

I put my arms around him, plant my face in his chest. 'So you've not met anybody? I thought you would have met somebody by now . . .' My voice is a squeezed, daring-to-be-happy wince.

I look up at him and his eyes ooze goodness and love. 'I never even looked.'

I'm terrified a breeze will stir up and this moment will be blown away on the back of this fateful summer day. 'But it's his child, Rob. How will you ever be able to forget that?'

He looks up over my head, shuts his eyes for a second, sighs, then looks right at me. 'Whose child it is, Jill, is just biology.'

I know Rob, he wouldn't mess me around. If he's saying this, he's given it a hell of a lot of thought and he really means it. 'Oh, Rob . . .' I squeeze my arms tightly around him, stuff my face in his shoulder again, claiming him, part panicked that he's going to suddenly change his mind. Maybe he'll say, 'Look, Jill, now that I'm touching you, now you're in my arms, I realise I don't feel it for you any more, and I can't forgive you. It was a mistake coming here . . .'

But when he plucks me off him, he's smiling. He

doesn't look pale any more. More like flushed. He gets down on one knee, and at that exact moment, through the sunshine, it starts to rain, a fine showerhead sprinkling.

'Oh, God, what are you doing?' I press the corners of my eyes to stop the tears.

'Jill Mallin. Will you be my wife?'

I pull him up by the shoulders of his shirt. 'I'll never be anything else.'

He hugs me. It brings back memories of that first time I touched him, many, many years ago. And I get the urge to run to the Millennium Bridge again and say *Tell me what you thought when you first met me.* And he will smooch me there, as senior citizens walk past us and scowl.

By the time we move apart, the shower has passed, as quickly as it came, and the sun is shining through.

I link arms with him and we go back into the small vestibule with its dark red, well-worn entrance rug. 'I'm underdressed,' he mutters. 'I lied when I said the car broke down. I actually wasn't going to come. I didn't think you'd have me. Not after all the rotten things I said to you.'

I'm about to say I deserved those rotten things, but then I think, no, Jill, don't go over old ground. Turn a new page. I go to enter the church and he pulls me back by my wrist. 'I'm all right, you know.' He turns me to face him, hands gripping my shoulders. 'What I mean is . . .' he whispers, 'Just in case you have any doubts, it's going to be all right. Everything.' His eyes roam over my face and for the first time in a long time, I see passion in them again. 'The old Rob is back,' he says and then he thrusts a great big kiss on me, and we stand there and have a big snog.

Every head in the place turns and looks at us as we walk in. The dog – who Rob tells me with a proud nudge has passed his obedience training with flying colours – has now finished ravishing the vicar and is sitting obediently by the altar as though in some moment of grace. I smile at Wendy. She looks from me to Rob, then beams a big smile. 'Here,' she says, passing Hannah over to him. 'Daddy.'

Rob beams and stares at the baby, presses the button of her nose with his big fingertip. 'She's got long eyelashes,' he says, infatuation all over his face. The only other person I've ever seen him give this look to is me.

'Do you think we can start now, please?' the vicar asks me.

I tell him we can. Rob says, 'Yes, but her name's Benedict now, Hannah Benedict.' He looks at me, smiles, his eyes lit up with fatherly pride. I look across to my dad, and his are too, for me.

Then I think . . . Hang on . . . Hannah Benedict? I don't like that. 'Wait a minute!'

'Oh!' goes Rob. 'You're not changing your mind?'

'Not about you,' I tell him, 'but, I – I think I would like to call her Rose.'

'Rose?' I hear my dad say. His face is screwed up and he mouths, 'That's awful.'

'But you've been calling her Hannah for ages now,' Rob says. 'God, she's going to be like the dog.' Then he apologises to the vicar for saying 'God'.

We put little Kiefer through several names before Rob finally landed on calling him after his favourite movie star. But then – like the plonker he is – he remembered his favourite movie star wasn't Kiefer, but Kiefer's dad, Donald. And we didn't have the heart to change the name again. Besides, Donald didn't work for a dog. I look at my daughter. 'Rose Benedict.' The more I say it, the more I love it. 'I mean, it's fine if I do that, isn't it? Rename her?' I ask the vicar.

'It's your party,' he says.

'D'you like it?' I look at Rob.

'You're her mam,' he says, and I shake my head.

'No, you're her dad.'

He holds my gaze, nods, 'It's awful, but somehow it works.'

I beam as I catch Rob looking at our baby with besotted father written all over him. And I feel something slip out of me. A flutter of a tensely-held breath. Giddy pride. 'Rob and Rose Benedict.' I say, gazing from one to the other, not believing this moment, but knowing I am a very lucky girl to be having it. 'My family.'

Little Rose looks at me and she cries for both of us.